Also by Peter Høeg

SMILLA'S SENSE OF SNOW

BORDERLINERS

The History

of Danish Dreams

THE

HISTORY

OF DANISH

DREAMS

PETER

HØEG

TRANSLATED BY

BARBARA HAVELAND

DOUBLEDAY CANADA LIMITED

Originally published in Danish under the title Forestilling Om Det
Tyvende Århundrede, copyright © 1988 by Peter Høeg and Munksgaard
Rosinante, Copenhagen

Canadian Cataloguing in Publication Data

Høeg, Peter, 1957–
The history of Danish dreams

Translation of: Forestilling om det tyvende århundrede.
ISBN 0-385-25549-7

I. Title.

PT8176.18.O335F6713   1995   839.8'1374   C95-931845-3

Printed and bound in the United States of America

Published in Canada by
Doubleday Canada Limited
105 Bond Street
Toronto, Ontario
M5B 1Y3

Contents

PART TWO

PART THREE

The History

of Danish Dreams

Foreword

THIS IS the History of Danish Dreams, an account of what we have dreaded and dreamed of and hoped for and expected during this century; I have endeavored to make it exhaustive and keep it simple and, as an argument for even so much as trying, I would like to mention two incidents.

One day in the early spring of 1929, Carsten was helping his father, Carl Laurids, to assemble a machine gun which, when it was finished, stood on a tripod and ranged from wall to wall of the pillared salon in the villa off Strand Drive. Anyone else might well have wondered at a machine gun in a living room, but Carsten saw it as a natural extension of his father's brutal elegance. Lying on his stomach, looking along the perforated barrel, he had the feeling that the weapon pointed, with the most liberating determination, into a hazy future. Then Carl Laurids said, "Well, kid, you're seven years old now, and old enough to be told my motto, which is: always look ahead because that's where the money is," and although Carsten was only five and had not understood a single word, still he listened, enthralled, because by this time it had become a rare occurrence for his father to address him directly. That is one incident.

The other took place at precisely the same moment, in a tenement building in Christianshavn, where Maria Jensen was watching her mother, Anna, cleaning. Anna had been engaged in this cleanup—which she intended to be the final, the definitive cleanup—for several years. Now she had borrowed, from the local doctor, a magnifying glass that allowed her to peer into the bottomless pit of germs on paneling she had believed to be clean and which she was now in the act of washing down with alcohol. Standing right behind her mother, Maria took a deep breath to conquer the stammer that had become more pronounced of late. Then she said, "Mom, wh-wh-why are you using that glass?" and Anna replied, "It's so this place can be really nice and clean." "But," Maria objected, "it won't do any g-g-good, because there'll always be more dirt," and Anna could find no good answer to this; she just stayed there for a moment, looking at her daughter.

The next moment, both incidents are past. Anna turns back to her interminable polishing. Carl Laurids dismantles the machine gun, and a day later he has disappeared without trace. It may not be a coincidence that their children have remembered these events and been able to tell me about them, but neither is it an indication that they were of any particular importance, since Carsten and Maria remembered so much else. The point is precisely that these two incidents resemble so many others. Nevertheless, I believe that, at the moment they occur, an astounding array of all the hopes of the twentieth century is assembled on Strand Drive and in Christianshavn. If I now carry on, in due course to return to Carsten and Maria, it is because I believe that encapsulated within many everyday events—and, yes, possibly any event whatsoever—lies the essence of an entire century.

Part One

CARL LAURIDS

The manor of Mørkhøj

Time that stands still

1520–1918

CARL LAURIDS is born at Mørkhøj one New Year's Eve—it has been impossible to discover who his parents were—and adopted, not long afterward, by the estate steward. At this point the manor has been shielded from progress for two hundred years, at least two hundred years, by a very high wall, topped by iron spikes, its gray limestone speckled with the remains of fossilized mud creatures. This wall encircles the estate and its buildings, which are constructed from the same stone as the wall and are further protected by a moat in whose greenish waters, on summer days, catfish as big as alligators can be glimpsed, lying motionless at the surface, glinting in the scant light that steals over the wall.

Most people believe that Carl Laurids was born in the year 1900, New Year's Eve 1900, although no one at the manor was aware of this. For here, in fact, time had been suspended. It had been standing still since the day the Count gave the word for work on the wall to begin and for all the ingeniously constructed clocks on the estate—which had, until then, besides time, date, and year, shown the positions of the moon and the planets—to be stopped. He then advised his secretary, who had hitherto been writing the history of the estate, that time had come to a standstill. Since, as the Count said, it is but a common, modern invention, anyway, never again do I want to see time on these premises; from now on, all time will be counted as year one.

The Count had never cared much for the passage of time and especially not these days, when his instincts were telling him that the old aristocracy were to be the main losers in this new age. At one point, during the course of his energetic youth among the folios and parchment scrolls of the great European libraries, he had discovered that the great natural scientist Paracelsus had once visited Mørkhøj and, while there, had disclosed the fact that the center of the world was to be found somewhere on the estate lands. This discovery might not cut much ice nowadays, and even for that time it was pretty farfetched, but the Count became obsessed with the idea. In those days, every educated person—and the Count was one such—was a bit of a historian and a doctor and a philosopher and a lawyer and a collector and a chemist and a clergyman. And it was because the Count was all of these things that he was able, more or less single-handedly, to build the big laboratory that he installed in the attic of the manor house. It was built according to guidelines laid down by Christian IV's court alchemist, Petrus Severinus. It was a full-scale laboratory complete with alembics and books and machines uniting Paracelsus' doctrine of Definitive Matter with the philosophy of Aristotle and Plato and the very latest mechanical aids. Besides which, it had running water and a bucket for shitting into. Once it was finished, the Count stayed in there among his star charts and geometric constructions, and rarely came out.

After what appears to have amounted, at the very least, to a lifetime, he succeeded in pinpointing the center of the universe quite precisely and accurately at a spot on the edge of the coach-house dunghill. Only then did he truly emerge into the sunlight, and have an iron balustrade forged and gilded and erected around the spot. His great moment had come. Now he would prove that he had not lived in vain and that his family, which had always been at the heart of things, reigned supreme. He must also have had some vague, muddled dream of coming up, in this way, with incontrovertible, scientific proof that God had assigned the world's paramount position to the aristocracy.

This idea strikes me as being both weak and unsound. Nonetheless, his contemporaries greeted it with some interest, and when the Count invited the court-shoe and powdered-wig brigade, they turned out to a man. That is to say, the scholars and the representatives of

Church and Crown and Parliament, not to mention Caspar Bartholin—Bartholinian mafioso and owner of the University of Copenhagen—and his son-in-law the great astronomer, engineer, inventor, and member of the Paris Academy, Ole Rømer.

The Count opened the proceedings by serving up fifty barrels of old Hungarian tokay, the grapes for which had been harvested when the Great Paracelsus was a child. He then described his epoch-making discovery and how his calculations had shown him that, were he to dig here, right at the center, he would discover a substance with which he would be able to produce the Philosopher's Stone, build a Perpetuum Mobile machine, and isolate a quantity of the Cosmic Seed.

The assembly sat on rows of chairs arranged around the gilded balustrade, listening to music played by the Mørkhøj orchestra. Before their eyes, twelve footmen in red silk stockings and breeches commenced digging inside the enclosure while the Count read aloud from the writings of Paracelsus. They dug until the hole grew so deep that the walls collapsed with a hollow belch and they were buried beneath the dunghill without finding anything other than the jawbones, picked clean, of a pig. Even so, none of the spectators laugh, all of them sympathize with the Count. Then the great Ole Rømer gets to his feet, totters over to him, lays a fleshy hand on his shoulder, and wheezes, "Tell you what, here's a tip, from one colleague to another: the earth is round, which means its center can be found all over the place, and all you'll find if you dig is shit." After which everyone takes his leave and the Count is left with the dunghill and the empty barrels and the gilded balustrade and the appalling melancholy derived from knowing that you are the only one, apart from God, who knows that you are right and that everyone else is wrong.

The next day he gave orders for the building of the wall to begin and for Mørkhøj's clocks to be stopped. These clocks, designed by Ole Rømer, were driven in ingenious fashion, by the water that passed, splashing and murmuring, through the fountains and the moat. With the flow of water now stemmed, the stone basins dried up and the moat was transformed into a murky morass in which poisonous water lilies and big catfish were the only visible sign of life. From then on, the only sound of time passing heard at Mørkhøj was the monotonous chant of the watchmen, and that, moreover, was in Latin, "since that's the way I want it," said the Count; "it's the only language fit for official use, *dixi!*"

And as time went on, the watchmen's song became all that was heard of the laborers and peasants on the estate, of whom there were around one thousand when the wall was built. They had never had any say in things before, and now, with the high wall throwing a dark shadow across the estate and keeping the outside world out, the only bright spots visible to them were one another's ever more indistinct features. By the time Carl Laurids was born, they had all but lost the power of speech and had intermarried so often that they were all one another's children and parents and uncles and aunts, and the awful fact is that eventually it became hard to tell the difference between them and the red cows. Having been equally deprived of any infusion of new blood, these had lost their horns and were wont, more and more often, to get up and walk around on two legs.

On those few occasions when a worker did recover his voice to protest and rebel, he was beheaded, and that was the end of that.

When all contact with the outside world was severed and the clocks switched off, time came to a standstill for the Count and his family. Dressed in his braided coat and with a face lined by a long life of fierce concentration, he entered his library and laboratory and, once there, launched himself back through history and out into space and down into the corrections of his own calculations in the hope of, at long last, being able to establish something. Occasionally he forgot what this something was, although it was, of course, the location of the world's midpoint. When he did show his face outside the main manor house, it was to take a drive in a little coach drawn by more and more of the decrepit horses and with a dumb coachman on the box. Wherever they went on these occasions, with the laborers dropping to their knees at sight of the carriage, the Count's face resembled the stone of the wall. By his side in the carriage sat his wife and his children, laced and powdered and transfixed in a seemingly perpetual youth.

Having realized that he had pressing business in his laboratory, the Count then entrusted the management of that time which he had had suspended to his two immediate subordinates. One of these was his secretary, Jacoby, whom the Count had sent for from England because he wrote such a marvelous form of cancellaresca script and because, after two or three or four bottles of wine, he could reel off Latin and Greek toasts and paeans and epitaphs and impromptus, and because he was a walking encyclopedia of the genealogy of the European aristocracy and was possessed of a profound insight into military history and Venetian double-entry bookkeeping. When the Count lost interest in everyday matters, Jacoby took on the keeping of the manor accounts—in which everything, absolutely everything, to do with the self-sufficient running of the estate was converted into Dutch gold ducats (in the Count's opinion, the only currency worth its salt)—and, most important of all, carried on recording the history and chronicle of events at Mørkhøj. This record was one of the Count's most vital sources. It confirmed that time had been frozen, was at a standstill, because look, said the Count, this is still, and always will be, year one, and if anyone has any other ideas we'll have him beheaded.

The other person who enjoyed the Count's confidence was Carl Laurids's foster father, the Mørkhøj steward, into whose hands the Count had entrusted the supervision of the medieval agricultural techniques, the stables, the storehouses, the tile works, the farm laborers' cottages, the manor chapel, the workshops, the grain mill—which was hand-operated because all of the water on Mørkhøj lands was stagnant—and the dairy where, in age-blackened churns, the ever-diminishing milk yield was turned into the estate's own small, tart cheeses. Then, too, he was the one man who could tell the Mørkhøj employees apart; who kept count of the stableboys and grooms and muckers-out and woodcutters and smallholders and gamekeepers and dairymaids and tradesmen and the pastor and the parish clerk and the eighty-two Polish girls and their *Aufseher* who had wandered onto the estate one day by mistake, while looking for work. They entered at a spot where the wall had collapsed, and once the estate closed around them, they continued to work, eat, sleep, give birth and die and drop to their knees at Mørkhøj, without ever remembering anything at all about the world they had left behind. This says something about how efficiently the Count had succeeded in realizing the dream of the Danish aristocracy and landed gentry, of time standing still with the hand pointing to feudalism and the rights of the few over the many.

At the manor house itself the steward kept an eye—once blue, but now gray with experience and the burden of responsibility—on the housekeepers, on the tally of Mørkhøj linen and lawn, on the kitchen maids and a cuisine that observed the conventions of the seventeenth-century French court. Hence, at evening meals—which the Count partook of aloofly and joylessly—marzipan was served before the roast, which was followed by a fish terrine (made, since nothing else was available, from the muddy flesh of the moat catfish) and candied fruit and smoked meat. The steward also saw to it that two men were constantly assigned to polishing the silver, which, despite the suspension of time, grew tarnished in the drawers and chests, and that butlers and servants and tapsters were chosen from among those of the estate tenants who could still walk upright with ease and who could be trained to balance the gold service, the colored wineglasses, and the dusty, monogrammed jars and bottles from the endless cellars of the manor house.

In addition to this, Carl Laurids's father was the only person at Mørkhøj who kept in touch with the outside world. It was he who collected letters sent to Mørkhøj from the gate, and brought them to Jacoby, who gave them to the Count—who always considered them so anachronistic. They concerned taxation, and compulsory schooling for the children of the estate tenants, and censuses and parish registers and the necessity of supplying soldiers. All of them concerned the things that Mørkhøj ought to be contributing to society, although the Count knew it was the outside world that ought to be eternally grateful to him. Even so, they made his blood boil. Fired by his indignation, he would dictate replies—in Latin and filled with elegantly turned insults—to Jacoby, in which he pointed out that his people were doing just fine in the black depths of their ignorance and that it was a ridiculous idea to count them because they could no longer be told apart and that he would never dream of supplying soldiers because he had need of every man for the defense of Mørkhøj and who did they think they were, demanding this, that, and the other of him, a man who lived at the center of the world? Jacoby made fair copies of these letters in splendidly convoluted capitals and in as many as fourteen drafts before the Count approved them and signed them and sealed them himself and finally, on the large, deckle-edged envelope, in his own hand, added the words "Virtue above All," believing thus to have plugged, in fine fashion, the little chinks in his dream, a dream with which we, too, are familiar: the dream of being able to shut oneself off from the state and the world and one's own time.

The letters were handed over to the steward, but Carl Laurids's father never sent them. Naturally he never sent them. He unsealed them and rewrote them. Carl Laurids's earliest memories were of his father hunched over the black script on the finely contoured paper, painstakingly writing, his pale face drawn and lined by the weariness of two hundred years and his sight partially ruined by his constantly having to keep an eye on everything and peer through the darkness of the estate, illumined as it was by nothing other than tallow dips and wax tapers. The steward knew there would be no point in mentioning the new moderator lamps and oil lamps to the Count.

I am sure that later, much later, Carl Laurids must have wondered what his father was doing on these nights with his superior's correspondence, but in those days he looked upon it merely as a natural expression of his father's omnipotent superintendence of life and death at Mørkhøj. So, at this early stage and with the benefit of hindsight, only you and I realize that the steward wrote to prevent the Mørkhøj house of cards from coming tumbling down.

Before the steward and his wife adopted Carl Laurids, their lives were totally bound up with Mørkhøj. Before that time they could not be said to have done anything other than fulfill their function in the service of the Count, apart, that is, from the small but essential detail of the rewritten letters, and even that constituted an act of obedience. But now here they were, adopting Carl Laurids, who may have been one of the smallholders' children. That in itself is odd—that a steward should adopt a smallholder's child—although it can perhaps be explained by the fact that it is hard to tell by looking at a baby how it is going to turn out. But that they did not, subsequently, stop Carl Laurids is something for which I have been unable to come up with any decent explanation.

It turns out that when he adopted Carl Laurids, the steward committed a crime, in that he persuaded Jacoby to record the child's name in the manor chronicle and keep an account of its age, which was an unheard-of and dangerous breach of the estate's one-year chronology. This breach made it possible, later on, to determine that Carl Laurids is seven years old when the steward draws up in the manor house yard one morning on a horse now so low-slung that his legs drag along the ground. And there he stays, stock-still, as the day wears on and the horse droops in the midday sun that rises clear of the wall, just for a little while, to cast the fuzzy shadows of the rusty iron spikes across the solitary rider in the tricorn hat and the gauntlets. When he is still there, rooted to that selfsame spot, the next morning, Jacoby makes his way over to him, to discover that he is as dead as a doornail and that rigor mortis is all that keeps him and his horse—which is wedged between his legs—upright.

On the day prior to his death the steward had taken his foster son—Carl Laurids, that is—out of Mørkhøj for the first time. They had driven in a little open carriage to the railroad station in the nearest town, which was Rudkøbing (although I would not have thought it had a railroad station). While Carl Laurids drank in his surroundings with eyes like saucers, the steward stared straight ahead, rigid and impervious to the shouts of the boys who ran along the road behind the carriage, and to the crowd that gathered around them while they waited at the railroad station, and to the town that struck him as being some demented magnification of the handful of low-roofed houses he remembered from his youth, 170 years before.

So there they stand, man and boy, with the little horses—dressed in the clothes of the previous century and utterly alone. And yet only the steward's hands are shaking; Carl Laurids is quite cool. Then the train pulls in and the horses nearly go berserk. Miss Clarizza has subsequently described how—just as she stepped down onto the platform with her hatboxes and suitcases and trunks and looked, aghast, at the steward in his wig and high-heeled buckled shoes struggling to force the muzzles of the little horses groundward—her eyes met those of Carl Laurids, which were fearless and brimming with a curiosity that knew no bounds.

From the train, besides Miss Clarizza, they collected a grand piano and a royal court photographer complete with his long-legged black instrument. It was Carl Laurids's foster father who had talked the Count into these acquisitions, by dint of which he believed they could more easily turn their backs on the outside world. By introducing photography to Mørkhøj he believed that it would be easier to prove that time stood still, because now, he said, even though the manor's resident painter is dead, we can produce a family portrait that can be placed alongside the paintings lining the stairway up to the banqueting hall, since pictures demonstrate, better than anything else, how everything is as it has always been. With the grand piano, which had been ordered from Switzerland, it would finally be possible to drown out the sound of the mechanical mowers and manure spreaders, which filtered across the wall ever more frequently and had been disturbing the Count's research work ever since the last of the palace musicians, whose playing had always accompanied his work, had collapsed over his instrument. Nevertheless, talking the Count into the photographer and the piano had taken some doing, and both concessions had weighed heavily upon him. And the only reason that he also permitted his steward to advertise for a governess—in newspapers he had heard of but never read—was that, one day, an airplane landed in the grounds of Mørkhøj.

The Count looked at this frail and rickety contraption and recalled, from his youth at the court of Versailles, a similar ungodly experiment involving a large bell filled with hot air. "I remember," he said out of nowhere, to the person standing next to him—who just happened to be Carl Laurids—"how the sinner was smashed to death on the cobblestones of Paris before he could get close enough to the sun for his craft to burst into flames." Carl Laurids made no reply. He just kept his eyes on the supernatural insect that had come over Mørkhøj's wall in a fog of noise, trembled like a bird with a broken wing, given a little dip, and then plummeted earthward like a stone. The pilot survived because the machine fell into the murky lake in the grounds. Under other circumstances he would have been beheaded on the spot, especially after the discovery, the following day, of several catfish floating belly up in the moat—these proud fish having been done to death by the shock wave from the crash. Now, however, the Count looked upon the airplane crash as a natural consequence of all the forces emanating from the Philosopher's Stone and the center of the world, and thus a divine pat on the back for him and his quest. So he had quarters organized for the pilot and had his leg fractures and internal injuries treated with leeches and by bloodletting and various diuretic agents while he attempted to question him, wanting to find out exactly what his position was when he was pulled downward. He was not able to discover anything, however, since the pilot turned out to be English. The Count himself spoke no English, and Jacoby had forgotten his native tongue two hundred years earlier. After a series of powerful purgatives the pilot's soul took off and flew back to where it had come from without him and his host, the Count, ever managing to understand each other.

After this episode, the Count gave permission to advertise for a governess who could teach his children modern languages.

On the day of Miss Clarizza's arrival, the first photograph ever was taken at Mørkhøj. In this picture, which is still in existence, the Count, the Countess, and their three children can be seen standing at the top of the Mørkhøj steps. There is no one on the next step, no one on the one below that, but on the next again stand Jacoby and the steward and his family. Where all the other faces have grown stiff in the knowledge that they are now being captured for eternity, there stands the boy Carl Laurids staring impassively straight into the lens.

The steward died the next day.

The Mørkhøj tenants had always buried their own dead. So, since the Count was busy calculating and Jacoby had long since lost the knack for anything of a practical nature, there was no one to do the needful for the steward's body. In his initial panic, Jacoby had the rigid rider pulled into the shadows, then tried to enter the death in the manor history. This, however, he had to abandon. The chronology would not allow it, it looked all wrong—the steward standing there in the full flower of his manhood, and then dying the same year. So Jacoby deferred this dilemma. As time went on, the air and the sparse light dried out the steward and his horse and the skin stretched over their skulls, making the animal look ever more intelligent and endowing the steward with an increasingly youthful and alert appearance. Both Jacoby and the Count stuck to their old habit of coming out onto the manor house steps at some point in the course of each day to address a couple of remarks to the steward. This was just as it should be, and that he remained silent was of no matter. They had both long since lost any interest in answers: the Count because, on that day two hundred years ago when his guests left him in front of the gilded railings, he had realized that he had all the answers; Jacoby because writing history had shown him that the truth always takes the form of a question. Besides, the steward had always been a man of few words, and even now, when the only sound he uttered came from the faint whistling of the wind in the shafts of bone sticking out, here and there, through the skin, the common folk still bowed respectfully to the motionless figure in the shadow of the main building every morning on their way to work. And they went on with their work knowing that those sandy-gray eyes were upon them.

On the day that the steward was moved into the shadows, Miss Clarizza saw Carl Laurids walk up to his father and take a long, hard look at him. After that, she did not see the boy again until, one morning, there he was, sitting at the back of the schoolroom.

I have been unable to discover how and when Carl Laurids caught the Count's eye or why the latter gave orders for him to take lessons in music and foreign languages from Miss Clarizza, along with his own children. Nevertheless, one day he was there, sitting at the back of the music room, which also did service as a schoolroom and was furnished with little desks fitted with sunken inkwells. Where Miss Clarizza and the three highborn children wore buckled shoes or button boots and frilled shirtfronts or cravats, Carl Laurids was attired in long oiled-leather boots and a shirtfront with a white collar—apparel never previously seen at Mørkhøj. He had walked across the cobbles of the manor house yard from the steward's quarters in this outfit, and the eyes of the workers had followed him all the way. When he disappeared up the steps of the main building, one of the footmen who still had the power of speech spat on the floor. "Ass-licking little Count!" he said.

But no one ever mentioned the boy's clothes to his face. To begin with, everyone expected the steward to bend down from his horse and punish the offending party with his riding crop. Later on, however, they stopped being surprised and only Miss Clarizza never forgot the boy's behavior. It had dawned on her that, in order to come by these clothes, Carl Laurids must have left Mørkhøj—which had always been strictly forbidden to everyone except the steward. That he had done so seemed a sure sign of a peculiarly blind faith in his own worth.

Carl Laurids could now observe these highborn children—who had, until then, shone for him in the glow of untouchable aloofness—at close quarters. From his seat at the back of the schoolroom he discovered that the two countesses, despite several lifetimes of teaching, still could not speak properly, and that the young count,

a boy of his own age, guided his slate pencil with both hands. It was
then that Carl Laurids perceived his own worth in the light of the
obscurantism of these aristocratic offspring. Miss Clarizza would
later maintain that it must have been in the music room, during her
classes, that Carl Laurids made the observation which was to determine the course of his life: that life was not arranged like the
Mørkhøj steps, with set levels; that it ought instead to be regarded
more as a slippery social slope; that an unfortunate combination of
coincidences had conspired to set him at its midpoint, and that it
was, in fact, possible to hang on and climb upward.

It was Carl Laurids's job, during classes—which were held in the
mornings—to close and open the windows and keep the fire going
in the big, open grate. For three years he carried out these duties,
and in three years he learned, without any effort, to read and write
in English, German, and French and to play the piano. He was the
most linguistically gifted child Miss Clarizza had ever taught. Initially, she treated him with firmness and condescension, but she
soon had to capitulate. In the course of those three years he became
the one person at Mørkhøj around whom all her thoughts and hopes
revolved, and behind the authoritative mien her face would glow
with a quiet joy when she looked across the vacant faces of the
Count's children and into Carl Laurids's knowing brown eyes and
said, "Shut the window, Charlie!"

One day Carl Laurids stayed behind after class to tell her, calmly
and politely, that he would no longer be attending to the fire or the
ventilation and that in the future, therefore, she was not to mention
either the weather or the room temperature when he was present
in the class. This was an outrageous request. Had the Count got to
hear of it, Carl Laurids's head would, in all probability, have been
forfeit, and Miss Clarizza did indeed stare at him, stunned. Her
mouth opened and closed in an attempt to come up with a sufficiently
scathing rebuff. Just then Carl Laurids's hands shot up and carefully
adjusted the black velvet ribbon she wore around her neck. At this
touch she was overwhelmed by the loneliness of her life at Mørkhøj
and by a previously unacknowledged tenderness and by the air of
resolve about Carl Laurids, and she threw her arms around him.
The schoolroom contained no furniture other than the desks and,
not wanting to dirty his trouser knees, Carl Laurids lifted his gov-

erness up onto the white grand piano, swept off the open music books in a single gesture, and raised his pitch to hers.

From then on, Miss Clarizza never mentioned the windows or the fire; Carl Laurids considered himself released from his duties. And from then on, the classes were held, according to the seasons, in baking heat or freezing cold.

Carl Laurids's feelings for Miss Clarizza are not known, but there is no doubt that no record of their romance survived. Whenever he left her he forgot all about her, and whenever, urgent with lust, he caught sight of her he was seeing her for the first time. With the result that his advances to her, in the years when he was her lover, retained the furtive, brutal nature of that first time. Miss Clarizza never understood him. It was as though, every time he reached out for her, he posed her the same insoluble riddle and this, together with her loneliness, was what bound her to him. Later, when Carl Laurids had been made the Count's secretary, he and the governess often met at the noble family's dinner table, and, more often than not, she was so terrified of his courteous indifference that she could not eat a bite. By this time she had given up making any demands on him, as she had done in the beginning. Then her tearful reproaches had induced a slight puckering around Carl Laurids's mouth. This had, over the years, hardened into a tiny, permanent line in one corner of his mouth; a little facial tic that he was later to conceal with the waxed mustache he was sporting by the time the world made his acquaintance. From that time onward, Miss Clarizza had grown so afraid of his calmness that she put up, unprotestingly, with his unpredictability.

One day Jacoby disappeared, and when the moat was dragged they found his bones, picked white and clean by the catfish. Nevertheless it was possible to identify them as being his with some degree of certainty, because of the extraordinary joints that had enabled him to produce such incredible flourishes in his handwriting and caused three cardinals, who had been personally acquainted with Ludovici Vicentino, to swear on the Bible that even the master's script had not been more beautiful. The skeleton's skull had been crushed, and it was deduced that Jacoby had been murdered.

Not long after this, the Count appointed Carl Laurids as his personal secretary in Jacoby's place. This appointment seemed only natural and reasonable, since by that time Miss Clarizza had given up trying to teach Carl Laurids anything. He had taught himself Italian and Spanish, and for the past six months Jacoby had been teaching him Latin and calligraphy. And yet there was something not quite right about this appointment. Even in the fossilized numb-skulls of Mørkhøj, suspicion of Carl Laurids smoldered. From then on, Miss Clarizza and the noble family and Carl Laurids's mother were the only ones who did not turn their backs when they saw him. Everyone else sneaked off as he approached, even the red cows with their udders dragging along the ground, and the decrepit horses, and the bald chickens that laid black, inedible eggs; and even the catfish, normally so motionless, slipped down into the mud when he walked across the drawbridge.

Carl Laurids sent Jacoby's bones to England, because the Count had the idea that the English court would raise a monument over the great penman's earthly remains. But in the winter following the summer of Carl Laurids's appointment, Jacoby returned to Mørkhøj. Miss Clarizza saw him arrive. He left no tracks in the snow of the driveway and stepped straight through the locked main door. That same evening she saw him sitting opposite Carl Laurids in the office that had once been his own, and after that she often saw them together, although she was never able to ascertain whether Carl Laurids was aware of the phantom's presence.

It was at this time that Carl Laurids learned about the course of history. Until then, time had meant nothing at Mørkhøj, or to Carl Laurids. All that the watchmen's song had conveyed was the rhythm of days and nights, which were sort of inside one another, if you see what I mean: before Carl Laurids was made secretary the days at Mørkhøj were not piled on top of one another. It was as though it were, in fact, the same day, or at any rate the same year, that kept coming around again, and so time led nowhere. But now Carl Laurids gained access to the one hundred folios containing the history of Mørkhøj, and there he unearthed the first clues to something that sent him delving into these books with their interminable record of recurrence. That something was transience. He discovered that in the midst of all this apparent regularity there were little things that sank and disappeared, never to return. There is no way of telling what first aroused his suspicions, but when it happened he had some kind of attack of total concentration. Night and day he sat reading in his office, and since, just at this moment, the Count himself was thinking that he was about to hit the bull's-eye, that he was now standing before the gates of truth, and was therefore seized by a rapturous, unrelenting lust for work, there was no one to disturb Carl Laurids, except for Miss Clarizza. Now and then she tiptoed into his office—although he may not even have noticed—to put fresh candles in the candlesticks and stand for a moment watching him. Now and again, when driven out of their chairs by their zeal, the Count and Carl Laurids would meet on the stairways and in the corridors of the manor amid the suits of armor and faded tapestries, and Miss Clarizza would see them pass each other without lifting their heads—the Count in a black robe and garters with rosettes, Carl Laurids in shirtsleeves and oiled-leather boots. On these occasions Jacoby was usually walking behind Carl Laurids with a somewhat mournful expression on his face and his elegant hands clasped behind his back. As they walked there, it was hard to tell whether they were alive or dead, and hence they resembled our own impression—and that of their contemporaries—that even then, at the beginning of this century, there was a ghostly air about the Danish aristocracy.

Carl Laurids began by reading backwards through the history of Mørkhøj, back to the erection of the wall and beyond, further back than anyone had ever read before, back to the great Paracelsus' visit, and to the founding of the estate, to that year when one of the Count's distant forefathers had kicked a rock out of the wall in the prison in which he had been incarcerated for lese majesty and had then fulfilled the sacred oath he had taken by walking in the direction of Rome for three days with the rock under his arm and, on the spot where he halted, laying the foundations for the church around which his new manor would be built. During his reading, Carl Laurids had registered so many changes, so many events that had taken place and were now, irrevocably, past, that he felt confident that time was a fact. It was from this point that he began his reconstruction of Mørkhøj's history. In dazzling flashes of clarity he understood what was hidden behind all those inky deletions with which Jacoby had masked Mørkhøj's original chronology. He recreated those moments at which the Count had resigned from all official posts and honorary political duties in order to devote himself wholeheartedly to proving that Mørkhøj stood at the center of a timeless world. He calculated his way to the date of the party at which the Count had presented his discovery to the world and had been let down. And after months of hollow-cheeked industry he drew up the chronology of Mørkhøj since the day the clocks were stopped. With this accomplished, Carl Laurids felt that the future had planted, on his forehead, the kiss that would awaken him fully from Mørkhøj's sleep of yesteryear, which he now knew to have lasted for exactly two hundred years. He was, at this time, eighteen years old and had been the Count's secretary for three years. He also knew that for the rest of the world the year was 1918.

It was at this point that the Count summoned Carl Laurids. The old man had been weakened by his work and thwarted expectations. In order to restore his vigor he had had himself bled six times in quick succession. Initially, these tapping operations had no effect, but shortly thereafter he was struck by a serious case of blood poisoning and septic fever, which led to a paralysis that spread upward from his abdomen. This is the usual direction taken by such things in Denmark—always upward from the abdomen, especially with elderly men suffering face-to-face with young men like Carl Laurids. Granted, he is not the Count's son, but still the situation strikes me as symbolic: the Count lying on his sickbed paralyzed below the waist, and Carl Laurids sitting on the edge of his bed—man of the new era. And what is he doing? He is reading aloud. The paralysis has also weakened the Count's sight, and when this occurs he is gripped by mistrust of his own memory. So he sends for Carl Laurids, to read the history of Mørkhøj to him and refresh his memory on certain points, such as what the great Paracelsus had said.

The bed in which the Count lay while Carl Laurids read to him had been set up in the laboratory under the big hole in the roof through which the Count's machines were directed toward the celestial equator. Now Carl Laurids began to read backwards, from the day when the Count's guests took their leave of him. But instead of reading exactly what was there on the page, he read with his own discovery of the law of change constantly in mind. During the readings, which went on week after week, he and the Count became closer to each other than they had ever been. What brought them together was the one crucial question—one that is also of interest to the rest of us—of whether time really does exist, and it was with a sense of fellowship not normally found between master and servant that they made their way together through the distances that had erased the great Paracelsus' words when he was carried up from the cellars where he had whiled away the time with tokay and three whores from Copenhagen, and had lifted his head from the stretcher and said damned if this wasn't the center of the world.

By the time they had got to this point, the Count was confined to bed and there was nothing left to stop Carl Laurids as he worked his way toward the present, reading of the inbreeding of the cows and the horses and the people and the death of the musicians and the cattle plague and the fungus against which Mørkhøj's medieval agricultural techniques were powerless and about such an incredible number of other events that he read right into the winter, even though he began in the autumn. On Christmas Eve, Miss Clarizza climbed up to the laboratory to call them down to the dinner table where the children and the Countess waited in fearful silence around the gold plate for Papa, who happened to be the Count and who had now been in the laboratory for so long that they barely remembered what he looked like.

She found them in the gloaming, with Carl Laurids reading by the glow from the luminous liquids in the alembics. When they became aware of her they sent her away again, saying that they wanted their food sent up; there could be no thought of breaking off just as they had got to a particularly exciting part: Carl Laurids recounted the dwindling of the Mørkhøj linen stocks, the steward's rewriting of the Count's mail, and Jacoby's registration of his, Carl Laurids's, birth, and if tiredness occasionally caused him to flag, he was immediately prompted by the Count, who never said a word during the reading but saved his protests and grew ever more convinced—even though the paralysis had now spread to most parts of his body—that he had never been closer to immortality. Carl Laurids recounted his education and his father's death, and all the times he had left Mørkhøj without permission, and his eyes never left the book, not even when the Count ordered the steward's mummified body to be brought up, horse and all, so that he could assure himself that it was in fact death that had endowed the steward with the sharp gaze under which life at Mørkhøj continued unchanged. While the paralysis was making it difficult for the Count to breathe,

Carl Laurids read of his affair with Miss Clarizza, pausing only for a brief moment to draw closer to the Count and drown out the weak wheeze of his breath.

On New Year's Eve the paralysis reached the Count's face, which stiffened into the expression of imperious arrogance that had only ever deserted it when he had been really drunk. And then Carl Laurids read about his discovery that even though the Count believed the opposite, time did in fact pass, and about how he had bashed in Jacoby's skull with the wooden sole of one of his boots and thrown him into the moat. Prompted by an evil glint in the Count's eye (this glimmer being now the only sign of life), he recounted how he had, just before he began to read, forged the manor accounts and stolen the last gold ducats from the cellars. It would be wrong to regard these admissions as calculated acts of malice against a dying man; the readings had long since elevated the Count and his secretary beyond the question of guilt and justice.

In the evening the children and the Countess and Miss Clarizza gathered at the sickbed, and then Carl Laurids reached the end of the last volume. The Count's cheeks were a hectic red, but Carl Laurids's were very pale and his voice remained intense and distinct as he read of the new law of succession which would come into effect on this night, New Year's Eve 1918, and which meant that, if the Count died on the other side of midnight, those few assets remaining would fall to the state. Just then Miss Clarizza heard the Countess sobbing, and when she felt a chill draft at her neck and turned around she saw Jacoby standing between the open window and the steward's corpse, which had been propped up against the wall. Apparently no one except herself had noticed the former secretary. As the Count's eyes veiled over and began to roll back, Carl Laurids turned the last page of the folio and read about this New Year's Eve and who was present and what had been served for dinner. Then the dying man opened his eyes for one last time and looked straight at his secretary. At that moment they heard the watchman singing down in the manor house yard. Carl Laurids stopped reading. As the singing faded away the Count's eyes opened wide and grew misty and gray as the wall around Mørkhøj. Carl Laurids straightened up. And in that same moment, as the draft rustled the pages of the book, he turned his weary face toward the figure of the former secretary and said, "Shut the window, Jacoby!"

AMALIE TEANDER

The house in Rudkøbing

Time that passes

1853–1909

IT IS A SUNDAY MORNING in Rudkøbing on Langeland. Amalie is four years old. At 11 a.m. precisely, on the dot, her grandmother has the big front door opened to admit the citizens of the town. They have been standing freezing in the street, which is a tribute, a mark of respect, a token of their humility in the face of Amalie's grandmother, the Old Lady, whom they know they are not going to see anyway. Now they are being allowed inside, where it is warm, now they are filing past the dim splendor of room after room and the life-size bronze lamps in the shape of young, naked men, and the aviaries full of brightly colored birds. They walk along endless corridors, lit by hissing gas jets, that lead them past the open door. On a dais, reached by ascending steps of white Persian marble, sits the first water closet in Rudkøbing, in Langeland—possibly even the first in the whole of provincial Denmark. It is mounted upon four lion's feet, and despite its weight the white bowl seems to float on a brilliant profusion of red painted flower petals executed with such skill that they seem, just now, at this very minute, to have been tossed into the air by a breeze. On the wall to the right of the closet hangs a clock, and beneath the clock, wearing a starched white dress, stands Amalie. Below the dress she is naked, a fact worth noting since the townspeople of Rudkøbing, whom it takes the entire day to file past, are all tightly buttoned up, every one of them, including the children.

Amalie stands with her back to the passersby. There is nothing strange in this. She is a little rich girl, there for decoration and to show the leading families in Rudkøbing that we, the Teander Rabow family, not only possess the finest privy ever seen but also have little cherubs who can turn their backs on your admiring glances. That is what the people passing by think, and that is what the Old Lady would have thought if she had been there, but that is not what Amalie is thinking. She stands with her back turned to observe the gently curved reflection of her audience in the faience of the toilet bowl. And here she makes a discovery. I might even go so far as to say: one of the greatest discoveries of her life. All at once she sees the reflected room collapse inward and fall into perspective, and behind the staggered amazement of the adults and the openmouthed wonder of the children appears a grassy meadow with strange, orange-colored animals, and beyond this she can just make out a purple forest from which comes a whistling sound, and just then something happens to her. It is hard to say exactly what it is; to me it seems as though, from that moment on, Amalie starts searching for just this whistling and just this paradisiacal landscape, which she must have felt was meant for her and her alone, even though, a moment later, it had disappeared. She stood on that platform all day, until the footsteps of the last visitor had wandered off down distant corridors, immersed in the memory of that landscape and filled with the triumphant melancholy of the chosen.

Amalie had never seen her grandfather, but her aunt, Gumma, had once shown her his photograph. Gumma was a cripple, following a badly healed fractured hip, and she negotiated the house's labyrinth of corridors and never-ending suites of rooms on a black-lacquered tricycle of complex construction. She had once given little Amalie a ride on this vehicle, and in one room—which they had entered by chance and which they never again succeeded in locating—she had pointed out to Amalie her grandfather, Frederik Ludwig Teander Rabow, in a series of daguerreotypes taken at intervals of several years from the time when, as a young man, he had won an old hand-operated printing press and some packs of yellowed paper in a nocturnal card game to when his muscular body began to blur at the edges and finally grew quite transparent. In the later pictures he can just be made out next to his wife, Amalie's grandmother, as a powdery cloud shimmering in the light of the magnesium flash.

By this time, the free broadside that had been his first publishing venture—possessed, as he was, by the illiterate's fascination with the printed word—had been transformed into a daily newspaper, and he had long been forgotten. As far as anyone remembered, Amalie's grandmother—of whom it was said that her father had been a refuse collector and nightman: in other words, he earned his living carting away shit—had always been the editor. For her own part, she no longer set foot outside the family home. These days the public encountered her vast and legendary store of knowledge about the town and its environs only in the newspaper. In its pages she could predict births and deaths and suicides and bankruptcies long before they took place, convincing the people of the town that their fates were in the hands of a Providence with which the Old Lady obviously had dealings. And so the paper hung on to its subscribers, even when the Old Lady disappeared from view and the printers and journalists stepped between her and the paper, which had, by this time, grown into a dream of a newspaper: six loose sheets, its accounts of the previous day's events scanned by more or less everyone in town, and the rest of Langeland, as they searched for their own futures.

It was at this time that the white house on the square was built. Barred, sheer and sharply gabled as a chalk cliff, this was the house into which the Old Lady withdrew, and the day on which the water closet was put on view was the first occasion in a generation that the house had been opened to the public. Only the oldest living residents of the town had retained a vague memory from the time when it was built, of a rectangular, unechoing courtyard, a covered well, and dim, hushed colonnaded galleries.

Somewhere among all those rooms and studies the Old Lady continued to dictate the newspaper's editorial to her secretary every morning, without herself ever learning to read or write, and in these rooms her husband, Amalie's grandfather—long since forgotten by the outside world—began to dissolve at the edges and, a few years later, disappeared completely. The Old Lady herself showed her face less and less often to her family, and through all her childhood Amalie saw her on only a handful of occasions. Scores of managers and secretaries—who had become necessary after the Old Lady bought up, first several other newspapers, and then printers and paper mills—received their dictated orders on slips of paper that they found on their desks in the offices and clerks' rooms—more and more of which were being set up within the never-ending confines of the white house.

Even on that momentous open day, even on water-closet Sunday, the Old Lady did not put in an appearance. Nevertheless, despite her absence (or, who knows: perhaps precisely because of it), the visitors had a strong sense of her presence, a sense they shared with the servants and with the Old Lady's own family, for whom the preparations for the great day had begun without any warning: the servants were taken by surprise, one day, by the sharp hack of chisels and the bitter smell of new wood. At the end of one of the corridors they had discovered six foreign workmen working intently and with great dexterity at a mysterious task and talking a language in which they sounded as though they were smacking their lips. At the end of two weeks they disappeared, leaving behind a locked room which, when it was opened the following Sunday, proved to contain this wonder, the water closet—at that time possibly Denmark's grandest premises for shitting in, ordered and paid for by the Old Lady, who had, in her youth, cut and sold peat, and had lived on a smallholding no better than a dunghill until her husband—Frederik Ludwig, now vanished—had, in a drunken haze, won a hand-operated printing press and begun publishing the broadside that would lead him and his family straight into that dream we all share of money, lots and lots of money.

In her own way, Amalie is just an ordinary child: a little girl from a *nouveau riche* family, with parents and an upbringing and a life to which we will return a little later. But she is also something special; she is a person who has made a discovery or who, at any rate, feels that she is special. And for this reason she causes a chord to reverberate inside every one of us, or at least inside me, and the note she strikes is a reminder of the loneliness of a child growing up in the belief that it is different; a belief that prompted Amalie to gaze into every shining surface: into polished harnesses and shop windows; into the varnish of the school desk, while her teachers called out her name without her hearing, so engrossed was she in trying to find a deeper truth in the reflected extension of her inkwell. The other girls teased her, trying to break through her far-too-adult and incomprehensible isolation, wanting to drag her out of it, until the day when Amalie came out of it all by herself and thrashed the biggest of them, cut off their pigtails and burned their fair locks in the school playground, showing everyone, the teachers, too, that they had confused her distraction with mildness and that, although she was a child and, at this point, just nine years old, her character was fraught with calculated brutality. After that they left her alone, or at least most of them did, even the servants and her mother, who often had to spend hours searching for her, only to find her, eventually, in some far-off corner of the house on a chair that she had dragged in front of one of the corridor mirrors, to sit with her elbows propped up on the gilded console, staring at a point beyond her ringlets and freshly ironed white collar. And to those who tried to drag her away from there, even her mother, she gave curt, impertinent replies that were both impudent and dreamy.

There is something baffling about a child's being able to keep a secret for so long. It is possible that Amalie did in fact confide in someone, but that is neither here nor there because here we are writing the story of dreams. Amalie would look back on her childhood as a time when she was utterly and absolutely alone, until the day when she discovered an ally in her father. Until then, silent and aloof, she had circulated, on the streets and at school, among people and surroundings that she hardly seemed to notice—and that is neither normal nor good for any child. She spent the long afternoons at home, endlessly wandering in search of glimpses of the orange animals and purple forests, and sometimes she lost her way and had to walk for days before chance, sooner or later, brought her into a clerks' room or a corridor that she knew.

During these years she makes some important discoveries. She soaks up the atmosphere of this Victorian home. Everywhere, in the diversity of these innumerable rooms, she encounters the same lopsided heaviness as that of tropical palms thrown off balance, and of immovable chairs floating on tasseled clouds, and of the libraries and studies where it seems that only the weight of the books prevents the bookcases and heavy desks from toppling over. Everywhere silence reigns. Even the sound of the gas lamps is absorbed by the shimmering drapes and the stiff portieres that keep out all the light and are too heavy for Amalie to pull back. Which is why, in all her wanderings, she never can tell whether the rooms she passes through face onto the street or onto the narrow, unechoing yard, or are situated in some inexplicable spot in the center of this bewildering edifice.

Sometimes Amalie would meet her grandmother, but on these occasions the Old Lady rarely noticed her granddaughter. Her sight was going, but still she bustled through the rooms, guided by some instinctive spatial recall, tightly swathed in wool like her furniture, on her way to her office—the location of which was known only to her and her secretary. There, every day, regardless of everything else, regardless of her increasing blindness and her impaired hearing and her isolation, she shouted out the paper's renowned editorial, which predicted any shifts in the political affiliations of its subscribers and adjusted its slant accordingly, with the result that the paper was regarded as being uncompromising and changeless when, in fact, from being conservative, and patriotic, and loyal to Estrup's dictatorship it had switched to being first critical and rebellious, then radical and revolutionary, only, later, to slip back to its original standpoint, in a smooth action that partly followed, partly anticipated that of its readers—who continually, therefore, found themselves, and only themselves, in its pages.

Amalie had, of course, always known her father. And yet it makes sense to say that she was about nine years old before she got through to him, and this expression "to get through to" was one she herself was later to use to explain her experiences.

It so happened, one evening, that she heard a sound somewhere in the house and followed it and discovered that it was nothing but the distant clattering of the servants and of Gumma's tricycle, so she went on and heard a second sound and followed that until she recognized her mother's tubercular cough, and heard a third sound and followed that, and then something happened. She entered a large, lit room that rang with the sound of raised voices. In this room something quite unique was taking place. In this room her grandmother, who normally fought shy of appearing in public except when it was absolutely necessary, was celebrating her company's anniversary, and at the moment that Amalie stepped into the room, her father, Christoffer Ludwig Teander Rabow, stood up to make a speech. Amalie rarely looked straight at her father, but now she stared at him and noticed a slight but disturbing resemblance between him and the portraits of his father that Gumma had once shown her. This resemblance lay in the fact that her father's, Christoffer Ludwig's, contours were so blurred and his form so elusive that it was possible to catch glimpses, straight through him, of the pictures on the wall behind.

From the moment he was born, Christoffer, Amalie's father, had been treated like a doll—left in the paralyzing care of the housemaids by parents too taken up with their work of writing and editing and printing and distributing the paper and doing accounts and investing and buying up property and mixing with those townsfolk who at that time could still remember buying peat from Frederik Ludwig and treated the family with a contempt that was gradually quelled as the balance sheets expanded to the point where it was necessary to take on office staff. When Christoffer's mother (later to become the Old Lady) looked up from the figures she controlled with all the poise of a juggler—notwithstanding her inability to read—and caught sight of her son, who was then just one year old, her first thought was: I wonder if he's old enough to deliver papers. So she had his long white dress pulled off, only to find that his chubby legs, which had been kissed raw by the housemaids and smelled of scented talcum powder, could not even support him because he was only one year old. After that she forgot all about him again until he was four years old, and then, seeing that he could now keep his balance, she had a suit of clothes made for him, complete with waistcoat, jacket, high collar, and detachable cuffs. Every day the maids had to take him from the nursery, along the corridors, to a private office next door to his father's. There they left the boy, on a raised chair, in a solitude broken only by sudden bursts of music from the musical cigar box on his desk, which was supposed to play whenever Christoffer offered his business contacts one of the Havana cigars, specially imported for the family, with which his mother had provided him, just as she had remembered to open an expense account for him—and all because she had not an ounce of understanding of children and their ways. This was also demonstrated by the way in which she and her husband took Christoffer with them to the grand dinners to which they were invited because the town's mayor and doctors and pastors and lawyers and consuls and industrialists and merchants feared these two parvenus, this odd couple, who still carried the smell of peat and cow barns with them wherever they went, accompanied by their son—that performing monkey, folk called him, that dandified dwarf, that tarted-up tot— Christoffer Teander. Thus he had learned, from a very early age, to conceal his disquiet behind a mask of courteous indifference until no one, no one at all, paid any more heed to him. Until the day when his father raised his head from years of hard work and realized that they must have made a mistake because his son's desk was covered, not by balance sheets or articles or charts, but by a forest of storybook creatures cut out of the pages of the newspaper. Frederik Ludwig would have demanded an explanation of his son, but by that time his contours were already starting to dissolve and his voice wavered as he asked Christoffer why he was not writing. From his son's hesitant replies he grasped the fact that he could neither read nor write but was, like himself, illiterate. And when, speechless with grief, he pointed at all the cut-up sheets of Christoffer's childhood lying scattered around the room in a layer three feet deep, the child answered, "You see, Father, it comes apart so easily, because the pages aren't glued in!"

Frederik Ludwig would have warned his wife, but his voice let him down. Not long after this she had the family's German doctor, Dr. Mahler, admit Christoffer to the nearest sanatorium, where he underwent Dr. Kneipp's water cure and contracted a dreadful bout of double pneumonia from the morning walks—barefoot, across the dewy autumn meadows—prescribed as part of this cure. This bout of pneumonia lodged itself in his skinny body in the form of a malignant fever that refused to release its grip on him, even after he had returned to his childhood home, where his father, Frederik Ludwig, was now no more than a vague shadow against the tapestries and high paneling. At this point, Christoffer lost his hair, even though he was not yet twenty, and thereby acquired a staggering resemblance to his father. And the fact that Christoffer was now the spitting image of his father may have accounted for Frederik Ludwig's dissolution's going almost unnoticed.

One morning, Christoffer woke up to discover that the fever had left him. Driven by an impulse to make his dreams come true in some way other than by cutting them out of paper, he decided to leave home. He hunted in vain for clothes, which were kept he knew not where—there always having been women around to help him get dressed—and all he found was a necktie that he could not tie. Dressed in slippers and pajamas, he left his childhood home, dismissing his worries with a wave of the hand. What was a tie compared to freedom of the individual. And it was late in the day before he gave up, having lost his way and wandered around the streets, being laughed at by people who pointed at him and knew that there went the editor's son, who couldn't even tie his own shoelaces. It was night by the time he found his way home, to a door that his mother had locked, and when he was let in the next morning a new and chilly calm had settled over his movements, previously so febrile and aimless. It was as though he had left his impatience behind, out there in the cold of the night through which he had sat on the doorstep, contemplating the twinkling stars. The next day, for the first time, he wore the Swiss fob watch he had had since his confirmation without ever learning to tell the time, and his mother— whom people were starting to call the Old Lady—felt convinced that he had sorted himself out. When, a week later, she asked him what the time was and he answered correctly, her eyes filled with a triumph reminiscent of what the rest of us would understand by happiness.

When she and her husband began publishing their broadside, she—who had only ever been familiar with the seasons and the difference between night and day—became obsessed with the passage of time, with the inexorable march of minutes and seconds. It may have been thanks to her visionary talents and the business sense with which these were inextricably linked that she realized, before anyone else, the significance of the relationship between time and financial calculations. She wrote away for Swiss-made precision chronometers and had them set up in all of the offices and, later, in all the corridors and communicating rooms of the house and, as time went on, in the bedrooms and the boudoirs and the water closets; and every morning—when she was always up before anyone else—she synchronized all the clocks. Hundreds of them were fitted with striking mechanisms that made the building vibrate every quarter hour with their crisp and utterly, perfectly synchronous chimes. When she first started to withdraw, she carved up the day for her employees. Everywhere—in the offices and the printshop and the editorial offices and the stockrooms—charts were discovered that seemed to have appeared out of the blue and laid down the time at which work should begin, the course of the working day, the brief lunch break, and the time to go home.

Christoffer Ludwig took to these straight roads of time so diligently and meticulously that his fondness for storybook creatures made of paper might in fact always have been a hankering after order of the kind he now discovered in the lists of accounts, the yellow filing cabinets, and the growing piles of orders, all of which he went through only in order to draw up the endless number of charts that appeared—without anyone's being able to clarify where the order came from—to be his one great and weighty responsibility. They were timetables, these charts, in which it was possible to look up any hour of the clock and see, in the first instance, what he himself would be doing. The first chart was a checklist of his own time, from that point in the morning, in his bedroom, when he was dressed by the maids—those intermediaries in Christoffer Ludwig's never-ending battle with items of clothing with which he never came to terms—until, back in the same place, he was helped into bed after a day spent in the big office or on his long walks along the maze of corridors that always left him baffled, and through which he found his way only because he was accompanied by one of the housemaids. The maids, for their part, always kept to the corridors with which they were positively familiar, and never went anywhere in the house without experiencing a pang of fear at the thought of getting lost.

First of all, Christoffer mapped out his own time—so precisely that there was an entry for every half second of the day (an onerous task for a man so averse to being in close proximity to women, since this involved three housemaids keeping watch at his bedside for several months, in order that he might map out his normal sleeping pattern). Then he turned his attention upon the other office employees—not because he had reached the end of the road as far as analyzing his own time was concerned but because his mother was urging him to get a move on.

Then, one day, the Old Lady disappeared. One morning she was seen by a few employees, who came in particularly early to clean their offices, following her son at a distance as he was escorted through the house, which had now become like one great smoothly running timepiece. Wherever he went, Christoffer's movements were synchronized with the innumerable clocks that he passed on his way to his office; and, for the employees, it was as though all the delivery dates, deadlines, and bill-of-exchange expiry dates hung around them in an atmosphere so concentrated that they could reach out and touch it. The Old Lady stood for a while at the double doors into her son's office, gazing intensely upon his hunched back. That was the last anyone saw of her. As she turns away and disappears into the labyrinth, all of those who see her go are struck, at the same moment, by the thought that under the straining satin dress and the stays that two of the brawniest kitchen maids have drawn tight every morning with the aid of a broom handle, her plump body moves with a waggish youthfulness that, in itself, blasphemes dreadfully against time. This thought, however, strikes them as being so unwonted that they all avoid one another's eyes and push it away.

The gap left by the Old Lady was filled by the way in which the business automatically continued to flourish. To begin with, the journalists were shocked when the necessary, but unwritten, articles seemed to materialize in the wicker baskets on their desks. Every morning the printers were astonished to find that deliveries of paper had turned up, inexplicably, all by themselves, and the office managers tried to conceal their amazement at the ever-swelling stream of orders pouring in, all unaided, from every part of the country and, as time went on, from distant continents with unpronounceable delivery addresses or postal codes written in exotic characters. After a while, however, their minds were set at ease by the thought that the Old Lady had merely withdrawn, like some Egyptian pharaoh, into a distant tomb or one of her luxurious privies, from where—from a gilded sarcophagus roomy enough for a body that was bound still to be as big and as agile as a rhinoceros's—she could keep an eye on them all. And they saw that it was possible for her to act in such a fashion because everything had been set into perpetual motion—in short, because she had succeeded in realizing the dream of the *nouveau riche*, the upstart, the parvenu, the tyrant, and the company president: that of having a total, one hundred percent firm grip on time.

Her quiescence must also, I think, have been reinforced because Christoffer Teander sat there, every day, bent over his columns, only straightening up to flick away a speck of dust that had fallen onto a lapel as immaculate as his unnaturally white collars, or onto his shirtfronts, which were stiff as the armor in the banqueting hall (fitted out to the Old Lady's specifications). Such small gestures, which would in others have indicated a lively interest in their outward appearance, made Christoffer look more like a puppet or a jumping jack than ever before, more than when he had, as a little boy, been the mute observer of his parents' social calls. And since he never spoke to his employees, it never occurred to anyone—not even the housemaids who surveyed his nakedness, without any curiosity, every morning and evening—that behind the lackluster forehead, the unseeing eyes, and the wavering contours there hid a human being. The announcement of his engagement did nothing to alter this impression.

One morning all the family's social and business acquaintances received a white card announcing the glad tidings of the engagement between Christoffer Ludwig Teander Rabow and Katarina Cornelius Bak, the dean's daughter. Everyone thought it was a joke. They all knew for a fact that Christoffer Ludwig and the dean's daughter had never met. For one thing, throughout his childhood and adolescence, Christoffer had only ever left his oversized office on a very few occasions. And for another, he had always been duly escorted by the servants or his parents. And lastly, Katarina had, at these times, been away, visiting the German spas, in vain attempts to cure a cough which, even then, sounded bad. Nevertheless, this card planted a nagging doubt in most minds, since, even though it bore no signature, it was printed in Venus Extra Bold. This typeface, together with the heavy, bittersweet scent of dried Australian carnations, reminded most recipients of Christoffer's mother and her grip on the future. The Reverend Mr. Cornelius himself was at first taken aback, then angry, then furious. Finally he calmed down and entered, instead, a mood of silent reflection in which, for some days, his thoughts revolved around his daughter, whose silence was broken only by bouts of coughing. At last he sought out Christoffer Teander, unearthing him in his office. Wordlessly, the dean places the invitation in front of him. Christoffer peruses it carefully; then he studiously compares the date set for the engagement with his timetables, and only after having done this does he look at the dean. "It is quite impossible for this engagement to have taken place, unless it occurred in less than half a second," he says without the trace of a smile.

Cornelius leaves him, convinced that the whole thing is nothing but a bad joke. In his opinion, Christoffer is an idiot, a complete and utter idiot. Amen.

A few months later the wedding invitation arrived. It had been delivered during the night, without anyone's seeing how this was achieved; it was tasteless and ostentatious; printed in gold on sheets of stiff deckle-edged paper embossed with the Old Lady's monogram—a silk scarf entwined around a miter; ornamented with cupids carrying champagne bottles in their chubby fists; the Rudkøbing coat of arms running all the way around the edge. It detailed every stage in the course of the great day, from the wedding itself—which was to take place at half-past five in the morning so that all the servants and office managers and printers, who worked on Sundays, could be back in time to start work—through the wedding reception, which would be held in the long courtyard, right up to the dinner in the evening, the schedule for which had been worked out right down to the very last second. It listed the names of the townspeople who would make speeches at this dinner and how long these speeches would be, along with a brief summary of their content and directions as to the length of time allowed for the applause before proceeding with the consumption of a menu—also specified—which presented a monstrous combination of the Old Lady's partiality for the dishes of her impoverished upbringing and her fascination with wealth. Barley gruel was to be served with the champagne, then a bacon omelette with syrup and crème de menthe, and wine jelly made with Château Margaux and marzipan preserved in duck fat. Coffee, cognac, and the refined potato aquavit that the Old Lady had persisted in preferring to liqueurs and fortified wines would be accompanied by indoor fireworks set off at the stucco ceilings. An eighteen-piece orchestra dressed in firemen's uniforms would provide music for the dancing. Pralines, whole coffee beans, white bread, pats of butter, and cold griddle cakes with blackcurrant jam would also be served, along with draft lager. With a mind to the close of the evening, four strong and rough characters, four real toughs from a remote village, had been hired and paid to stay sober until daybreak, at which point they would assist the last of the guests to leave the premises; said guests being mentioned by name, both those who stepped willingly into the gray dawn carrying the last barrel of lager between them, and those who would offer resistance and refuse to go home, thus hindering the tidying up that would allow Monday to start on time. These last would have their bottom teeth knocked out by the toughs, who would then bash their heads against the white beech parquet floor before throwing them out into the street, where they would lie in the gutter in their own blood and snot until a specified time at which they would crawl away. Thus the big house at the end of the square would greet the rays of the morning sun with gleaming windows and an air of industry implying that nothing had occurred, apart from the happy event. That is all, and very best wishes, wrote the Old Lady, particularly to those who have been invited to the dinner—of whom there now followed a list, at the foot of which she had signed her name.

The people of the town accepted this invitation with the same resigned wonder with which they would have observed an eclipse of the moon. Even those who found themselves, to their own surprise, on the list of speakers yielded to the weight of Fate and the Old Lady's authority and started jotting down headings in line with the summaries provided in the invitation, and the three lawyers who saw that they were going to have their teeth knocked out and would be crawling home from the party made appointments with their dentists and put signs in their windows saying that they would be closed on the day after the wedding. The Old Lady was accorded such great respect that only the Reverend Mr. Cornelius offered any resistance. Into his sermon for the following Sunday he wove a reminder to everyone, in a passage declaring Woe to Ye that laugh at this bad joke and Woe to Ye that are rich, for it will be the worse for you. Then he dressed in black and walked across the square. He found the main door of the house locked, and no one answered when he tugged the bellpull, but it seemed to him that all the windows of the house stared blankly at him. Boiling with rage and primed for a fight, he arrived home to find his daughter in the act of trying on a wedding dress that had arrived from Copenhagen, though no one could say who had placed the order. It fitted her perfectly. It even had an intricate mesh of whalebone worked into it that straightened her crooked back and endowed her figure with a surprising, stately carriage. Similarly, a pad soaked in spirit of camphor had been fixed inside the stiffened bodice. This, together with the peppermint oil which came with the dress and with which the veil was to be sprayed, was intended to ensure that the wedding would not be spoiled by her coughing. Then the Reverend Mr. Cornelius—who had otherwise walked sedately throughout his life—ran to the church, only, on his arrival, to have his rage consolidate around his mouth in a foam that turned blue when he learned that word had been received about the time at which the coach and the other carriages would be arriving; just as the binding of the wreaths had begun, since the Old Lady, unlike other people, would not have fresh floral decorations, but wreaths of dried carnations and orchids that had arrived long before from Madeira; just as the organist had received a list of what was to be played, including not only the usual hymns but also a number of popular old ditties. But the dean was not yet beaten; he had God on his side in the battle against this woman, this horned monster who had never shown her face in church; whom he had never trusted; who, everyone knew, could not conceal her lack of breeding and who now went so far as to demand that improper songs be played in the church. Well, not if he could help it. Then he saw that among the papers pertaining to the wedding—which also contained, apart from the organist's list, instructions for his, the dean's, nuptial address; instructions into which had been inserted, within brackets, the points where he would clear his throat and the points where he would raise his head and look out over the congregation—there was a sheet of paper enjoining everyone to remember their umbrellas, since a light shower of rain would fall, as a sign of heaven's blessing upon the bridal couple and the guests when they were leaving the church. As a final, panic-stricken protest, the dean grabbed the church register, imagining that by removing it he might prevent the wedding. It flew open in his hands, and his anger ebbed away, leaving behind a weary sense of despondency as he read of the wedding between Katarina Cornelius Bak and Christoffer Ludwig Teander Rabow as though it had already taken place. As he leafed farther away from the written pages toward the blank and unforeseeable pages, he found, in his own handwriting, the record of the birth and christening dates of the three daughters to whom Katarina—to her own astonishment and that of everyone around her—would give birth. Then he realized that the universe was against him. For the first time ever, he felt worn out, old, aged; for the first time ever, he felt his age creating a gap between him and the outside world. This feeling stayed with him as, later, he erased the words of criticism in his sermon, the tone of which softened further in the days prior to the wedding as he acknowledged the advantages of marrying his tubercular, weak-chested daughter to the crown prince of a dynasty, even if that prince was as much of a fool and a nincompoop, as much of a nonentity, as Christoffer Ludwig.

The wedding went ahead according to the guidelines laid down in the invitation. At the church, the dean himself led his daughter to the altar where Christoffer stood waiting. He had been accompanied to the altar by Dr. Mahler because he had no family and because no one could trace any friends. He had, after all, grown up alone, among adults. At the altar the two young people look at each other without showing any sign of recognition, and to those standing nearest it looks as though Katarina, her sight possibly hampered by a veil saturated with peppermint oil, clutches at the doctor's arm in the belief that he is the man she is to marry. No one will ever know for sure whether these two young people had ever laid eyes on each other before. The Reverend Mr. Cornelius sticks scrupulously to his written instructions and the two young faces remain expressionless, apart from during the coughing fits that rack Katarina's body on several occasions, despite all the precautions, and the absentminded disquiet with which Christoffer's eyes flicker forlornly several times around his room bereft of clocks. The rain that started to fall as the married couple left the church continued throughout the night with a mysterious energy that had, by morning, transformed the gutters into rivers that carried the drunk and bleeding lawyers away from the deserted square, so that everything could come to pass as it had been foretold.

At no point during the celebrations did the Old Lady put in an appearance.

Amalie was born the youngest of Katarina and Christoffer Ludwig's three daughters and grew up without ever doubting for one minute that her father was an automaton. The only change brought about in Christoffer's way of life by his marriage was that every evening after dinner he was led into a sitting room, to his family, where previously he had sat alone in a smoking room where he did not smoke. But his face retained, unaltered, the expression of indifferent courtesy that it had borne since he was a child, and, as always, his eyes were riveted to one of the clocks in the room as though he were following the movements of the hands—which, in all probability, is what he was doing. Opposite him, on the sofa, sat his wife. Because of her infirmity, even embroidery—the only thing in which she had ever shown any interest—was beyond her. On only a handful of occasions did Amalie hear her parents speak to each other. From when they were very small, the three daughters were trained in silence and stillness. The housemaids—who toiled in vain, day and night, to rid the vast house of dust and the compromising smell of the stables that the brown soap and dried violets never quite succeeded in quelling—would often pass through the room, feather dusters in hand. On these occasions they would run a duster over the family group in the belief that they, just like the life-size copies of classical Greek figures, were part of the furniture; an illusion shattered now and again by Katarina's feeble cough or one of the increasingly more pronounced fluctuations of Christoffer's silhouette. Nevertheless, it is important that we steer clear of the idea that the Teander family residence was a dead house. Certainly the family are not particularly active; they seem, undeniably, dull as dishwater, but this may be because life in this family—as in the rest of middleclass Denmark at this time—has been shifted from the outer persona of individuals to their inner persona or to their surroundings and, in particular, to the clocks. Thus this waxwork-like couple and their three children exemplify the dream of uniting the unforeseeable in life with the mechanics of clockwork and standard time.

From a very early age, Amalie had populated the silence surrounding her with deafening dreams in which she conquered the world, but not until her grandmother opened the doors of the house to let the people of the town admire the water closet did Amalie discover that her dreams were images of a reality residing within mirrors. It was then that she began her wanderings through the great house. To begin with, her mother tried to prevent it, but she was too weak. Her tuberculosis, already bad by the time of her marriage, had been aggravated by the three times Christoffer had heard his mother's voice. Like everyone else, he had stopped thinking about the Old Lady. There were those who believed that he had stopped thinking of anything whatsoever, other than time, which is, in itself, such an abstract concept that it dissolves at the thought. So it must have come as a shock when, one night, his mother spoke to him and forced him to get up in a darkness his eyes could not penetrate, and led him, naked, through the deserted house, through empty rooms lit by the moon where Christoffer could see that there was no sign of his mother other than the imperious voice that brooked no denial but led him to a white door, which he opened. Only when he reached the bed did he see that it was occupied by his wife. Christoffer felt the Old Lady's breath on the back of his neck and obediently lay down on top of the sleeper.

The third time this happened, Katarina committed a crime—for the first and the last time in her life. While paying a visit to her childhood home she stole an old, rusty revolver from her father's closet, one that she remembered from her childhood but that her father had long forgotten about. After such an exertion she had to wait months before she was strong enough to assure herself that it was loaded, and not until just before she gave birth to Amalie did she release the safety catch and tuck the gun under her pillow, firmly determined, in the future, to shoot at anything that opened her bedroom door after she had retired for the night, even if it should be her mother-in-law's ghost.

This precaution proved to be unnecessary. Christoffer Teander heard his mother's voice only once more after Amalie's birth, and then it was almost unrecognizable.

It happened at the celebration held for the Old Lady's business anniversary. Word of this event had not been announced in advance. Instead it manifested itself in the minds of the fifty-two guests, all of them men, as fifty-two simultaneous and identical feelings of conviction that they had been invited and that all they had to do was to turn up. They gathered, on time, at the Rabow family home in a large oval dining room lit solely by candles. The room's large oval table was spread with a black velvet cloth edged with Valenciennes lace. This interplay of black and white was echoed by the identical white-tie-and-tails outfits worn by the fifty-two guests. Once they were there, the thought struck all of them, simultaneously, that they did not know which anniversary they were celebrating today—because the dates of all the Rabow family triumphs had been forgotten—and that this oval room filled with candles appeared to be decked out for a wake. Only then did they notice the Old Lady. She was sitting at the head of the table with her body, which was bigger and more shapeless than they remembered, squeezed into a dark, carved oak armchair. It looked for all the world as though she were sitting in her own upright coffin, awaiting her burial—an impression reinforced by her having placed, against one wall, her own tombstone on display. This ceiling-high slab of Swedish granite bore as yet—in all modesty—nothing but her name, a detailed list of all the personal and official victories of her life, a salute in verse from a famous Copenhagen poet, and three crosses and a dove inlaid in marble—all burnished to a gleaming, preternaturally dazzling sheen.

Not a single word was spoken during the serving of refreshments, which followed, with unerring accuracy, the program with which all the guests were somehow familiar and which made every word superfluous. These refreshments consisted of a sweet, heavy vintage Madeira and small slices of dry cake.

Nothing was said until the moment for the judging of the competition arrived. This competition had been the only public intimation of the Old Lady's anniversary. It had been announced on the front page of the newspaper along with two lines of verse:

> *This newspaper's praises are easily sung,*
> *But if fault with it we must find*

and all the guests had known beforehand that they were supposed to bring with them a suggestion for the completion of this poem. The entries were now read out one by one by Christoffer's father-in-law, who kept going until all fifty-two had been read. Then it became clear to everyone, at one and the same time, that Dr. Mahler's suggestion was splendid, the best, the winner, and the two golden lines were recited in chorus:

> *It has to be said, when all's said and done,*
> *That nothing springs to mind.*

After this, everyone fell silent as the room shook with the simultaneous striking of all the clocks in the house. A last round of refreshments was then offered, and the fifty-two guests all looked, as one, at the Old Lady—who had not uttered one word, nor would, according to the program—and everyone knew that this would be the last time they would ever see her. For a brief moment, of previously determined length, their thoughts left the room and they recalled how they had known her in their capacities as judges and department heads and doctors and lawyers and chartered surveyors

and town councilors and pastors and magistrates and company directors and landowners and captains, and then they reached for
their glasses to toast the woman who had, like some great clock-
maker, set in motion a mechanism which did not need to be wound
up but which could continue to run for all time.

Then two things occurred that one can never completely guard
against. The first was that Amalie opened the door. The second was
that Christoffer got to his feet and, as one, the other fifty-one guests
put down their glasses. Each in his own way, they understood that,
for the first time since his wedding-day "Yes" in the church, Christoffer Ludwig was going to say something in company and that, for
the first time ever, he was himself going to make a speech. This had
not been foreseen in the Old Lady's schedule.

"Ladies and gentlemen," says Christoffer—and everyone remarks
upon how surprisingly clear his voice is—"I would like to submit
another possible solution, outside of the competition. My poem goes
like this:

> *"This newspaper's praises are easily sung,*
> *But if fault with it we must find,*
> *Then of all that is writ in the Danish tongue*
> *Know that ne'er was a rag so lacking in spine—*
> *Please, glue it and bind."*

After which he sits down and the party's schedule vanishes in a fog
of chatter and murmuring and voicing of opinions. Just at that moment the house clocks start to chime, far too early and all slightly
out of step with one another, as though Christoffer's breach of time
in the oval room has spread to the rest of the building. Everyone
talks even louder to drown out the grating dissonance of all these
timepieces, and, amid this din, only the Old Lady and Amalie were
silent: Amalie because, for the first time ever, she was thinking that
perhaps, at heart, her father was not, after all, constructed out of
weights and pulleys and springs and soulless machinery, as the
mechanical chess player she had seen demonstrated in one of the
markets of her childhood had been; the Old Lady because she was
in danger of bursting with indignation. Not until much later, when
the last of the Madeira had been drunk and the guests had taken
themselves off, singing (because the Old Lady had been so confident

about the way in which the evening would be conducted that she had not hired the bouncers), and after the last candle had burned down in its holder and the room lay in darkness apart from the faint glow of the tombstone—which the Old Lady did not notice because she had long since gone blind—did she say, out into the emptiness inhabited now only by herself and Amalie, "That abominable racket, it sounded like Christoffer!"

The next morning the housemaids found her in the room, dead. Her body was stiff and cold, but about the cracked but still full lips there hung a contented smile that made the servants think that she had, at the hour of her death, made a particularly advantageous deal with the Devil himself. That smile was kept in place by the rigor mortis that also made it impossible to pull her body free of the chair. Which is why they had a cover of oak made for it, and buried her sitting up.

It has not been possible for me to reconstruct the events immediately succeeding the Old Lady's funeral. Once they were over, the people of the town forgot them in the same way that they forgot the cholera epidemics of the nineteenth century, and what occurred left no traces other than two extraordinary editions of the newspaper and a series of evasive answers. All we can be sure of is the beginning and the end. The Old Lady's will was read aloud to Christoffer, Katarina, Amalie, and her sisters in a room that would be used on only one further occasion, after which it apparently ceased to exist. At the instant that the lawyer opened the big brown manila envelope that had been lying in his safe for three years—although he had not the faintest idea how it came to be there—he recognized, to his astonishment, his own handwriting and the Old Lady's impatient dictation style. And at that same instant all of those present, and the rest of the town, were given a glimpse of eternity. The will was written on fine, almost transparent sheets of rice paper, and as the lawyer read out the date it became evident that this was the final, the definitive list, because this date contained no numbers. Instead, in the lawyer's neat hand, it said: "From this day and for all time." From the opening words of the will—which the lawyer read with quavering voice because he both recognized his own handwriting and yet felt sure that he had never written the document before him—both he and the family knew that this was the Old Lady's most inconsiderate, most arrogant masterpiece: a complete record of the Teander Rabow family history for all time.

The Old Lady began by stating the date, the hour, and the place for the reading of her will to her vapid son and his ailing wife and her two grandchildren and Amalie, the willful one, and how the townspeople would realize that these precise moments had been predetermined. The lawyer looked up because the thought had suddenly occurred to him that he was reading to a group of waxwork dummies, and only the quick glance Amalie shot at her father made him go on, although he did not understand that this particular glance had not been predicted in the will before him, which otherwise contained detailed notes for every moment of the reading of it.

There followed a description of the Old Lady's funeral; a description more deafly earsplitting, more impatient, and more detailed than ever before, and everything was as she said it would be, right down to her despotic and arrogant indications of where, in her funeral sermon, Christoffer's father-in-law, the dean, would pause, distracted by the memory of the previous night, in the chapel, when he had wanted to unscrew the lid of the coffin in the futile hope that that disagreeable smile would have forsaken her face, never again to haunt his memory. After this came an account of the future of the newspaper, the printing plants, the offices, and the accounts and expansion projects and new acquisitions and investments— being particularly mindful of a new and promising world war— there you are; and here the will was as gracious as though this war were a gift to the bereaved, in their sorrow. Next came a month-by-month recital of the front-line positions, so that, when the time came, the newspaper could be first with the news. This will was a true catalogue of eternity. The Old Lady had not even considered it necessary to exhort her audience to listen and take all her words to heart. Nor was it necessary, since, during the reading, the terse sentences had retained all of her effrontery, to such an extent that now, before her family, she loomed large in the room, a solid specter that made them all sit even more improbably still than usual. Even Amalie stopped glancing at her father as the will set out the family's private conditions and decreed which parts of the house they could frequent and specified their bedtimes and departures from these and when they might take sleeping drafts and where, under the bed, they could place their chamber pots and how Christoffer was to dress and the way in which his cuffs would fray: a never-ending number of details that were then discussed in greater depth in the footnotes. After having unfolded the course of Katarina's illness and given a precise description of the last stages of her tuberculosis— during which Christoffer was to carry his wife's bloody sputum to the public sewer twelve times a day, to prevent the children from being infected—this part of the will closed by predicting that the lawyer would pause at just this point because Katarina would have collapsed in a tearful coughing fit and because the reading could just as well continue another day, since it involved a catalogue of eternity, after all, and eternity does not change from one day to the next. So we can continue, the Old Lady snarled from the rice paper, we can carry on after the twenty-one days of mourning, which will be conducted as previously stated, and that's that!

To begin with, everything went as it should. For one week the newspaper was published with blank white sheets, meant, along with the broad black border that edged them, to remind everyone of the Old Lady—which they did.

The following week the newspaper printed all the obituaries and poems and blessings and condolences written by important person-ages in Copenhagen. These letters gave the first clear indication of what a powerful influence the Old Lady had exerted, even over people who had never met her: there were letters from bishops and professors and landowners and company directors and famous sur-geons, and a violin sonata composed for the Old Lady by the great violinist and virtuoso member of the Royal Theater orchestra Fini Henriques, and a poem in hexameter stanzas, filling four closely written pages and hailing the Old Lady as the Odysseus of the turbulent waters of politics, written by the country's Minister of Justice, former counsel to the Supreme Court Peter Alberti, whose political career the Old Lady had at all times supported.

During the third week the newspaper published the tribute from the town, and for this it expanded to include two extra sections in which everyone who could read and write wept publicly for the town's patroness, our dear mother and grandmother and mother-in-law, benefactress of the hospitals, protector of the poor, patron saint of the chamber of commerce, angel of the dairies, fairy god-mother of the banks, lady bountiful of the fire brigade, good Samaritan of the sanitation department, and among all these tears, besides the sorrow, there was an element of fearful trust, inasmuch as many of these people still found it hard to believe that the Old Lady, remembered by them as a wise woman, was dead. Especially when they heard how warmly and teasingly she had smiled, from her coffin, upon those who came to pay their respects.

On the following Monday the newspaper was to be published as normal. On that Sunday the journalists got on with their work, suspecting nothing and unaware of the electricity in the air. They wrote their articles, all of which still dealt with the way the town grieved for its lost daughter and mother, and how it would take a while for it to recover from its loss—as predicted in the will, which was also mentioned—and then they went home. And from that moment things started to go wrong: that night they slept a sleep filled with oppressive dreams, and this sleep ran on and on into an endless night that was morning for others in the town. With the result that the journalists did not turn up for work at the time that was, for some, the next day.

Do not expect me to know what happened to Rudkøbing on that night and in the time that followed. The best I can do is to say that time apparently lost its significance. It is possible that at that very moment, and purely by chance, Rudkøbing passed through one of those points in the universe where time stands still. It is also possible that this confusion arises because I have to rely upon Amalie's and Christoffer's memories of what happened. Because in one sense they were, of course, obedient; in one sense they were the Old Lady's son and grandchild; but they were also rebels, and it is quite likely that their greatest wish had been to see the Old Lady's laboriously maintained timing fall apart. If so, then Rudkøbing's chaotic time was actually Christoffer's and Amalie's dream. But if that is the case, then it was a discreet, almost covert dream, since, initially, time administered a severe shock to Christoffer. He was the first to arrive at work, the first to see that something was wrong. He noticed that the journalists had not shown up, and when he opened the morning paper he discovered that it bore a date from a lifetime ago and was filled with articles on people from a bygone age who had died long ago in places that no longer existed. He had risen from his chair to walk over to the printshop when a sudden impulse made him pull back the curtain to see the morning sun coloring the roof of the

white house on the other side of the dark courtyard. Instead he saw
the stars, and as he walked through the building on his way to the
printshop he passed through rooms facing onto the square, where
dust particles danced in the winter morning sunlight—yes, we all
heard it right, winter *morning* sunlight. And when nighttime and
daytime are present simultaneously, then something is really wrong.
Then anyone less well schooled than Christoffer, or less odd, would
have quit the place. But not he. He went on to the printshop, which
he found deserted apart from four printer's apprentices, who had
suffered no ill-effects from this crazy merger of night and day other
than some slight headaches.

The gap between these four men and Christoffer was very wide,
one might almost say colossal. It had been part of the Old Lady's
lifework to create the gulf across which her employees and her son,
Christoffer Ludwig, now regarded one another. Furthermore, there
had never been any need for them to speak to one another, since
the Old Lady's commands rang in all their ears. And so Christoffer
circulated among his workers like some solitary sleepwalker, trying
to recall whether these unexpected difficulties had been predicted
in his mother's will. Finally he leaned up against a big printing
press, looked into the expectant faces, and said, "Gentlemen, you
will have to write the newspaper."

The Old Lady had always made sure that everyone employed by
the family could read and write, for the very reason that she herself
had never mastered these skills. But, faced by the white sheets of
paper, all that the printer's apprentices could call to mind was the
fragmentary schooling from the distant days of their childhood.
When the journalists awoke from their sleep to a light belonging
neither to day or to night, in which the bells of the town's churches
were ringing for morning or evening prayer, they awoke to a paper
full of hymn stanzas and quotations from Luther's catechism and
the dates of Danish military victories and the announcement that
the great violinist and virtuous member of the royal orchard Fine
Henriksen—as the printer's apprentices put it—would be paying a
visit to the town. Here was a mystery that the journalists wanted to
have cleared up. On their way to the square they bumped into one
another in streets filled with people who were rubbing sleep out of
their eyes, or on their way home to bed, or who had just finished
eating dinner. Outside the taverns, drinking cronies fought over what

time it was, and they had to jump clear of the cobbled roadway so as not to be run down by a coach whose driver had collapsed in a heap on the box, weary with confusion, or trampled by horses whose riders had left them to go in search of some anchor to cling to in their lives. Wherever they went, they were pursued by the echo of the church bells, chiming at one and the same time for all the holy days and religious festivals of the year. This clamor pursued them all the way to the square, which, though it had been morning when they left their homes, lay bathed in moonlight. Beneath the stars, in the chill blue light, the stall holders were selling vegetables that were not in season, and here they met Christoffer Ludwig. He was sitting on the box of the newspaper's big four-wheeled cart, his eyes were bloodshot with weariness, and the clothes that he had been wearing for a space of time as indeterminate as everything else were covered with a layer of lead dust from the printshop. But his eyes were shining as he—who had never learned to drive a cart—left the horse to find its own way around to the newspaper's sub-scribers, delivering the morning's paper, which he had written and corrected and typeset and made up and printed, folded, and glued all by himself, and if his eyes were shining it was because he was now sure that this was exactly what the will had predicted. He had, in fact, been reminded of the wording once the printers had fallen asleep at the presses after working nonstop through a night that would never come to an end and during which, after having written and printed the paper, they then had to deliver it because all the paperboys, bar one, had joined the frantic commotion on the streets. As he stood alone in the printshop with the sleeping workers, who looked like victims of a fire—slumped, arms poised to lunge, covered with lead dust, scraps of paper, and printing-ink stains—Christoffer's gloom and doubt were dispersed by a dazzling light and he heard his mother's voice reading aloud the section of the will which declared that the responsibility now rested on his shoulders.

Christoffer thought he had better check this. That he succeeded in finding his way back to the room in which the echo of the lawyer's reading still hung in the air, and the will lay, undisturbed, on the desk, seemed to him like some sort of confirmation, as though his mother had reached out a hand to him. Christoffer wanted, first of all, to count the number of sheets of rice paper, but he never succeeded. As he lifted the white bundle, the paper crumbled into dust between his fingers. He left the room not knowing that he would never find it again and without noticing that there was something very wrong with the furnishings. The tapestries and the rough wooden furniture and the torches on the walls and the chessboard-patterned marble floor belonged not to his own time but to another. For the first time, on his way through the house, he did not look at the clocks, and so he did not notice, either, that they had come to a standstill. Just as he did not hear the housemaids panting as they ran from room to room winding up the precious timepieces to keep them going, while their dinner was sticking to the bottom of the pots in the kitchens, and rooms and windows and doors appeared in the wrong places only to vanish immediately once more.

Christoffer headed straight for his office, where, all on his own, he copied out the next edition of the newspaper, in accordance with the dictates of the will, as far as his excellent memory had retained them. He did not allow anything to interrupt him, not even the shrieks of the kitchen maids who, turning to look at one another after trying to stir the food in the pots in the soot-blackened kitchens, found that they had all, suddenly, grown terrifyingly old. Now they were tearing along the corridors, colliding with footmen and house-maids whose teeth chattered in their heads because they no longer recognized a house that was now in a constant state of flux. This was demonstrated by the way they ascended spiral staircases and walked through rooms they had never seen before, decorated in styles they had never come across, only to find that the water closets and some of the offices, not to mention their own rooms, had disappeared.

Naturally, they then left the house. Passing through boudoirs and living rooms and along the corridors outside Christoffer's office, they snatched everything that could be stuffed into their pockets or bags, because they knew they would never get what was owed them from this intolerable house where poltergeists ran amok. With trembling hands they cut the pictures out of their frames, rolled up the carpets, and attempted to haul away paperweights and epergnes and silver paper knives because, they reasoned, that lunatic Christoffer Lud-wig, who just sits there writing and writing in the midst of this mixed-up time, is never going to need any of it anyway. When Christoffer got to his feet, clutching his completed draft, he crossed rooms that were deserted and empty and bathed in a light that was neither one thing nor the other. In the printshop, all by himself, he printed the newspaper that he was later to throw to the journalists in the square. In the rays of the emerging sun, shivering in the wintry chill, they read a newspaper that contained something of everything the Old Lady would never have countenanced: an apology for, and disclaimer of, the previous edition of the paper, followed by a résumé of the year's great international discoveries and sensitive political situations and an article reporting that the country's Minister of Justice, our very own Mr. Alberti, had been arrested for fraud and that this man, wrote Christoffer, this archetypal modern-day careerist, had never wanted anything for himself except as much as possible in his own capacious pocket, as much as possible on his lapel, and as much as possible on himself in the Official State Yearbook. None of the journalists recognized Christoffer's voice in the cool, concise language of the newspaper; Christoffer the milksop, the cowed lad who had, apparently, said here, for the first time, exactly what he thought, and about a government minister at that, a good friend of his mother's. And that is what turns this action into a dream, our dream, Christoffer's dream—a revolt against those who dictate.

The journalists gazed hopelessly after him as he drove away. Before going their separate ways they met the mayor and Dr. Mahler and the lawyer and the Reverend Mr. Cornelius, all of whom were in the act of erecting a sundial in the square in the hope of seizing hold of time with a flash through the drifting clouds. Together they kicked open the post office door—which had been so firmly shut that it seemed as though it would never open again—and woke the telegraph operator, who was asleep on a bed of blank forms scattered about the floor, and forced him to telegraph Copenhagen. The reply they received seemed never-ending and its content was lost in the crackle of static—all but the last part, which stated that Christoffer's last article was nothing but a pack of lies, since the Minister of Justice could be found—supported by the trust of the people and the judicial system and the government—in the Ministry of Justice and in Parliament and in and out of the meetings of the countless boards chaired by him. And always, since the Old Lady's death, dressed in black. And with that they had to content themselves. On their way home they met Christoffer and the horse, although Christoffer did not see a thing because his thoughts had run on far beyond their own time, preoccupied as he was with carrying out what he believed to be his mother's last wish. Later, while the journalists and the mayor and the doctor and the lawyer and even the Reverend Mr. Cornelius drank themselves into apathy in a café full of weeping adults and silent children who had given up asking for explanations, Christoffer woke his daughters and took them, oblivious to his wife's gurgling protests, to the printshop. Once there, he had them proofread his articles and then work the big printing presses. In the meantime, he wrote to the family's other printing plants and ordered the expansion and the new acquisitions, predicted in the will, which he considered would be necessary in order to fulfill the stream of orders that was, at this moment, during these weird days, pouring into his office. And strange orders they were: for the printing of books by authors as yet unborn, from countries that were not yet nation-states, in languages that as yet boasted no alphabet, and dealing with events several future generations removed. In his letters Christoffer also described where the printers were to set up the big rotary presses which he had ordered from abroad and which were to meet the demand for newspapers described in the will, the contents of which had also been determined. While Amalie, with shining eyes, was making fair copies of her father's letters and recognizing in them her own dreams of a world in which she and now her father, too, were the celebrated focal points, Christoffer was at the station collecting the photoengraving machine he had ordered from Copenhagen. This arrived with a railroad car full of liquids and bowls and all the equipment necessary for the etching of printing blocks, and Christoffer was able to illustrate that very day's edition of the newspaper—or was it the next day's?—with his own drawings, which resembled the creatures he had, once upon a time, cut out of paper. No one except Amalie, who did the proofreading, ever saw these last issues of the paper.

When Christoffer drove out to deliver them he saw for the first time, with bemused wonder, all the people hanging around in the café doorways and those who were sitting on the doorsteps and those who were lying on the sidewalks and nearly freezing to death, as though they had always hung about and sat and lain there, and all of them seeing the town ripple before their eyes. The houses outside which the horse stopped so that Christoffer could deliver the paper metamorphosed into thatch-roofed, mud-walled hovels, then wooden shanties—if, that is, they were not burned-out sites turning into churchyards or the overgrown backyards of buildings from the future. Onlookers saw Christoffer's cart transformed into one of the Old Lady's automobiles, then to a handcart, and, finally, back to its original form. And all the while Christoffer was throwing the paper—which, according to all accounts, contained nothing but illustrated ditties and nursery rhymes of his own invention because that was what the will had foretold—into mailboxes from which they were never collected because people had taken refuge indoors. There they could watch, through their windows, as their surroundings liquefied and the streets turned to rutted, churned-up tracks, and then to mud-filled mires, and then into a river that forced its way up their steps and over their thresholds before disappearing and leaving instead a path bordered by winter-brown blackberry bushes that grew up beneath the bubbling mailboxes in which Christoffer's newspaper lay untouched. Night fell just as the sound of the church bells was starting to fade away, since the churches would soon be transformed into cathedrals, which would be replaced by wooden huts, which would dwindle into nothingness. And when everyone was sleeping, except Christoffer and his daughters—who were busily engaged in producing the next edition—the snow came, gently falling straight to earth. The snowflakes were flat and so big that they piled up one atop another, layer upon layer, but at the same time they were so light that they rose like a cloud around Christoffer and the horse and the three girls as they drove off to deliver the paper to the sleeping town. The snow heralded the end.

No one knows how long the night lasted, or whether it even had a length, but when people woke up it was light and the street rang with bugle calls that made the powdery snow fly up in fine clouds that caught the sunlight glinting off the army now entering the town. They had been summoned by the silence and vague rumors, and because in Denmark, in those days, the cavalry turned up regularly and willingly, and often at just the right moment. It took a whole day and a whole night for all the regiments of hussars and honor guards and royal cavalry and engineers and transportation corps to enter the town, where their tents and kit and horses and gun carriages filled all the streets and squares, leaving only a narrow pathway open. Along this pathway walked the general who had been called in, his face hardened by lack of understanding. A little way behind him walked the Reverend Mr. Cornelius and the mayor and the lawyer and Dr. Mahler, and while these five men are walking slowly through the town, time returns to normal. They come through the slums and past the post office. They make their way down to the harbor, where the ships are covered in white snow against which the dark skins of the foreign seamen show up like black holes. Everywhere, people look at their feet and give the evasive answers that become one of the few traces left of the disaster, once the footprints in the snow have melted away and the dampness has soaked through Christoffer's newspaper. All that is found when the mailboxes are opened is a greenish-blue mold.

Around this time, Christoffer is sitting in his office staring vacantly into space. For him, too, the disunited sections of time are reassembling. To me there is something remorseless about this situation, and I, too, stare vacantly into space as the sound of the five men's footsteps draws nearer. I, too, have a dream of living in a chaotic universe where hours and minutes have no place, just as Christoffer succeeded in doing. I, too, feel like trying to run from time, but it catches up with us all, even with me. Even I cannot dwell any longer on the will to life in Christoffer's rhymes, because now the steps are coming closer. There is only time enough for me to say that on the paper before him on the desk he has written:

> Die Juristen sind böse Christen
> Die Medizinen sind grosse Schwinen
> Die Theologen sind worse than any of them

At this moment Katarina, Christoffer's wife and mother of his children, suffocates during a prolonged bout of coughing and somewhere in the town three accountants raise their insect-like heads from calculations that show that Christoffer has squandered the family fortune; that at some point in the spiral of time he has succeeded in losing everything. So now he is bankrupt and a widower with three young daughters and an obscure responsibility for a murky passage in the history of Rudkøbing. All that remains is the sound of the general's riding boots on the marble tiles and the dry rasp of the lawyer's elastic-sided shoes. The men walk through the empty rooms plundered by the servants and, somewhere in the building, they find Christoffer. Much as I might like Christoffer to utter one last line, his lips remain sealed in the face of these five men, these representatives of time and regularity. Amalie is at his side. Wide-eyed she watches the five men, and it is quite clear to her that this is the first time that anyone has entered this house unbidden since the day in the distant past when the Old Lady opened her doors to show off the first water closet in Rudkøbing.

ANNA BAK

The fishing village of Lavnæs

The new Virgin

1898–1918

THE THOUGHT THAT Anna Bak should have been chosen to bear
the new Messiah first occurred to the people of the fishing village
of Lavnæs around the shoemaker's deathbed. The shoemaker's soul
is the last one in Lavnæs to have been won for the Lord, an event
that came about after Anna's father, Thorvald Bak, the village pastor,
had lain in wait all through one lifelessly cold and frosty night behind
a tree until the shoemaker appeared, riding home—and lolling
drunkenly on his mount—from Rudkøbing. Then, from among the
trees, Bak called out, "Dismount, shoemaker. Your Lord wishes to
speak to you!"

Sobered by terror, standing barefoot in snow that is as loose as
powder and burns like poisoned needles, the shoemaker hears the
voice of God issuing from the black forest and shattering the frozen
branches like glass. He returns to Lavnæs burning with fever and
filled with religious visions. A week later he dies of pneumonia with
the pastor and the villagers standing by his box bed, where they are
afforded wonderful proof of the divine life that has been aroused in
the dying man. Nevertheless, his soul is about to slip through their
fingers. As his life ebbs away he wavers, appalled by the thought of
an eternity without alcohol, and calls for aquavit.

That is when it happens. All of those present see how the pastor's
daughter, Anna, who is at this time only seven years old, splits into
two people. One moment there is just the one Anna, standing next

to her father, and the next there is, apart from her, another Anna, who sits down on the edge of the shoemaker's bed. And at that moment it is as though those present *see* Anna for the first time. Obviously, they have seen her before and know that she is the pastor's daughter. But what they now perceive is that this child who has just split herself in two is exceptionally beautiful and that she, quite literally, radiates an innocence that puts them in mind of the Holy Virgin and causes the memory of their former dissolute lives to manifest itself as a metallic taste in their mouths. Then they all understand, without having exchanged a word on the subject, that she has been created for some higher purpose.

Seemingly oblivious to their stares, Anna places her hand on the shoemaker's forehead. His craving for alcohol is replaced by a sense of comfort he has not felt since childhood, and then he dies.

Anna's father, Thorvald Bak, received the word that he was to be the pastor of Lavnæs in a revelation straight from God. It came to him when his mother's portrait fell off the wall while he—full of loathing for the hollowness of existence—was standing at the washbasin in his room in Copenhagen, rubbing his member with a searing salve supposed to cure him of syphilis. It was so long now since he had arrived there from Rudkøbing to study theology at the university that he had long since lost his rural accent, and lost sight of his birthplace in the fog of debauchery into which he had plunged. Which was why he listened, feeling nothing in particular, as the girl who lay on his bed read out extracts from the letters from his childhood home which had been arriving, regular as clockwork, at the rate of two a week ever since he left for the city, and which he had stuffed, unopened, into his straw mattress. It was from there that the girl had now pulled them, stained by spillages of spiked coffee and the juices of lovemaking.

"Your brother's been made a dean," said the girl, wrapping herself in the flimsy stuff of her negligee.

"The Devil looks after his own," replied Thorvald.

"Your sister got married," added the girl and slit open a fresh envelope with one long, grimy nail.

"I hope she gets eaten up by cancer," mumbled Thorvald absentmindedly.

"Your father's dead," said the girl and looked up from the sheet of paper.

"To hell with him," said Thorvald, and at that instant the watercolor depicting his mother's features—faded by the tobacco smoke that hung in the room and all the swearwords uttered there—tumbled into the washbasin. As the colors ran together like a dream being wiped away, Thorvald Bak woke to a new life.

It is difficult for me to comprehend such sudden changes of heart. They remind me, just a little, of virgin births, inasmuch as nothing out of the ordinary seems to have preceded them. Nevertheless, that *was* how Thorvald Bak viewed his salvation, as a bolt from the blue, striking his life in the capital. And later, when—together with Vilhelm Beck, that great champion of the common cause—he became one of the founders of the Danish Evangelical Mission, this was precisely the sort of conversion for which he campaigned. Now, however, he did not utter a sound. He dropped the salve into the washbasin and his knees slowly gave way under the weight of that blend of arrogance and humility derived from being, at one and the same time, the Lord's anointed and chosen one and the most contemptible of men. Then, in a vision, he saw the fishing village of Lavnæs, which he had never heard of, even though it lay not that far away from Rudkøbing. What he saw was a cluster of dark houses situated on the boundary between land that was barren as a desert and a sea that surged grayly below a perpetual blanket of storm clouds—and all shrouded in the stench of rotten fish.

Up until now, Thorvald had attended the university only in order to have a laugh, along with his drinking cronies, at the way in which the professors of theology attempted to establish, on scientific grounds, the falsity of biblical texts while at the same time testifying to their profundity. These days were now at an end. He was about to turn over a new leaf. Filled with the strength of his conviction, he sat his final examinations and passed with top marks, after just one year; a year during which, into the bargain—in the little free time left to him—he had made the rounds of all the taverns where he had previously drunk from the poisonous tankards of sin, in an effort to convert his acquaintances.

In the sermon he gave on graduating from the theological college, Thorvald took hell as his subject. He spoke before the bishop and several professors of theology who had come, drawn by the rumors of this young graduate who preached with all the remorselessness of a Jesuit. His sermon made a powerful impression on those who heard it. It caused distant church bells to peal and the organ pipes to sigh darkly and the inside of the church to smell of red-hot iron filings and singed linen. None of those in attendance would ever forget the way in which Thorvald Bak had, at one stage, worked his way up onto the edge of the pulpit, where he had then hunkered down, hovering like a big bird of prey, and said, quite softly, "Hell shall be the coals under the boilers of faith!"

As soon as his sermon was over, Thorvald asked the bishop to procure him the incumbency of Lavnæs. The old man hunted fruit-lessly through the registers for this benefice and finally discovered it hidden away among the lost causes—those where the solution had now been left in God's hands. He saw that there had been no pastor there for many years and that the post had been occupied by thirty different incumbents in the past hundred years. The dreary climate and the village's stubborn ungodliness had dragged every new pastor to the bottom in a maelstrom of melancholy and alcohol in which he forgot to send his reports to the ministry and, before too long, was not even in a fit state to seek his own dismissal.

When the bishop asked the advice of the dean regarding Thor-vald's request, the latter replied, "If we don't get rid of him now, he's going to become another Ignatius Loyola."

Thorvald Bak paid a farewell visit to the bishop, to thank him for the post and for the wagon with which the ministry had supplied him, wanting to make sure that he would reach Lavnæs, where the idea of building a road had been abandoned. It would only be washed away by the sudden floods, covered by the dreadful snow-storms that struck the town even in the late spring, or made im-passable by chasms left by the earth's apocalyptic subsidences. When the bishop asked Thorvald why he had applied for this particular post, the young pastor replied with pride, "Because these are the very souls that I have heard screaming in hell."

The bishop recalled Thorvald's sermon and shook his head wear-ily. "God created heaven," he said. "Hell is the work of man."

Unyielding, Thorvald shook his superior's hand.

Prior to his departure from Copenhagen, Thorvald Bak married. He had met his wife a year earlier at a revival meeting that he himself had arranged. She was the closemouthed daughter of a middle-class family, ten years his senior, under whose pale skin the veins gleamed greenly. As a young girl she had considered becoming a nun, and Thorvald became betrothed to her because her skinny frame and chronic cough appealed to those feelings of compassion for humanity as a whole that his faith had aroused in him, and because he was sure that—consisting as she did of so much soul and so little body—she would not upset his equanimity. He discovered, immediately after their betrothal, that in this he was mistaken. First her big dark eyes started appearing in his dreams; then her whole form invaded his nights. These were already short, because of his studying and pastoral work, and now they were passed in wakefulness, as his conscience tormented him—until he found peace in the knowledge that the Lord had chosen him by punishing him. During the time remaining before their wedding it was possible for him to take her hand without losing his self-control—after months of shivering in his shoes at the mere thought of being in the same town as her. He had come to terms with the thought of having, for the rest of his life, to suffer a passionless marriage. On his wedding night, however, he discovered that his wife's embraces were as passionate as her blessings. When, for a moment in the bed, he brought time to a standstill, stopped moving, and supported himself on his arms to see the glow in her eyes, she said, in a voice both loving and enticing, "Descend to me and let the Lord's will be done!" That night, Thorvald Bak realized that she loved him both as a man and as a soldier of the Lord, and when, a week later, sitting atop the wagon, she saw Lavnæs emerging out of the damp mist and said, "You would think we were going down into the Kingdom of the Dead," Thorvald Bak answered proudly, "We'll be fine, my love. It won't be the first time a warrior returned victorious from hell!"

At the time that Thorvald Bak arrived in Lavnæs, the village comprised around eighty stone-walled houses roofed with three-foot-thick layers of seaweed, these being the only materials capable of withstanding the flood tides, torrential downpours, snowstorms, and droughts that succeeded one another, regardless of the seasons, with senseless, interminable monotony. In this capricious climate, where fishing was a difficult and risky business and it was almost impossible to grow anything, the people survived, faint from mal-

nutrition, on a diet consisting mainly of aquavit and potatoes, and
worn out by deficiency diseases and the raging epidemics that returned again and again to the village even after they had been
eradicated from the rest of the country. In Lavnæs, cut off from the
outside world by fog and wind, the stench of fish and incredible
poverty, the course of the year had evolved into a series of celebrations. At these gatherings, drunken villagers tried, through the
snatches of song handed down to them and well-worn tales into
which the raging elements penetrated deeper and deeper, to hang
on to a hope long since swamped by a seemingly never-ending
poverty. And, in fact, the inhabitants were able to endure such conditions only because of their pigheadedness and the notion they had
formed that Lavnæs was surrounded by a host of legendary monsters. They had but the haziest notion of how these creatures looked,
but they associated them with the towers, far off on the horizon, and
with the high wall, a corner of which could be glimpsed on a hill
high above Lavnæs and which was, in fact, the manor of Mørkhøj
—although no one now remembered this.

When the Count at Mørkhøj had the wall built, Lavnæs was, to
all intents and purposes, cut off from the outside world. The fishing
village had originally been part of the estate, but thanks to his ab-
sorption in his research work, the Count had lost any inclination to
exercise his right to the first night with every new bride in the district.
Then, too, the smell of fish was—even from a distance—quite of-
fensive. So the estate wall gave a wide berth to Lavnæs, which was
thus forgotten by the outside world, attracting attention only on a
few occasions, as, for example, when one of the state tax collectors
found his way to the village. Well, of course a tax collector—who
else?

He was a single-minded sort of man, a former army officer who
still felt and thought like a soldier. Having noted the fact that
Lavnæs's name was listed in the ministry registers but did not appear
in the local district court reports, he fought his way through to the
town on horseback in a thunderstorm, in an atmosphere so charged
with electricity that it made his sword hilt sing out ominously. The
storm had also transformed the village streets into an impassable
mire in which floated the swollen white bodies of skinny beasts that
had perished in the floods preceding the thunderstorm. The village
was still numb from the wake held for the flood victims. The tax

collector sought out the biggest and best-kept house and stepped inside. On a packed-earth floor saturated by the rain, an old man was sitting by an open hearth, boiling up a thin soup of seaweed from his roof. The tax collector glanced around at the furniture, which looked as if only the inveterate stubbornness of the room were holding it together.

"What do you live on?"

The old man looked blankly at him, his eyes watering in the smoke from the burning dung.

"We eat our own shit," he replied.

The tax collector turned on his heel and left Lavnæs to its poverty.

Although Thorvald Bak had never set eyes on Lavnæs, he found the place exactly as he had seen it in his vision. As the wagon reached the first houses, the mists were dispersed by a burning sun which, by the time they had driven to the other end of the village, had dried the mud into a cracked crust, and people were sitting outside their houses, on the golden-white sand, playing cards for coins that had gone out of circulation fifty years before. Inside the dilapidated church a man was lying on the altar steps. Thorvald Bak nudged him with his foot. The man opened his eyes onto the painful light falling through the broken windowpanes and asked, "Who bought the last round?"

This man was the former pastor of Lavnæs.

In that first year, not a single soul came to church. For a year, Thorvald Bak's wife—despite the fact that she was pregnant and was growing both heavier and more gaunt—was the sole witness to his preaching. His sermons grew ever more radiantly animated and full of conviction, despite the howling gale and the chill of the building, which left them both with the coughs and sneezes of chronic colds. At the end of the year she gave birth to a daughter —this was, of course, Anna—only, right after the birth, to be hit by a violent coughing fit, during which she coughed her soul to death. Just as he heard the child cry out, Thorvald saw the soul rise upward and soar through the cracks in the ceiling like a big white bat. When he christened his daughter, the only witnesses were his housekeeper and the church frescoes.

That same autumn he fell victim to dreadful saltwater sores, which the wind from the sea prevented from healing. When it rained heavily on the patch of earth on which—with great difficulty and with fortune, it seemed, smiling upon him—he had managed to grow some turnips, and when these were then covered by three feet of water and rotted away within the week, the first of the villagers turned up at church to lay bets on how long the pastor would stick it out.

During the winter, Lavnæs was hit by a cyclone whose icy winds swept past at lightning speed, freezing the crests of the waves. Like miniature icebergs, these then crushed several of the boats in the harbor. The same winds sent one of the parsonage gable ends flying sky-high and showered the area with a lethal hail of rock. In their wake they brought so much snow that—when it was melted the week after by high summer temperatures quite unnatural for mid-November—it flooded the parsonage and the church, forcing Thorvald Bak and his baby daughter and his housekeeper to take to the attic in one of the wings.

On the first Sunday after the flooding, when, despite everything, he still succeeded in sailing to the church in a flat-bottomed barge of his own construction, and—standing on the altar in seaboots that reached to his crotch—gave his sermon for the crowd of people who had sailed to church, all bets were off. No one in Lavnæs had dared to bank on his being there. There were those who were genuinely shocked by that Sunday. The widespread betting was an expression of how they looked at life: as a chain of coincidences in which the only sure thing was suffering. There were many in the village who threw the dice every morning to see whether they should get up or stay in bed on their seaweed mattresses and await the day's quota of pain. What the people who had come to church now saw was Thorvald Bak's serenity. For the first time ever they did not play cards or drink in the organ loft. Instead, they listened to the sermon.

They heard themselves. They rediscovered words they themselves had spoken and songs they themselves had sung. In Thorvald Bak's description of hell they recognized Lavnæs, and when he painted a picture of heaven they remembered the dreams they had clung to during all those get-togethers and Christmas parties and spring revels. Then still more turned up at church, and there were those who asked to receive Communion at the Lord's table—which had by now dried out—and so the conversion began. It happened, not because Thorvald had put the people of Lavnæs in touch with another reality, but because, in his serenity, he was stronger than anyone they had ever come across and because his euphoria was more powerful and more imaginative than their own. They converted because they could see that Thorvald Bak was in the hands of the same forces as themselves, and they took to religion with the same energy and obstinacy with which they had searched for the stairs to hell. They developed an unbelievable level of patience in which they could, with exalted tranquillity, watch the waves rise, topple their fishing stakes, and carry them, nets and all, out to sea, while they did not lift a finger because it was Sunday and they were observing the Sabbath and keeping it holy. Thereafter, with heartfelt joy, they could thank the Lord for having chosen them to suffer, rather than the people of the surrounding towns or of Mørkhøj, whom they had, for one hundred years, thought of as the menacing, wingèd monsters who made leaving Lavnæs a dangerous business. Now, however, Thorvald Bak could reveal that they were in fact miserable sinners, squandering their existence in calculated acts of ungodliness and excess. They congregated for Bible reading and confession in the ecstasy of a new day dawning. There they had the opportunity both to recall the crowning moments of their own past sinfulness and to savor the sweetness of denouncing others.

Thorvald Bak was wise enough not to interfere when these meetings developed into appalling relapses during which these saintly souls would start giving themselves alcohol enemas and singing disgusting songs, before going on to tear down the mission house, rip off their clothes, and hare around the village—stark naked and with seaweed from the roofs in their hair—on the hunt for kerosene, because the aquavit had run out. When that also had been drunk, they rubbed their gums with axle grease, which drove them right out of their minds. Thorvald Bak waited until their ravings subsided because he, too, was familiar with sin and knew how closely related it is to remorse, and remorse to loneliness, and loneliness to a longing for fellowship, and fellowship to the religious submission that brought these righteous folk even closer together. Then he could preach to them and berate them until they wept and wailed and had to put their hands over their ears, because all around them they heard the laughter of hell.

Over the years these relapses occurred less often, as the people of Lavnæs gradually became aware that they were the chosen ones, and even though this awareness manifested itself more slowly for them than it had done for Thorvald Bak (when his mother's portrait fell off the wall), nevertheless it was every bit as strong. They understood that they had been chosen to suffer more than anyone else, that their fortitude was to be tested. It was then that they went back to work (after centuries of progressive idleness): to making nets and building boats and planting potatoes, obsessed with the idea that though they might have lived in poverty, they would die wealthy. In just a few years they grew tremendously tight-fisted. They resumed commercial links, severed long before, with Rudkøbing and had virtually all of their meager crops and salted fish carted off to the town while they and their children ate soup made from the seaweed off the roofs. Only in their gifts to the church and the mission house did they retain their former generosity, because they felt that this house belonged to them all, and constituted a safe way of conserving their assets.

Through all of Thorvald Bak's early years as pastor of Lavnæs the town was obsessed by divine stockpiling. All the inhabitants were seized by the conviction that they were, by dint of their hard, fruitless labor, their exceptional powers of endurance, and their pious conversation, making a divine investment that would one day be redeemed, with interest, in the sunlit groves of paradise. Even the climate seemed, during these years, to alter, as their new love for one another and their passionate faith cast golden rays of sunlight over the frozen deserts of winter and a protective shade across the heat of summer. Brimming with fresh energy, they turned their eyes upon one another, there to drive out the sin that they sensed as a faint tremor in the subsoil and a particular smell off the sea. They put a stop to all sales of alcohol and the lethal axle grease in the town, and naturally they took away all the musicians' instruments and put a stop to the Saturday night dances (they knew all about music and how it begets lust). Then, when Anna was six years old, all the true believers of Lavnæs painted their houses black and took to wearing the same clothes of coarse linen—its stiffness against their skin meant to remind them of the difference between good and evil, while its color, together with that of the houses, was intended, in its monotony, to ensure that eyes remained fixed on the future and were not sidetracked by earthly misfortunes. They counted the converted souls meticulously and with pleasure, and by the time Anna was seven years old only the shoemaker and the former pastor still had not been saved but lived as though dead. And just after this, the pastor did in fact die.

Thorvald Bak visited the old man in his cottage by the sea and found him lying in his own excrement, which had frozen into an icy couch. He had survived on a diet consisting solely of aquavit since being removed from his post a lifetime before. On his deathbed his lips remained sealed to the end, at which point Thorvald Bak, moved by this proof of God's retributive will, leaned over and planted a kiss on the dying man's forehead. At this the former pastor opened his eyes and looked up at Thorvald Bak just as he had looked up at him once before from the floor of the church, and said, "Now I know I must be Lazarus, if the dogs are licking me."

After having hunted out sin within one another, until the fishy smell that had always hung over the village disappeared, leaving them free to sniff at an unfamiliar emptiness in the air, the people of Lavnæs turned their gaze inward, upon themselves and the sin in their own hearts, where they ferreted out every urge to exaggerate. Thus the last women to have retained any weakness for painting their skin or outlining their eyes now attended Bible study with scrubbed faces and contrite gaze. They discovered how profligate they were with words and, in rapturous unison, ceased talking, except during Bible study meetings and prayers and when it was of practical necessity. A purified silence settled over Lavnæs. Where previously they had tried to drown out the storms, they now met them with an expectant silence in which they exchanged only the minimum of practical remarks. Even these they endeavored to restrict, by weaving brief messages to one another into grace and evening prayers, along the lines of "Thy kingdom come. Thy will be done, Anders, remember to muck out the stables after supper, in earth as it is in heaven."

And yet it was emptiness, not happiness, that flourished amid all this silence and faith and testifying and dark colors and loving one another and work. It was a longing for a sign. They began to feel that what they needed was some sort of divine statement of account to confirm their hope that they were on the credit side. So exhausted did they become from gazing into the future that this longing grew even stronger.

This future and the change they had wished for were presented to them by the shoemaker's deathbed, when they saw the vicar's daughter, Anna Bak, sit down next to the dying man's head while still standing at her father's side. Faced by this miraculous duplication, they closed their eyes and shook their heads, remembering, from the days before they were saved, the unreliable illusions induced by bingeing on kerosene, which they now feared had returned. But while they stood there with their eyes closed, every one of them had the feeling that the little girl was standing next to them, like some multiple expression of maternal comfort. They also noticed that odd metallic taste in their mouths, and when the light of utter purity emanating from the child seared through their eyelids, they understood that she had been chosen to bear the new Messiah, in their midst, as a reward for their self-restraint. Lavnæs would be the new Bethlehem and they would be the new disciples.

When the shoemaker's heart stopped, they were all so filled with the Holy Spirit that they lifted Anna up onto a wagon and placed her on an improvised throne. Then, driven by the ardent faith that enabled them to see through the houses of Lavnæs, and through the blue-gray clouds that had hung over the village for weeks, and through the hills to far-off regions where the heathen languished, they pulled the wagon through the muddy streets and over the impassable drifts of shifting sand and over the heath to bring religion to the godless. At their head danced Thorvald Bak, preaching as he went, seized by mighty forces (as on the day when his mother's portrait fell off the wall). With them, in their procession, they had brought pots and buckets, which they beat with wooden spoons in a spontaneous, insistent rhythm. "The world awaits us!" cried Thorvald Bak. But when, in the middle of the night, they reached the nearest farms, they found them deserted. Long before this, the farmers had heard a muffled racket that had been taken for the raging of a storm until the procession hove into sight. With all the dark-cowled heads and the light from the child on her weird vehicle and with the pallid faces covered with scabs from the saltwater sores forming pale, disembodied patches in the gray mist, it looked like some ghostly procession. So the farmers had packed up their belongings and fled into the hills.

As the missionaries were returning to Lavnæs through the darkness of a night into which the rain lashed white streaks of foam, they noticed how the storm yielded to Anna, so that she seemed to sit on the wagon surrounded by a protective film. Flower petals

fluttered down upon those who pulled the wagon, and as they neared
the sea, the clouds—which were so dense that it was almost impossible to breathe—parted, and the light from Anna's form beamed
across the sea and was sighted by a big ketch that had disregarded
the dark patches on the sea chart and then been caught in the storm.
The sailors saw the light and confused it with that of the lighthouse
on the hill above Rudkøbing. They turned the ship around, intoxicated by the thought of their imminent deliverance, and ran straight
onto the wicked sandbars lying in wait off Lavnæs, there to be
smashed to smithereens. For a long time afterward driftwood and
pieces of rigging were regularly washed up on the shore, along with
the occasional yellow bone from which the tears of joy the seamen
were shedding as they went aground still ran in a clear liquid, thick
as resin. And even though these events do seem a bit farfetched—
even for me; just bordering on where I would have to say, "That's
damn hard to believe"—nevertheless, that is just how those who
were there at the time remember it.

At the service for the dead seamen, Thorvald Bak said that they
had perished in the light of God. But, referring to the missionary
work, spreading the word of God and taking the news of the new
Messiah to all the corners of the earth, he said, "The world is not
yet ready. We will quietly await our reward."

It is quite likely that Anna never really understood her own significance. She moved with a natural innocence through a world of
prayers and silence, amid her own miracles and the expectations of
others, and she does not seem to have noticed the crowds of people
who followed her wherever she went, to protect her and stand guard
over her every step and read omens in the way that she scratched
her nose. All she did was smile when, in Sunday school, she was
placed on a tall throne next to the Sunday-school teacher's desk,
and the other children shied away from her, dazzled by the light
surrounding her and shocked at the thought of the weight that lay
on her shoulders. In church, during Thorvald Bak's services, her
voice, soaring like a paradisiacal silver flute above the congregation's
chorus, sent a number of the faithful into fits. Then, as the victims
were carried out—with hymnals wedged between their straining
jaws to keep them from biting off their worshipful tongues—she
would artlessly turn her shining eyes toward the pulpit. She seems
to have been what I would call divinely naïve. When Thorvald ex-

empted her from physical labor she spent the endless run of foul-
weather days in her room, playing by herself. The wealth of gifts
and toys delivered to her every day, for which the brethren had to
sacrifice what little they had and once again appease their hunger
with seaweed soup or by sucking on the shells washed up on the
beach, do not appear to have interested her. Instead she played with
a Christmas crib built out of matchsticks and raw potatoes which
Thorvald Bak's housekeeper had made for her and which was evidently sufficient for her in her solitary state. For many years Thorvald Bak noted only one predilection in his daughter, and that was
her love of the sea. Now and again she would leave her room, and
usually he would find her on the beach—watched over by a crowd
of the faithful—gazing out to sea, playing with the bleached driftwood from the sunken ketch, or digging in the sand for fragments
of the drowned sailors' bones.

As time went on, the distance between her and other people grew
wider and wider and she stopped talking altogether. Before this she
had greeted people on her way down to the sea, but, after her duplication, respect placed a circle of emptiness around her and she
walked in silence through the village followed by people who rolled
on the ground where she had trodden or tried to come past her on
the lee side and catch a whiff of the scent that hung around her or
spied on her as she shit, then collected her excrement and took it
home to keep as a relic.

For a while, therefore, Anna talked to the sea gulls instead. She
spent her days on the beach and taught herself to imitate their cries
to perfection. Eventually, however, she became tired of calling across
the gray sea. She grew silent and shut herself away in her room,
shrinking from all those who dogged her footsteps. Thorvald Bak
finally came to the conclusion that his daughter was slow-witted. It
was a source of wonder to him that God should have chosen to
bestow his great blessing on such an unassuming instrument, but
he took comfort in telling himself that it is, after all, the poor in
spirit who shall inherit, and so on and so forth.

Anna was heard to pray for the first time when she was twelve
years old. It happened at a mission meeting. By that time the only
sound anyone could ever remember hearing her utter had been
during the hymn singing that Thorvald Bak had had to forbid, because it induced too much in the way of hemorrhaging and swoon-

ing among the congregation. Nevertheless, she now stood up at the mission meeting and prayed. Speechless with amazement, they heard how moving and fluent her prayers were; how they put them in mind of cloudless skies long forgotten, and awoke memories of the funerals and weddings of their past until the hair on their heads stood on end. From then on, Thorvald Bak took her with him on his missionary expeditions to the villages closest to Lavnæs, and during church services he permitted her to pray. She always spoke standing on a tall white-painted stool. Her words flowed like music, and in her almond-shaped eyes the congregation saw tears glinting like pearls in the light from her face. They gurgled, every one of them, with the taste of metal in their mouths before, overcome by tears, face-to-face with this white-clad girl, the scales fell from their eyes and they saw their former lives as a quagmire of iniquity. Then they collapsed, racked by sobs, and beat their heads against the church floor and created scenes of mass hysteria that I would have refused to believe could ever occur in Denmark—in Danish country churches at the beginning of this century—if it were not, however, that evidence does exist: eyewitness accounts and written records and photographs, forcing me to admit that this is precisely what happened. And all the while, Anna Bak surveyed these scenes of pandemonium, though I doubt whether she realized that the screams and the conversions that accompanied them were engendered by her presence.

In Lavnæs she no longer left her room at all. The congregation had built a round tower for her, from which she could see the sea. It had tall windows and could be seen from every house in the village, so they could all keep her in sight at all times. Thorvald Bak was convinced that his daughter sat in her tower waiting for the Divine Conception. When he took her with him to the mission meetings, even he kept his distance from her, overwhelmed by the thought of what lay in store for her and anxious because, more and more often in recent years, she had made him think of his time in Copenhagen and of his wife's soul as it winged its way up to the ceiling.

He received his first warning one evening as he returned from a meeting with other like-minded pastors—one of the meetings that saw the start of that powerful national movement the Danish Evangelical Mission. Anna was sitting opposite him in the boat as they sailed over the flaming carpet of the sunset. Then, with his eyes on his daughter, he becomes aware of something outside of the boat. He turns his head and sees Anna walking beside the boat on the slivers of burnished gold with which the sun has coated the sea. When he calls out to her, she does not come back but walks off toward the sun, continuing until it seems that the darkness will drag her down with it into the sea. Trembling with fear, Thorvald has to grasp the hands of the daughter before him, to convince himself that she is still there and that he has been left with at least one copy of her.

Terrified rather than delighted by this miracle, he had a fine gold chain forged for Anna's neck, and when she left her tower—which he had had fitted with locks—the other end of this chain was always fastened around his wrist. Now, to us this may seem barbaric, but as he himself said when explaining it to Anna, "It's for your own good." Where, hitherto, he had taken pleasure in his daughter's refined silence, now it struck him that perhaps this was, in fact, a bad thing. He tried to get her to give testimony at the mission meetings, to confess her sins. But this proved impossible. Anna's shining eyes gazed kindlily and guiltlessly upon the faithful, but not a word escaped her lips, and Thorvald Bak eventually came to the conclusion that she was so pure and innocent that she was incapable of even speaking about sin. Nevertheless, she followed the testimonies of the others with interest. Thorvald Bak had divided the faithful into two groups, men and women, whom he had confess separately so that nothing should be concealed but everything brought out in the open. He and Anna were the only ones who listened to both the men and the women as they related how and when they had indulged in one thing and another. Sometimes God's Spirit would descend into the midst of the faithful, and then men and women would flock together and pour out of the church, led by Thorvald Bak, to continue their meeting in the open air, at the edge of a wood, where they prayed and gave testimony and sang hymns under the gathering storm clouds which, more often than not, attended the inhabitants of Lavnæs. Then, while the rain poured down, they would continue their interminable confessions, by means of which they endeavored to drown out the rain and one another. Finally they would stand thigh-high in mud singing and singing until, humble nonetheless, they sank to their knees as Thorvald Bak or Anna prayed in their behalf.

After one such meeting, Thorvald Bak and Anna found themselves alone together, for once, after the rejoicing throng had departed, and Anna looked into her father's face, streaked as it was with rain and mud and strain, and asked, "Why do they confess?"

Thorvald Bak looked quizzically at his daughter. Hardly ever did she ask him a question.

"To be cleansed of their sins," he replied.

"But behind every sin there's another one," said Anna. "It never stops."

Thorvald Bak could find no good answer to this crazy notion, but he ordered a silver-plated cage from a goldsmith in Copenhagen— where he would never normally have bought anything—and kept Anna locked up inside it, in an attempt to stifle the elusive element in her nature. Anna put up with this new arrangement without comment. Now she undertook the long sails along the coast on the decks of fishing boats in her shining cage, peering through its bars—although there is no way of determining what she herself was thinking, or whether she had any thoughts at all about a pastor in Denmark in this enlightened age keeping his own child locked up in a cage.

One night Thorvald Bak's dead wife, Anna's mother, came to him in a dream. She appeared in the shape of nothing less than the Angel of the Lord, bathed in the roseate glow of dawn and hovering on white bat wings. Through the taut skin of the wings green veins could be discerned. She scattered the storm clouds that hung around Lavnæs, along with the smell of fish that had returned in the dream, and showed him a town floating on an enormous, luminous crystal of yellow sulfur. Thorvald could see the signs above the taverns and the anonymous doors of the brothels. With Anna at his side he walked into the town. Behind them the song of the angels rose above the chink of bottles, a cross was reflected in the pools of beer on the floors, and the women's nakedness was draped in white muslin.

Thorvald awoke from this dream seized by a restlessness he could barely contain until the following Sunday, at which time he told the congregation of his vision.

"The world is ready," he said, in a voice that brought flakes of damp plaster tumbling off the walls. Once again he gave them a vivid description of the godlessness of the towns. Surprising himself with his own assurance, he recalled incredible details of his youth in Rudkøbing and in Copenhagen; he described how people lived by stealing from one another; how the nation's leaders got drunk on government premises and painted blasphemous pictures on the walls with fingers they had dipped in their own excrement; and how the servants of the church kept domestic animals in God's house and in the churchyard and always wore short boots into which they could shove the hind legs of the sheep and the pigs while having their lustful way with these defenseless creatures. After this sermon, the congregation fetched rakes and axes and scythes, and flintlocks that had belonged to their forefathers and were so eaten away by rust that they fell apart when taken down from the wall. Then they gathered outside the church and insisted that Thorvald Bak, with Anna at his side, should lead a new crusade, with Rudkøbing as its target. That same night they set sail from the small, unprotected harbor at Lavnæs: not, however, before Thorvald Bak had, on the quay, grown uneasy at the sight of their hate and the bloodthirsty note in their voices. Unaccustomed to anything other than prayer, they had now, at the hour of departure, grown brayingly loquacious as they yelled to outdo the wind that had risen at sunset. Thorvald Bak appealed to their compassion and spoke of abused and enfeebled heathen mothers and of their fatherless children who, with the towns so ravaged by the demons of hunger, could never be sure that they would not one day find themselves being boiled up in a pot with onions and devoured. Eventually the faithful were reduced to tears. They threw away their weapons; then they all climbed aboard their boats, the very sails of which were black. Anna's silver-plated cage was lashed to the deck of the little bark carrying Thorvald Bak. They sailed out of the harbor and the wind howled, louder and louder, seeming to come directly from hell. And the sea swelled up into shifting inky-black mountains of water that towered over the little boats, then broke and crashed down onto the pale upturned faces, sweeping overboard everything that was not lashed down. Then Thorvald Bak woke Anna, who had been sleeping, miraculously sheltered from the icy cascades, with her face tranquil in slumber. As she got to her feet, the turbulent waters subsided, thereby making the dream that faith can remove mountains come true. All through the night—until the moment when the distant city of sin rose out of the sea, just as Thorvald had seen it in his dreams—Bak kept his daughter awake. The strange light around her face lit up the little boats and the dark cowls of their passengers, with their restless eyes and fierce obstinacy.

This obstinacy turned to fear as they slipped into Rudkøbing's huge harbor and its tentacles closed around them, pushing them toward a depravity beyond anything they could ever have imagined, with harborside drinking dens and brothels, and alehouses built like palaces with pillared colonnades and magnificent entrances and towers and spires and bay windows floating on clouds of gleaming copper. Later, when they came ashore, the savage cacophony closed over their heads, split them up, and drew them into a stream of humanity dressed with unbridled extravagance; into streets where Jewish peddlers hawked nails just like those with which the Savior was crucified. Not only that: on display they had a large crucified dummy, resembling the Son of Man, into which one could hammer one's nails. In these streets animal tamers presented creatures from Noah's ark: giraffes, hippopotamuses, elephants, and a unique monstrosity: a long-legged, misshapen duckbill platypus—all of these trained to make obscene gestures and to copulate with one another before the very eyes of the spectators. Now here I have to step in to say that I have had a hard time recognizing Rudkøbing, that respectable provincial town, in this, a description drawn from the annals of the Danish Evangelical Mission. Nevertheless, that is what the faithful later remembered having seen.

As they made their way through the town that evening to the service, which Thorvald Bak's irresistible powers of persuasion had ensured would be held in the church, they huddled tightly around Anna in her silver-plated cage. This they pushed, on a little handcart, through a darkness constantly rocked by the sound of brawling from the wine cellars; the burbling of the organ music emanating from the theater, which sounded like the gasps of a couple making love; and the screams from the whorehouses as clients were smitten by rare tropical venereal diseases that spread through the body like galloping gangrene. They made their way through a reddish mist that by no means veiled their view. On the contrary, it made every outline stand out with heightened clarity. This mist gave off such a stench of corruption that the people of Lavnæs had to hold their breath, until their lips turned violet and their eyes were bulging out of their sockets; then they were forced to surrender and fill their lungs with a mist that went to their heads, bombarding them with memories of vices that their forefathers had given in to in a far-off century. And then they had to let themselves be drawn after the cage while they tried to catch a glimpse of Anna's face.

At a street corner they pass a boy. He is standing leaning against a lamppost, staring vacantly into the mist, immersed in his own innermost visions. What he sees in his mind's eye is the sea. He has come to town with a traveling theater. As wave boy in that unparalleled stage success *Sigurd's Great Voyage around the World* he is responsible for creating convincing waves in the blue sheeting upon which the steamship *Mongolia* sails. He has stopped for a moment on his way to the theater, and his mind is now filled with wavy patterns. And while he is leaning against this lamppost and his body is swaying gently in tune to the interference of the waves, he looks into a world of unimaginable blueness, and out of the depths of soft, endless, permeable blocks of crystal floats a face. At first this face is but a white ruffle in a chasm of blue, but gradually it comes closer and closer, until it can clearly be seen. It is the face of Anna Bak.

On seeing the rapt boy, Anna's first impulse is to pray for him, then to sing, but when she sees the sea in his eyes, she senses that neither prayers nor song would be enough. And so her spirit duplicates itself. While the procession of cowled brothers and sisters is swallowed up by the interplay of light and shade in the streets, together with Thorvald Bak—who has withdrawn into his shell and is committing to memory the hell that he is going to conjure up in his sermon—and the cage in which Anna sits surveying her surroundings, Anna Bak—or, now how else could I put this; at any rate, a different Anna from the one in the cage—glides barefoot across the cobbles and falls into step next to the wave boy on his way to the theater.

The religious missionary movement of which Thorvald Bak was to become co-founder—the Danish Evangelical Mission, that is— was henceforth to celebrate the anniversary of Thorvald Bak's sermon in Rudkøbing church as one of its most significant founding dates. And in later years he himself always remembered his speech as being one of the most miraculously inspired he had ever given. Even in the shadow cast by subsequent disasters it would always shine in his memory as a mysterious sign from heaven. Likewise, Anna never forgot her night at the theater. From her place in the wings she, who was so fond of the sea, was moved to tears by the sight of those scandalous theatrical illusions and by the cavernous auditorium in which white shirtfronts and coquettish bosoms, powdered and bare, floated like small icebergs on a sea of black tailcoats and satin gowns. Lifting his eyes from the pulpit at that same moment, Thorvald Bak looked out upon a packed church. Rumors of the cowled fishermen and their fiery faith had spread, and people had flocked to see the child sacrifices, the speaking in tongues, the laying on of hands, and the transcendental frenzies of which they had heard; if, that is, they had not simply bumped into the fearful procession and then tagged along with it. Others had been lured by the sight of the actors' parade and rumors of the incomparable stage production of *Sigurd's Great Voyage around the World* in which the Princess Aouda appeared, to all intents and purposes, naked; a fact which Anna was, to her delight, having confirmed at that same moment—seeing the near-naked beauty being painted brown as a native and wound in her skimpy shroud. Paupers off the street had followed Thorvald Bak into the church believing that they had joined some gala procession, and the steadily swelling throng had been joined by seamen from the foreign ships anchored in the harbor. Before him Thorvald Bak now beheld more sin than he had encountered in his entire life, and he would, at that moment, have lost his composure if Anna's face, at his side, had not begun to radiate a white light, even as, at the theater, she was watching the playacting seamen and remembering the bones she had collected on the beach at Lavnæs. The white light from the face of the Anna in the church intensified, and Thorvald Bak began to speak. While Anna took the wave boy's hand and the dramatization of *Sigurd's Great Voyage around the World* proclaimed the triumph of civilization and modern transportation methods over time, Thorvald Bak spoke of his audience's journey into the wilderness of depravity. So penetrating and clear were his words that they were not apprehended as sounds but turned into images in the mind of each individual: pictures representing a cavalcade of the sins of his or her particular life, bathed in the white light emanating from Anna. And they all had to close their eyes. Meanwhile, at the theater, Anna was aware of the wave boy's closeness and how he smelled of fresh-baked bread. She looked up at the blue sheeting as it was lowered over them like a starry sky, and at that moment Thorvald Bak was speaking of the liberation of death, in such a way that everyone heard the tolling bell and the oration from his or her own funeral. By the time he was telling them how it was possible, while still on this side of death, to face up to life and salvation and carry the faith to others, Anna had learned how to let the graceful undulations ripple across her body; undulations that created the amazing impression of the stormy sea on which the explosion of the steamship *Henriette* raised a pillar of flame and tossed pieces of wreckage all over the stage. The actors then swam through them while water was poured on them from up in the flies, making their skin, by the time they were rescued, as wet as the faces of Thorvald Bak's congregation while they screamed at him that he must tell them the truth about life and he lifted his hands to still them and said, "The world awaits us." While, under the blue sheeting, Anna edged closer to the wave boy, and there was not one person in the church who did not understand Thorvald Bak's words; even the flock of Brazilian sailors who had brought their whores along dropped to their knees and beat their curly heads upon the church floor and, in their remorse, tried in vain to re-member how many murders they had committed. These men were later to form the nucleus of the Seamen's Mission, which spread from the town to some of the remotest corners of the earth and which was, in time, to make the Evangelical Mission one of the Danish dreams that would encircle the globe. When Anna, her face close to the boy's and her fingers in his curly hair, gave in to the irresistible urge to see what lay behind things and unbuttoned his trousers, the intensity of the atmosphere in the church shattered the stained-glass windows and carved doors and forced the crowd out into the streets, where groups of people roamed for the rest of the night, singing songs of praise while searching for Thorvald Bak and the divine girl, of whom their only clear memory was a bitter taste in the mouth that gradually faded.

They never did find them, because they had already left. Weak from exhaustion, Thorvald Bak had staggered out of the church, protected by those members of the faithful who still had all their wits about them. They had Anna's cage in tow and were so intent upon reaching the boat that they did not notice the two children, standing closely entwined at a street corner, who pulled apart sud-denly just as they passed by. Then, looking as though there was something she had forgotten, Anna glided across to her cage and merged with the girl who rested on the silver plating, worn out by the service. Dawn had broken when their ship left the harbor.

After their return to Lavnæs, Anna resumed her habit of taking long walks, and it was not long before Thorvald Bak realized that she was pregnant and about to fulfill her destiny. He said nothing but let people discover it for themselves. As they did, they formed a guard of honor, which was changed four times a day, to escort Anna through the scorching days and ice-cold nights that persisted throughout the summer.

She gave birth one night, without warning and without help. Thorvald Bak was the first to see the child. He found some trivial excuse to send home the guard of honor, which had gathered around the bonfire outside the tower. Then he left the building. He pleaded with his God and summoned up all his spiritual strength. Only for one brief moment did he lose his self-control, when, on his way back, he met his housekeeper, her face now moldy with age.

"Our Savior is a girl," he said.

He stayed away until the sun came up. By the time he returned to Anna's room—where the night chill had already been replaced by intolerable heat—he had regained his strength and the enduring fortitude of his faith. He found the bed vacated and, later, discovered that the mission box was empty. Then, understanding that he would never again see Anna or the child and that all of this must be a punishment for some appalling mistake he had made—without having any idea of what this might have been—he bowed his head toward his housekeeper's deafness and screamed, "The Lord gave, and the Lord hath taken away; blessed be the name of the Lord."

ADONIS JENSEN

On the run

Living outside the law

1838–1918

RAMSES JENSEN'S entire life turns into one long flight. And at one point, when he is well along in years, this brings him to Rudkøbing.

One moonless night he unscrews the hinges of a little arched door in the Teander Rabow family home; closes it carefully from the inside; glides across the black-and-white marble floor and up the wide staircase and along the long corridors without making a single sound. He has a peculiar gift for never leaving any traces of himself, a gift that is to make life difficult for the judges and lawyers and prosecutors from the courts of inquiry set up on the few occasions when he is arrested.

He collects all the items he intends to take on the floor of one large room, finding the things he seeks with instinctive assurance and without at any time being distracted by the house, as it sighs and moans in the night, or by the noises issuing from the bedrooms, where the Old Lady's snoring sounds like laughter and where Christoffer Ludwig is memorizing his columns of figures in his sleep and where Katarina tosses and turns wakefully in her bed, with her hand on her father's revolver.

In the tall chiffoniers his sensitive fingers find bed linens; in the kitchen cupboards, brushes; and elsewhere, down-at-heel shoes. These he chooses, in preference to the embroidered table runners, the bolts of lawn, or the silverware, just as he steers clear of the secret compartments where the jewelry lies in leather cases and where valuable toilet sets, complete with yellowed manicure sticks of silver and ivory, rest in wooden boxes lined with velvet. This seemingly unnecessary restraint arises from his deep and lifelong distrust of wealth.

Now and again he pauses in his work to consider the ponderous trappings of affluence that the Old Lady has amassed, perhaps fearing that her life would take to the air like a balloon and drift off toward the North Pole: the carved oak cupboards that had been on display at the World Exhibition, the shepherdesses on their epergnes of Meissen porcelain, the suits of armor that line the walls of the room, and the marble busts, in whose gaze Ramses Jensen sees the reflection of his own brooding gravity.

His character had possessed an introspective side ever since his incarceration—a very long time ago, when he was still a young man—in the new state prison at Horsens, where he had spent one whole year in total isolation. At that time the prison, which had been built according to the American Philadelphia principle, was not yet completed. Ramses had been moved there from one of the Copenhagen houses of correction because the prison warden was eager to put his principles into practice.

This star-shaped prison complex lay on a windswept stretch of countryside. Every single one of its—empty—cells was equipped with a toilet and running water. The plates of colorless potatoes and iron-hard crusts of bread seemed to edge their way into the cell of their own accord, without any human intervention, and the only person whom Ramses ever saw was the warden, who was a doctor of theology. Each Sunday he held a brief religious service in the prison assembly hall for Ramses, who stood bolt upright during the sermon, strapped into a wooden sentry box, his face covered by a special helmet that left only his eyes exposed. This saved the warden from being distracted by the face that confronted him and Ramses from being hurled back into a life of corruption by seeing his own reflection in the steel prison bars.

The warden was a brutal and gloomy disciplinarian who firmly believed that his sermons, the strict isolation, and the prison diet of bread, water, and potatoes would direct the prisoner's gaze inward, toward his own brutality and debasement, and elicit repentance, despair, and a change of heart. He dabbled secretly in the occult, and his sermons were always based on the Book of Revelation, which he considered to be a talismanic text. He was convinced that, as he spoke, his words were converted into magnetic rays that penetrated the prisoners' cerebral cortices and induced chemical changes in their criminal physiology. So he had acquired the habit during his sermons, when he had said something particularly important, of opening his mouth wide in order to direct his magnetism toward the prisoner.

Ramses spent his year in prison digging a tunnel from his cell to freedom, and recalling all the crimes he had ever committed. To help him endure the loneliness of the vast prison, he reviewed every one of his burglaries, ridding them of creaking doors and toppled furniture and tricky locks and alert guard dogs, and all the mistakes he had made. Within himself he discovered unexpected powers of recall, and so, once he had perfected all his own crimes, he went on to review those of his father and his grandfather and his great-grandfather, right down to the last detail. He kept this up through all the long nights, when he could hear the wind outside tearing at the heather. He kept it up during all the sermons, with the warden referring to the creatures from Revelation as symbols of punishment and justice until Ramses reached the point where he was no longer sure what was more real, the great assembly hall filled with delirious visions of the Apocalypse—in the midst of which the warden's mouth opened and closed like a landed fish gulping for air—or his own dream locks and fantasy rooms, which he negotiated as effortlessly as a dancer before departing, leaving no trace of himself other than his urine. He maintained his forefathers' practice of emptying his bladder at the scene of the crime, this being the most infallible means of evading detection.

At the end of a year his tunnel was finished. Unlike those prisoners later to be accommodated in the prison, who would eventually leave it staggering or crawling or feet first, Ramses Jensen strolled to freedom with a back as straight as when he arrived. All that was visible on his bold features was the pallor of his prolonged imprisonment, pride at the skill he had acquired through his imaginary burglaries, and the wrinkles on his forehead, the consequence of so much time spent deep in thought.

In addition to this, he had had confirmed the distrust of the outside world he had harbored ever since being arrested at the age of twelve, while burglarizing a mill not far from Copenhagen, together with his father. The twelve policemen who had been lying in wait for him had carried him off, bleeding like a stuck pig, while his father stood by, a passive and indifferent onlooker. Then Ramses heard him laugh his unrestrained rogue's laugh and understood, in his child's heart, that his father must have informed on him.

During his lifetime, Ramses' father, Caesar Jensen, stole the credit for so many crimes and charitable acts that he can no longer be discerned behind the thirty-five crimes against King and Crown, the seventeen violations of other people's liberty, the one hundred and forty-four instances of slander, the seventeen murders, the five hundred charges of breach of the peace, and the one thousand and forty-four cases of theft and looting and robbery and threatening behavior of which he was convicted. This sentence was not passed until he was an extremely old man, when he had allowed himself to be caught, after having learned to read and write, so that he could, like the great thief and murderer Ole Kollerød, with whom he had once shared a cell, scratch the grossly exaggerated story of his life on the walls of his cell. These walls were later taken down and produced in court as admissions of guilt, although this was, in fact, unnecessary. All his life, Caesar Jensen had longed to be in a position where he could confess to this incredible multitude of crimes, which led to his execution's being postponed for five years—that being the time it took the court to form an overall picture of the offenses to which he had confessed and for which, as one of the judges said, we could have him executed five hundred times over. His execution was witnessed by one thousand of his fellow prisoners. As the iron rings were placed around his neck, he broke out into peals of uncontrollable laughter, and only Ramses (and perhaps you and I) understands that Caesar Jensen's dying with such arrogance was due, not to that courage ascribed to him by the world, but to his having succeeded in fooling everyone.

It was impossible for Ramses (just as it is hopeless for us) to uncover the truth behind the extravagant boasts that Caesar Jensen wove around his family history, which—like his dress, which consisted of tight white trousers, boots, a fur-trimmed scarlet, fitted jacket, and a broad-brimmed hat—appeared to have been borrowed from cheap broadsides describing the master criminals of history. Throughout Ramses' life a gulf was to exist between the man he encountered in the capricious fantasies of the storytellers—a man represented as being his father—and the Caesar Jensen he knew from his childhood, with his petty pilfering and spur-of-the-moment, panic-stricken burglarizing of elderly folk on isolated farms.

The truth, as the rest of the world saw it, was that Caesar Jensen personified the romantic dream of a criminal; that his career represented the culmination of a long line of arch-rogues who had, down through the generations, spit on the executioner and egged on the six horses that were still not powerful enough to tear them limb from limb; and who, after their funerals, continued to throw the soil off their graves until at last they succeeded in creating someone like Caesar Jensen. Throughout his life, on his interminable travels, Ramses came across his father in legends of the poor man's protector, the intrepid adversary of the rich Caesar Jensen, the cosmopolitan, who had known the Italian Meomartino and the gallant Ròsza. At one point it dawned on him that even the rolls of all the penal judgments in the land hailed Caesar Jensen as a thievish and theatrical messiah, and that he, Ramses, was the only one to see through all the contradictory tales of the seducer, the solitary and fiercely religious avenger—a man who washed his bloody hands in the stream of his own pious tears every Sunday in church, and taught in several Sunday schools—and see his father as he had actually been: a cynical little thief who confessed to everyone else's murders, real or invented, but never to his own sexual offenses; a man whose only grand crime lay in the sum total and quality of all the lies he told in court in order to go down in history as the most infamous criminal of the century.

Late in his life, Ramses visited Copenhagen one last time. One night, in the light from the gas lamps that had, in his old age, made his housebreaking a more and more risky business—he caught sight of his father's name calling out to him from a poster hanging right next to WANTED posters offering prodigious sums for information leading to his own apprehension. The poster carrying Caesar Jensen's name was an advertisement for a play. So, for the first and only time, Ramses attended a performance at the Royal Theater, dressed in an evening suit he had stolen from a house just a few hours earlier, along with a cane and money for the cab that drove him to the theater. There he saw his father's life staged as a ballet. The King and Queen were also present for this performance, in which Caesar Jensen's seventeen false murders and one hundred and forty-four undeserved instances of slander and one thousand and forty-four phony thefts had undergone a metamorphosis: one whereby they were resurrected in a tragic tale of unrequited love and unfortunate—and fatal—misunderstandings, acted out against a backdrop of dewy forests and ancient burial mounds; all of this lit by a stage moon beneath which a hollow-eyed, effeminate boy danced the part of Caesar Jensen. Even though Ramses found the theater and the crowds repellent, that evening he understood that this was what his father had always dreamed of. History had come around in a semicircle, transforming those crimes about which Caesar Jensen had so painstakingly lied into deeds of national renown, their fame transmitted by word of mouth across the length and breadth of the country. They were reenacted before full houses in the finest theater in the land, bathed in the light which Ramses had shunned all his life and surrounded by the sartorial elegance of which Caesar Jensen had always been so fond.

There was one other thing that Ramses noted, prior to his disappearance into the darkness, just before the interval: in the gilded tableaux on the stage and in the tears of the weeping violins he recognized the same sentimental faith he had detected in his father, at their last meeting. This did not take place until some years after the burglary at the mill, Ramses' arrest, and the ensuing court case, during which he had been accused of several of his own break-ins plus a good number of his father's, as well as those for which his father was by then starting to take credit, and those of his dead forefathers. Ramses kept his mouth shut, because he had never been to school and did not understand the language of the court. His silence was therefore taken as an admission of guilt, and he was sentenced to eight years' hard labor, since no one believed that he was only twelve years old. The eight policemen who had arrested him had displayed in court the cracked skulls and broken arms and smashed kneecaps he had inflicted upon them with his left hand while with his right keeping a tight grip on the two-hundred-pound flour sack with which he had been about to make his getaway.

He spent two years in Christianshavn prison, making wood chips for textile dyeing and lending substance to our picture of the innocent but pensive child by gazing through his barred window, wondering at his fate. Until one of the women held in the female section of the prison—who were hoisted up into the cell, every night, through a gap in the loose floorboards—let Ramses see that she had a revolver. Up until then he had only ever regarded women with the elusive curiosity of a child, and the sound of prison lovemaking had never previously disturbed his slumber, but that night he lay awake, and stole for the first time in two years. The next day, just around midday, he rose from the wood-chip table, shoved the barrel of the revolver into the mouth of the guard on duty, and slipped from our picture of the innocent child into our vision—and that of all fairy tales—of a mettlesome youth as he forced the guard to let him out into a little yard behind the prison, from which, after a hazardous climb, he escaped into the crowded streets. For two months he searched for Caesar Jensen. The latter's notoriety, which had doubled and redoubled, kept leading Ramses on wild-goose chases. That he did, nevertheless, track him down was thanks to his habit of always following up the least fanciful of all the tall stories until, one night—all the significant events in the story of Ramses' life take place at night—in an inn near Holbæk, he kicked down the door of his father's room.

Caesar Jensen recognized his son without surprise, and when Ramses pointed the revolver at him he looked fearlessly down its barrel. Ramses had never been much of a talker and in prison he had grown practically dumb, but his question was written all over a face now covered by an incipient beard like a cloud of dark memories.

"I had to teach you to be on your guard," said his father and turned back wearily to the table, where the picklocks and skeleton keys and lead strips were arrayed on a piece of cloth. He picked up a stolen fob watch and said, "That's the only way to survive. Don't trust anyone, not even your father."

Ramses cocked the revolver. His father adjusted his stock, wanting to die looking his best, and added, "Oh, by the way, there's a price on your head, of fifty rigsdalers."

Ramses lowered the revolver, foiled by this argument, and because he realized that he would have done the same thing. Besides, he could not stand the thought that he might be the one to dispatch Caesar Jensen to the immortality of which he dreamed. He turned on his heel, having laid eyes on his father for the last time, and disappeared into another of our pictures—that of the lone fugitive

—and into a world which from then on he regarded as a prison. In this world he viewed everyone as either a judge, a guard, a policeman, or, at the very least, an informer; and he was always on the move while still, in every sound, seeming to hear the cell door slamming behind him.

In the years that followed, Ramses traveled and worked alone, supporting himself in his forlorn state with his pictures of his forebears. His father he dismissed as an aberration, while himself conscientiously avoiding every form of excess, to the extent that the entries in the court records from those occasions when charges were brought against him—if they had contained the facts—would have amounted to infinitely lengthy but nonetheless humble lists of cheese, cheap linen, used brushes, plain tobacco pouches, pawned shoes, old iron, new-laid eggs, and cows milked in the fields, because these, and only these, were the things that Ramses stole.

Now and again, in Copenhagen or one of the larger provincial towns, he would break into some large villa or manor farm. Then, however, he was not after the silver drinking vessels or the West Indian coffee sets or the pear-shaped earrings given to a young girl in the family, once upon a time, by one of the Emperor Napoleon's exiled generals. Ramses skirted all of these and, instead, lit a stump of candle. In its light he would hunker down in front of the massive escritoire and dream. The drop leaf of the escritoire was decorated with a motif, inlaid in wood, depicting the view through a door, which led to a garden, which ran up to a house, which lay bathed in a moonlight such as Ramses believed he remembered from his childhood. This light fell through the fine curtains of a villa that was almost transparent with domestic bliss. And it was this bliss that Ramses sought during these break-ins, when he took nothing, stealing only the opportunity to linger close to people living within his and their own and our picture of domestic bliss. On nights such as these, Ramses could spend hours in a darkened room, listening to the laughter from the adjoining rooms without being any more certain than we are whether what he was hearing was only what he longed to hear, or whether there really were young girls accompanying themselves on their little pianos as they sang of the lonesome young men of the windswept highways. By the light of a candle or a match, Ramses was also able to admire the paintings on the walls. It was as though he saw himself there, in a cloak he had never laid eyes on before, wearing a tall hat he had never owned, staring out across a plain that ended in a forest that opened onto a lake whose farthest shore was lost in a mist of promises. And these paintings represented the middle-class picture of just the sort of life that Ramses led.

Even while being attracted by the domestic idylls into which he steals, Ramses is also repelled by them. He will never acquire the gift of the gab, will never really master the spoken word, so he will never be able to provide a coherent description of the middle-class homes he beheld. Which is a pity, since he beholds more than most. Nevertheless, by piecing together his sparse observations, we can see that he must have entertained a certain suspicion of the Bourgeois Danish Family: his sharp ears caught the hysterical undertone in the young girls' laughter, and his sensitive fingers discovered that furniture which was meant to look genuine and solid was veneered inside and out, and that those pictures, supposedly of inlaid wood, which depicted a father reading to his wife and children were nothing but pasted-on pieces of industrial speculation. There are so many such details that do not stand up well to closer inspection. And always he experiences a sense of quiet satisfaction, as though he has evaded some danger, some risk, when at last he urinates onto the embers in the hearth or into the drowsing spinets, before gliding off, under a white moon, across the flowery carpets of the villa gardens, back to the solitude he endures because he cannot picture anything else.

During these years, Ramses developed the Pride of the Danish Artisan. He explained this to himself by saying that he was practicing an age-old craft, one for which his forefathers—whom he gradually imbued with a life not even his father could have faulted—had been convicted according to laws still based on the Ten Commandments, and then executed as martyrs of a sort. Furthermore, he told himself, in practicing my trade I am demonstrating the same moderation and the same Christian humility as everyone else—apart from my father. Ramses might even have forgotten Caesar Jensen were it not for the fact that his own Christian name, taken from a book his father had once appropriated, stood as a constant reminder of how Caesar Jensen would steal anything whatsoever from anyone whomsoever.

Ramses succeeded in hanging on to his honorable outlook on life only because he was extremely wary and extremely obstinate. He ran, but his reputation was always one step ahead of him, at first boosted by his father's reputation but later growing of its own accord. It was at this time, too, that he had to give up keeping count of his crimes. From then on, he only ever found them added up and enumerated on the WANTED posters that, complete with his portrait, grinned down at him in dusty provincial towns. The portrait had been drawn by one of his prison cell mates, since, despite his size, Ramses had become as supple and silent as a cat and no decent citizen had ever seen his face. Thus the portrait preserved a childishness quite at odds with the robberies and, eventually, murders, too, for which he was wanted and which he knew he could not have committed, but which did explain a reward so generous that it would have tempted most of those with whom Ramses ever came into contact. It even tempted him to turn himself in. This he only stopped himself from doing because he realized that the size of the reward proved that the authorities were mystified and that they had been taken in by the baroque exaggerations of his crimes and charity in the broadside ballads—packs of lies, the lot of them—that he heard sung on street corners on the rare occasions when he ventured into any good-sized town.

The only human society Ramses sought was that of vagabonds, ragmen, and Gypsies, in whom he seemed to recognize his own restlessness and wariness. They, for their part, always treated him with respect. They were convinced that he was possessed by gods, because he always slept with his eyes open and his hand over his mouth—although, in actual fact, this was because his wariness had grown so deep-rooted that he did not even trust himself, but feared that he would confide in someone in his sleep, thereby dispelling the veil of invisibility his anonymity accorded him.

It was thanks to this penchant for seeking company, despite his pride and his taciturnity, that he one day fell in with three horse-drawn covered carts driven by dark-skinned men of the same race as those who would, sometime in the future, build the Old Lady's water closet. The ragtag appearance of this procession made him feel so safe that he fell asleep that afternoon on the roof of one of the carts; and slept on, his open eyes and the hand over his mouth notwithstanding, while the carts crawled through resin-scented pine forests and small, suspicious villages where the washing was taken in as the carts trundled past like some traveling exhibition of the dingy squalor of the wayfaring life.

Ramses awoke to the fleeting notion that he had landed in paradise. Before him the Pearly Gates lit up the night, with glittering letters spelling out the words "National Theater" and "Art Exhibition"; words that he could not read because he had never been to school. He thought he was entering the sunlit glades of Pison when he slipped, unseen, past a German ticket lady dressed up as the Roman goddess Minerva. Only then did he realize that he had entered our dream—and his, and that of his time—of the circus. He was encircled by a black sea of people, all of them facing a ring in which horses pranced on their hind legs like men, and submissive cattle allowed themselves to be twisted into unnatural shapes; while donkeys, walking upright, sold autographed copies of scenes in which scantily clad women posed as Polynesian queens.

Despite all the temptations, Ramses would have fled from the light and the noise and the crowds if the bust of a woman, suspended from the infinitely distant tent roof by thin steel wires, had not screeched at him that happiness awaited him here, in this very place—happiness. And so Ramses Jensen stayed where he was, in this circus, somewhere in North Jutland, somewhere around the middle of the last century. There he stands amid the crystallized dreams of Exotica and Erotica and Freedom and Paradise, all of which must have unfurled from the flaking unpretentiousness of the carts.

In the circus there are two levels of seating, for the two different levels of audience to be found in Denmark at this time: the run-of-the-mill spectators, who have paid the standard price, and the quality, who paid whatever they felt was appropriate—all of them having stumped up knowing full well that this world into which they have stepped is not without its risks. It is a world in which—apart from those things I have mentioned, and the music—they might be exposed to insults of the kind now being hurled by a quick-change artist, a man who appeared at first to be attired in some sort of evening dress gilded by the lights of the circus ring. He said he had the honor to welcome them to this acrobatic pantomime, this zoological extravaganza which was about to get under way, weather permitting, and which would include the launching of what was in all respects the most perfect aerial sphere. This thirty-thousand-cubic-foot aerostatic balloon, as empty on the inside as the heads of the most esteemed members of this audience, would rise far beyond the understanding of the honorable members of the public, all the way up to the roof. Beneath this balloon would be his daughter, a twelve-year-old maiden, hanging by her teeth and one of her perfectly formed fingers. And, he promised them—while changing first into the costume of a maharaja, then that of Harlequin—from this position she would execute—might he shrivel up and rot on the spot, together with this esteemed audience, if he were lying—a triple somersault. Then his daughter appeared.

The sight of the girl slipped around Ramses' silence and his pride, past his penchant for introspection, and broke the lock on his heart. As she stood there in the ring, and then when she started to dance, he recognized the same skepticism and contempt that he had heard in her father's, the quick-change artist's, outlandish accent and hissing sibilants. When the audience did not applaud, when she did not receive the required ovation, off she waded into the midst of all the booing men and hissing women and howling children, fired off two pistols, and then began to let fly with her fists at all those in her immediate vicinity. After that, terror-stricken and led by the claque, everyone applauded and Ramses had to stay, having been gripped by what he had seen and by the dream of circus-ring passion and flying-trapeze love affairs which we all nurture, and which Ramses Jensen's contemporaries endeavored to keep within the bounds of the circus arena.

He remained there for the rest of the evening while his beloved rose into the air under the balloon, illuminated by fireworks representing Mount Vesuvius, with the red-hot lava from the volcano's eruption igniting the royal monogram. As the twelve-year-old dangled beneath the balloon, so high above the floor of the ring that her body was barely visible—although her acrobatic feats and reckless, death-defying somersaults could clearly be seen—more than one member of the audience wept from fear. But not Ramses Jensen, who was, just then, filled with the sort of serenity which corroborates the myth of love at first sight and of love's utter contempt for death, and which endowed him with enough presence of mind to sneak away before the pantomime, the climax to the festivities, in which all the performers appeared, dressed up and painted with cocoa and

soot mixed with grease, to resemble the Danes' picture of the southern Europeans they in fact happened to be. This they did in the
subtle knowledge that neither in the circus ring nor, for that matter,
in this account of actual events do our wishes ever appear in their
totally scrubbed and natural state. Then they left the ring, not in
their shabby carts, but floating on a flying carpet, pursued by officers
dressed in the gaudy uniforms of Cromwell's time and ushered out
by the triumphant laughter of an audience which had, to its complete
and utter satisfaction, witnessed the ousting of everything conjured
up by the evening's performance.

Ramses awaited his circus artiste in one of the collapsible wooden
caravans that had sprung up around the circus tent, surrounded by
imitation flowers and ripped tights and the scent of eau de cologne
and many another thing he did not notice because his heart had
risen into the air with the balloon. When the girl opened the door,
Ramses saw that the light had distorted her proportions. She was
now very small and just as broad as she was long.

"I shall be the first and the last man in your life," he said, without
knowing how he came, suddenly, to be so eloquent.

The girl regarded him fearlessly and laughed quietly at finding
herself face-to-face with such naïveté.

"You're too late to be the first," she said, "and too early to be the
last."

"But you're only twelve," said Ramses.

The girl gave him a thoughtful look. "I'm thirty," she said. Then
her head arched backwards and her body grew soft as india rubber.
When her head emerged between her legs, she had a lit cigar between her lips and a glass of wine in a hand attached to an arm
that she had wrapped twice around her neck.

"Are you a man," she asked him, "or are you a butterfly?"

Ramses stood up. In one single movement he shook himself free
of a momentary giddiness, and of his loneliness and his introspection
and the smell of sawdust. Then he bent down and kissed the girl's
mouth. When she disentangled herself and put her muscular arms
around his neck, and when they slid down onto the four-poster bed,
with its canopy embroidered like some distant circus dome, he
thought: This may be the only thing in life that can't be stolen.

They spent three days in the caravan, behind closed shutters, and
when they opened the door on the third day they discovered that

their vehicle was standing in solitary state on a hillside from which, in the distance, they could see the sun rising over great forests. On this hillside, with our—and to some extent their own—longing for uninhabited countryside spread at their feet, Ramses asked the circus princess about her life. But she did not answer him, neither on that occasion nor later, although it was evident that she, too, listened for the slamming of doors in the song of the larks and the murmur of the wind through the wheat; and that, even at a distance, she dreaded the very forest boundaries because they reminded her of walls. And even then Ramses accepted that she was to constitute the lock in his life for which no skeleton key existed. From that day on he journeyed with her without knowing her name.

She was as nimble as he. The only time they were arrested it came about because, while hanging from a fifth-floor balcony, high above a crowd of onlookers and police officers, she had suddenly been overwhelmed by circus fever and by her father's, the quick-change artist's, love of mocking his audience and hearing them gasp, while teetering on the brink of death. And so—suspended between heaven and earth, and even though she was, by that time, getting on in years—she re-created the vaults and somersaults of her youth. By the time the fifty policemen reached her she had wound herself around the railings so many times that they had to be cut away and taken into custody along with her and Ramses, whom the police had been able to pluck like ripe fruit, so absorbed was he by the Princess's death-defying aerobatics. These had left him feeling as passionate and yet quiescent as they had done when he had witnessed them for the first time as a young man. He felt as though he could just as easily have dropped dead on the spot as gone on living, since at that moment he wanted for nothing. Instead, he was totally taken up by the Princess, who had long since become his wife. They had stolen the marriage documents and kidnapped a pastor to fill them in and enter their names in the parish register.

Following their arrest, they were charged with eleven hundred offenses in ten countries, even though these charges were the result of the chamberlains and recorders from the courts of inquiry having listened—amid all the hubbub that followed Caesar Jensen's boasting and all the hush that followed the Princess and Ramses—to tall stories and superstition. Thus, even these charges for crimes they had not committed contained a modicum of truth, inasmuch as

Ramses and the Princess had, together, covered great distances and crossed more borders than they could count, all in an effort to escape from their own reputation—a reputation that nevertheless traveled ahead of them—and to keep up with their yearning for a love as free as air, a yearning that was theirs and is now ours. But we must not forget that, like all professional criminals, they spent every minute of their lives on the move, for three reasons: fear of hunger; a vague, directionless anger; and that yearning which brought them the life we are able to use, here, as an example.

As a kindness to a sympathetic jailer they stayed in their cells for two days, the longest they had ever been apart. On the third day they vanished without trace.

Ramses never made any effort to arrive at a final tally of his children. Once the Princess had given birth to their eleventh son he stopped keeping count of them or trying to tell them apart. He had never had a head for figures or any sense for the diversity of the human race, so, from then on, the only two of his children whom he ever remembered were his one daughter and Adonis.

Adonis was an afterthought. He was born some years after the last of their children had left them to their own devices after a succession of years that Ramses recalled as being endless and full of children, thanks to the fact that, by being constantly on the move, he and the Princess not only stayed clear of other people but also outdistanced consumption and cholera and the English sweating sickness and all the other epidemics that ravaged Denmark during the second half of the last century. All they had to worry about, therefore, was food and an ever-changing series of roofs over their heads, to sustain both their children and their own joyful passion. Their love burned brightly in haystacks and barns and out-of-the-way inns. It was grand and intense and quite at odds with a life that was in all other respects very, very modest; an existence at all times hand-to-mouth.

Whenever the children reached the age of twelve, Ramses would force a pastor to confirm them. It never worried him that this act, having taken place under duress, would subsequently be declared invalid. Likewise he never, despite his pensive streak, thought twice about the fact that he—who had turned his back on his father's bogus piety and who had never said a prayer and who had broken one of the Ten Commandments on an almost daily basis, often out of mere curiosity—should, even so, now risk hunting up a man of the cloth to bestow an invalid blessing on his unbaptized children.

Nor did Ramses understand his children. He tried to teach them his craft, but they showed no interest in locks and hasps and forged keys, just as all his attempts to teach them his stealth were in vain. After that, he regarded them just as he regarded everyone else: with wary reserve. If we reproach him for this, then we stop short of the truth and our sight is blurred by the sentimental wish that parents should love their children. And then we lose sight of Ramses, because, introspective though he may be, his personality is devoid of sentimentality. So we cannot blame him, either, because many years later, on once more coming across his eldest son, he did not reveal who he was. Indeed, he did not even realize that this was the eldest until the Princess told him. It happened in Rudkøbing, where, later, he was to break in to the Teander Rabow family home, and where the fates of so many of those whose history we are narrating cross. And this tells us something about the association, in real life, between chaos and order; something that Ramses also read in the eyes of this man who was his son but who bore an appalling likeness to his father, Caesar Jensen. Ramses' sons (and his daughter) had long since erased every trace of their past, changed their names, and purported to come from law-abiding families of many generations' standing. Sooner or later, all of them succeeded in becoming wealthy or at any rate famous, although only we realize that they were the offspring of the Princess and Ramses. The boy in the square at Rudkøbing, holding forth to a large crowd from the back of a cart, called himself Pio and—even though the Princess was sure that it was not so many years since he had still been in diapers—Ramses realized, as his speech was coming to a close, that his son was talking about the ideas behind socialism.

During this speech, Ramses was so busy emptying the pockets of his son's audience that he barely caught what his son was saying: there would be no more putting new patches on old clothes. And that was why he was now appealing to all those who were listening, to all of you who sway like reeds in the wind, he said, while, from their pockets, their watches and cigar cases and hip flasks seemed to vanish into thin air. The man on the back of the cart described the hard roads they would have to take, roads which would at first be strewn with thorns and thistles rather than roses, but which would soon grow easier. For, said Pio, from all sides, the cry of the awakening masses rises to greet us, like the dull roar of the sea before a storm.

Something about this torrent of words touched Ramses' heart. It made him think of the piano playing of his own youth. And it kept him there, even when it started to rain, to hear his son yelling at the listening day laborers and shopkeepers and journalists from the local newspaper, and Christoffer Ludwig, as yet just a small child dressed like a grownup, listening through the open windows of his office. Now the workers were no longer going to drain the bitter draft, now the rich would no longer be able to cry, like the French court: *"Après nous le déluge,"* now there would be an end to religion and woolly-headed notions, shouted Pio, now reality was hammering on society's doors. And though these were the doors whose locks Ramses had otherwise always picked, this speech moved him. So while his son bawled through the rain at the gathering that the workingman is nature's firstborn, her stoutest son, Ramses put all the stolen combs and watch chains and clasp knives back into their rightful pockets.

When the rain stops and the police gallop into the midst of the gathering and disperse it, and then handcuff his son, it is a thoughtful Ramses who reluctantly makes his retreat. He has so much to think about: he has seen his son seized by what he himself considers to be some sort of religious frenzy; heard him talking exactly like some revivalist preacher. That his message is different, or at least to some extent different, is something that Ramses is unable to grasp. His own life, his own distrust have blinded him to the misery that feeds the dreams his son is now well under way with dreaming.

In one sense, all of Ramses' children acquire the same way of looking at the world: even though they all end up at widely differing points on the social pyramid, they all still come to regard the world as a piece of wax in which one can set one's seal. This faith in their own abilities derives from the kind of upbringing they have had as sons of a couple of exceptionally cunning and unpretentious petty criminals. From when they were very small, they have known the power and the wretchedness of being homeless. They have stopped believing that anything stands still forever, with the result that all of them, in their own ways, end up working to set in motion that weightiest of all things, namely society itself.

To Ramses this work is an outrage since, despite his lawless life, he has maintained an unshakable belief that society is now, and will always be, the best of all pyramids and that its stability will not be affected one whit by his forcing a door here and there on its upper stories. This is more or less how he was thinking that day, after the subversive meeting in Rudkøbing at which his son had spoken. Then he did as he had done so often before in his life: he pissed up against a bush and went on his way.

After this experience, Ramses stayed away from towns, which he was not sure he understood, anyway, and which now and again caused him to have a particular dream: a dreadful wish, which he never mentioned, that some monster, or one of the creatures that Caesar Jensen had boasted of having encountered, would obliterate these collections of houses. It so happened that the Princess had the selfsame dream—which they were never aware of, since the only thing they did not share with each other was their dreams. The writer Steen Steensen Blicher (who was by this time dead) dreamed the same dream, as did the writer Hans Christian Andersen (who was dying), and so do I, to this very day. It is a hopeless dream. There is no future in it, and yet it has to be spoken of.

Because of their isolation—in which they only ever met beggars and ragmen, and in which Ramses only ever heard his native tongue spoken in adjoining rooms, during his burglaries—he and the Princess lost touch with their own legends. It was as though they had broken free and finally disappeared, only to reappear early one May morning, when one of the Gypsies in their company, who could read, recognized Ramses from a portrait in a newspaper. "You've been pardoned," said the Gypsy and held the newspaper out to him. Ramses' eyes never left the Gypsy's face as he said, "It says you won undying glory in the war." Ramses gripped his arm tightly. "Read it to me," he ordered. It was a long article, in the Old Lady's Rudkøbing newspaper. It stated that he, Ramses Jensen, had fought valiantly in the war and had then disappeared. That he had, in fact, always been on the side of freedom and that the King himself had decided to pardon him, at the request of a group of important personages who had publicly protested the erroneous impression the general public had been given of Ramses, thanks to Caesar Jensen's misdeeds.

Ramses had not kept up with what had happened to his sons, but now it dawned on him that they had become important men, capable of arranging whatever was necessary, even such a falsification of history. From that day, and until Adonis was born, he and the Princess shunned all human society.

Adonis was born after a series of seemingly premeditated coincidences, which may have started with Ramses breaking into Mørkhøj.

I do not know what made Ramses do it. Normally, he would have avoided a place such as Mørkhøj. It was, at one and the same time, too gloomy and too ostentatious for his taste. So he must have been prompted by something out of the ordinary. It may have been that he saw a faded WANTED poster, for himself, on the wall. Or it may have been out of curiosity, or long habit, or the challenge presented by the height of the wall. No one can be sure now. What we do know is that by this time Ramses was, by the standards of his own century, an old man. Even so, he effortlessly negotiated the iron spikes that had kept time out until that moment, even though they shattered at his touch, eaten away by rust. He glided across the dark green lawns of the manor grounds just at one of those rare moments when the golden light of the sun filtered through the tops of the oak trees to create a veil of light and shade that covered him, and left him free to witness, all unseen, the laborers singing in the fields, the cows in the meadows, and the fair hair of the young countesses, all of which could just be discerned in the shadow of the trees, and all of which were part of a wish that Ramses did not share and that therefore made no impression on him.

Ramses had never dreamed of manor-house idylls. So it would not have made any impression on him either if he had come within earshot and discovered that the working songs consisted not of words but of meaningless grunts and that the red cows were no bigger than badgers and that the countesses' two-hundred-year-old reveries were but an empty ritual. What Ramses, who had no home, savored was the silence and the coolness of the secret pathways which had been forgotten for three centuries but which he found without any difficulty. These led him to the overgrown moat and through the cellars where the great Paracelsus had drunk with his whores and up narrow staircases in the thick walls of the main building. From there, through concealed spyholes in the canvases of extinct painters, he could watch the dumb footmen polishing the silver, and peep into the white-and-gilt room, and over Jacoby's shoulder, at the ink drying on the already yellowed pages of the castle's history. From here, too, he spent a long while watching the Count, who was working in his laboratory. Ramses may even have felt as though he knew this man, who had decreed, and later witnessed, the execution of one of Ramses' forebears in the square outside Copenhagen Cathedral in a time before that with which we are here concerned. It was, as it happens, on that occasion—outside the cathedral and face-to-face with a criminal from the lowest rung of humanity, who just happened to be one of Ramses' forefathers—that the Count had formed some of the ideas on the structure of the universe that now kept him tied to his work in the laboratory, surrounded by retorts and alembics, one of which Ramses now takes. It is the only thing he takes, before vanishing just as silently as Jacoby's ghost will—in a not-too-distant future—make its return.

That Ramses should have picked up this particular alembic is yet another of those important coincidences. He takes it, on impulse, from a table behind where the Count is working. But even when being impulsive, he remains true to his principle of modesty and takes an alembic containing nothing but air beneath its stopper. Later, he and the Princess unstop the alembic in the bedroom of an isolated house into which they have forced their way for the night—just this one night. That it should be this particular house is yet another coincidence, and now they do, in fact, open the alembic. The air pent up inside it is so old that it smells of violets and prussic acid, and out of the bottle there rises the faint echo of the lonesome music played on a cello by the last of Mørkhøj's dying race of musicians.

This situation comprises elements from so many different places. Once again, so many dreams come together here: the house is large and empty and far away from everything. Outside, the wind howls, reminding Ramses and the Princess of how awful it is to travel at night and what a burden it is always to be on the run. On the table before them there is a lit candle and the remains of a modest meal—possibly porridge and pork cracklings, but at any rate definitely something hot. The Princess never skimped where food was concerned; she and Ramses and the children had always eaten like regular folks. And then there is the alembic, and the scent of the past, and distant music. This last calls to mind for both of them the mazurkas and Hungarian folk dances that the drunken Belgian circus musicians had played in their youthful days on the hilltop. It causes them to slide down next to each other, and what happens next is that Adonis—son of two ragged-trousered proletarians—is conceived in this bed, which had been shown at the big exhibition of Scandinavian art and industry. What happens in this bed, apart from that, is none of our business. So instead let me just say that its upholstery and rosettes and heavy hangings heralded a new age. This bed represented a last attempt at camouflage on the part of a middle class that would never make the acquaintance of Ramses and the Princess. I should also mention that both the bed and the deserted house, with its medieval turrets and curved bronze window frames, had been designed by one of their own sons, an architect who had disowned his father and mother by taking the name of Meldahl and who would, in time, become both principal of the Academy of Fine Arts and a member of the Copenhagen municipal council—all of which indicates that the parents' love and their children's achievements are in some way connected.

As a child, Adonis brought his father and mother much sorrow, through his compassion for mankind. Ramses and the Princess must have become aware of this compassion very early on because, as a baby on his mother's back, if he saw his father walking off with a piece of canvas or a salami that did not belong to him, he would break into the infant howls that summoned the dogs and armed men whom Ramses had spent a lifetime avoiding but from whom he now had to run, just as he had done when he was young, by wading through streams, up to his waist in water, to cover his tracks. And all the while he struggled to understand how children could be so impossible by nature; why he had never succeeded in getting just one son to follow in his own, invisible, footsteps, which were, instead, now being followed by sheepdogs and men with hunting rifles because of whom he was forced to stay in the water for so long that he contracted pneumonia—an illness that was still plaguing him when they met the Princess's father, the quick-change artist.

This meeting took place at a cattle market, when the puppets in one of the puppet theaters that had been set up started to shout after

Ramses, who had just set foot in the streets for the first time in three weeks. Behind the gilded proscenium of the theater they found the old circus manager, who now spent his life behind puppets. In a voice hoarse from an entire life of bawling out insults, he congratulated Ramses on how well he looked and told them, with some feeling, how, in another part of the country, he had come across tales of his daughter, of whom it was said that she was a witch. Before setting off, on foot, with his theater folded up and strapped to his back, he gave the baby the name of Adonis. So full of authority were the furrows, thick with soot, that age had etched in his face that Ramses accepted the name, even though it reminded him of Caesar Jensen. Nevertheless, he made just one bid to persuade his father-in-law to change his mind, shouting after the departing theater, "Every policeman will remember that name!"

The impresario waved his hat and answered him, without turning around, "It's an artist's name. Women will never forget it!"

And thus he left Ramses and the Princess to hopes and expectations that were kept alive when Adonis proved, as he grew, to be the obedient child of whom every parent dreams. He became as stealthy as Ramses and as nimble as the Princess. With his instinct for soothing all living things, he sweet-talked the cows in the fields while Ramses milked them, and then helped his father to carry home the milk, to the extent that Ramses was able to harbor a fragile hope, which he preserved by never really putting Adonis to the test. And so his hope remained unthwarted until the night when he broke into the Teander Rabow family home—which is where we began this chapter. For when Ramses tore his eyes away from the marble busts in the Old Lady's house in Rudkøbing in Langeland, he discovered that his sack, which lay on the floor, was now so flat that it could only be full of emptiness and nothing but emptiness. Beside it, in the moonlight, stood Adonis. It was quite clear, there was no denying, that the boy—his own son—must have broken in after his father and crept through the house even more silently than Ramses himself; in fact, with such extraordinary stealth that the boy's presence actually muffled the house's own natural sounds. Thus, even Katarina dozed—although her finger did not leave the trigger. Thereafter, Adonis had put back everything; thereafter, he had stolen from his own father and put the worthless fabrics and brushes and shoes back where they came from, while his old father was staring at statues as old as himself, recalling that past in which he had supported a family so large that the precise number of children escaped him—though they had all let him down by becoming important and immoderate men with strange names and extravagant dreams of changing the world, and had left him and the Princess, his heart's darling, alone with the fragile hope that now, before God, had been most decidedly shattered, now that Adonis had abused his gifts and dealt his father this blow. Even now Ramses, who, since his youth, had never spoken during a break-in, merely inclined his head silently toward the empty sack on the dark floor, lit by a white moon. And it was Adonis who broke the silence.

"These things don't belong to you, Father," he said.

Ramses raised his hand as though to hit him, but was held back by the feeling that some higher form of justice does exist, a feeling he had acquired from living outside the laws of man. Instead the outrage he felt in his heart found its way to his lips. "You young whippersnapper," he hissed, "you'd see your own parents lying in the streets with their bones picked clean before you'd spare them a crust." The sound of his voice carried to Katarina, who woke up and fired her pistol at the door, believing that her husband or her mother-in-law, or more likely both of them, were trying to take her by surprise. Then Ramses and Adonis made a run for it. Ramses was so shaken that he crashed into tables and chairs and stools. He became separated from his son and was unable to regain his bat-like sense for finding his way in the dark. At one point a door yielded to his weight and sent him into the arms of a police chief who had spent his whole life chasing him. This police chief arrested Ramses personally, even though he was befuddled by rumors that the King wanted to pardon him, and by all the tall stories about his magnanimity.

During the two months of his imprisonment, Ramses never uttered a single word but remained as silent as in his youth. He was transferred to Copenhagen and placed in the same cell as the Princess. She had turned herself in to be close to her husband and to show her contempt for the authorities, who were now trying to make this stay in prison as pleasant as possible for these two celebrated criminals by decorating their cell like a bridal suite, fearing, as they did, the couple's influential sponsors, who were, of course, their sons. Three times daily they were served meals from a fine restaurant, and they were visited by pastors and journalists and lawyers whom Ramses detested.

In this elegantly appointed cell, at one point, they were also visited by their children, and even Ramses could no longer fail to see how well things had gone for them. They had become mathematicians and doctors and lawyers and prophets of doom and inventors. They had tried to forget their upbringing by shoring up their wavering times with morality or with brilliant machines or with legislation that Ramses had never respected or understood. Moreover, he could never quite understand how they had managed to secure his pardon. Nor, when it came right down to it, did he show any sign of recognizing these tall, self-assured men wearing the clothes and symbols of power. He accepted that they were his sons only because the Princess said so, and all her life she had been right. One after another they approached him in the cell to receive his thanks for a favor he had never asked of them. He looked in wonder at these penguins, whose strides had grown short, stiff, and measured from their regular visits to ministries and courts of law, and at his only daughter, who, like her brothers, wanted to change the world. In her the Princess's courage and urge to scandalize her contemporaries had developed into an urge to change the world by improving the status of women, as she explained proudly to Ramses. And while she was speaking, he was shaking his head and wondering if he was losing his mind. He refused to understand the woman who now stood before him dressed provocatively in loose-fitting clothing; who was not only an agricultural consultant but also a horse trader and member of the jockey club *and* smoked cigars, not only here in front of her parents but out in the streets, too—to shock people.

Ramses shut himself out from the world (if, indeed, one is prepared to accept the possibility of putting oneself even further out of touch than he already was). He forbade the Princess to read aloud from the newspapers delivered to their cell in the days before their pardon was granted. In these they could read their own story, illustrated with etchings that portrayed them in a transfigured, mythological light, dressed as some royal couple from a distant and legendary age *à la* Regnar Lodbrog, against a backdrop of misty mountains and dusky blue fjords. Only once did he speak to anyone in that stream of visitors—when he recognized Meldahl, the oldest of his sons, now architect to the Danish court and a Knight Commander of the Order of Dannebrog. He had also, as it happens, designed the out-of-the-way house in which Adonis was conceived, and had succeeded in creating for himself a totally watertight past, to the extent that no one now knew that he was Ramses and the Princess's son. Ramses saw the Dannebrog Cross on the breast of his tailcoat, and in his eyes he glimpsed the reflection of all the villas and churches and lunatic asylums and prisons and palaces that he had designed, and whose building he had supervised; all the buildings in which, in granite and slate and sandstone and plaster and stucco, he had endeavored to express his desire to forget his childhood. And yet here it was, facing him, in the shape of his own father, who was imprisoned in a prison he himself had built, with a façade camouflaged to resemble a Swiss chalet. Ramses turned away from him in anger, and the architect extended his hands in a helpless gesture, unable to understand what was happening. "You have built walls," Ramses said tonelessly. Meldahl left without saying anything, and they only ever saw him on one other occasion. That was when he returned with Adonis, who had given himself up and tried to claim responsibility for his father's break-ins, and now the authorities were at a loss as to what to do with him.

That same night, not wanting to hear the result of the petition for mercy, Ramses and the Princess broke out of prison with that hopeless child—Adonis, that is. They did not, however, manage to slip out of town unseen. Around daybreak, a group of journalists, who had been waiting in the street for just such a turn of events, spotted them driving north. In the press the next day, their departure was presented as a triumphal procession: the grand old man and illustrious war hero making his dignified exit. The family had been captured for posterity in etchings that depicted them smiling and waving as they left the town by way of Søtorvet—a square designed by Meldahl along Parisian lines. In the background, barely discernible, were the churches and ministries and hospitals—also Meldahl's work—frequented by the sons of Ramses and the Princess; those pillars of society who would, not long after this, be sending telegrams of homage and condolence to Rudkøbing, on the occasion of the Old Lady's death. That event occurred just as the coachman lashed the horses with his whip and the coach trundled past the journalists' faces. Ramses shook his fist at them until he could no longer see them.

For the first few months, Ramses and the Princess traveled southward. On their way through Europe they put one after another border behind them in an attempt to elude this modern age in which criminals were looked upon as heroes, where they ran the risk of at any moment finding their long and arduous lives screeching at them from cabarets and vaudeville shows in big cities, and where the Princess recognized her sons' names on the works in bookshop windows—works of scientific research into the criminal physiognomy and the prison system and agriculture and the development of machines. The racket from these last, which she and Ramses abhorred, constituted one of their reasons for making a definite decision to keep to the country areas. They traveled south because they wanted to get away and because the Princess retained a vague memory, from the stories of her childhood, of shady countries like pleasant gardens. Instead, on foot and in uncomfortable stagecoaches, they passed through regions bathed in a dry and all-revealing sunlight in which garrulousness and the tendency to exaggerate, from which they had fled, seemed to flourish like a tropical flower. Here the dust still held the imprint of footsteps from the time when their sons had traveled through Europe on grand tours, paid for by the state they would later come to support or try to overthrow, but at any rate to change—by transplanting what they had seen on their travels into Danish soil. And this explains why Ramses felt as though, everywhere he looked, he saw prisons: because when he designed his prisons, Meldahl had drawn inspiration from the Italian villas and Greek temples and Turkish mosques in the towns through which his parents were now passing. And it was in such places that they met the hardy revolutionaries whose ideas had fallen upon the embers smoldering inside their son the Socialist, ideas that had transformed his nagging dissatisfaction into the gasoline blaze that would send him to prison and then exile him to America. In fact, he was on the point of departure just as Ramses and the Princess were traveling past wretchedness the likes of which they had never seen and which they still did not see because, now and for the rest of their lives, they lived in the belief that the world around them was the best of possible worlds and that everyone ought to keep to the place allotted him—everyone except themselves, since they were under the singular obligation to remain eternally on the move.

Before giving up all hope of understanding Adonis, the only child left to them, Ramses tried to teach him, in various European capitals, the art of picking people's pockets and of appropriating brass-bound leather suitcases in intolerable railroad stations. Adonis mastered every new trick so quickly that Ramses—who was looking for anything, the slightest hint, that his son might become a criminal, like his father—told himself that the boy picked up everything as if by some sort of intellectual theft, inasmuch as he could, with one swipe, appropriate foreign vocabularies and grammar and win the confidence of foreigners with his blue eyes—which could turn almost green with goodwill. Such skills, together with his carefree nature, make him seem, to us, like another Aladdin. And that is how he would have seemed to his parents if it had not been for his honesty, which was inclined to manifest itself in baroque fashion for as long as Ramses kept on trying to overcome it and make his son understand that the world had to be met with skepticism and distrust and a permananent state of readiness. Sometimes, because Ramses insists, Adonis complies with his wishes, as when, in the square in front of St. Peter's in Rome, he slits open the coat pocket of a passing gentleman with a razor, grabs his fat wallet as it falls out, and then laughs, proudly and happily, at his father, who is hidden in the crowd, observing his son. Naturally, Ramses is proud, but his pleasure does not last for long. When they return to their *pensione* it becomes apparent that Adonis no longer has the wallet. While still out in the vast square, with his father standing there delightedly nodding and smiling, Adonis had with his free hand slit open his victim's other pocket, slipped the wallet back, and then sewn up both pockets—all of this while the man was walking past him, and the entire operation executed so dexterously that not even Ramses saw it. This done, Adonis walks over to Ramses, a happy man who has, in actuality, nothing to be happy about except the fact that his son has at least left no trace of himself, other than the two rows of stitches that the coat's owner will discover and wonder at some months later. These stitches are Adonis's attempt to repair his youth, in which he—like so many others whose stories we have told—is torn between his own nature and his father and mother's abstemious obstinacy.

When Adonis was nine years old, he met his grandfather the quick-change artist. They met in Turkey, at one of the garish bazaars that were a nightmare for Ramses. They seemed to hover on a cloud of dust, and, as Adonis moved through them, his fair curls made the women cry and the stall holders presented him with cakes sweetened with blood and honey, just to see him chew, while trade came to a standstill and everyone pushed and shoved to get a look at this divine child.

That was to be the day when Adonis left his parents. Somewhere, amid the canopies and waterskins and dried cheeses, a man stepped out of the dust and the noise to alternately mock and flatter spectators in what was not quite their own language but something like it. During the clamorous applause, the man peeled off his face and Adonis realized that it was a mask, and that under that there was another mask, and then he was sure that this must be his grandfather, of whom he had heard but whom he had never met—if we disregard that time when he was very small and was given his name. To begin with, it was not his standing face-to-face with his grandfather that mattered to Adonis. The crucial factor was the effect the mask had on the audience. During the impudent performance Adonis did not look at his grandfather but at the audience, and here, for the first time, he saw the moisture in the eyes of the veiled women and the shaking hands of the men. I think I can say that it was at this moment that Adonis, who was just a little boy, saw, in a flash of understanding, that his life was bound to masks, and to the theater. I deliberately use the expression "flash of understanding" because that is what it was, and it was the only one of its kind that Adonis would ever experience in a life in which decisive moments were rare and imperceptible transitions the norm. When the old man disappeared into the crowd, followed by the applause, Adonis was right behind him. In a little red-and-white-striped tent he revealed his identity to his grandfather, who answered him in a language Adonis did not understand. Even in the cool peacefulness of the tent, the quick-change artist's face was so distorted that Adonis wondered whether one of the masks he had been slipping on and off all through his life had finally got the better of him.

It was evening when Ramses and the Princess found Adonis. They had followed the laughter rising from around a little dais where he and his grandfather were staging a piece of improvised comedy that Ramses and the Princess did not understand. Nor would they have recognized their son if the Princess had not glimpsed his hair shining above his mask, just for an instant, when the light from the oil lamps caught it. Once Ramses had had his son pointed out to him and realized that the boy was actually standing on the stage, he suddenly remembered the moment when, as a young boy with a year in prison behind him, he had stood facing his father. Now, too, he yielded to the sense of his own impotence—and left.

That same night he and the Princess headed east. Some sort of melancholy defiance made them move in the opposite direction from the great constellations known to them from the innumerable nights when they had watched over their prodigal sons and their one impossible daughter. They traveled because they wanted never again to have to look their children or the world they left behind in the eye, and because they were driven by their wanderlust. This was something they themselves found harder and harder to understand as, gradually, they wandered farther and farther away from Europe. Their progress turned into a journey through a wilderness of snow-covered mountains and steamy rain forests, where the inhabitants were so poor that it was impossible to rob them. Instead, they showed such hospitality to Ramses and the Princess that they were forced to accept, even though it pained them that, with every free dish of unfamiliar vegetables, their status became ever more clear: namely, that of two increasingly feeble vagabonds, plagued by dysentery, malaria, parasites, and, most of all, the loneliness of these foreign lands and the dream of their homeland that blossomed slowly out of Ramses' introspection and the Princess's sorrow. And because of this dream they were childishly delighted when, one day beside the sea, they came upon a trading post flying the Danish flag. They were given a warm welcome by Danes who said that at least Ramses wasn't a damn Negro or an Arab and that even the Princess looked more like a white person than the natives of this region, whose dirty fingers had cultivated the spices or felled the trees that were shipped back to Denmark via this trading post. The post belonged to the Danish East Asia Company, which most graciously deigned to provide Ramses and the Princess with passage in return for their chipping away rust and splicing ropes and tarring and scrubbing and smearing on red lead. After all, the company had no time for loafers, freeloaders, or stowaways, as Ramses and the Princess learned from the president of the company, H. N. Andersen, who was sailing home on the same ship. He amused himself with these two strange old characters—Ramses and the Princess, that is—because, since they at least spoke his mother tongue, he could explain to them that the company had become what it was only by honoring Duty and Work, the sole true gods, which were to replace the ridiculous idols of the natives in these Hottentot countries. He told Ramses and the Princess (who had until now been under the impression that the world was infinitely vast) that the company had now circumscribed the globe, making it so comprehensible that even Ramses' limited intelligence could encompass it. At this point he tapped the old housebreaker's sweaty, rust-covered brow, and Ramses would have wrung his neck if the Princess had not held him back. It had dawned on her, long before this, that the president was one of their own sons: one who had gone to sea many years before and who had, ever since, made such a good job of camouflaging his origins and upbringing that, as far as everyone was concerned, he was the son of a shipmaster from Nakskov. He had also partially succeeded in himself forgetting where he came from, which was one of the reasons that he at no time recognized his parents. But the Princess remembered him, and understood that his absurd dream of world supremacy was yet one more unfortunate manifestation of the family weakness. For the remainder of the voyage she kept a tight rein on Ramses whenever Andersen visited them, at their work, to tell them of his poor childhood and his parents in their thatch-roofed, cottage-garden idyll in Nakskov—this being just part of the lies about his native land that he had created in order to withstand the dreadful solitude of tropical nights when the wind whistled through the rigging of his ship and he imagined he heard the vicious snarls of the whores on the floating bordellos that he had sent up the rivers of Siam to lay the foundations of his fortune. He had spent a long time away from Europe and more especially from Denmark, which was now, in the transfiguring glow of his memories, rising out of the ocean like the sunken city of Atlantis. He urged the Princess and Ramses to continue with their work while he talked, since idleness is worse than death, worse than syphilis, worse than Negroes, as he explained to his countrymen, his father and mother; to whom he also boasted of how the company understood how best to exploit war, through the transportation of troops and weapons; and all in order to bring glory to the Old Country, as he called it. It was quite evident, from the turns of phrase that he employed, that the feet of this son, too, had long since lost touch with that earth which he maintained could be circumscribed in less, much less, than eighty days.

Adonis and the master of masks made their way north to Denmark, and crossed the last border as Adonis's brother the president was telling the Princess and Ramses about the croaking frogs and calm straits of his homeland. And so, as luck would have it, during these weeks three generations of the same family are all, at one and the same time and unknowingly, converging upon one another and the Danish Summer, which H. N. Andersen pictured as a kindly, motherly woman whom he would not for one moment have connected with the creature sitting before him, chipping at rust—but who was in fact his real mother.

Adonis and the quick-change artist came home to this summer without recognizing it—just as they retained only a vague memory of the country, since both were at a forgetful age. During the suffocating heat of the summer months they tramped the length of Jutland, which the old showman found so densely populated that it left him feeling unable to breathe and which was so rife with mosquitoes that he believed he had seen nothing like it since the malaria-ridden plains of his childhood. Those he had left, once upon a time, to avoid being tormented by the very insomnia that now struck him. And in his wakeful state, the cool pricks of the mosquito stings induced a cold, sweating fever that left him tossing restlessly on his straw pallet, next to Adonis.

Adonis, on the other hand, adjusted quickly and soon reverted to his native tongue. And it was he who realized that it was necessary to shift from one sentimental dream to another: hitherto, on their way through Europe, it was as though Adonis were an apprentice of sorts to his grandfather. Their relationship had resembled our picture, and that of their day and age, of the old man helping the orphaned child—an image they exploited, wherever they appeared, to draw a crowd. This picture now needed to be replaced by another: that other image—also extremely popular—of the child leading the doddering old man. This change took place when Adonis encountered hunger for the first time in his life, and that came about because the quick-change artist, because of his great age, could no longer live up to the expectations of his audiences. In this flat country—Denmark, that is—even the smallest villages through which they passed had heard of the picture palaces. And, from magazines, everyone knew about an art form other than that of the old circus manager: one composed of wistful dramas and pictures of dreamy-eyed young ladies in tasteful states of undress, as opposed to the old showman's baroque masks, which were not even seen in his own country now and which here, under foreign skies, took on an increasingly aggressive and wicked appearance when confronted with silent audiences who less and less often paid to see them.

For a while they survived because Adonis made up and acted out mawkish romances, or sang tearful and jolly ballads that compensated somewhat for the gestures with which the old showman tried to wring a response from his audiences, whom he had begun to fear, suspecting them, as he did, of being some sort of cold-blooded, two-legged, upstanding salamander, endowed with a power of speech they used only sparingly—just like the ones with which his grandmother had filled the nights of his childhood and which he had thought he would never run into; until now, that is, in these squares and marketplaces. More and more often he had to break off in the middle of a performance, lay his mask aside, and place a hand on one of the bystanders to reassure himself that this man with the leather waistcoat and dead eyes was not some clammy amphibian but a real person. That summer, for the first time, he saw his own age, objectively, in the eyes of these people; a sight that led him to doubt whether he had ever been young. He was seized by the uncertainty that strikes us all sooner or later, and particularly those of us involved in recounting unlikely extracts of the truth. He was no longer sure that he had once actually roamed these parts with his own circus and presented the wonders of the seven seas and wild beasts from far-flung continents and the world's most beautiful women to these yokels whom he now endeavored to delight by imitating the roars of his long-lost lions and by telling them of his circus princesses—all dead—whose radiant beauty had once had their yokel forebears' tongues hanging out. Now they did not so much as flicker an eyelid, believing as they did that, in newspapers and books and at the great exhibitions, they had seen all, or at least almost all, there was to see.

The old man gave his last performance in a town of red brick situated on the very same gently sloping hill on which his circus tent had been pitched the night that Ramses first saw the Princess. This was mere chance, and a coincidence that the old showman may well have noted. But he was not, as we are, surprised by it, presumably because, unlike us, he was not aware that, throughout the history of Denmark, parents often go back to the spot where their children became engaged, to die. He performed in a market-place surrounded by so many spectators that the surrounding countryside was completely hidden from view; to an audience that swelled and swelled he acted out his bittersweet tale of a pig who wanted to go on the stage and sing arias, and the one about a writer who becomes lost in his own books, while his son looks on.

No one laughed.

When Adonis saw the old man's tears saturating a mask that also depicted the face of an old man, he tried to catch his eye, behind the mask. But there was no eye. He sat where he was, quite still, and perceived that at this moment, in front of this crowd, his grandfather was the loneliest person in the world. And in this loneliness he presented his picture of the country's first circus manager: himself. The members of the audience usually became involved in this show, but here, in this intolerable country, the old man found no people to participate in the grand finale of his life, only stony faces that reminded him of ancient graven images he had once seen, at the beginning of the previous century, half-buried in the sand, when his parents had taken him to the seaside. Adonis watched his grandfather circulate among the impassive farmers, stepping out jerkily like a timid bird; hidden behind a Harlequin mask and tentatively peddling a show that had been performed when parents of this audience were small. Then he took off his hat and held it out. When, out of pity, one of the farmers tossed a coin into the hat, the old man lifted it out. On finding that he did not recognize it—remembering now only the coins with which he had been paid when he was young—he pulled off his mask. Under it was the pig mask, and under that the mask of an old man, and under that an obscene red monkey, and under that the smooth, expressionless features of a young boy. And with that Adonis's grandfather disappeared. For beneath this last mask there was nothing but thin air, and this—together with a little heap of dark cloth—was all that was left of the quick-change artist.

The spectators turned and left, without paying. They were so well acquainted with a world where everything disappeared that nothing less than a resurrection would satisfy them. For the rest of that day and all through the long night, Adonis sat on, beside the abandoned masks. And sitting there, with nothing left but memories and his resilient adaptability, he is the forsaken youngest son of the fairy tales who must now set off into the world alone.

As morning approaches, he gets up (not wanting to be in the way of the sunlight), walks across the square, and enters the town theater. Well, of course he enters the theater, and what he is looking for is work—wishing, in no way, to be a burden to anyone—preferably work that keeps him out of sight: a prompter, for instance, if only he could read, or some invisible extra; just as long as he can once more savor the happy upturned faces of the audience and the cheerful tolerance of the theater. He walked through a door fitted with panes of black glass and along corridors as quiet as a hospital. Sweaty men tiptoed past the boy in their stocking feet, without noticing him or his wonderment at the smell of burial and dashed hopes that surrounded him—this last due to the appearance at the theater of a company, on tour from Copenhagen, whose leading lady had announced that she was indisposed and refused to go on. Adonis passed by the door of her dressing room; edged his way around the director and the conductor and the doctor and a playwright, all trying, through the closed door, to persuade the Divine One to give one more performance; to just once more, for her public's sake, give herself up to that blend of tearful smiles and madness for which she was adored and for the sake of which audiences had time and again unharnessed the horses from her carriage and themselves pulled her, in it, from the Royal Theater. In the basement—while she was once more screaming, "No, no!" and "Let me die in peace!"— Adonis came across the theater's stagehands and craftsmen: Italians and burned-out actors whose scars and prison pallor gave them the look of extras in some show, which, from time to time, they actually were. He inquired about work, and when he could see that they thought he was too young, his forehead took on the color of years he had never known and his mouth grew taut from sorrows far removed from his carefree nature and his jaw set with a distaste for life that he would never feel. Then he told them he was eighteen, and looked older as he said it. So they asked him if he could work, and his back bent under loads he had never carried, and they took him on. After a week when he had done nothing but sweep up, they asked him to shift fifty huge bolts of blue canvas, and his cover was blown. He seized hold of a bolt, but it would not budge. Then, when he realized that the stagehands were watching him, he assumed a stoop and started swinging his hands in the air like a veteran and made his voice deeper, but still they could see he was just a boy.

Nevertheless, the theater retained Adonis. The stagehands entertained toward him the same curiosity that has prompted me to tell the story of his fortunes, wanting, as I do, to look behind the roles that Adonis spent his whole life playing in his efforts not to disappoint any living soul, nor, if possible, the dead. In actual fact, there were very few things he asked of life: to share in the joyousness which surrounds all actors—and which he had first discerned surrounding his grandfather in that far-off Turkish bazaar—and at the same time to remain practically invisible and on no account to be in the way. So when the theater gave him the job of wave boy in a tremendously successful play, he felt he had achieved his heart's desire.

The name of the play was *Sigurd's Great Voyage around the World*, and it had been put together by that great poet Holger Drachmann, in one of his innumerable attempts to keep everyone, absolutely everyone, happy.

This piece was an unparalleled compromise. Drachmann had lifted the plot, with some minor alterations, from *Around the World in Eighty Days*, but it had as its central character Sigurd Jorsalsfar, from the great romantic drama of the same name. The dialogue was taken from several of his own unfinished dramatic works, and he had supplemented the entr'actes with brief episodes from contemporary, and rather risqué, satires, the language of which he had toned down, just as he had made sure that nowhere in the piece did the word "German" appear; this being something which, because of the tense situation in Europe, the Foreign Ministry would never have permitted. To ensure the goodwill of the royal family he had taken out all tavern scenes and any reference to prostitution. To save offending Vigilia, the Society for Moral Rearming, who kept a careful eye on the theater, he had himself written and inserted five uplifting ballads set to modern hymn tunes. In the same way, he found it necessary to cut out Phileas Fogg's marriage to the widowed Aouda. Instead, he had her die on the pyre alongside her husband. Then, owing to much theatrical intrigue, it was decided that the piece should be directed by a professor of literature who was almost totally blind; that the sets should be designed by a pupil of the Academy of Fine Arts' principal (Adonis's secret brother Meldahl), and that the part of the hero, Sigurd the traveler, should be rewritten for a woman, since the theater owed its leading lady a plum role. The piece had been a triumph for the theater. At the premiere, with the next fifty performances and the nationwide tour sold out, the director turned to Drachmann.

"You are a great artist," he said.

The poet ran his fingers through his hair, which was white and soft as whipped cream, and smiled dementedly. "I'm a great whore," he said.

It was Adonis's job every evening, along with seven other boys, to roll out and agitate the blue canvas sheeting that passed for the sea in the scenes that took place on board the steamship *Mongolia*. This task he performed to everyone's satisfaction. Without himself being tempted, he watched his fellow wave boys acquiring the same habits as the actors. They drank alcohol and placed themselves at the disposal of older men and women trying to prolong the enchantment of the performance by purchasing brief dominion over these boys, who sold themselves as much from greed as from curiosity—wanting to see the underside of public morality and the dress suits and trains and long gloves. He refrained because he did not want to disappoint his parents, whom, by now, he had difficulty in remembering; and because he believed that the theater was in fact a huge and ingenious machine designed for the ennoblement of mankind. Every evening he enjoyed the transformation that took place in both actors and audience. Every evening alcoholism and hysteria, suicides (contemplated or carried out) and brutal egoism underwent a metamorphosis, to be distilled, every one, into tears and cries of joy and music and cannon fire. And these, like some form of alchemy, made the auditorium weep and shout, or fall silent with quiet nobility, until the only sound to be heard was the tiptoeing of the theater attendants carrying out, on stretchers, those officers who had swooned with emotion at the words "Danes we are, and Danes we shall remain."

After having taken part in sixty performances in sixty days, Adonis was sure that his life would never be any different. Because of his unobtrusive willingness, which led the director and the stagehands to forget his age, more and more tasks were assigned to him. Every evening, after he had played the last of his increasing number of walk-on parts, he was sent on—by the last train or the last mail coach or, occasionally, on horseback or by bicycle—to the next town to make sure that the local property man had solved the perennially hopeless problem of procuring, free of charge, the antique sofas and majestic chairs and big triumphal arches required for the next day's performance. In order to fill the theaters and lure the last of the townspeople, and to save anyone's being disappointed, it had been necessary to expand the repertoire. Holger Drachmann had cut the original play by half—smiling as he did so—to make room for *Under Ideology's Banner*, which dealt with the plight of the workers. The bitter message of this piece was then sweetened by the final item on the program, *The Corsetiere's Daughter*, which no one could help but be amused by—and everyone was, especially Adonis. It made him weak at the knees every evening, and left him pale-faced and quivering like jelly with joy over the laughter and the applause.

At no time does he appear to have been offended by the contra-dictions of the theater. At every single performance he allowed him-self to be taken in by the illusions without ever being distracted by the odd furniture, or the local crop of extras who took to the stage in clogs and fell into the orchestra pit, or all the weird houses in which they played. Often it would be a gymnasium or a barn where nailed-up oil lamps swung above the steamship *Mongolia* and a blue sea which the actions of the wave boys brought so convincingly to life that spectators in the front rows gathered up their skirts and lifted their button boots off the floor so as not to get them wet. To Adonis, the scent of the theater represented the truth, even though it was the scent of powder and escaping gas and the tarred rope used for the wigs, and of dust from the wings, and of the benzine with which Adonis himself had removed the stains from the leading lady's gloves and crinoline gowns. And all of this acts as a reminder, to me, that Denmark is not, as is said, a land devoid of passion. Quite the contrary: it is the most unhinged place in the history of the world. What other culture has ever embraced a contradiction as false as that which existed between the actresses' conduct in the wings—where Adonis sponged their fancy dress, with them fondling him and whispering that they would teach him something about life, and he wriggling, eel-like, out of reach—and their stage roles, in which they played sensitive, quietly touching young girls with a fine, pure poetry that prompted their admirers and co-actors to brave the smell of benzine in their dressing rooms and shower rose petals down their partially exposed cleavages? What other culture, I ask you, can boast such an absurd moral standard?

In one of those flashes of memory to do with his grandfather that Adonis had retained, the old man had said, "Life, my boy, is a journey from one square or marketplace to the next, and the most one can hope for is that just once in every place, God will descend and possess the actor." Adonis was too cautious to believe in divine beings, but he had not taken exception to these words of wisdom. He had grown up with his parents' paradoxical view of honesty, and he had learned to live amid apparently irreconcilable contradictions. Now he felt that, after all, his grandfather had been right. His own life, too, had taken the form of open spaces. And in his mind these had merged with the theaters, which grew steadily in number, after the director managed to have his grant renewed and extended the tour to the point at which Adonis would meet Anna.

To Anna and Adonis, their meeting was like a miracle; one which, later on, they would never grow tired of mulling over and calling to mind. They were convinced that it had, in some way, been planned, foreseen, arranged—and it is a tempting thought. Like Adonis and Anna, we, too, have a need to believe in some higher purpose, or at least in the possibility of some quite-out-of-the-ordinary coincidence. Unfortunately, this is not possible. In fact, it turns out on closer investigation that Adonis's and Anna's paths had crossed many times before they met, and that Adonis had on several occasions performed in a town where Anna's father was preaching, with his daughter sitting beside the pulpit. The only miracle we can discern is that they did not meet each other earlier—although this can possibly be explained by Thorvald Bak's having steered clear of the theater, which he regarded as a den of iniquity; an attitude fostered by his distorted memories of the vaudeville shows he had seen in Copenhagen as a young man. These were the only theatrical presentations he had ever witnessed, and he now looked back upon them as a sequence of tableaux populated by wine-soused maidens and horned monsters. For his part, the theater's director dreaded

Bak's Evangelical Mission. So the two men never met and thus never became aware of what is so obvious to us: that, in fact, these two—the preacher and the impresario—each in his own way wanted the same things. The pastor also wanted to entertain his audience, and wooed them with promises of illusions and anecdotes and baroque dialogue; and the director was also a missionary, anxious to spread the word of the Eternal Art to the very tiniest of hamlets. Part of the truth about the director and all the rest of that traveling theater—by which, for a time, Adonis was totally absorbed—was that they all dreamed of opening their audience's eyes to a nobler, a finer, view of the world so that, one day, theaters might be built on the ruins of these barns and outhouses where they now performed; and that it might be possible to fill these theaters with a literary and enlightened public, with the same good taste as the citizens of Copenhagen: a public for whom it would no longer be necessary to perform these ghastly histrionic potpourris reminiscent of exotic beasts. Driven by this dream, and by the perennial financial problems that form another part of the truth, the theater and Adonis traveled the length and breadth of the country, playing anywhere they could, anywhere at all, since art must not scorn humble surroundings. And on these travels, their path—which follows the meandering railroad tracks and which I am now laboriously retracing—crosses any number of times with that of Thorvald Bak. On several occasions he has been on the same train, and sat only a few cars ahead of Adonis's compartment, with Anna by his side and her chain in his hand. But not until Rudkøbing were all the elements in place: the elements of a situation that would under any circumstances have arisen. Only then did Adonis come out onto the street for a moment, to be alone; and that because he, who had always traveled on land, had happened to think of the sea—a thought that had long filled Anna's life, because the sea reminds the captive that imprisonment need not last forever; and because no Danes can ever shake themselves free of the sea around Denmark—not even Adonis and Anna. And now we have reached the moment when they stand face-to-face on the street in Rudkøbing.

As they stood there, facing each other, with the crowd of believers proceeding toward the church, Adonis cast a momentary glance after the cage and Thorvald Bak and the dark-clad men and women. Then he asked, "Won't they cry when they miss you?" Anna took his hand. "They'd do better to cry for themselves," she said, and then walked on to the theater with Adonis.

I have no way of knowing whether it was Love at First Sight. This is of some interest to me, since this particular type of love is said to be something quite special, although to me it seems like an instance of the same sort of illusions in which Anna participated, later that evening, when she helped Adonis make the blue canvas sheeting move. But knowing this is not important. What is important is that, the next day, as Adonis was about to board the train that would carry him away from Rudkøbing, his feet would not budge from the platform. At that precise moment, Amalie's grandmother's last will and testament was opened, and the other actors and most other people in the town were struck by the feeling that they were in the hands of some higher power. But there was only one sensation that could make any impact on Adonis at that moment: the knowledge that he had to see Anna Bak again, and soon, preferably immediately. And this although, at that moment, he did not even know her name.

Part Two

ADONIS AND ANNA

The tenement in Christianshavn

Poverty

1919–1939

DURING THE MONTHS that followed, for the first time in his life Adonis experienced that yearning, so prevalent among Danes, to be somewhere other than where he was. Joylessly he carried out his ever more onerous duties. He grew thinner and thinner, his appetite ruined by night after night of witnessing stage romance and the dubious morality of the two ballad operas, all of which he had once enjoyed but which now made him throw up. He fell ill but nevertheless carried on working, his sense of duty to the situation at hand proving stronger than his yearning; as it is with many people, including myself. Had it not been, I would not have had the patience to follow the theater company on its journey through provincial Denmark to that performance during which Adonis—under the blue canvas sheeting, just after the explosion of the steamship *Henriette* on the seas off Liverpool—might well have succumbed to the fever had he not felt a hand on his brow and, in the darkness, seen Anna's face close to his own.

How Anna had found Adonis is a mystery. When the curtain fell and the lights went up, he could see that she was covered with the yellow dust of the highways and that she had walked the soles off her shoes and that she carried an infant in a shawl wrapped around her shoulders. So exhausted was she that she could not speak. But the eyes she turned on him gleamed with the metallic glint of love and of a willpower that brooked no argument: the same willpower that motivated him, the next morning, to ask for his pay. Not wanting to arouse any suspicion, he said he wanted to send his mother embroidered tablecloths and picture postcards of the theater—an excuse thought up by Anna. Immediately thereafter they took the first train out of town, and in so doing, Adonis committed a breach of contract. He himself would never have dared to do such a thing, but Anna knew that they had to run away, because the company would never have accepted her or let her travel with Adonis. Instead, they would have sent her home because she was a child and, more especially, because she was an unmarried mother—the last circumstance being the most damning, since this was precisely what the majority of plays acted out on the stage every evening warned against.

To keep her happy, Adonis complied with her wishes. He was deeply disturbed and full of wonder, it never having occurred to him that he might possibly be in charge of his own life. Nor was he, since it was Anna's willpower that carried them, by train, away from the town and the theater, out of childhood and provincial Denmark and into Copenhagen.

In a sense, the city was waiting for them. This idea of the waiting city is not just an image; it is also a historical fact. In a way, Copenhagen was a fateful city for Anna and Adonis—although that was not evident at this point. When they set foot in it for the first time, they did not even see it. They drove into that mountainous landscape of stone and iron without experiencing any of the usual shock of the country dweller, mainly because Adonis had eyes only for Anna—while she, Anna, looked straight through everything, focusing on what was, for her, their true goal, the spot to which she led Adonis from Central Station. She has never been there before, yet she finds her way down to the harborside, to a windswept quay that just happens to be Langelinie. And here they come to a halt. Here they stand side by side, these two young people with the baby and no luggage to speak of. It is an important spot, this quay. It is the quay of dreams, designed by Adonis's brother Meldahl and envisaged as a symbol of Denmark—at one and the same time inviting and imposing, adorned with monuments to the past and constructed along elongated modern lines that stretched into the future. By this stone wharf sits the ship *Frederik den Ottende*, bound for America.

They arrived there an hour before departure time. For an hour they stood watching this huge ship, whose white paint had soaked up the sun of foreign climes, and for that hour they shared the hopes of an entire continent: hopes of log cabins and gold and the endless stretches of highway that had welcomed so many others who had, like themselves, made mistakes and broken the law. Anna had sought out this spot because she knew, instinctively, that it was necessary to put at least an ocean's width between her and the youth she had never had. That they did not sail on that great ship after all, that, after all, they remained on the quayside as the ship headed seaward like some solid, burnished promise of freedom, was because Adonis held her back.

At the last moment, just as Anna had finally made up her mind, he remembered something that made him stay where he was, instead of conforming to his nature and tagging along. He was restrained not by any thought but by something seemingly insignificant. It was a picture that kept flickering across his mind, a picture from one of the break-ins he had carried out, as a boy, with his father: a picture of an old man he had glimpsed through the half-open door of a scullery that he and Ramses had come past, laden with coils of rope and a Bible that Ramses had taken to help one of his sons prepare for his confirmation. They may have stopped beside the scullery door because Ramses wanted to show Adonis that not even time itself need be hurried—even here, when they are caught between incarceration and liberty. But what Adonis remembered, standing on the windswept quay next to the great steamship, was the sight, on the white scullery table, of the medieval castle the old man had built out of silver American coins, and the lifelessness of his face as he stared at it. That was what made Adonis detain Anna on the quayside—within sight of the Voyage to America—and then walk briskly away from a harbor that both enticed him and filled him with a fear of all things foreign and of long journeys; a fear with which I, too, am familiar, and which is one of the reasons that I write, here, as concisely as possible and always stick to the facts. It was after this that Anna and Adonis made the acquaintance of Copenhagen.

They moved into an apartment in Christianshavn, in a building that backed onto a narrow canal. Its front was reached by negotiating a maze of courtyards and buildings in the rear and passages and gateways. The first time they saw this building, its upper stories were lit, high above, by the evening sun, while the blue haze rising off the canal made it seem as though this vast edifice were about to sail off across a sea of fog.

"It's a boat," said Anna.

And at that moment she was struck by the powerful sense that this place was going to sink. But she said nothing. In order to obtain these two rooms both she and Adonis had had to present themselves at a small and dusty office in an out-of-the-way part of the city, where some menial clerk had made them sign their names to a statement saying that they were not Socialists and that they were and would always remain childless and law-abiding. And all the while he was telling them of his fear that the poor would breed like rats, spill out of those buildings which he had the onerous task of administering, and plague the city like ghosts rising from their graves.

This property was situated in a forgotten part of Christianshavn that the police had long since stopped patrolling; where the only street lighting was provided by whale-oil lamps from the previous century—and even those were never lit, because the lamplighters dreaded the narrow streets every bit as much as the policemen. For the first time in his life Adonis had a roof over his head without having broken in and without having to move on the next day; and he was happy, because being in love had numbed his senses and because in the afternoons he could open his door with a key that was not false. Then, together with Anna, he could drown himself in a love through which he could escape his family's fear of interruptions and exposure and slamming doors.

Although she would never be able to express what she thought to other people, Anna sensed right from the start that they had moved into some sort of Atlantis. And for me, her insight casts fresh light on the doomed world of the slums—as, for example, with this building. I had always assumed it to be a jerry-built tenement, a study in gray of city depression, inhabited by people whose lives consisted of one long, formless overclouded day—when, in fact, Anna perceived the truth of the matter: this entire community was on the move; all its residents—all the whores and workingmen and children and housewives and those on the dole and small tradesmen and consumptives and dogs and rats—all of them assumed that their home, this rocklike tenement block, might at any moment cut itself adrift and sail off with them across the sea to warmer and happier climes.

For a time, after they first moved in, Anna and Adonis lived on their love and the money Adonis had drawn from the theater. The money soon ran out because their lovemaking made them gluttonous and led to their buying port and fruit and cake. These they consumed during the brief spells when they got out of bed to look at the sun on the yellow walls of the buildings or the moon over Our Saviour's Church, just opposite the prison from which Ramses Jensen had once escaped in order to revenge himself on his father: a fact which once again acts as a reminder of how short the distance is between the sins of parents and their children's love affairs. In due course, Adonis started to work and Anna began to explore her surroundings.

The first time she attempted to walk all the way around the tenement block she became lost in the maze of courtyards and side streets. Wherever she went, she found ground-floor and basement premises occupied by wine cellars and cafés and dance halls named after strange and exotic places. On the walls of these establishments hung cages containing parrots and geckos brought home by the sailors who sat on the stairways and regarded the young girl impassively. Anna returned their stares fearlessly, thinking, as she did so, that even these men—who had seen the whole world and were sunburned for life—even they retreat into dreams. And Anna was right. The exotic names of the wine cellars helped them recapture the velvety breezes of Beckway and Paramaribo and Bahia and later, in another street, the sudden storms of Tierra del Fuego and the traveling walls of water found along the fortieth parallel, before they were carried off to bed, there to continue their dream of a voyage that never got under way. With her child in her arms, Anna negotiated the long corridors where whores plied their trade. Here, through the open doors, she saw the cheap prints of improbable South Sea islands, passage to which the prostitutes imagined could be bought by selling a love which, since it was Danish, they also knew would probably lead them nowhere but to hell. In all of the little apartments she visited she found the same running in place, the same gazing on some distant goal. In an effort to combat poverty these apartments had been turned into gambling dens or given over to small cottage industries, with families manufacturing gas lighters or clothespins, or writing letters to Freuchen and Amundsen, offering to take part in their next expeditions.

It seems likely that Anna understood this longing—which no one expects to be fulfilled—because it reminded her of her childhood, and because the poverty around her was like the poverty of Lavnæs. In the midst of her own happiness she would find herself waking in the morning with a feeling that her sympathy for these people— and for herself and Adonis, whose circumstances were, in fact, similar—was about to suck the marrow out of her bones. Such sympathy is something I must handle with care, since it can blur our perception of history. Nevertheless it is vital that we, like Anna, realize that all the residents of this big building believed they were moving toward all four corners of the world at once. This was, however, in no way a consistent dream, because, while wishing themselves far away, they believed that the world around them would, sooner or later, be transformed into the Danish countryside. They all cherished their own or their parents' or their grandparents' memories of the region from which they hailed. These memories, which had grown rosier as time went on, prompted them to fill their tiny apartments with potted plants and led them to believe that the frail blades of grass which succeeded in pushing up between the cobblestones were signs that the countryside was making inroads into the city. So they founded cooperative gardening societies on the island of Amager, and there on their little plots of land they grew vegetables which, when brought home, were viewed as signs that now, at long last, the city was shrinking. And only Anna and we who can look at it in retrospect realize that all these onions and potatoes and strawberries signaled the direct opposite.

And, again, only Anna could pinpoint the moment when she and Adonis merged with the city. One morning, not long after they had moved in, they awoke to the certainty that they had dreamed the same dream, not just as everyone else in the building, but as everyone in Copenhagen. Their dream—like ours—was the dream of the Village. It is undoubtedly sentimental and in all probability it is also false, but it is nevertheless appealing—even to me. On that morning it also wakened Adonis's brothers—H. N. Andersen of the Danish East Asia Company; Alberti, the former Minister of Justice; and the ghost of Meldahl the architect, who that morning saw his buildings for what they were: heavy façades overlaying rickety skeletons, like fragile dreams of security and dignity; dreams which, on that morning, seemed like a nightmare behind which he wished to see only rivers or islands or one of the ditches where, as a child, he had eaten with Ramses and the Princess. At that moment all of them heard the distant chime of church bells in a silence they had forgotten. At that moment they were brought together, everyone in Copenhagen and—by no means least—these alienated brothers, who would not have greeted one another in the street, not even if they had recognized one another. It might seem hard to believe: that people can be united, in spite of everything, by a common dream, the dream of an idyll that has never existed. But the way I see it, we have reason to feel proud; after all, where else but in Denmark can people ordinarily at loggerheads be united in the dream of a dream with no foundation in reality? One would imagine that of all these dreamers—and they amount, more or less, to the entire population of Copenhagen—a few might have learned something from this yearning for fellowship and the countryside, but that does not seem to be the case. No one, apparently, remembered much of it, and certainly not Meldahl, who could not even remember what his father had once said to him in prison. He never even reached the stage of being amazed, as we are, that he had laid out half of Copenhagen and spent his whole life designing regular buildings in order to circumvent the far side of nature's irregularity, while all the time fantasizing about gardens. Thus he had dispelled one dream by means of another, which he had then counterbalanced with a third, until it became extremely rare for him to catch sight of reality. Nor did he sight it that morning, when he mopped the sweat from his brow with the lace collar of his burial shirt, touched the cross of the Order of Dannebrog—which he had with him in his coffin—and wondered for whom the bells tolled.

The one who remembered this incident the longest was Anna, but in time even she forgot it.

At first glance, Adonis's life during these years in Copenhagen seems to have been sunshine and roses all the way; a sort of cascade of happy coincidences. Which leads me to consider whether fortune might in fact be a sort of river, just like the stream of time. Because in that case the explanation might be that, as a child, Adonis had been swept up by a wave that carried him along and brought him,

here in Copenhagen, to his job with the Danish Sugar Refineries—
just at the point when he and Anna had spent their last krone. This
position was terminated after four days because the factory burned
down, only to be immediately supplanted by another, a job that
resulted from a crystal-clear and quite absurd stroke of luck: on the
night when the fire broke out, Adonis had been sleeping the sleep
of the dead in Anna's arms, and so he did not hear the shouts, and
so did not happen to be standing around the factory throughout the
night, like the other workers, watching the glowing streams of sugar
running like lava onto the hoarfrost on the streets. By the time he
arrived for work, everyone had left to face unemployment in the
bleak light of the dawning day, and so he was the one who was
photographed by the reporters who had turned up to take pictures
of the devastation in the light of day. By that time the sugar refinery
had been transformed into a gutted stalagmite cavern, the water
from the fire brigade hoses having frozen as it ran off the charred
ruins of the building and formed huge stalagmites. Adonis was
photographed sitting on these, like Aladdin in his cave. His picture
appeared on the front pages, above reports in which the journalists
more than hinted that he had led the firefighting, while the truth
of the matter was that he had arrived too late for everything and
had done nothing except steal chunks of caramelized sugar that he
managed to break off the sidewalk. As a result of the picture and
the newspaper reports the president of the sugar refinery sent a
personal letter of thanks to Adonis along with a cash reward and
the offer of a job at the new sugar refinery that had been built at
the end of Langebro, not far from the area where Anna and Adonis
lived. He took the job because it was there, right under his nose,
and so as not to disappoint the president, and because he was drawn
by the aroma aboard the three refinery ships. These transported the
sugar from Cuba in two-hundred-pound sacks that the waves of the
North Atlantic ripped apart, dissolving the sugar. It, in turn, dried
into a brown crust, hard as marble, that had to be hacked to pieces
with picks and drills before once again being shoveled into two-
hundred-pound sacks and carried ashore. All of this made for tough,
physical labor—which Adonis succeeded in steering clear of. In the
tropical heat of the big melting vats, where everyone else had an
hourly quota, he was appointed as a sort of foreman, an inspector,
walking around at his leisure. And for this there is no explanation

other than that fortune's fan cooled his sweating brow. This same fortune led him, after a week, to leave the factory floor on a sudden impulse just before a copper pipe on the ceiling burst and covered everything in a rain of boiling sugar that forced the refinery to close down for a long while. Adonis did not even have time to pick up his termination papers. Just as he stepped out into the spring sunshine of the street, one of the Carlsberg brewery drays came driving past, and as Adonis closed the door behind him the driver crumpled up, felled by a heart attack. Loathing death, Adonis looked in the opposite direction and started to walk away. But luck was with him. Some passersby yelled at him to lend a hand, and so, to humor them, he jumped up onto the driver's seat and took the reins. Sitting there, he resembled the onlookers' picture of the young hero reining in the runaway horses. He sat on, to humor the horses, but it was only because they knew the way and needed no directing that Adonis (who had never driven a horse and cart) arrived that evening at the brewery in Valby, where he was once more hailed as a hero and rescuer. He was offered the dead man's job on the spot and could do nothing other than accept, since that was what was expected of him.

That is how I see Adonis during these years: on a stalagmite, or on a catwalk or the box of a dray, driving through Copenhagen. He is always aloft; it is interesting to note how he is always to be found on a stage of sorts; he is always *spotted* by others wherever he happens to be and he is always surrounded by an airy elegance accepted by all those who come into contact with him. Even when working at the sugar refinery or driving a cart for Carlsberg or the ice plant he never ever wears a uniform. He is always dressed in black and white, with a lace cravat that dates from his theater days. If one considers how the rest of Copenhagen, around Adonis, looked in the twenties, then his life during these years truly does deviate from his surroundings. One might even wonder whether Adonis is still in the theater, playing the leading role. These are the years when the journeymen carpenters and smiths and bakers come out on strike. People are dying of starvation where Adonis lives, but he does not seem to notice them. It is as though they are merely part of the scenery, as though they are all extras for a show in which Adonis plays the part of the Happy Worker.

But this is probably not a fair assessment after all. Even for Adonis, life is not nonstop playacting. But it is clear that he manages better than others, even though there is no way of telling why he should. I, at any rate, cannot explain it, but I can see how, every morning, he drives past the long lines of unemployed waiting outside the shipyards in the hope of salvage work—imagine, lining up every morning for the chance of burning out rivets. He drives past the endless processions of protesting workers, who are pushing Denmark in the direction of our own day and age. Cool in summer or swathed in wool in winter, from up on his box he bids good day to the men, waves to the girls, talks to the horses, and radiates contentment.

Adonis never gets drawn into a fight, is never involved in a road accident, never becomes a member of a trade union; and he and Anna never have a quarrel. In one way or another, Adonis is always *on the outside.* He never holds a position of authority, is never a subordinate; whenever trouble is brewing, his back is already turned as he heads off into the sunlight. His life is like a dream: the dream of the individual hovering above the crowd; and this dream is part of the truth. But at the same time I am quite certain that hovering does not come cheap. It has its price. Although I have no proof, I am sure that Adonis purposely turned his back on trouble, and ran away, thus continuing his parents' never-ending flight. I imagine Adonis, during these years, as someone constantly having to take very long strides in order to straddle a chasm—not that this mode of walking seems to bother him. Most of the time I am afraid that he is walking with his eyes only half-open, or even closed. He might well be Aladdin, but he is also blind, and this is a disturbing combination; a blind Aladdin perpetually smiling at a world he cannot properly see.

One particular incident brought this home. It took place on a glorious summer's day, when a young girl with almond-shaped blue eyes tossed a large orange up to Adonis on his box. Naturally, he grabbed for the fruit as it hung in the air like a big orange sun, and when it burst between his fingers like a soap bubble riddled with rot, he recognized the girl. She lived in the same building as he and was married to a syndicalist, a political agitator. Ever since she had tried to persuade him to join a union, Adonis had kept out of her way. He did not want to offend either her or his employers, and he had been shocked by the three skulls nailed to her wall. These, she told him, had belonged to the last three policemen who had forced their way into the building to arrest one of the whores. Now he meets her contemptuous gaze among the crowd, but he does not fly off the handle, he does not stand up, he does not shout at her. Instead he gives a shrug, a little twist, as though dodging something or squeezing himself through some narrow opening, wincing as he does so. Then the memory is gone, the girl is already far behind him, the horses' hooves are freshly tarred, Adonis is smiling again, and only one single, minor irritation remains, just one tiny detail: the stench of rotten fruit.

Adonis and Anna named their daughter Maria. The first years of the child's life were passed amid the secure alternation of bright days and nights black as pitch: the unreal nocturnal light that had, thanks to the glow from the grand city stores, always hung over this darkly shrouded quarter had been extinguished, because of gas rationing. It was thanks to Anna that the adult Maria knew she had been born into such a darkness, and it was Anna, too, who explained to her daughter that the rationing was a consequence of the World War, something she seemed to know all about without ever having looked at a newspaper or left the neighborhood. Unlike Adonis, who avoided the news because it was almost always bad, or forcing him to speak out against something or other, Anna harbored, behind her quiet reserve, a tremendous curiosity. And it was this that drove her to go roaming through the vast tenement and is responsible for her—like Adonis's mother, the Princess, and Amalie in Rudkøbing—becoming one of those women whose characters possess a roving streak; a trait that makes it a mistake to imagine that only the men in Danish history are on the move.

That sense of security disappeared from Maria's life one Sunday morning, when Anna heard a song she did not think she had heard before. This happened while, deep in thought, she was watering a plant with water from an empty port bottle. The first line of the song was about Tahiti, but only after she heard the second line did she realize that it was she herself who was singing. Then she noticed that the plant on the windowsill in front of her was an orchid. She turned around and, for the first time, really saw the prints on the walls of the volcanic landscapes of the Azores, and the travel memoirs by Amundsen and Høeg on top of the closet. Then she stood quite still. All of this Maria had observed from her bed, and it is to form her first memory of her mother, a picture of Anna gazing around in bewilderment, struck by something or other.

Until this moment Anna had been an onlooker. She had roamed around the big building without feeling anything other than curiosity, something I, too, feel for this place. It was a universe within which, if one looked, one would discover every facet—absolutely every facet—of existence. Anna had even attended the whores' prayer meetings, offshoots of the Evangelical Mission which Thorvald Bak had helped found and which had now also spread to this place. Here Anna was reminded of her childhood, recognizing as she did the Lavnæs mixture of lust and pain and convoluted morality in one of the whores screaming from the rostrum, "So long as I dare to embrace my Saviour and have my hands and can spread my legs, I need never beg or be a burden to anyone."

Anna never told anyone, but she knew that the word "mission" is crucial here. Even those suffering from the DTs and the wife-beaters and dealers who sold absolutely anything—even they believed they had a mission. There was not one person in that building who was not working for the betterment of the community. Even those with a sneaking aversion to gainful employment, who had pledged their lives to waging war on the police, and who lurked in doorways armed with lead pipes wrapped in newspaper—even they were convinced that it was possible to batter one's way into a better life. Only on the question of which approach to adopt did they disagree with the union agitators, who were strolling along the path to peace in the company of the cigar sorter and member of Parliament, Minister of Supply and Control Thorvald Stauning, who also lived in this building. They negotiated that path on foot—not least Stauning, who strolled to the ministry every morning and who, when traveling abroad, walked on his own two feet from the station to his hotel, suitcase in hand, while the other members of the government were driven in a carriage. And all of this just goes to show that, on closer inspection, this neglected property in Christianshavn is a place from which hopes take to the air like freed balloons.

Yet, until that Sunday morning, Anna had never herself believed that she had any kind of mission. Now, however, it manifested itself. What struck her first was a definite sense of slipping away. When she looked at the tropical flower and the books and the prints it occurred to her that she and Adonis and Maria were also about to take off, and then two things happened. First, she split up. Before Maria's eyes she slipped away from herself and spread out in several directions. This disintegration lasted only for an instant, but for that brief space of time Anna was with her child and at the whores' prayer meeting and among the market stalls and with the women washing clothes in the backyard and in the apartment next door where the carpenter's wife and children lay in wait armed with cudgels for the man himself, the children's father, to come home drunk. For a brief moment Anna's heart bled for all these people, and not just for them but for all the poor of Christianshavn and for all the children of the world and for the strangely pathetic and faded Sunday sunshine on the peeling walls. And at that moment Anna was a symbol. Just as she had beside the shoemaker's deathbed in Lavnæs, she represented the dream and the story we all share of a mother whose compassion knows no bounds. This is, unfortunately, a fragile dream, for while at that moment on that Sunday everyone else felt Anna's presence, what Maria felt was that her mother had disappeared, leaving nothing behind her in the room but an impotent figure that left her, Maria, alone. And I am afraid that Maria was right, because how could Anna possibly feel for the entire population of the world without disintegrating, particularly when surrounded by as much misery as now resounded in that room around Maria, with the woman and children beating up the carpenter on the other side of the thin wall while, in other corners of the building, children wailed with hunger and the prostitutes' clients whined about the going rate? How could she possibly stay whole and protect a child like Maria, who was even now, though still so young, an enigma, inasmuch as even in her cradle she had alternately followed Anna with imploring eyes and gnashed her teeth at her. For Anna this was, of course, an impossibility, so there is no reason to shed tears over Maria. All we can do is wonder at the capacity of all poor children, and especially Maria, to cope and survive. As on that Sunday morning when Anna was dragged away from the room and Maria encountered loneliness for the first time in her life.

Granted, Anna's disintegration lasted only momentarily. It may be that all the four corners of the earth did not require her presence and her compassion for more than a few minutes, but for Maria the

length of time was not important. What mattered to her was the
experience itself, the child's sudden certainty that she had been
deserted. She faced the loneliness in silence, staring, without crying,
but with an obstinacy totally alien to Anna's gentleness and Adonis's
acquiescence: a quality that neither of her parents ever truly understood. And thus Maria's destiny comes to resemble the lot of several
others of the children in this tale. Their parents did not understand
them either. And perhaps that tells us something about the twentieth
century, where things change so rapidly that parents' experiences
are totally and uselessly outdated by the time their children have
need of them.

As time went on, Adonis was the one who grew to understand
Maria best, because he treated her with the same absentminded
cheeriness that he displayed toward everyone else. He showed his
tenderness for her in special, gently comic rituals—imitating bird-
calls, for instance, while she watched him shaving. After which he
would say, "Maria, scoot down and check whether the dogs are
peeing on my bike," at which Maria would walk down the back
stairs (where the homeless were, by this time, starting to pitch their
tents on the landings) to Adonis's black bicycle. More often than
not, there would be a little clutch of women waiting for Adonis who
had seen him on the box of his cart or had sold him something or
who had simply, from several streets away and above the noise of
the traffic, heard the echo of his laughter. Thereafter they had been
drawn along because in Adonis's slipstream there came an enticing
call, as of a distant promise of love and luck and a meaning to
existence. And now they were waiting for him—pleading, desperate,
eyes heavy with sleep—and Maria had to walk at her father's side,
accompany him outside, to show that he had a family to keep and
had to be protected, not least against his own tendency to give in to
these pallid faces and red lips. Holding Adonis's hand, Maria could
look so small and so pathetic that the women made way for them
without a word and refrained from pursuing him. Which is why, on
such mornings, there was a touch of ceremony about his departures,
something reminiscent of a funeral. And now and again they were
even accompanied by the chimes of Our Saviour's Church, which
would start up when least expected. They were ringing, too, that
morning, when the women had left by the time Adonis came down
because Maria had walked straight up to them and said, "Scram!

Beat it! Get out!" and they had gone. There had been a brutal air of menace about the little girl which even Adonis, that morning, could sense, but which he had immediately shrugged off. After all, why burden oneself with such worries?

That was the morning on which fortune failed him for the first time. It was not a serious failure, not a real example of misfortune, but it was a hint that good fortune can run out, or at least that whirlpools can occur in the current of luck. He turned up for work to find his place of employment closed down. At that time Adonis was a driver for a coal merchant, in which capacity—among workers who looked like Africans, their skin covered by a fine layer of coal dust—he succeeded in keeping his cravat utterly and perfectly white. It was his job to deliver coal and coke to Tivoli, the last place of amusement to be exempted from fuel rationing because it is just in such dark times that national symbols need to be seen shining brightly. But on this morning, when Adonis had only just had time enough to forget the brutality shown by Maria, the coal merchant's windows were boarded up, the sign bearing the company's name had already faded, and unemployment and the generally prevailing poverty were closing in on Adonis.

He asked around among the residents of the narrow street only to discover that the city's amnesia had already spread to cover the coal merchant's. Although it had been there just the day before, only a handful of people could remember it. Anyone else would have despaired, but Adonis was not for one moment daunted. So used was he to propping himself up on his destiny that the only thing that smarted was being told by an old man that the coal and gas for Tivoli had now been rationed, which meant that the enchanted gardens would have to close as early as 11 p.m. On hearing this news, Adonis slumps against the coal merchant's locked door, and it might be imagined that he is thinking, but he is not. He is waiting for fortune. He is waiting for life to come to him, and at this moment he makes me think of a Trobriand Islander or an Aztec or a Kikuyu waiting for rain. On this morning, as on previous occasions, there is something outlandish about Adonis's trust.

There he stands and waits, possibly for an hour, possibly for two, but nothing happens. For a moment the illusion bursts and a hole appears in the dream of Aladdin. Adonis has to cycle home on his black bicycle, and now he is not riding so high as he usually does.

Just at this moment he is about to come down to earth among the rest of us. But it is not very long before a new wave lifts him up. Only a quarter of an hour later he is president and co-owner of a bakery that one of his acquaintances and admirers has set up in one of the buildings in the rear courtyard. Here, from now on, he and Adonis turn out genuine Amsterdam spice cookies—*speculaas*—which they then cart around the markets and sell. In no time, Adonis is flying high once more—and still keeping his hands clean, since it is his partner who makes the cakes. It is Adonis's job to drive the cart and flash the customers his lucky, golden smiles, just like the one he gave Maria as he drove through the gateway on his new cart the next morning. It was a smile that had forgotten everything and learned nothing.

It was not long after this that Anna started to clean. This is a historical fact and, no matter what I do, history is history. Nor do I need to excuse anything over which I have no influence, but I do have to say, beware of this "not long after" because it reminds me that time—while establishing a context in an account such as this —seems so unreliable, especially because, when this happened, it was viewed in quite a different light—not least by Anna, who would have maintained that she had always had this need for order. And so it is Maria's, her daughter's, time that we relate to, in our belief that not long after this, Anna was seized by her cleaning mania. Although this last word isn't right either, since there is no reason to believe that Maria ever used it about her mother, or that she so much as knew the word, and it may not even be particularly indicative. Nevertheless, it is the closest I can get. It is the word that best describes how, through year upon year of her childhood, Maria was to see her mother: as a person seized by a mania that forced her to make everything fantastically, spotlessly, totally clean.

There is no doubt that Anna had always been a tidy person. It had upset her, as a child in Lavnæs, that she was not even allowed to clean her own cage. But her love of order had been nothing out of the ordinary; she had accepted the world as a whole, dirt and all. In order, therefore, to explain how she changed, we must take a look at the day when this transformation took place, that day—again a Sunday, with Adonis somewhere in North Zealand selling his spice cookies—when Anna became aware of a heavy, soggy smell that cut like a knife through the walls and floors of the big tenement, to the second floor, where Anna and Adonis's apartment was situated. She followed the smell to the ground floor, which housed a dance hall, and then farther down, to the basement rooms occupied by homeless waifs and strays, and still farther down, to the subbasement. This was so deep down that not even the cats ventured into it, and there Anna found dense darkness and a monotonous bubbling sound. By the light of a match she saw that the floor was covered by a layer of pale mud. She assumed that this must have penetrated from the canal outside, until she sensed the floor moving—as only someone of her exceptional sensitivity could have registered it—and realized that the floor had sunk; that this entire enormous tenement was ever so gently descending into the earth and that, in fact, this house was not about to sail off across the sea. Instead, it was in the process of sinking straight down into the mire.

That very same Sunday she tried to warn the residents. Pale and solemn-faced, with Maria in her arms, she made her rounds to tell them all: to tell the whores and the shopkeepers and Mr. Stauning, Minister of Supply and Control, and all of those who had no vote because they were on the dole. But it was no use; no one believed her. They listened politely to the child-mother with the great dark eyes, but did not take her seriously. After all, who is going to believe a young girl who tells them they are living in a sinking Atlantis, when everyone knows their home is a tenement, a beggars' stronghold, a workhouse in Christianshavn. The only place where Anna found herself understood was among the sailors in the taverns. They believed her, because they themselves lived right next to the basement and had noticed the fatal freshwater smell of the mud, and because they had lived long in the company of superstition and lies more blatant, considerably more blatant, than the yarn served up to them by this sweet girl, and had thereby got into the habit of believing everyone, including this Madonna.

Late that night, Anna attempted to warn Adonis. Her worries had at first been forgotten, because he had come home bubbling over with glee from his cookie-selling—an occupation that presented him with the opportunity to perform before an audience again. He had lifted her onto the bed, and wafted the quilt as a reminder of his days as a wave boy, and then they had forgotten everything, absolutely everything, even the child. They had had eyes only for each other, and had stayed awake until dawn. Then Anna had grown grave again and had told Adonis about the building and how it was sinking. But what was he supposed to say to her? The future was not the time for Adonis, who was now, at this very moment, in the Monday sunshine, wallowing in the smell of almonds and *speculaas* spices and Anna's nakedness and Maria. So he swept her worries aside with his gaiety. "Don't worry, little miss," he said; "today the skies are blue."

That was the morning Anna began her cleaning. She started by washing the varnished floor, one floorboard at a time, until it had acquired a deep, reflective sheen. And she carried on from there, quite calmly. Anna never grew frantic; her mania did not lie in hustling and bustling but in keeping at it, cleaning on and on and on, with tenacious thoroughness, until the windows were so gleamingly clear that pigeons flew into them, thinking that there were openings running right through the building, and were killed. And the corners of the rooms sparkled, so white that it seemed as though she had succeeded in polishing away the dark shadows of light itself. But still she cleaned on, with quiet perseverance, on the trail of grime that only her eyes could discern. She followed it out of the apartment and down the stairs, where, gently but firmly, she requested the homeless squatters to move their cardboard boxes and straw pallets while she swept underneath them. Maria and Adonis found themselves, because of her, moving ever more carefully around the small apartment, with its three rooms solemnly marking time, like a hospital waiting to perform some vital operation that required just this obdurately gleaming floor and just this metallic sheen from the shining kitchen walls. Adonis and Maria grew ever more silent, fearing as they did that too much talk or laughter would cause particles to come adrift from the polished surfaces. Anna never scolded them—her cleanliness never took an aggressive turn—but once having put Maria to bed, she would then painstakingly erase every trace of the evening meal and the day's activity and pack everything away. And all the while Adonis would watch her, unable to fathom this quiet zeal which, in his opinion, made their home look like a family tomb.

So Maria is the only one who, as time goes by, conceives some notion of what is happening to her mother. Everyone else is filled with admiration for Anna on those afternoons when she is stooped over the big copper kettle in the rear courtyard, wringing out the

sheets with such concentrated, no-nonsense strength that they could
be put straight into the linen drawer, without drying, if it were not
for their having to bleach in the sun. On such afternoons, the tenement residents hang out of their windows to watch Anna. Her
sheets, hung in the sun to bleach, are a symbol, because what is to
be bleached is something as intimate as bed linen, an expression of
this lovely girl's managing to realize the dream of the Danish Housewife, who can combine passionate lovemaking with the smell of
brown soap. Her apartment forms the frame around a picture representing honesty and passion and neatness, and that despite her
youth and the fact that this apartment, this Garden of Eden, is
situated in this area, in this infested tenement, just above a dance
hall, next to the whores' corridors, and facing directly onto this
courtyard.

Only Maria noticed that Anna's calm tenacity did not derive from
her having found her place in the scheme of things; that she had,
on the contrary, set herself in motion. The only time Maria said
anything to her mother was on that previously mentioned occasion
when Anna was down on her hands and knees, methodically cleaning the wall paneling with alcohol. Seen through Maria's eyes, she
was like a scientist, an ardent zoologist, and even to me it is obvious
that she is not a woman who has resigned herself to anything but
she has set herself a goal. This goal is the lamentable petit-bourgeois
dream, doomed in advance, of getting to the bottom of things and
exterminating the last, the very last, microbe. At this point, Maria
was five years old, but already, her stammer notwithstanding, she
possessed a command of language to which neither Anna nor Adonis
would ever aspire. And so, when she had asked about the g-g-glass,
Anna had paused, once she had given her feeble reply, and tried to
remember what this exchange of words reminded her of—to no
avail. This was the last time Maria broached the subject, feeling as
she did that there was no point. And she was probably right, because,
from then on, Anna grew more and more grim. Even though she
told Adonis that she was simply changing her tactics, that she was
now going to roll up her sleeves so this can be a nice home and
we'll be able to say we may be poor, but we are honest and we keep
a very, very clean house.

And although Anna sounded plausible and convincing, it was a
mania. Because she now borrowed the doctor's magnifying glass,

which enabled her to peer down into a fresh hell. One day, when Maria came up from the courtyard for a bite to eat, she found the door locked and sealed with gummed paper. Anna was fumigating the apartment, using gas, pest-control cartridges. The place was barely aired before she sealed it again and burned some yellow powder on a plate on the kitchen floor. This filled the rooms with a smoke that defied every airing, hung beneath the disinfected ceilings for weeks, and forced the family to sleep with the squatters on the landings, and even there it stung the throat dreadfully.

After seventeen days they were able to move back into the apartment—seventeen being the precise number Anna had been able to predict, because she had started taking omens. In so doing, she punctures the myth that the city of Copenhagen, now a good way over the threshold of our enlightened century, is a place where religion and superstition have been exorcised, and where the only temple that exists is raised to progress. Because Anna was not alone in her superstition. While she was arriving at the number seventeen by surveying the movements of the birds in the blue sky above the courtyard, Privy Counselor H. N. Andersen was taking omens from how long it took his staff to turn their faces toward the wall when they met him in the corridors of the Danish East Asia Company. Meldahl, too, had taken the omens; and in Christianshavn, Stauning was determining certain areas of government policy by the progress of his cigar smoke toward the blackened ceilings. So Anna was not alone, but she felt as though she were, and therefore said nothing. Which is why it was only to herself that she predicted the seventeen days they lived on the stairway landing and the poverty that was closing in on the family, now that Adonis was finding it increasingly difficult to dispose of his cookies.

Adonis registered Anna's new anxiety as an increased attentiveness to daily trivia. He noticed how in the mornings she woke early and lay quite still with her anxious eyes wide open, waiting to hear what the very first sound from the menacing courtyard would be; and how in the midst of making a meal she would stiffen and just stand there, watching the dust that persisted in dancing in the sunbeams, despite all her cleaning. Once, when he asked her if she was afraid of something, she looked at him with eyes that were pitying, sorrowful, and triumphant, all at once.

"We're sliding into the mud," she said.

After that, Adonis leaves her in peace, does not press her. He would do anything to keep the shadows away from those beautiful eyes. Instead he pats her cheek, the portion of her anatomy that seems to suit the occasion; a pat of the housewife's cheek turning the whole thing into a bee in Anna's bonnet, the odd notion of a woman weighed down by poverty and work.

To me it is like a photograph: Adonis patting Anna on the cheek. But in that same moment he draws his hand back and his smile stiffens. Although, strictly speaking, it may not be in that same moment but a week or a month or six months later. But from where I am standing, it looks as though he draws his hand back in that same moment and, for an instant, turns solemn, realizing as he does that the building in which he lives, his child's home, the frame around his love and those long afternoons of fluid lovemaking, is sinking.

This dawned on him when he discovered that the dance hall, which was situated under the family's apartment, had disappeared. The place was called Cape Horn, a name selected by its proprietor, former heavyweight wrestling champion of the world Søren M. Jensen, because it reminded him of the pictures of palm-fringed lagoons that had adorned the walls of a dressing room from his youth. It was there that the great Bech Olsen had predicted that he would one day open a tavern, because wrestling and bars went hand in hand. Later, when he learned the truth from sailors who had sailed around the real Cape Horn and who still, a lifetime later, remembered that rocky coastline as an iron-gray skull, battered by gales and set amid a boiling sea, he kept the name anyway because he felt the very sound of it contained a bitter longing well suited to the place. During the day it was a bar and wine cellar, with gambling in the dimly lit premises to the rear, where well-groomed men from distant parts of town accepted bets. On Fridays and Saturdays, Søren M. Jensen cleaned the place up and opened his doors for workingmen's club dances, and on those evenings the place had, to all appearances, undergone a transformation. Then violins, flutes, and pianos replaced the sailors' crude songs because, even in this poor district and even within the workingmen's own organizations, there existed a strict moral code which demanded that parents accompany their daughters to the Cape Horn and come to fetch them—all because they sensed something that we, at a later date, can clearly see: that virtue was a sort of shell around these young people, and that it could crack and burst open, with the result that Adonis, on those increasingly more frequent evenings when he came home late, was in danger of tripping over couples lying on the stairways or on the ground itself. Later, when these lovers were married to each other, or to someone else, or found themselves alone, this moral code would be reconstituted among most of them until the shell reformed and could be passed on to the next generation. To me, all of this is downright incomprehensible, but right now, on these summer nights when Maria is running to meet Adonis, the Cape Horn possesses an atmosphere akin to that of a Roman orgy or a Renaissance ball. Adonis and Maria stand together in front of this radiant palace, reveling in the chandeliers and the red plush and the unbridled laughter, which Maria will never forget. And then there is the seductive music, which also rises to the apartment above, to Anna, who is smiling sweetly but abstractedly, because by now she no longer knows what kind of a place she has beneath her feet.

From one day to the next, the place vanished. One morning Adonis said hello as usual to the heavyweight wrestler. The latter was sitting on a low stool in the sunshine, and the tavern's bow windows and faded sunshades and the peeling yellow frontage and the sign with the palm trees all still looked as they always did, more or less as they always did—with the possible exception of the entrance, which Adonis later remembered was in fact sitting remarkably low. The next day no trace remained of the heavyweight wrestler or the dimly lit premises or the bookmakers or the palms. They had all completely disappeared.

At first Adonis thought that the frontage had been redone, that during the night the Cape Horn had undergone one of those panic-stricken alterations attributable to poverty and competition, but then he realized this could not be the case because it was not just the Cape Horn that had gone but the other wine cellars, too—the Palermo and the Cape of Good Hope and the Barony Café—leaving nothing behind but the sign that had hung over the brothel, bearing the name Batam Grande in yellow letters on a green ground, and the marble rollers from electric mangles that had been rescued from the laundry and set up on the sidewalk.

There Adonis stands, surveying all this, and I have a feeling that I am expecting something of him. It is as though the time has come

to recognize that his luck has all but run out and that it is not possible
to survive in the Copenhagen of the 1920s on the conviction that
everything comes to him who waits, because the only thing that will
come, automatically and without fail, is dismal wretchedness. At the
same time, I know very well why I am thinking such thoughts. My
own sentimentality is running away with me, making me cry out
across the endless number of years and across all the barriers that
separate me from Adonis, not least the barrier between life and
death, "Dammit, man! Pull yourself together. Try to remember that
you have a wife who's being swallowed up by a mania that makes
her clean and clean as though she were an attendant in a bathhouse,
and a daughter who has developed a brutal nature unlike that of
any of the lawbreakers in your family. It's time for you to listen to
Anna's predictions now, because this is the last call, the final act,
because your home is sinking straight into the earth!"

But it's no use. And anyway, I have no idea of how to set about
building a bridge back into history, but one thing is certain: emotion
won't do it. I will have to relate, quietly and calmly, the state of
affairs as it stands: that Adonis was as shaken as I am to this day
by this mysterious fatality. After all—even if it is just one huge,
jerry-built monument to the pursuit of profit—a whole house does
not just start to sink into the ground. That sort of thing happens
only abroad and usually in the southern latitudes, as, for example,
in Venice, where the boy Adonis made a halfhearted attempt to
empty the pockets of gondola-riding tourists in an effort to please
his father. But Venice was far away, a city built on pilings and sand,
while Christianshavn rested upon something more solid, namely,
shit and rubbish from the days of Christian IV.

We cannot help but wonder, along with Adonis, at the staying
power of the residents whose apartments had just, within the last
twenty-four hours, been swallowed up by the earth and who have
already moved, with their belongings, into the buildings in the rear
courtyard or onto the back stairs to join the squatters. In spite of
everything, these people preserved exceptional reserves of patience,
which enabled them to accept that they were now homeless. So
much so that they already appeared to be forgetting they had ever
been anything else, as they settled down on the landing to cook over
open fires—an arrangement that assured that every day this firetrap
of a building continued to exist constituted a miracle.

For a while the racket made by the squatters drew Anna back to reality. Filled with compassion, she left her cleaning and Adonis and, sadly, Maria, too, to accompany strange men and women and children around Copenhagen as they wandered through the wilderness, begging their way around the unemployment benefit offices and welfare offices and Copenhagen's Benevolent Society. The supervisors of all these bodies refused them help because it struck them that these supposed paupers asked for money with an obstinacy that seemed alarming; and that this, along with their ragged clothing, appeared to camouflage a secret prosperity and bohemian lifestyle, when the truth was that several of them were close to dying of starvation. And so they had to keep going, on to the Salvation Army and the Women's Aid Coffee Carts, who fed this strange band with the unnaturally pale girl at their head with coffee and five Danish pastries. The only stone Anna left unturned was that of the Evangelical Mission, because she could not bear the thought of being recognized, but even so the expedition bore no fruit. All they brought home with them were admonitions and more admonitions. That night Anna cried for so long and so inconsolably in Adonis's arms that she was unable to answer his question about what most surprised him: something which struck him once night had fallen and which prompted him to get out of bed and cross to the window. From there he could see the mirror image of the moon in the canal. Its light, cast on the building walls in the form of restless reflections, revealed that his eyes were not deceiving him, that their apartment was still on the second floor even though the whole building had sunk by one story.

For a moment Adonis remained standing by the window, looking out at the night and the moonlight while Anna wept softly and despairingly behind him. Then he went back to bed and lay down beside her without asking any questions—questions which it is not even certain that Anna could have answered.

Through the time that followed, the little apartment would appear to have remained suspended at second-floor level, with Anna never for a minute seeming to be disconcerted by the upper floors sliding past her, although this meant she could never be sure, when she opened the door in the morning to clean under the doormat, whether it would open onto the stairway or the squatters or the whores' quarters, or onto a corridor she could not remember ever having seen before. She never commented on this, and even if she had she might not have been able to give as much of an explanation as I would offer: that her love of order and her profound and desperate desire to hold her family and her home together kept the apartment hovering like some spotless celestial sphere while everything else sank. Not, of course, that that explains it; that won't make anyone any the wiser.

And yet, though Adonis could have asked her, he did not, in part because he was preoccupied with his work. He had started performing again. Compelled by circumstances—it was becoming increasingly difficult to sell anything at all, never mind spice cookies—and driven by his old urge to perform, he left his partner and the cake stall in favor of performing in the marketplaces, just as he had done as a child, on the road with his grandfather. He constructed a small collapsible platform that could sit behind his bicycle seat, and made himself an instrument consisting solely of a tin can across which he had stretched a piece of piano wire. There were pictures on the tin can of ships sailing across silken-smooth seas under blue moons, pictures strangely akin to the songs Adonis sang. He had no idea how he came to recollect these songs. Often they would not spring to mind until he started to sing them. They were songs about desert nomads and jungles and coral islands and love that cannot be but on the other hand might just make it. And they all had melodies capable of moving audiences to tears, so much so that there were times when they had to beg the handsome, dark-haired man—Adonis, that is—to cease his singing, because it is so sad and so beautiful, they wept. Adonis accompanied these images on his instrument, which produced a fine and tremulously wistful tone that detained his listeners (most especially the women) in the square long after Adonis had cycled off, in the hope of finding him and comforting him. They thought he shared the longing that filled their hearts when in actuality it so happened that this melancholy bore not the faintest resemblance to Adonis's own life, the keynote of which was contentment. And yet there was no hypocrisy in his singing. He took great pleasure in treading the boards once more, and he himself could be brought close to tears when he performed, although these tears arose from his gratitude at having an audience and from the women's tears of emotion, and not from some private and secret sorrow—although that is what more or less everyone believed. He would never have had the heart to cheat them. Like Ramses, his father, Adonis was uncompromisingly honest, and this sense of right and wrong was what kept him clear of bad company in marketplaces that had altered beyond recognition from when he was a boy. Faced with an increasingly blasé public, the traveling showmen had lost all faith in the possibility of giving pleasure. All that remained of the quick-change artist's magic was the shock effect. This had now become the sole means of surprise, practiced by confidence tricksters who stood behind little tables spread with green baize and dice and leather cups, awaiting their public with the same studied innocence that the caged Bengal tigers had shown on these same churned-up squares a century before. And yet Adonis never looked back. As far as he was concerned, hindsight barely existed; life, audiences, family—all these lie ahead of you. But it did occur to him that the difference between then and now was that the public had become the enemy, not just of the confidence trick- sters but of those showmen who netted more than anyone else be- cause they had grasped that the biggest shock could be derived from the modern age and its technology. So they rode motorcycles around the inside of a big wire-mesh globe decked with brightly colored illustrations of countries and continents. Round and round they would go, vaulting and looping the loop, while reading newspapers or smoking Turkish cigarettes or taunting the spectators. And the audiences wished for nothing more than the liberating crash that would give them their revenge, release the tension, and check this rush around a wall of death that bore such an alarming resemblance to life, inasmuch as once you have started, you have to keep going and can never slacken speed.

It was not indifference that kept Adonis away from Christianshavn for longer and longer stretches. He was by no means either irre- sponsible or callous. It was more as though he had become ensnared by his joy in his work and had, after all, sensed, through his opti- mism, that something was not quite right. In his sterile apartment —the windows of which Anna had now unequivocally nailed shut —he may have sensed a vague, sneaking unease at the way in which he was defying gravity, along with Anna, the wife whom he some- times had difficulty in recognizing because of her sadness and her struggle against their decline.

Adonis is away from home and Anna works. During the spells

when she is not working, she stares into the dancing dust particles, trying to take the omens for a future of which she expects only the worst. And so a void opens up between Adonis, slipping away from his family because he has always tried to steer clear of disaster, and Anna, who is becoming lost in the tough battle presented by the here and now and the calamities ahead. And it is in this void that Maria grows up. Without being sentimental about it, I can say that she lacked security, to such an extent that I am amazed by the way she coped and survived and left enough of an impression for me to be able to trace her story, and for her to become a central character in this narrative. It is not a problem when she is small. When she is small, Adonis is riding high on luck; he has a job and comes home every evening. During these years, Anna is as close to being happy as she will ever be. Maria follows her on her tours around the tenement, she helps with the cooking and the laundry, and the only portent I have been able to unearth of the bad years ahead is one particular Sunday when compassion almost tears Anna to bits. This Sunday apart, all three recollect those years as being bathed in endless sunshine, and, they say, the sun even shone on that dreadful Sunday. We just have to look at the newspapers from those years to see that, in a sense, this cannot be true. Those years saw some of the cruelest winters ever. Nevertheless, that is how all three were to picture that time, and this I must respect. Maria saw her earliest childhood as being one endless summer, and that is all that matters here. Once rationing was discontinued, all the nights were bright; even the darkest of them were illuminated by the glow from Copenhagen's city center and from Tivoli and the dance halls and the reflection of the moon in the canal. The darkness did not fall until later. It is falling now, as Anna starts her cleaning; which was exactly what she had been fearing: that the darkness would settle in the corners.

I do not know whether, before this, Anna had been afraid of the courtyard, that wide and partially built-upon space surrounded by the walls of the tenement. I do not think she had. I cannot know for sure, but I do not think so. It is, however, a fact that she tried to prevent Maria from playing or even going into the yard. It sounds insignificant, it sounds like a mere detail, but it is important. Because everyone uses the yard—not least all the other children but most of the adults as well. That a mother, Anna, should want to stop her child, Maria, from doing what everyone else does is something that sets Anna apart, not only in her own imagination but for us, too. It proves she is not like the others; some might say she has no business being here at all in that case because her life and her dreams are not typical but unique. In answer, I would say that averages are only ever representative when they appear in statistics. What I, on the other hand, have to look for here is whatever it is that makes the common factors *visible*. Often this is achieved by just such unique instances as Anna's forbidding Maria to set foot in the courtyard—an irresistibly tantalizing place, ringing with the sounds from the stands set up by unemployed workers and from the little manufacturing businesses and courtyard singers and peddlers, and from the other children. Anna's prohibition made no impression; it must have come when Maria was about seven years old, by which time Anna could no longer see her clearly; by that time her maternal solicitude had been reduced to clichés and her Danish dream of protecting Maria from becoming like the other children had already grown hazy. If it had not been so, then she might have noticed the brutality in her daughter that made her, even then, in her own way, worse than the worst of the children from whom Anna endeavored to protect her. And then she might have seen that there were two sides to Maria's character: a sunlit side of girlish coyness and cheerfulness, much like my, and Anna's, and, by no means least, Adonis's dream of the perfect daughter, and then the other side, which is black as a winter morning in Copenhagen in the 1920s and possessed of an exceptionally intelligent and indomitable brutality—the same brutality she had vented that morning when, with a single gesture, she chased her father's devotees out of the very courtyard from which, shortly afterward, Anna would attempt to keep her away. Anna never saw this side of her daughter, thus joining the ranks of all those parents who have, at some time or another, ceased to understand their children. We cannot blame her for this, we can only note that that was the way of it; that it was not exceptional, neither in this chapter of Denmark's history nor anywhere else; that it was a recurring motif. Not that it just happened; nothing just happens. There came a point when Anna noticed that Maria no longer obeyed her, and then she realized—perhaps for a fraction of a fraction of a second—that she was looking at Maria as though she were a stranger. Not that she let her daughter go without a fight. There is some indication of convulsive attempts to get through to her; many attempts, all of which failed. As, for example, when Anna sent Maria to school.

She was somewhere between the ages of seven and nine, that much we know. And in any other part of the city the police would have come to fetch her long since, so that Adonis and Anna could fulfill their obligation to make sure their child received an education. This was an obligation of which Adonis, at any rate, had never heard and which, in fact, carried no weight in this area of Christianshavn, since the police never came here and since children had to earn their living from a very early age. So when Anna sent Maria to school, it was for her, Maria's, own good. It was an attempt to take care of her daughter—albeit a misguided attempt, because Maria stayed there for only one day. I repeat, one day.

The school was on the opposite side of the canal. It had the corridors, tiny rooms, and stinking toilets of a barracks and the high ceilings, arched doorways, and dark, Latin-inscribed niches of a Gothic cathedral. Amid these gloomy surroundings, Maria experienced the first morning assembly of her life. To her it seemed a depressing ritual that made the patriotic songs sound like some muted mass, because none of the pupils joined in the singing and the teachers barely did. Instead they muttered the words. More or less everyone muttered the words, even the principal, who stood on a podium under an array of his predecessors' death masks and the inscription "Under the shadow of thy wings." In a classroom that was as dark as night because it faced onto a rear courtyard and because lighting was rationed, Maria sat alongside pupils whose heads had all been shaved on account of virulent outbreaks of head lice. This made them look like convicts or novice monks and nuns, bending under the knowledge imparted to them by dusty men and women who had long ago lost touch with the world outside and subsided into the dream world of an outdated tradition. It was a tradition rich in valiant Norse gods, physical violence, vacuous Greek ideals, and the few victories of Denmark's history—and the countless defeats. And even these they managed to interpret afresh—the cloistered and endlessly repetitive life of the school having opened their eyes to the new, inner, spiritual wealth contained within this succession of military and political disasters.

Maria immediately sniffed out the weak spot in the reality embraced by these intellectual mentors, and she would have left the school of her own accord. If it had been necessary, she would have got to her feet and left, never to return. But circumstances got ahead of her. In the middle of the lunch break; right in the middle of the inedible grated carrot served up every day by the private benevolent society that also supplied the delousing powder for the bald pates of all these children; amid all the racket of the playground, in which Maria's menacing stammer could be heard, holding the curiosity of the other children at bay; in the midst of all of this, the school was discreetly appropriated to provide accommodations for the multitude of homeless souls in Copenhagen, a body whose numbers swelled with every day that passed. Maria witnessed the way in which long rows of pupils, and then teachers, had to file out through the gate to make way for the homeless. And here we have a significant moment; with the state and the city forced to close this temple of learning and turn it into a hotel, a central station for the homeless. It is a historic moment, but it belongs to a story other than ours, and is mentioned here only because it took place on Maria Jensen's first day at school, a day cut short because of it, before Maria herself could put an end to it. The only truly interesting item of knowledge she brought home with her was the sight of this long string of children walking and running out through the green gateway carrying their book bags, or just books strapped into a bundle—and behind them the teachers, who seemed to be having difficulty in moving. Like insects found under an overturned stone, they were not really equipped to deal with the light or the street, which boasts no lecterns or tall desks or inscriptions and is almost bereft of elevation.

And here I have to pause for a moment. From this point onward certain problems arise in writing Maria's story: I would like to depict her as a coherent individual—well, in one sense or another we are all coherent—but this proves to be impossible. It has something to do with the writing of history. History is always an invention; it is a fairy tale built upon certain clues. The clues are not the problem, not even in Maria's case, where they consist of what Anna and Adonis remembered and what Maria herself remembered, together with the school register, then the police reports, and later the files of the child welfare committee, and later still other pieces of information—to all of which we will return. These clues are pretty well established; most of them can literally be laid on the desktop for anyone to handle. But these, unfortunately, do not constitute history. History consists of the links between them, and it is this that presents the problem. And the link is especially opaque when, as here, we are dealing with the History of Dreams, because the only thing that anyone—and that includes me—can use to fill in the gaps between history's clues is themselves. In the case of Maria Jensen, the problem becomes pressing because it is not possible—at least not for me—to cover all the gaps, not even roughly. We know that she was between seven and nine years of age when Anna sent her to school, and now some of the clues do point in one direction: Anna and Adonis did not remember anything except that she continued to go to school. To them Maria was our little blue-eyed, fair-haired girl, who has grown up surrounded by a haze of pet names, and who runs to meet her father and takes his hand while they stand gazing into the brightly lit rooms of the Cape Horn, and who—when she is very small—follows her mother everywhere, first with her eyes and then on her little legs, and who is, in every way, a little angel with whom no fault can be found other than that she can at times be a bit quiet, not moody, but quiet in a way that left her parents with the feeling that they did not really understand her. Being a model child, she is also predictable, which is why Anna is able to foresee her fate. And it bears all the marks of the twenties dream of a small girl's future. Maria would float through life. If it became necessary for her to work, for a little while, then it would be in a confectionery store in some distant, pure white part of town, and there she would meet the man in her life, whom Anna, strange as it may seem, pictured on horseback—an equestrian statue coated with a respectable verdigris of courtesy and honorable intentions. That was the extent of Anna's dream, particularly in the days before she embarked upon her cleaning, and it should be noted that this impression of Anna is, in all probability, absolutely correct. It is part of the truth. But it is scarcely the whole truth. Because, while a girl—Maria—is growing up in a family that is, all things considered, a model family; while her mother and father are watching her float-ing around the silent, spotless rooms like some tiny genius or a fairy or a skinny Baroque angel; while all this is going on, letters are being written. There are letters from Maria's school to the Children's

Panel and from the Children's Panel to the Child Welfare Services, and a succession of interesting police reports are completed. All of these I have been able to see, and they are now lying before me, on the desk. Ostensibly, they have nothing to do with Maria. They refer to a group of children between the ages of ten and eighteen, probably resident in Christianshavn, probably all from the same tenement block, who are totally out of control. They are all truants, given to smoking cigarettes and roaming the streets. Furthermore, the police reports describe countless infringements of the penal code. It has not been possible for me to have a word with any of the individuals who then belonged to this group. I have been able to follow them just so far—up to their last spell of detention, from which they are never again released into moral depravity but are taken into care. From this point, however, their trails diverge. Some were put into reform schools, while others fell under paragraph 62 of the poor law, underwent compulsory sterilization, and were then assigned to the Department for the Education of the Subnormal. Still others were sent to prison, but all have disappeared, all trace of them has been lost. Which means we have no witnesses. There is no possibility of starting up a conversation that might shed some light on the part played by Maria. All I can say is that the reports in front of me speak of a girl nicknamed the Stutterer, a girl whose real name and family circumstances were never established although she was arrested several times and on one solitary occasion brought before the Children's Panel. Of her, the forms state that she appeared to occupy a leading position in this bunch of depraved, neglected, unkempt children; that she had headed the band's sorties into other properties on Christianshavn, as well as its shoplifting expeditions and retaliatory attacks upon the police. In a letter to the Children's Panel, Police Chief Jespersen writes that the girl is probably about fifteen years old but looks younger, that she is slight of stature, and that she has blue eyes. We cannot know for sure whether this was Maria; all we know is that Maria did not go to school. Every morning she picked up her packed lunch and her books, set off down the back stairs, and disappeared into the light and the day, not to return until late in the afternoon, and sometimes even later. She did not go to school, this we know. There is no doubt that she skipped school, but we can only guess where she spent the time. And this guess is supported by the reports and files.

It seems likely that Maria grew up in the courtyard, which makes the brutal streak in her character that we have glimpsed easier to understand, and not just that but certain subsequent occurrences. It requires some effort on our part to understand the group of children around Maria; understanding does not just happen. Part of the truth about this league of degenerate children is possibly their solidarity, and it was this that Maria was to remember. It is depicted in many a children's book: the poor children plotting against the adults and coming out on top, high jinks on the ramparts around Christianshavn, and the fantastic, avenging forays into other neighborhoods. And this dream, even if it is romantic, may well be accurate. But there is also another truth, and that is the truth about flight: if we look at the life of the adults in the tenement in Christianshavn we can see that it is a journey—in many different directions, but at any rate a journey. But to the children it is flight. When I read the police reports I can see that they all deal with attempted getaways. Take, for example, the case of Maria's lieutenant. One winter's day, this boy ran away from the magistrate's court. He ran and ran, all through the night; he contracted gangrene in both feet and had to have both his legs amputated. From then on, he hops through subsequent reports on crutches and is, because of his disability, constantly being discovered and caught. Or what about all the others who run away from prison or from reform schools or hospitals; who employ all their ingenuity in trying to get away from, or eluding, or wriggling free of people who are going to catch them anyway, all of them without exception, sooner or later.

There is a photograph of all these children, taken early one morning. They are standing behind a shed. There is a grayish cast to the light and most of them are wearing dark clothing. Who took the photograph is a mystery, but it has been taken from an awkward angle, possibly from an outhouse roof. There is a somewhat matter-of-fact air about it, this picture, coolly registering its interest. Several of the children are carrying books and lunch bags, and they have gathered behind this outhouse so their parents will think they have gone to school. In the picture, their faces are white, very white. There is no mistaking that they are undernourished and malnourished, and it is quite evident that they are on the move. You can tell by the positioning of their feet and their arms that this group of children is about to make a move. But they are not setting out to conquer the world, they are heading away from a blow or a grasping hand, and this, too, can be sensed in the picture. They are under a strain, this group; a strain imposed, not just by God's Avenging Finger or the Long Arm of the Law or the Firm Hand of School, but the strain of a child's life in the Copenhagen of the 1920s. Even now, today, I find this photograph oppressive, and it makes me wish I could interpret its message. But it's no use. Every time I open my mouth, up pops sentimentality, like a historic lump in my throat. So far better to let their time do the talking: not long after this picture was taken, Maria (if indeed it was she) was brought before the Children's Panel because, even for those days, hers was a very representative and instructive case, and because the child-loving members of the panel were, quite simply, curious and wanted a look at the Stutterer. On that occasion, the doctor in attendance, Dr. Dambmann, said these children, this army of wretches, responded to a natural law, more specifically Boyle's law, which says that pressure times volume equals a constant. In other words, in response to the pressure from the world around them, these children had built up a considerable and tough resistance and . . . er . . . um . . . an exceptional inner pressure. This sentence, uttered by a scientifically educated children's friend, is in many ways interesting. It assumes that society and man form a kind of pressure chamber and, moreover, that they respond to natural laws—an academic dream worth noting, among other reasons because it may, to some extent, be correct. The flock of children in the picture radiates toughness as well as the inherent discipline required in order to live, the latter quality being upheld by their leaders, of whom Maria is one. She is standing at the edge of the picture; on her head she has a police helmet that hides her fair hair. Pretty brazen, isn't it, making a getaway with a police helmet on your head? It says something about how malevolent this group was and maybe also something about a foolhardiness that is not without humor, not without an embittered grin.

That photograph is lying in front of me, and next to it lie my blank sheets of paper. It is as though the children had already moved on; as though the whole group had disappeared, leaving a gap between a winter's morning in Copenhagen and that March day when Maria was arrested and taken to the Copenhagen authorities, to be brought before the Children's Panel. I am abandoning all thought

of filling in that gap with anything other than the facts gleaned from
the police reports: that the infringements of the penal code perpe-
trated by these children amounted to fifty cases of theft (including
the handling of stolen goods), five cases of indecency, ten cases of
unnatural practices, forty cases of assault and battery, sixty-eight
cases of wanton destruction of property, forty-two cases of trafficking
in minors, eleven cases of breach of the peace, and fifty-two cases
that were not proven, or of which the police had not been able to
make head or tail. We do not know what Maria had done; strictly
speaking, we do not know whether she had done anything at all.
Only one—I repeat, one—report does more than just mention the
Stutterer in passing. And although it makes more detailed reference
to her, it is rather muddled and falls into the "not proven" category.
Otherwise only rumors and suspicions exist about this little girl with
the faint stammer and her hair hidden under a police helmet.

Maria was arrested in March, on the same day that Kofoed, the
sexton who was later to become so renowned, opened his handicrafts
school in Christianshavn. The report states that the arrest took place
in the cellars of the tenement where she lived. It might be thought
odd that the police were able to make an arrest within no-man's-
land but if it happened at all it seems only reasonable that it should
have happened in the cellars. Naturally, Maria went where no one
else would go. She knew these seething shafts, the lower regions of
which were now filled with pale mud, and she, and possibly the
other children, knew that one day all of it was going to go under.
They caught her in the cellars and brought her to the police station,
where they took away the police helmet that had betrayed her identity as the Stutterer. The next day they brought her to the municipal
authorities. No explanation is given for why the meeting should have
taken place there, in the shadow of the town hall. Which is strange,
since the Children's Panel was so skeptical of municipal bureaucracy, which is then, as now, opposed to everything, almost everything, at any rate if it involves change. It may be that the meeting
was called at the last minute because they believed they had caught
a ringleader, a trailblazer, a particularly hardened specimen, and
so there was nowhere else for them to meet but here, in this large,
high-ceilinged chamber, in the center of which Maria—if indeed it
was she—now stands, lit by the March sunshine falling through the
window. Around her sit the members of the Children's Panel: Mayor

Drechsel; Mr. Bayer, the lawyer; the industrialist and wholesaler P. Carl Petersen; the merchant Martin Hansen; Dr. Dambmann— shortly to mention Boyle's law; the headmaster Knud Christensen; the Reverend C. Wagner; and Mrs. M. Hauerbach, housewife. These are joined by a senior municipal clerk, a man whose name is not mentioned in the minutes and who remained silent throughout the proceedings. They all stare at the girl before them. She is standing in the sunlight but seems to be lit from within. Her hair is long and fair, her eyes are breathtakingly blue, and she looks very, very young. This much they all see, all nine adults. But—her hair and her age apart—they each saw their own vision. A few of them scribbled their impressions in the margins of their notepads and so we know that the Reverend Mr. Wagner felt that he was face-to-face with a feminine version of the boy Jesus in the temple; and that P. Carl Petersen, the wholesaler, found himself thinking of his masseuse's daughter; and that the headmaster thought of the Little Match Girl and the housewife of certain broadside ballads; and the only thing that all these associations have in common is the impression that Maria is innocent. During those first few minutes, when Maria simply *stood* before them, with no one saying a word, the meeting's outcome was settled. During those minutes the Children's Panel members felt as though they understood that of course they were not confronted here by a criminal but by a Little Red Ridinghood of sorts, or a lost lamb. To me the situation seems symbolic. Looked at from a particular angle, it presents us with the most significant feature of the nature of the Child Welfare Services in 1920s Denmark. At this moment, in this chamber in the municipal buildings, all these people have different objects in mind: financial, political, erotic, religious, and charitable, most definitely charitable. But a great gap exists between them and the girl standing before them, a kind of chasm, and it is this they are attempting to bridge with the aid of the term "innocent."

After that it was just a matter of form. They asked a number of questions that Maria answered in monosyllables: no, she did not understand why she had been arrested; yes, she did know her parents; yes, she ate every day; yes, she was washed at least once a week; yes, she went to school. The minutes of the examination make strange reading. They did not ask Maria her name, nor did they ask her parents' names or which school she attended—or at any rate, if they have asked, then they have not made a note of her replies. This can perhaps be explained by the impression Maria has made; the paralysis that spread throughout the chamber when they realized they were faced, not with the Stutterer, but with a creature who spoke directly to their hearts, because that is what Maria did. The amazing thing is that the Children's Panel had not understood her—"innocence" is not a good description of a child—but Maria had understood them. With singular adroitness she has grasped the nature of these people; has penetrated it and given them exactly what they had always dreamed of: Little Red Ridinghood without the wolf, Gretel without Hansel, the dream of the Innocent Child.

This situation is somehow familiar. The air was filled with the same emotion as when Anna testified for the brethren, at some seaside spot, and when Adonis, traveling through Jutland, had sung to the farmers: a mysterious combination of honesty and calculation and naïveté and insight—all of which, when put together, produce a wistful sigh, a sigh on the brink of tears, a sigh which, on that day, hung vibrating under the lofty ceilings of the Copenhagen municipal offices.

Thereafter, several members of the Children's Panel made speeches. Now, this was not standard practice, but there was something remarkable about this situation, and it must have been this that called for the speechmaking, during which the housewife, Mrs. Hauerbach, deplored this wrongful arrest and regretted that Maria was not her daughter, and P. Carl Petersen announced that he would bequeath his sizable property at 263 Strand Drive to young people with no home of their own, and Dambmann spoke of Boyle's law —and which was rounded off by the headmaster. His speech is important because it deals with the correct sort of education on sexual matters. Now what, you may ask yourself, does that have to do with Maria? Why is sex suddenly being brought into the picture? And the answer, possibly, is that it has always been there; that when they found Maria innocent—and other children before and after her—it has something to do with the Children's Panel's attitude to sex, as now defined by the headmaster. With regard to sex education, he said that "this ought to be provided by the parents—though they may perhaps not be up to the task; the schools avoid the subject, and so nothing is done. I bring this up," said the headmaster, "because it is most important that guidance given at this stage should

be combined with a moral inducement, an appeal to the individual
not to jump the gun but to wait until both mind and body are fully
developed and mature enough to sustain a lasting marital relationship. Young people should not be instructed by the publications on
such subjects sold at newsstands and tobacconists. I am not suggesting that the members of the Children's Panel should impart
such instruction personally, but the Children's Panel ought, if possible, to ensure that it is given, in whatever way can best be arranged
and in the appropriate surroundings.''

And here his speech ended. In order to understand it, it has to
be seen not only in the March sunlight that gilds Maria while the
headmaster is speaking but also in the light of Maria's own experience of sex in the building in Christianshavn, where she led the
way in the basement undressing games; and where she came and
went as she pleased in the whores' quarters; and where at home she
had witnessed her father and mother's uninhibited lovemaking.
Most of all, however, we ought to note that the headmaster speaks
of restraining oneself and not jumping the gun and waiting until
body and mind are ready and willing, and *that* must have sounded
a bit odd to Maria, this advice to take it easy, very easy, and not to
make demands, but to bide your time until blah, blah, blah . . . It
does not have quite the same ring to it for the headmaster as it does
for Maria, who hails from a place where a lot of people, if not most
people, find it hard just to get enough to eat and where everyone
learns from infancy to grab all he can.

With this in mind (and not just this), Maria listens to the headmaster's speech. Then she goes home, leaving behind her the Children's Panel, of whose members it can be said that, in this case,
they had not understood a thing. Of course, there had, both before
and after this, been other meetings that were different—also meetings about Maria—and, of course, on other occasions they understood a lot more. But on this afternoon in March, in Copenhagen,
in the late 1920s, they understood practically nothing.

Then we are left with just one more isolated incident before disaster strikes and everything comes to an end: Maria's encounter
with wealth. She came upon it one spring afternoon when she was
roaming around on her own and had thus wound up in a far corner
of the courtyard. There she bumped into the owner of this property
and of several other properties in Christianshavn and of half of

Vesterbro: Andreasen, the owner of a trucking company, a bent, worn-looking man in blue coveralls. By then he had become a legendary figure, and to those who can remember having heard of him he still is. Few had ever seen him, but Maria knew straightaway who he was. He was sitting on the top of the dunghill he had had deposited on this particular section of his property because here, in those backcourt buildings that even he could not rent out, he kept a three-story cow barn, only two stories of which were still above ground. When Maria saw him, she stopped dead in her tracks and for a long, long time she just stood there looking at him while the man on the dunghill returned her gaze. And that is about all there is to say about that meeting. I do not know enough to guess what Maria was feeling and nowhere near enough to know what the trucker felt. There is no reason to believe that Maria sensed the dreadful loneliness of this man, which would later move him to leave his fortune to the local Masonic lodge (to which he had never belonged) merely in order to arouse, in some quarter at least, some emotion other than dislike. As likely as not, Maria has not known, either, that he did not realize that the property was sinking or that *that* was why the cooped-up cows lowed in complaint more and more often—through the night, too, now. But one thing rooted itself in her memory: on the dunghill, around the trucker, hopped his free-range hens, and in his hands he held one with a broken leg. Now, Maria knew that anyone else would have wrung that hen's neck. But not the trucker. A dead hen is a loss, not a great loss, but still a loss. Which is why, just then, up on the dunghill, he was fixing a stick he had cut to the hen's broken leg: a splint to support this leg that would never heal. While the two of them are exchanging glances, his hands automatically finish the job and set the hen free. And just before Maria turns and walks away, the hen runs past her, squawking as it stumbles off into the sunshine. This sticks in Maria's mind, this picture of the hen with its wooden leg hobbling into the sunshine. It is something she will remember.

Then all we are left with is the end.

It came one spring, in May. Long before this, the residents had begun to leave the tenement. Even these people, who had nowhere else to go, left this property, where only the uppermost floors still remained clear of the earth. It can hardly have been because they knew what was happening. It was still only the children and the sailors and Anna who knew where all of this was leading. But there must have been something in the air, maybe the smell of the mud, the freshwater aroma of decline which, to begin with, merely added a fresh touch of unease to life. Amid this fresh uneasiness the number of suicides rose. People leaped out of windows or hung themselves in the attics, and wherever her rambles took her, Maria encountered the smell of gas from apartments where the residents had switched on their ovens to gas themselves—whole families. And since they could hardly all get their heads in at the same time, Daddy had to support the little ones, and even then it was touch and go. Afterward the gas seeped out into the corridors until someone struck a match, all the apartments in that section were blown sky-high, and the neighbors had to put out the fire themselves, because not even the fire department dared to enter the area. Later on, they began to vacate the tenement: first the squatters, then young married couples with no children—although initially only a handful actually left. Most of the residents still believed that one day, and possibly one of these very days, the building would sail away. They would not admit that the property was sinking; they believed that the street and the sidewalk were closing upon their floor, their windows, because what had been solid ground was now rising in waves; and that this was because the property was about to break free of poverty and depression and unemployment. And indeed a singular sense of optimism did reign in Copenhagen during that month. It was a quiet month for stocks and shares. The newspapers printed pictures of Europe in festive mood, with Mussolini making speeches to thousands of uniformed youths. And over it all arched a clear blue sky. The very fact of the sunshine made it hard to admit that anything could be wrong. Its yellow light fell like glittering confetti, or melted butter, on the solid, enigmatic figure of Stauning as he vacated the building. It did not look as though he was fleeing; he carried a suitcase in one hand, nothing else. And, of course, he left on foot. It was a morning like any other; no one could have known that he would not be coming back. He was followed, at night, by the rats —a broad, dark, living river that momentarily washed over everything and then was gone. Later that same night, the cows broke loose and fled, bellowing, and over the next few days and nights the property slowly emptied.

No one in the Jensen family really understood what was happen-

ing, neither Maria nor Adonis, and not even Anna, because, in one
way or another, they were all absent or preoccupied. Those days,
Maria rarely came home. She had started sleeping in the railroad
yards, in railroad cars and sheds, because the disinfected apartment
made her feel ill and because she felt uneasy about the change that
had taken place in her mother. Anna had had a revelation. Weighed
down by her cleaning—which, instead of helping her get to the
bottom of things, seemed continually to wind deeper and deeper
into itself, like a labyrinth—she had sought comfort at the whores'
mission meetings. To begin with, she was merely an onlooker, but
after a while she was seized by the urge to help and to tend. She
helped found an African Mission for the purpose of sending a missionary to the needy black children. To this end, after mission meetings, a collection was taken in a carved and painted figure of a Negro
boy with an enormous red mouth, into which the faithful, Anna
included, popped their coins. Her revelation came shortly after the
founding of this mission. After having given up trying to make the
others see that the building was sinking, after having given up everything other than keeping her family suspended, at one of the mission
meetings she had received a message from God: a message that
made her feel she had been both heard and understood. She had
seen paradise. In the twinkling of an eye she had been swept away
from that room and had seen Lavnæs and the part of the country
around which she had traveled as a child. These manifested themselves to her not as she had viewed them in those days, through the
bars of a cage, but as welcoming meadowlands. And on these meadows she saw the forgotten faces of her childhood: Thorvald Bak, and
the brethren and the young men who had gazed through the bars
of her cage with hungry, wistful expressions, as though they longed
to be held captive. All these faces she had seen, and after that she
kept coming back to the mission meetings. She did not come to
pray. As far as she was concerned, prayers formed a veil of words
behind which lay nothing but a resounding emptiness, and this
frightened her. What she sought was a repetition of those pictures
from her revelation, of the childhood she had never known. And
this she was given. She did succeed in seeing the meadowlands
again. The second revelation did not manifest itself until long after
the first, but thereafter the revelations occurred with increasing regularity. She did not tell anyone about them, partly because there

was no chance to, since Adonis and Maria were seldom at home, and partly because her visions were so fragile that words might eradicate them completely. She discovered that her work around the apartment secured them. It was as if her soul consisted of the same smooth surfaces as her walls and floors and kitchen counters and windows. By dint of her incessant cleaning and polishing, the mists disappeared and out of the gloom stepped the golden pictures of those lost days. Maria also appeared in these pictures; not Maria as she looked now, with her knowing eyes and watchful air, but Maria as she had been when she was very little, or at any rate as she had sometimes been: a ball of fluff with no attributes other than beauty and helplessness. That is how she appeared in these visions, which Anna was seeing more and more frequently, and it was to this image that Anna spoke when she occasionally saw Maria in reality—never noticing the police helmet that Maria no longer bothered to hide and never noticing her bumps and bruises or the makeup which, now and again, Maria stole or borrowed from one of her girlfriends.

Maria could see that Anna's journey was now bearing her away, back in time and consequently away from her, Maria. And so she distanced herself from her mother. It scared her to see Anna talking to thin air, to ghosts that only she could see, so Maria withdrew from the hovering apartment and from the property, in which fewer and fewer children were to be seen because they, too, had disappeared—withdrew to the nights in the railroad yards. And it was here that she met Adonis. It happened in a marketplace that had sprung up just on that spot because the city of Copenhagen had imported an Indian village. The importation was the result of its being spring, and of the general interest in the lost colonies and all things foreign. It was sponsored by H. N. Andersen, Maria's uncle, who wanted the Danish People to experience something of the Orient. He had therefore financed the introduction into the country of this exotic dream: an Indian village, all-inclusive, with elephants and snake charmers and women weaving and men hacking at the earth between the railroad tracks, all smiling those wide, gilt-edged smiles that confirmed what the Danes already knew: that these weird Hottentots enjoyed the most carefree of lives, full of merriment and in tune with nature.

On the square, between the mud-walled huts and surrounded by vendors and snake charmers and bonfires fed by the dung from the holy cows, Maria met her father. Adonis was standing on his stage, singing, and beside him stood a woman. Her hair was coal-black, plaited and oiled and smoothed back over her scalp, like a gleaming helmet. It framed a foreign-looking face of indeterminate age, unlike that of the ancient man sitting at the foot of the platform, his hands trembling with age. These two aged characters were Maria's grandparents—Ramses Jensen and the Princess. Adonis had come upon them in a railroad car—well, of course, of all places, in a railroad car. It had been parked at Sydhavnen and it belonged to an institution called the Heavenly Express that collected money for the down-and-outs of society and thus, also, for Ramses Jensen and the Princess. When Adonis found them they were cowering together in a corner of a bunk, looking for all the world like the hope cherished by the Danish National Evangelical Lutheran Church and the Danish judicial system, that justice be done and the wages of sin doled out.

We can perhaps detect a certain fatal irony in that these two old people—after having spent their entire lives dreaming of Domestic Bliss around Hearth and Home, while still remaining lifelong fugitives—should end up in a social welfare railroad car; a temporary hut on wheels that might, at any moment, start to roll. But they themselves were not capable of finding this irony amusing, and Adonis certainly was not. He reveled in this reunion, with a simple delight undiminished by all the years since they had last seen one another, years about which Ramses and the Princess had nothing rational to say. After their arrival in Denmark the years had vanished without trace, as though, while they grew slower with age, time traveled faster; as though their life had become a tunnel that sucked up the years into a vacuous darkness. Moreover, Adonis was not curious, so when he received no replies he stopped asking questions and concentrated instead on the matter at hand, on reality, in the shape of the brilliant idea he had just had. He would put his parents on show in the marketplace; he would enrich his little stage and his musical numbers by the addition of these living legends, these museum pieces—and so it was agreed. Adonis had always been able to persuade everyone, or at least nearly everyone, to do anything, and the Princess and Ramses were old. Without comprehending that their life had made a gradual, sinuous turn away from all those incredible, invisible break-ins and had, at long last, been turned upside down, they allowed themselves to be drawn out into the light they had spent all their life avoiding. They became visible in much the same way as they had disappeared when their reluctant renown forced them to flee the country, but now they were not fleeing any- where; now they met the sunlight and the upturned faces with that patient resignation which, by all accounts, comes with age.

There is a poster from those days, a four-color print, commis- sioned by Adonis. It shows Adonis himself standing in the back- ground with his arms reaching out in a gesture of embrace. His mouth is open, he is singing, and in the poster he looks like a 175- pounds-lighter, long-haired version of the great tenor Caruso. Be- neath him sits his father, Ramses Jensen, selling tickets from a little table. In the poster his hands seem perfectly steady. Right at the front, in the foreground and twice the size of the other two put together, hangs the Princess. She is suspended by one arm, her left, from what looks like a balcony and is gazing intently upon the onlooker. This poster reflected a dream that never became a reality because Adonis had not absorbed the fact that his mother had aged. Ramses was an old man, of that there could be no doubt. His youth- ful knack of freezing to the spot and becoming absolutely one hundred percent motionless had now been replaced by this feverish trembling which made him appear to be in a hurry or anxious to draw attention to himself, when in reality what he had in mind was the exact opposite. But the Princess was serene; her hair was black, as were her eyes. She had not changed; she looked like the girl of her youth. There was a certain ceramic indestructibility about her, and it was this that led Adonis to believe that she could perform a wall-scaling number. He would build a climbing frame from which she would hang and swing with all the apelike agility of her girlhood. In hopes of this, the poster was printed, but it never amounted to anything other than a splendid depiction of a misunderstanding. The Princess was old and in no fit state to cling to anything except the simplest facets of existence, and even those she took in small portions, one day at a time. Nevertheless, Adonis pasted up the poster and the public did not feel cheated. All the indications are that they were well satisfied with Adonis's singing and with Ramses' trembling and with the Princess, who stood at the very front and just *gazed* out, across their heads, with those black eyes which still, in spite of everything, no matter what, remained as relentlessly bold as when Ramses first saw her, long ago in the previous century.

There turned out to be many who remembered the old people. The memory of them had passed through the shredder and converter of the new century, the new press, the new memory bank, which transforms and blanches all facts before inflating them with noble gases. Thus the rumors of Ramses and the Princess's incredible, grasping crimes hung above the marketplaces like swelling hydrogen balloons which could be seen a long way off and which drew the crowds, particularly in the provinces. It was never a thriving business, because Adonis never learned how to make money, not even in a small way. But it aroused interest, interest and a curiosity tinged with fear.

Only we now, so many years later, can detect the pattern guiding this family's steps in one direction: the footlights. It is as though they must get up there, whether they want to or not. They all end up as performers, even Ramses, who finds himself selling tickets next to the stage, which is itself like art, a pedestal and a platform for the displaying of dreams. And thus, for the first time in his life, Ramses, too, comes in from the cold and joins society. But at the same time the Jensen family's fate demonstrates that the footlights coincide with the edge of the precipice, just at the point where it is hard to see where solid ground ends and the void begins. To think that Ramses and the Princess's life—which had been one long series of criminal offenses and one great yearning after darkness—should, still and all, have wound up bringing them into the light. Just imagine!

One evening, Maria was standing in front of the platform, listening to her father sing. When Adonis's eye fell on her he inserted bird-songs and other little references to the past into his songs. Maria watched him impassively, and afterward, too, when Adonis took her to speak to her grandparents, she seemed entrenched within herself. That same night, Adonis packed up his stage and bundled it and his parents onto a truck, in which he drove himself and his props and Maria and the two old people over to Christianshavn.

That night, while Adonis was singing to Maria, and then packing up; that night, the last residents left the property in Christianshavn. Last to leave were the chickens and the squatters and the sick and the whores and Andreasen the trucker and those children who, like 5,424 others in the country in that year, had been sentenced to compulsory removal from their parents' custody. They had hidden in the building and stayed there until the last minute, in an attempt to evade the child welfare committee and the official guardians and foster families, but now they were being forced out anyway, because anything is better than death, even in Christianshavn.

It was a clear, moonlit night and Anna was the only one left in the empty building. Naturally, she was working; by the moonlight alone she was running a dustcloth over the wall paneling. She had been working for a long while—I do not know how long, but a very long while—and she kept at it, unflagging. On this night her loneliness was transformed into energy and a sense of how everything is connected. She finished shortly after midnight, by which time the last sounds from outside had faded away and the last irregularity fled the apartment, and Anna was surrounded by the totally clean, microbe-free, and harmonious space for which she had been longing. Stiffly, cautiously, she straightened up and put down the dustcloth. Everything had been accomplished, and all of us who believe that one can never get to the bottom of things have been mistaken and must bow our heads. At that instant, Anna's spirit condensed and all the voices that had been calling to her from all sides throughout her life fell silent. Gingerly she walked around the rooms, filled with the sense that life was not a battle against impurities but a delicate balancing act in empty space. She had now gained her balance, and while she was balancing, she had the impression that the apartment bore some vague resemblance to the silver-plated cage of her childhood. At that moment the last of the building went under, and the canal flowed past outside Anna's window. Then she stepped out, through the bars, and set off across the water, along the path of molten silver formed by the moonlight. Past the sleeping boats she went, out toward the sea, feeling nothing but curiosity and sadness. It was not death that Anna wandered into, there is no need to be sad, there was no talk of suicide, no talk of anything other than that Anna wandered off to look for the youth she had never known.

By the time Maria and Adonis got there, the building had completely disappeared. It was totally and utterly gone, with not even a
chimney sticking up. The moon had set, but in the feeble dawn light
the mud shone grayly. The lot was deserted, empty, and incalculably
large, and in the empty space above it there still hung a weightless
memory of the lost tenement. It was as though it went on living,
somewhere else; as though, during the night, some giant had picked
it up and hurled it into another dimension—one that occupied the
same spot, though on a different plane, as the one where Maria and
Adonis stood gazing at the cold gray light of morning; a winter
morning in Copenhagen, and the sort of light that is no longer seen
but that is the most appropriate for what happens next. Which is,
that Adonis looks at Maria. There is no doubt that he wanted her
to come with him. After all, he was her father. She could sit in the
back of the truck next to her grandparents and the collapsible platform; maybe he could devise a number for her; they could perform
together, she and Adonis—wouldn't that have been beautiful, the
dream of father and daughter and grandparents huddling together
in the face of 1930s Denmark, after the mother had disappeared,
at that. Wouldn't that have been beautiful. It is how I would like to
see things turn out, but it would not have been the truth, and here
truth takes precedence over everything, even beauty. What does in
fact happen is that Maria turns away. She takes off her police helmet
and wipes a brow dampened by the moisture in the air; then she
turns away, as though there were no more to this story. But of course
there is, there is always a sequel, and most decidedly a sequel to
this moment. I am familiar with some of this sequel—the part that
follows the progress of Maria's life—but I know nothing about the
immediate aftermath. Whatever happened during that dawn has
been forgotten. Maybe they ran, Adonis and Maria; maybe they
raced through the narrow, sleeping streets searching for someone
—Anna, mother and wife—whom, one assumes, they knew to have
vanished, finally and irrevocably. Maybe they even went to the police. It is not unthinkable that Adonis, at any rate, might have done
so. Whatever they did, they did not remember it. In their memories,
that morning would consist of nothing but the cold and the gray
light and the simple fact that Anna had gone, and that gesture of
Maria's. Maria—wiping her brow as she turned away from Adonis
Jensen and the silent figures in the truck and made off, through the

gradually swelling crowd of sightseers and unemployed workers and message boys and representatives from the child welfare committee and official guardians and newspaper reporters—although these last deemed this event, the sinking of this property, worthy of only the very briefest of mentions.

CARL LAURIDS

AND AMALIE

The villa on Strand Drive

Prosperity

1919–1939

CARL LAURIDS AND AMALIE met one warm day in May 1919 on a meadow next to a racecourse outside Copenhagen, from which Carl Laurids had organized a balloon ascent. Well, naturally, a balloon ascent—nothing less would do. The balloon had been constructed at von Zeppelin's workshops in Friedrichshafen on the shores of Lake Constance and bore a plaque with the inscription "From one sportsman to another," signed "Ferdinand"—a detail undoubtedly designed to create the impression that what we are dealing with here is quality goods; a product, what is more, of our mighty neighbor Germany, with whom, now that the war is over, we may share everything, even such new, technical advances as this balloon. Even so, there were several guests who, like me, had their doubts as to whether this flamboyant craft really had been a gift from Count Ferdinand von Zeppelin to Carl Laurids. This was the first they had heard of the latter; they knew even less about him than we do. But there he was, in their midst, wearing white tails and a flying helmet, willingly answering any and all questions, except the key question: Where did he come from and where did he get the money to stage such an extravagant event.

Later on, standing on a improvised podium of champagne cases, Carl Laurids gives a speech that has been preserved in the newspaper reports. It was a speech none of those who heard it would ever forget: elegant, incisive, and yet imbued with that remarkable air of com-

172 [The History of Danish Dreams

posure so characteristic of everything to which Carl Laurids turns his hand—a quality made that much more difficult to understand by the fact that here, on the grass outside the racecourse, he is but nineteen years of age. He closed his speech by saying that this balloon was a symbol of the new century's acknowledgment that the lighter a thing is, the faster it will rise into the air. After which he was roundly applauded, his words having touched the hearts of his guests—this collection of speculative businessmen and blushing maidens, all of whom had, during the Great War, amassed fortunes from various forms of tin cans; these writers and politicians and actors who, each in his own fashion, earned their livings from singing the praises of progress and modern technology and who were now watching, enraptured, as the balloon was filled with hydrogen, thereby revealing itself to be, not round, but cigar-shaped and topped by a silver-plated cupola. Seeing the glittering reflection of the afternoon sun on this cupola, one young actress was moved to turn to her neighbor—that great author and subsequent Nobel Prize winner Johannes V. Jensen—point at the huge silken structure rising hesitantly off the ground, and say with a giggle, "It looks like that thing men have between their legs."

Along the side of the balloon, in large letters, ran the legend "Carl Laurids Mahogany. Import—Export." This event must have represented a major investment, and no small risk, on Carl Laurids's part. He may indeed have staked his all on this balloon ascent, which was supposed to secure him goodwill, contacts, and a place in the sun. And hence there is something rather sinister about him on this afternoon. Before, during, and after his speech; during all the backslapping and arm-waving; among all these influential men and lighthearted women—on whom, he must have known, his future depended—his smile and the cordial greetings he dispensed to all and sundry seemed touched by the icy indifference of a man who, even amid such an admiring throng, right in the middle of the most decisive moment of his life, is totally alone.

Right from the start, Carl Laurids had had the confidence of his guests. He may even have gained it in the days before he met them for the first time. There is reason for believing that he had already won them over with the invitations he sent out. At first these had elicited chilly smiles: who was this stranger by the name of Mahogany who had the temerity to send invitations to them? Nevertheless, they eventually accepted, thanks to the handwritten invitations, and that surname, Mahogany (recently assumed by Carl Laurids), and to the words "Import—Export"; none of which betokened anything other than precisely that self-assured ruthlessness for which they were all searching and which they had now found in this boy in his white tie and tails, and his flying helmet.

None of those who were present that afternoon had believed in Carl Laurids. They were not really interested in knowing whether the balloon truly was a gift from von Zeppelin, or what Carl Laurids's airy fortune derived from, or who his family really were. They were interested in something quite different, namely, that very ruthlessness, that overweening belief in oneself, and, perhaps above all else, that coldness about Carl Laurids which every one of them could sense and which filled them with the hope that here, on the champagne cases, was a man who could protect them against the fear which is part of the history of that spring day. Nor were they disappointed, because, from his podium, Carl Laurids let his composure fall upon them like a gentle shower of rain and it was obvious that he understood them; he knew whom he had invited and who had turned up: everyone in Copenhagen and its suburbs who was not afraid to run a risk and whose wealth, like Carl Laurids's—if it did, in fact, exist—was founded on luck and love, or on property speculation; on absolutely anything other than strong family connections or a sound business or a good education. And even those in the crowd who might possibly have had one of these advantages were, notwithstanding, afraid.

It is not easy for me to describe the fear lurking inside these people. It has no definite form—in the way that, for instance, Carl Laurids's balloon has; it is diffuse yet complex; besides which, it lay camouflaged beneath liberally rouged feminine cheeks and tall black moleskin hats and beneath Johannes V. Jensen's view of history, which he is in the act of enlarging upon to the young actress; the gist of his theory being that when the last Ice Age swept down across Scandinavia, all those people who were small and dark traveled south and became Negroes—not to put too fine a point on it, *Negroes*—and those who were tall and broad-shouldered and blue-eyed and had hair on their chest headed north to become forefathers to us, who can, without exaggeration, be called the master race and who dare to take risks.

The disquiet that afternoon was caused, among other things, by things outside Denmark going from bad to worse—particularly in Russia—and Germany's not having as yet signed the peace treaty that would safeguard Danish exports and provide all the Danes with just a smidgen of security; give them a breathing space—right here—after having made their fortunes to the distant musical accompaniment of the shellfire, with the stench of the blood from the trenches in their nostrils. All of that they wanted merely to forget, along with their impoverished beginnings. And it was this forgetfulness which Carl Laurids dispensed to them that day. In the double, testicle-shaped gondola suspended beneath the balloon he had arranged for the serving of a lavish repast, concocted by two French chefs—two international celebrities at whom he fired instructions in authoritative French. The menu consisted of exotic dishes from the remotest colonies, from the very places where wars raged and revolts were staged; from the flashpoints, the sources of all the threats. These dishes were devised and derived from large, dangerous animals, as a way of showing everyone that they could relax; and that is exactly what Carl Laurids said as the last moorings were cast off. He invited them to relax and enjoy this meal; *enjoyment* is the name of the game on this balloon trip. Now, things might be looking pretty ominous on the international front—that he would be the first to admit—but we have plenty of reason to feel well pleased, he said, and to let our hair down, because we have tamed technology, tamed the forces of nature. With the result that I am able to serve giant crabs from Madagascar and elephant consommé and fillets of bear masked with lobster sauce, and an entire stuffed boa constrictor served in its own skin with a Negro warrior in its mouth, a Negro warrior whom it was in the very act of swallowing at the moment of its death, at the second it succumbed to a rifle bullet—a well-aimed shot that also killed the Negro, the kind of shot that will always occur and redeem the situation, said Carl Laurids. And as for the wine, ladies and gentlemen, it's champagne, champagne all the way.

His last words were "Eat, drink, and be merry"—and they did not have to be told twice. These words did not seem to shock anyone, apart from us and one of the prostitutes who had been brought up in a religious home. But neither she nor we can help but view this remark as being yet another cool and detached touch of malice on the part of Carl Laurids, who said it knowing full well that he was quoting Christ's parable of the rich man who decided to eat, drink, and be merry—but whom the Lord warned, tomorrow you die! eat, drink, and be merry, for tomorrow you die!

The balloon was equipped with big gas lamps designed to heat the open gondola to room temperature, enclose the guests within a pleasant bell of light, and make them feel that they were floating in a—in all senses of the word—self-sufficient bubble in space. At the last moment, however, just before Carl Laurids lit the lamps, they had a clear view of Copenhagen. Bathed in the rays of the setting sun, as the city was at that moment, it looked like a gold mine—which indeed it was and had proved to be for most of those present. And yet just then every one of them had the feeling that the city was threatening them; that it also had the look of a grave, or a whirlpool, or some huge beast lying in wait, stiff with menace. Then Carl Laurids lit the lamps and invited them to help themselves from the buffet, and they turned toward one another, in relief, feeling that there was no cause for concern when the world and, for that matter, Denmark contained men of Carl Laurids's caliber, who could mask wild beasts in lobster sauce or cover them with whipped cream or present absolutely anything, anything at all, they thought, on a puff pastry base, even the disturbing fact—which had, until now, been in all their thoughts—that the longshoremen were on strike, despite the eight-hour day, despite the lowering of the voting age, even despite the strike's having been declared illegal by the permanent arbitration tribunal. One of the members of this tribunal —a representative from the employers' association—happened to be among those in the gondola; a slightly built fidget of a man who would later that evening confide to his neighbors that he saw himself as an exorcist and that this time he was going to drive out the demons of communism and syndicalism by fining the longshoremen 800,000 kroner—I repeat, eight hundred thousand—many times more than the cost of this balloon trip. But by that time no one was listening to him; up there, as they floated between heaven and earth, all their worries had been thrown overboard along with the first of the balloon's sandbags.

At the last minute, just before the tall flight of steps leading up to the gondola was rolled away, the last guest arrives—a woman in a white dress, coming toward them across the meadow, fluttering

erratically like a leaf caught by the wind. And that is just what she
is. She has been caught by the wind, and as she draws nearer, the
reason becomes clear: she is thin, alarmingly thin, nothing but skin
and bone. And so, weighing next to nothing, she is totally at the
mercy of the spring breeze that carries her along, in the direction
of Carl Laurids's searching gaze. She manages to latch on to the
steps and, for a split second, hangs there. What she must have seen,
at that moment, was those eyes, scrutinizing her from between a
flying helmet and a white bow tie. What Carl Laurids saw was a
figure reminiscent of the legend, from his childhood, of the White
Lady of Mørkhøj. But both must, in addition, have seen something
else, because, all at once, Carl Laurids climbs out of the gondola
and down the steps, takes her in his arms, and carries her back up
the steps, without her offering any resistance. Once they are inside
the gondola, the steps are wheeled away and the balloon lifts off.
The girl in Carl Laurids's arms was Amalie Teander, and her search
had now led her to him, to no one but him.

To Amalie, the journey she made as a child from Rudkøbing to
Copenhagen had become a triumphal procession. It had been paid
for by the Reverend Mr. Cornelius and by other members of the
family and by a number of other influential townspeople. The official
reason was, of course, that they wanted to redeem the family's good
name, and give Christoffer Ludwig the chance to exercise his en-
trepreneurial skills elsewhere, and let the children have a change
of air, blah, blah, blah. But the real reason why so many dipped
into their pockets—including the family's creditors, who were so
stingy that the coins stuck to the lining—was that having Christoffer
on their doorstep filled them with a sneaking dread. His presence
chafed away at the raw patches on their consciences, reminding
them of the spate of newspapers issued after the Old Lady's funeral.
It made them distrust one another, and society, and the little hand
and the big one, and their own senses. They would not feel safe
until Christoffer was out of sight altogether. It was with no faith in
their own schemes that they raised funds for him, found him an
apartment in Copenhagen, packed up the family's few belongings
—including the printing press that Frederik Teander had won in a
card game; the one that had laid the foundations for the white house
and the water closets and the Old Lady's will—and piled the lot

onto the back of a truck, one of the first trucks in Denmark. And even while they were helping Christoffer aboard, and after him his three daughters, and finally Gumma and her tricycle, they kept expecting that something dreadful would happen: that their scheme would somehow go to pieces, and that Christoffer would turn out to have yet another couple of daggers up his sleeve.

Amalie could sense this dread and it made her smile. It enhanced her departure from Rudkøbing, a departure already distinguished by the large crowd it attracted, just as on the day when the Old Lady granted the townspeople a peek at her new water closet. It came at just the right time for Amalie, who now realized that these people would never understand her. What she was thinking on that chilly autumn morning, as she sat in the back of the truck, was that she had deigned to be born in their town, she had descended to mingle with them, in all modesty, and had let their mirrors and window-panes reproduce her image—her ringlets and her doe eyes—in all modesty. But they had let their chance go by, they had been caught napping, and now it's all over, it's time to leave, they've missed the train, she has left them—together with a radiantly calm and contented Christoffer, Gumma, and her two sisters, who had, here in the triumphal coach, abandoned themselves to numb despair. The previous day, for the first time in their lives, they had had to do their own shopping. They had returned in tears to the Reverend Mr. Cornelius's parsonage (where the family was staying while the business and their financial situation and their life in general were being straightened out) and asked Christoffer, through their sobs, "Why must we suffer so and where is Mother and where is the white house and where are all the servants?" Christoffer had spread his arms wide—his movements had grown somewhat capricious and spasmodic—and replied, "Easy come, easy go!" This remark did little to quell their tears, and I, too, find it a bit much. How can anyone who has just lost his wife—a bankrupt, who has frittered away a family business built up over two generations—say such a thing? But Amalie was delighted by it. She savored it as she warmed herself with the thought of how she and Christoffer had worked together on the last issues of the newspaper. And so, as the truck drove away from the town, and her two sisters and Gumma curled up like animals and went to sleep, it was to her father that Amalie related her dreams of the future.

Her words fell on deaf ears. When Christoffer felt his mother's will crumbling between his fingers, while still hearing her voice continuing to make prognoses, it was the last time in his life that he ever listened properly to anything. He had witnessed the breakdown of clock time and the Old Lady's vain attempt to determine the future, and this had filled him with a distrust of both plans and memories. And so, although he looked lovingly at his youngest daughter, he was not really paying attention to what Amalie was saying.

What she was trying to convey to Christoffer was her picture of the city. What she expected to find in Copenhagen, Amalie explained, was genuine, heroic poverty. This she pictured as consisting of lines of people slowly tramping on and on to the tune of the funeral marches she had heard played in the houses of Rudkøbing. At their head walked gaunt young men with long, flowing locks. Their eyes were fixed on the horizon, as though, out there, they spied victory over their oppressors, whom Amalie pictured as being doctors and clergymen and lawyers. They were followed by weeping mothers and starving children with smoldering eyes, and over the whole scenario hung a faint pall of smoke from the fires of revolution; a smoke screen which, for a while, hides the last group of people from view. They carry a young woman seated in a basket of linked hands; her features are veiled, but this is obviously the queen of the revolution, a Danish Joan of Arc. She draws nearer, close enough for us, and even for Christoffer, to see who she is: yes, someone known both to him and to us—guess who, well, Amalie, of course. And here she is, sitting in the back of a truck, telling her father how sure she is that some new and regal status awaits her.

Now, at this point, Christoffer could have set his daughter straight, or made some sort of protest, but he did not. Everything other than his own inner peace and warmth had lost all significance. Which is why only we are in a position to shake our heads at the absurd arrogance of this girl who, even now at the age of eleven or twelve, believes that the world, even with all its misery, exists solely for her benefit.

It had not been difficult for Amalie to nurture these clear-cut notions of being one of the elect, growing up, as she did, comfortably distanced from reality, in a hothouse environment that gave her no reason to doubt her fantasy of being an orchid in a world of frogs

who never seemed to get around to turning into princes. Her grandmother had always been of the opinion that paupers had only themselves to blame, which is why Amalie had sided with the poor.
Gumma had told her wildly exaggerated tales of the Paris Commune
and of riots in the big cities, and her reading of French novels had
gradually swelled her fantasy even further. All of this had steered
her in the direction taken by so many dreams (though it is counter
to my own), namely, away from reality and toward a hopeless faith
in the People and poverty such as she had never witnessed at close
quarters.

What she found in Copenhagen was normal, everyday life. It lay
waiting for her between tall houses, in Dannebrogs Street—a narrow
street, the nether regions of which lay wrapped in a perpetual chill
and a twilight that knew no season. It was here, in this street, that
an apartment had been found for Christoffer, and it was here that
he opened a small printshop.

Amalie spent just one day searching. For twenty-four hours she
roamed the streets of the city, wide-eyed, looking for the barbed
wire, the guillotine, the barricades, the Commune, and the gaunt
young men. Then she understood. Although "understood" is perhaps not the right word; it might be more correct to say that it dawned
on Amalie Teander that Copenhagen could not meet her demands;
that these people passing her on the street could not live up to her
expectations: they were not dressed in rags; they wore thick gray
overcoats. She could not see herself mirrored in their eyes, nor
glimpse any reflection of the fires of revolution, when they all kept
their eyes on the well-worn paths they followed along the sidewalks;
paths that their fathers had trod, and their fathers before them. There
was nothing to suggest that they would lift her up and carry her on a
basket of hands when they had a hard enough job lugging around
their own worries about making ends meet. Amalie had been expecting to live among factory slaves and coal trimmers and chimney
sweeps' boys and firewood gatherers and little match girls. What she
found were barbers and shopkeepers and pawnbrokers and tradesmen. And all of these extinguished souls were making their way to
cooperages and cigar shops and offices and shops selling caged
birds, which they had taken over from their parents, who had taken
them over from their parents—whose stories, like the cobblestones
and the gray buildings, are lost in the mists of the previous century.

At this point Amalie is in an interesting situation. She is twelve years old, but she is faced with the same painful prospect as so many Danes, both before and after her, who have, like her, grown up in the singular belief that God knows we're not all cut from the same cloth. Her prospect is the prospect of people other than those she had encountered as a child in the bell jar of her conviction that she had been chosen. In there, no one had ever told her that the most obvious place to look for love and recognition is here, right here, close to home—and so it never occurred to her. In her father's printshop, which was set up in a room that lacked both windows and daylight, and on her wanderings through the streets of Copenhagen, Amalie made a choice she was to abide by for a long, long while. Or at least, that is how it seems to me, although I might be mistaken: perhaps Amalie had no choice, perhaps it is my dream, our dream, of the place of free will in history that makes us imagine that Amalie withdrew into her own contempt through choice. Faced with the painful prospect of ordinary people, this little girl actually chooses to stick to her childhood belief in being chosen, regardless of the fact that no one she meets understands her.

With a forgetfulness that was, to Amalie's mind, animal-like, Gumma and her sisters had adapted to their new way of life. Within three days they had stopped crying, within a week their plaintive wails had abated, and a month later Amalie noticed how their evening prayers were filled with sincere contentment with their lot. It was just by chance that she happened to overhear their prayers. Even when she was very small, her inner visions had supplanted the usual picture of paradise. Besides which, she had never had much faith in her mother's insipid accounts of heavenly bliss. Katarina Teander struggled and strove to kindle the faith in her daughters, but, for one thing, her struggles were choked off by fits of coughing, and, for another, Amalie had found that even when her mother spoke of heaven, she seemed to be staring down into her own grave. And so Amalie had decided to trust only her own visions, and had become accustomed to defying every objection and leaving the nursery when her sisters and Gumma were praying—the girls on their knees, with their elbows propped on the bed; Gumma with her hands clasped over the handlebars of her tricycle.

That night, after she had heard their prayers, Amalie did not fall asleep. Wide awake and alert, she lay there in the dark, between

her two sisters and their deep, contented breathing, and allowed the
sense of a wasted life to course through her body. Around daybreak
her patience deserted her. She got out of bed without making a
sound, dressed, and climbed up to the street, from where she could
see the odd star glinting above the rooftops. Then she heard a noise
in the distance, a heavy rumbling, and out of the gloom trundled a
vehicle—a covered wooden cart, drawn by four scraggy horses. Four
men accompanied this vehicle—four old-timers—and the entire
spectacle was enveloped in a prehistoric stench. The cart pulled up
outside the gateway of the building and, without so much as a look
at Amalie, three of the men disappeared into the courtyard. They
reappeared carrying what looked to Amalie like dark bundles, and
it suddenly struck her that they might be robbers, but even as she
thought this she knew it was not the case. She stole a little closer
to one of the men, and when, just at that moment, she saw something
fall from his bundle, something that hit the pavement, she called
out, "You dropped something." The man inclined his face toward
her and said, "You can keep it"; and as he did so, Amalie saw that
this was her great-grandfather, the Old Lady's father, the nightman,
whom she had never met; and she saw that the burdens the three
men toted were, in fact, the building's latrine buckets. Thanks to
this godforsaken part of Copenhagen being one of the few still not
provided with sewers—progress having passed it by—their night soil
was being collected by an apparition to whom she was related.

Prompted by this encounter, Amalie went in search of Christoffer.
He was not in his bed, but she found him in the printshop. He was
sitting at a round table, in the narrow circle of light thrown by an
electric bulb with a lacquered-paper shade, surrounded by a dense
darkness that hid the rest of the room. On one of the first days after
they had moved in, Amalie had walked farther and farther into this
darkness until the lamp was just a bright spot in the distance, and
had then turned back because, instead of walls, she had come upon
an infinite space filled with piles of books and the echoes of Christoffer's anecdotes, and permeated by the dry, acrid scent of paper.
Now she caught her father's eye. "We're not all cut from the same
cloth," she began, and went on to explain her point of view to her
father. She was so sure that he was on her side, that he supported
her and would agree with her that their family—or at any rate she
and he—was surrounded, here, by underdogs and nonentities, who

encircled them like the bars of a prison cell, hindering the development of their own brilliant personalities. And at the same time, these creatures blocked their view of the real people, those burning, uncontrollably crude souls whom she and he, Amalie and Christoffer, would have understood; and who would have understood them, if only they had been able to find one another in this desert of mediocrity that could not even boast a sewer.

Once again, I feel that Christoffer ought to have quashed his daughter's overblown notions, but he did not, even though he found the idea of complaining utterly absurd. Because, here, in this circle of light, beside the little printing press, Christoffer was content, very content, more content than he had ever been before. So he merely waggled his head as an avowal of his love for Amalie, who was describing to him—Papa—the true state of affairs, which, as she saw it, was that she, who had been born to float, had been cooped up between houses which, with every day that passed, crowded closer together around streets populated by people so common that—and at this point the little girl swore for the first time—it might not be such a bad idea to hang the whole damn lot. All these people ever thought about was eating their fill, stuffing their guts with produce from the butchers' shops that made the whole area stink of pork crackling. These people believed—and at this point the little girl swore for the second time—that they could damn well guzzle their way into paradise, or down to hell; or else they were so stingy that they believed they could save their way to it, or fight their way out and up by washing other people's clothes behind windows that were so covered with dust and grime that she, Amalie, could not even see her reflection in them. These people hardly knew what a lavatory was; these people—and at this point she swore for the third time— had nothing but a damn bucket, a bucket, a bucket that had to be emptied by her great-grandfather.

Christoffer regarded his daughter vacantly. He had never understood women and it had never occurred to him that his children might harbor secret hopes. So now, as his youngest daughter presented him with hers, he stared at them, unable to fathom them. That anyone might consider herself to be a cut above her neighbors was beyond him. All his life he had felt that he was inferior to everyone else, and this feeling had stayed with him until those last hectic months when he had edited the *Langeland Times*, and then

it had been replaced by the certainty that he had found his
All he had grasped was that his daughter had come across the
soil cart and that this had scared her. He was in a daze—b
he had lost all sense of time and had worked the long night
through—and the only thing that occurred to him was a song from
his youth, which he now proceeded to sing, in a gentle, cracked
voice, like an adult lulling a child to sleep:

> *"The clock strikes ten and from afar*
> *Comes a rumbling that gives you the jitters.*
> *It could be thunder, it could be a war*
> *Or just a good dose of the skitters.*
> *Here it comes, it's drawing near*
> *Out of the night; what have we here?*
> *Why! There you have them, clear as clear,*
> *Our trusty chums the old nightmen!"*

For a moment, Amalie stared at her father, and in that moment she
made her final decision; in that moment all contact was severed and
this little girl made the decision which was, for someone of her age,
such an unreasonable one: that when it came to finding forests,
animals, and worldwide devotion, you had to do it alone.

The next day, Amalie stopped eating. She threw away her school
lunch bag, and during the evening meal she watched, intent but
passive, as Christoffer Teander and Gumma and her two sisters ate
fried salt pork with parsley sauce. The days went on, and still she
did not eat a thing. Every morning she made up the sandwiches for
her lunch, and then gave them away at school, in order to watch
with interest as her classmates polished them off. And every evening
she sat at the dinner table, silent and impassive, while her family ate.

Initially, people around her were perturbed. Gumma peered into
her eyes and far down into her throat, looking for signs of illness,
and at school the teachers approached her desk and felt her forehead, but after a while they left her alone. There was no denying
that she grew thinner and thinner, but she was as conscientious as
ever and much sweeter and more pleasant. Besides, fasting was the
furthest thing from anyone's mind. So the schoolteachers were sure
that she ate at home, while Gumma comforted herself with the
thought that at least she ate her lunch at school.

Actually, what had happened was that Amalie had decided to
starve her way through adolescence. And even though she feels that
she is entirely alone, she thereby falls into the same category as a
number of other Danes, a category composed mainly of women,
and most particularly of young girls who dream that the best way
of demonstrating their individuality is to put their skeletons on display. Offhand, this may seem like a crazy idea—I mean, if there is
one thing we all have in common it is our bones, and no two things
are more alike than a couple of walking skeletons. But on closer
inspection, the attraction in starving oneself becomes easier to understand; closer inspection reveals that the starveling is in fact rewarded with a new inner plumpness, and that is what happened to
Amalie. After a few days she was overwhelmed by a giddy weightlessness, like an intoxicant that sharpened her hearing and amplified
the distant music that had rung in her ears since childhood. And
gradually, as the weeks went by, the world around her grew a little
vague. Her inner landscapes, on the other hand, grew more and
more distinct until finally, one day, after three months of total fasting, when she was on her way to school, they stood out quite clearly.
It happened just as Amalie stopped outside a shop—I do not know
which one—and just as the clouds were dispersed by the sun of a
season that is not clear in my mind because there was a vagueness
to the seasons in that part of town, and because Amalie had lost all
sense of the weather. Thus the only thing that registered with her
was that the sun could now penetrate her closed eyelids and disturb
her visions. She lifted her hand up to shade her eyes, and when the
sun shone right through the palm of her hand, making her bones
stand out like sharply etched silhouettes on one of those modern
X-ray pictures, she realized that she was now at death's door.

She is standing on an edge, the edge before the void, and as she
now walks on, mechanically, toward school she is still teetering on
the brink of the precipice, unable to decide. She is tempted by that
enticing music—it is stronger than ever now—but at the same time
it gladdens her to walk like this, lost in her exclusive, blossoming
giddiness. And when, a few minutes later, she makes her move, it
is back toward life that she turns—with just the shortest, the daintiest
of steps—the credit for which must go to the piece of licorice root
she most graciously accepts from a girl who sits next to her in class.
This girl, whose name she has never bothered to discover, runs a

little business in the form of a dish of sugared water in which, for a small fee, she would restore pieces of chewed licorice to their former power and glory. Hence it is this tiny drop of sugared water that for a while brings Amalie Teander back to the classroom, the sun, and life with the rest of us.

From then on, and through the years that follow, she evolves into an artist, a starvation artist. When people in the outside world, or Gumma, or her sisters offer her anything, especially anything to eat, she will as a rule, and quite decidedly, say no, no thank you, I don't feel like it, take it away. But now and again she will say yes, a very tiny yes. By dint of this alternation between a large number of refusals and a very few acceptances she learns to play upon her body as a musician plays upon his instrument or, to give a more exact representation of her particular megalomania, as a conductor plays upon his orchestra. She becomes an artist who can advance upon death by starvation in little leaps, only at the last minute to backtrack toward life by means of a hard candy or a piece of fruit or just a cup of tea with lemon.

On two occasions during these years, the district medical officer visited the school to examine the girls. Amalie was the first to be seen, since their names were called according to their ranking in class: in other words, by their cleverness. Amalie's position at the head of her class had never been threatened, partly because she was a quick learner and partly because her teachers interpreted her giddy air of distraction as a sign of quiet intelligence. Consequently, both they and her classmates treated her with a respect and a consideration that were not without a trace of fear, all of which suited Amalie perfectly, when she was in a fit state to perceive it. When the doctor put his stethoscope to her chest and heard her bones grating against each other at the joints, he had her admitted to the hospital. In a white hospital room Amalie's hallucinations merged with reality, to the point where she believed that the room, the bed, and the two nurses were all a part of her own true paradise. As a reward for their efforts she allowed them to talk her into eating more than she normally did, until her weight increase caused them to lose interest in her. Then she left the hospital. Some years later, when the doctor wanted to admit her again, she said no—a pure and simple no —with the same authority as that with which she declined food. The doctor did not dare to argue with her. Instead he explained,

in a long letter to Christoffer Ludwig, that from a professional standpoint his daughter was as good as dead. He made the mistake of
giving the letter to Amalie herself to take home. That same afternoon
she threw the letter away because she was in the middle of an
interesting experiment and did not wish to be disturbed. This experiment consisted of an investigation into whether it was possible
to survive on half a cup of strong black coffee per day. She also
threw it away because it predicted that her growth would be stunted
and her development inhibited. And so we and Amalie are the only
ones ever to learn its content.

The doctor was proved wrong. No matter how absurd it may
sound, Amalie's physical development followed its natural course.
She grew to normal height, and going by what happened later, there
is reason to believe that if she had not been so alarmingly emaciated,
so atrociously thin, she would have looked just like any young girl.
Instead she resembled a walking scarecrow with eyes that glowed,
deep in their sockets, like carbon arc lamps. At school she was
continually having to shift position in her chair because she did not
sit, as the others did, on muscle and fat, but right on her protruding
bones. Nevertheless she grew at the same rate as other girls of her
age, and never, not once, did she succumb to pneumonia or tuberculosis or any of malnutrition's other faithful companions in the
Copenhagen of the early twentieth century. And contrary to all that
is reasonable, and in spite of the doctor's professional standpoint,
her first menstrual period also arrived. So copiously did she bleed
that it all but killed her—in toying with her own health, she had
not foreseen this eventuality. It came at a time when she really could
not afford to relinquish anything at all, and certainly not this sudden,
unexpected trickle of blood. She told no one about it but stanched
it with a cotton rag and accounted for it, to herself, by seeing it as
a parallel to Christ's tears of blood in the garden of Gethsemane.

If one asks oneself, as I have so often done, why her family did
not somehow try to get through to her, then the best answer I can
give is that they were suffering from that Danish family syndrome
which we all fear: to be, at one and the same time, so close to one
another, and yet so far apart, that there is no possibility of helping.
Amalie had finally distanced herself from Gumma and from her
sisters—against whose puppy fat and, later, mature bodies she usually warmed her chilly, fleshless frame at night—and she had, in a

sense, despaired of her father. In order not to founder on her tremendous disappointment over his failure to transform her into Cleo-
patra or a revolutionary queen or at least into a dazzling success,
and over his failure to bring her to a temple or a palace or the
barricades—not even to a big white villa on Strand Drive—she had
placed him in a drawer in that strange highboy where so many of
us hide our dreams. Packed away with him in this drawer were the
images of that unfortunate citizen, the total failure, who is neither
a proper businessman nor a proper father, nor yet a proper man.
Instead he is something of a wimp, a weed, of whom the best that
can be said is that he is kind to animals and always wraps up warmly.
Such a way of perceiving another human being is always risky;
bottom-drawer perceptions are always risky, and in Christoffer Ludwig's case they did not go nearly far enough, because Amalie had,
thereby, overlooked her father's powerful imagination, his mastery
of time, and his great love of the world—all attributes that she, in
her fit of pique, had forgotten and was no longer capable of recognizing. Sometimes on sleepless nights she relived their brief collaboration in Rudkøbing. Once again she would see him hunched over
his articles or the printing press, or standing beside the big desk in
the act of reading his proposal aloud to the Old Lady. Sometimes,
when this happened, Amalie would get up and walk across the cold
floors and into Christoffer's bedroom to look at her father. But she
always went back to bed deeply disappointed, convinced that her
memory must be playing tricks on her, because—lying there in the
wan light from the street in his white nightshirt, and with his cat,
Mussovsky, spread in slumber across his chest—Christoffer looked
like nothing at all. In sleep his features were so slack that to Amalie
he looked just like a defenseless baby, and in them she could read
nothing other than the grounds for her own disillusionment.

And so we arrive at the moment when she sees him for the last
time, or at any rate the last time in a long while.

This encounter took place in the printshop. Amalie did not exactly
know why she went there; nevertheless she did so, wending her way
along a narrow corridor of books, which seemed to have piled up
without anyone's being able to say how they came to be there, and
which now made it difficult to gain access to the room with no walls
where Christoffer sat, as always, at the round table. Its surface was
now hidden under a thick layer of orders to which he had never

responded and forms he had never completed and final demands he had never read, and the paper cutouts of mythical creatures that he had recently gone back to producing. The sole aid to timekeeping in the room of this man—who had once upon a time endeavored to pin his life down to a tolerance of less than half a second—was a tear-off calendar displaying a date from two years before. On this occasion, Amalie did not speak to her father; she merely stood there, having her prejudices reinforced. Then she turned and left.

Walking out of the printshop and down the narrow corridor, she stepped straight into her last day at school. Now, this is a physical impossibility, because her school was situated some way from her home. Nevertheless, even if this does seem likely to be a halluci-nation brought about by her famished state, still we must respect it because what we are going by here is Amalie's mind and not the Copenhagen street directory. And so, as I was saying, Amalie stepped straight from her father's printshop into the school auditorium.

At various times in Amalie's life it happens that she walks in upon a party in celebration of something or other, although always just a little on the late side. And so it is on this occasion as she enters the auditorium and quietly finds her place among all the other people. At first she understands nothing. She has not eaten for three days, which is why she catches only very brief flashes of what is going on around her. These flashes seem to show her what she is used to seeing: the principal making a speech, the students singing, and the teacher walking along the rows to pull the hair of those not singing clearly—although of course she bypasses Amalie. No one pulls Amalie's hair. Then something begins to filter through to her: she sees that the flag is flying outside and it dawns on her that it is springtime. Then she enters into the situation and realizes that this is the last day of school; that all these children sitting here in front of her are waiting to receive their diplomas, waiting for their pre-dictable futures to overtake them. Amalie knows how they picture these futures. She knows that these girls have built themselves flimsy, illogical dreams out of cheap romances: dreams that leave only one question unanswered, that being whether the man who comes to carry them off will be a doctor or a lawyer. This knowledge makes Amalie smile superciliously, here amid this assembly of red-cheeked, shiny-eyed, white-clad girls, her contemporaries. She delights in her splendid insight into what awaits these country bumpkins: the Institute for Domestic Servants, factory work, apprenticeships to tobacconists, and a life of interminable grayness.

And then she hears her own name. The headmistress calls it out, and a moment later the summons comes again. Amalie focuses with some difficulty on the stout figure of the principal, Lady So-and-so, who is standing in front of a large picture depicting Delling opening the gates of morning, and realizes that it is she who is being referred to, that she is a hairsbreadth away from having to walk up to the podium and receive something or other. She is never quite sure what. It might be a prize for diligence, or a reward for keeping quiet, or for being so well behaved year in, year out, or for top marks in the school-leaving exam. Amalie has no chance to hear what it might be because, just at that moment, she sees herself and her own contempt from the outside. All at once her image of herself as something ethereal and unique—as someone at death's door, rendered transparent by their own inner life—crumbles away, and instead she sees a dreadfully thin girl, sitting in the midst of this blithe company, sniggering and mocking her companions with a smile that is idiotic, condescending, and full of the smug conviction that she is something quite special, because she has starved herself and because she thinks she has seen through the banality of existence.

This clarity lasted only for an instant, but in that instant Amalie was overwhelmed by self-loathing. She was called to the podium, but by then she was gone. She had disappeared so swiftly and discreetly that no one had noticed, not even the girl sitting next to her who passed her hand two or three times through the air above the chair Amalie had vacated to make sure that they were not simply overlooking her because she had grown even thinner and more transparent. But sure enough, Amalie had left the hall. The moment that she had seen this vision of herself as a fool, she had walked out of the hall and into that picture representing the last day at school as being somehow special, a red-letter day; as being a time for rebellion or clarification, or for making decisions such as the one Amalie has now made—which is that she wants to die.

Without touching up the impartial picture I am here attempting to paint of Amalie I still cannot help but wonder, again, that something as elusive as unfulfilled, grandiose ambitions can drive someone like Amalie to the kind of despair that now moved her to lean into the wind and surrender herself: a despair there was now every reason to take seriously. Previously, Amalie had been acting out some sort of tragedy in which she had endeavored to carve out a place for herself in life and to extort admiration and sympathy from the outside world. But now she had given up; now she no longer believed that all of this could lead anywhere. And if she occasionally checked her dash through the city by grabbing hold of streetcar stops or railings along the way, it was not in an effort to stay upright but solely in order to be quite sure she would have time to appreciate fully how it felt to die.

The city seemed to her to be deserted. As life was departing from her, as the toes of her shoes were being dragged along the pavement and, at times, lifted free of it, she perceived Copenhagen to be devoid of life. There was no traffic in the streets; houses and stores stood empty; the statues seemed more animated than anything else. As the wind swept Amalie through the outskirts of the city and out of it altogether, she instinctively saw the grim irony in that she, who had, ever since she was just a little girl, pictured herself wallowing for life in a sort of bubble bath of other people's admiration, should die, at the age of seventeen, with no one looking on.

Now, it cannot be the case that the city was deserted. This notion must be put down to hallucinations arising from Amalie's weakened state. From anyone else's point of view, Copenhagen was jam-packed with cars and bicycles and pedestrians and horse-drawn vehicles, many of which now had to brake and veer around her as she was carried through the streets like a withered leaf. She got in the way of a march of girls her own age demonstrating for the right of women to join the ministry, and a hansom cab driven by Adonis Jensen—although that is only mentioned here as an interesting coincidence. The passengers of the cab, all of them attired in frock coats and top hats, had just returned from the big peace conference in Paris, at which they had represented Denmark. Among their number, strange as it may seem, was H. N. Andersen, privy counselor and Adonis's secret brother. The two brothers did not recognize each other on this occasion either.

At this point Amalie lost consciousness, and all her actions thereafter were carried out as though in her sleep.

When she awoke she was lying down, and Carl Laurids was leaning over her. He had forced a few drops of brandy between her bloodless lips, and this spirit was now running through her veins like a river of molten metal. She studied him carefully, then turned her head away dismissively, closed her eyes, and fainted once more. When the brandy seared her mouth for a second time she opened her eyes, and this time took a look at her surroundings. The gondola was bathed in golden light. The last rays of the setting sun had tinted the sea dark red, and on the shining horizon she could see the misty silhouette of Copenhagen rising like distant blue mountains. In the darkness beyond Carl Laurids's face she could just make out the huge form of the balloon, moving gently in the evening breeze. The whole craft seemed to be swimming through the ether. Six musicians dressed all in white were standing on a dais, playing waltzes, and it occurred to Amalie that she must be dead. At long last, and more by accident than by design, she had crossed over to the other side, which she had, until now, only ever beheld from afar. She thought she recognized the music playing around her and the scent of food fried in butter and the flashing of the women's jewelry and Carl Laurids's soothing touch and the taste of brandy. At long last she had died and at long last she had entered that paradise which she had spent her whole life gazing upon and which was— one hundred percent—her due.

Carl Laurids did not sit with her for long. He had other things to see to. He had lifted her on board on the spur of the moment, on a whim. He was the sort of person who could afford to trust his intuition and give in to playful impulses because chance was never allowed to gain the upper hand in a life he was convinced he ran with forethought and common sense. Which is why he administered some brandy to Amalie and watched as she closed her eyes coyly and swooned; and why he called her back to life once more and stared, with a smile on his lips, at her thinness and listened with half an ear to her disjointed story of water closets and rare beasts and a long journey and distant purple forests. Then he asked one of the waiters to keep an eye on her and went back to his guests.

He was under the impression, when he turned away from Amalie, that he had forgotten her. Without the slightest suspicion of what lay in store for him, he circulated among his guests, greeting this one and that, immersing himself in the warmth and the enjoyment evinced by these businessmen dancing or chatting to the prostitutes;

and the representative of the employers' association divulging the names of leading syndicalists whose arrest was in the offing; and Johannes V. Jensen, the writer, who was warning the young actress against the threat from homosexuals, while his right hand was struggling to prevent his left from feeling its way up the tight jersey trousers of the young waiters. Nodding and smiling to right and left, Carl Laurids stepped up onto the dais, in front of the musicians—not to interrupt the festivities but rather to give them an added boost; to show that he was still monitoring the proceedings and that they could all abandon themselves to one another and the food and the champagne and the music and the feeling of simply floating. And at that moment he felt a sudden pain in the left side of his chest. At first he was convinced he had been shot, and while he was reeling and trying to regain his balance he fumbled under his tailcoat for the little snub-nosed revolver he always carried. Only then, as his hand ran across his shirtfront and his fingers told him that it was as dry, white, and stiff as when he had put it on, did he realize that the pain and trembling were caused, not by any outside agency, but by the beating of his own heart. He managed to get off the dais without anyone noticing anything untoward. He found a glass of champagne on a table and drained it while cold-bloodedly registering how his hands shook uncontrollably and the wine tasted like water. Not since his childhood bouts of scarlet fever and measles had Carl Laurids ever been sick, and since he was quite convinced that his willpower and self-confidence formed an impenetrable armored shield around him, he came to the conclusion that one of his guests had succeeded in poisoning him, and that the poison had now reached his heart. With his hand on the butt of his revolver, he embarked upon a slow progress from one huddle of guests to the next, looking for a pair of shifty, and obviously guilty, eyes—so that he might have the chance to avenge himself, here on the deck of the gondola, before the poison devoured him from within and felled him like an overcooked vegetable at the height of his popularity.

During these moments when the fear of death has Carl Laurids in its clutches, he looks like an animal. Hunched up, making no attempt to conceal the revolver that he cleans and oils and loads with small, evil-looking lead projectiles every morning—including

this morning—he moves from group to group looking for his murderer, only to find nothing other than frenzied gaiety unfolding like
a flower. At this moment I am tempted to say, there you are, now
Carl Laurids is showing his real self, now his thin shell of humanity
has cracked and he is reduced to nothing but a mass of instinct;
now the cynic displays his true nature, consisting of fear and hate
in equal parts. And that is precisely what the writer Johannes V.
Jensen is thinking. He is the only person in the gondola who is sober
enough to see that something is wrong with Carl Laurids. Furthermore, all those trashy novels he had written in his youth had
given plenty of practice in the study of human nature, helped by a
handful of crude theories that he now employs in explaining to the
young actress, damned if we're not going to see some action now,
see, there's the beast, there's your instinctive, bloodthirsty proletar-
ian, and with a giant club of a revolver in his hand; now all the
parasites and petty hucksters will be wiped off the face of the earth,
because here's someone looking for revenge, and that someone is
Carl Laurids.

This view of that moment, and indeed of Carl Laurids in particular, complies with a dream we all have, and that is the dream of
being able to say that certain people are inhuman. But in this case,
in this case at least, it is a poor explanation. Here, in the gondola,
high above Copenhagen, we are never going to get anywhere near
Carl Laurids by declaring him to be a beast, when, during these
minutes, what is making him tremble and bringing the palms of his
hands out in a cold sweat and causing him to peer searchingly into
flushed and powdered and expectant faces that take neither his dour
demeanor nor his revolver seriously is not in fact a thirst for revenge
but the fear of losing something. Carl Laurids, too, is just about to
recognize that this is the case, after having made a survey of all his
guests without coming up with anything other than what he himself
pulled out all the stops to achieve: intoxication, lechery, gourman-
dise, abandonment, gratitude, and a tenuous, short-lived sense of
security—all suspended beneath the huge balloon. Having passed
the last of the Romeos and Juliets—who have hung their furs and
tailcoats over the gas lamps and subsided onto the darkness of the
divans—and the last of the barons—so drunk on champagne that
they have forgotten their newly purchased titles and have rediscov-

ered their identities as cattle drovers and are swearing and arm-
wrestling and finger-pulling and hanging one-armed over the edge
of the gondola—Carl Laurids arrives at the wickerwork chaise
longue on which Amalie is lying. And here he stops, because his
symptoms vanish: his heart slows down, his palms dry up, and he
notices that he is hungry. He clips the revolver back into place next
to his waistcoat pocket and tells himself that he has suffered some
sort of inexplicable attack that has now, absolutely and most definitely, blown over.

But actually this was only the beginning. No matter how strange
it may sound, by that time Carl Laurids was a goner. Even though
I harbor serious doubts about Fate, I would say that, just then, Carl
Laurids's hour had come. And what lay in store for him was love.
Not the contradictory turn-of-the-century dream of languorous,
ever-faithful wives and spirited but steady and strong-willed husbands; nor yet our ideal of two mature and liberated individuals
striding side by side, heads held high, into the pale green future.
What faced Carl Laurids Mahogany and Amalie Teander was a
romantic quagmire, a steamy morass of emotions that would never
become clear.

If anyone had told Carl Laurids this—now, in his moment of
triumph, just when he had regained his equilibrium—he would have
given an affable but dismissive wave of his hand. He was back on
top, back on a firm footing. He winked roguishly at Amalie and
promised himself that if he remembered this pale-faced girl after
they had landed, he would have her fed up so that he could com-
memorate the success of this balloon trip by screwing her, without
running the risk of knocking the last spark of life out of her frail
body. Then he gave the balloonist the order to take the balloon
tenderly back and down, while he made the rounds of his guests,
ensuring that no one would be disturbed by the noise of the pro-
peller shaft, or by the fierce hiss of the hydrogen being released.
He knew, you see, that for these people—who were all fundamen-
tally neurotic and plagued by constipation and various, baffling types
of nervous disorder—a soft, imperceptible landing was every bit as
important as the ascent. To his satisfaction, he found that the party
had been such a success that they did not even notice the landing.
Their screeching and singing and cheering, together with the racket
from the orchestra, which had now turned to playing jazz—some of

the first jazz ever played in Copenhagen—completely drowned out the engine noise and the bumps and hissing of the valves.

As Carl Laurids carried Amalie off in a cab, the party was still going strong in the glittering gondola, now tethered in the meadow; and far down Strand Drive, as they drove through that beautiful night, they could still hear the scintillating music.

Carl Laurids had the cab drive to the grand and expensive Hotel d'Angleterre (designed by Meldahl, of course), where he hired the bridal suite for Amalie. That he should have headed for this hotel in particular seemed rather rash, since it was from here that he had, only the year before, absconded from the biggest hotel bill ever reneged upon in Denmark. It was not all that long since he had been forced to pay up, after a lengthy lawsuit, and the astronomical bill itself still hung in its frame above the receptionist's desk in the foyer, as a warning to all and perhaps also as an extravagant joke totally befitting such an ostentatious establishment. I think, in other circumstances, Carl Laurids would have been ejected on the spot, and it is, at any rate, hard to imagine the hotel's welcoming him with open arms after that traumatic lawsuit. To begin with, the police had found it almost impossible to track him down; then the magistrate's court had even more difficulty in establishing whether he was solvent, whether there actually were any funds to draw upon behind all the trade names and companies that had screened his business activities during the two years since he had come to Copenhagen from Mørkhøj. Nonetheless, Carl Laurids is now met by nothing but open arms and courtesy, and this, I think, must be put down to the aura of confidence that surrounds him. With every hour that has gone by since he met Amalie his spirits have risen, until by now he is irrepressible—although he cannot say why he should have been seized by such restless euphoria, or why this should put it into his head that of course she'll stay at the d'Angleterre, it's the obvious place for fattening her up. This confidence is the only explanation I can offer for everything's passing off as well as it does —and some such explanation is necessary, since Carl Laurids meets no opposition whatsoever. Quite the contrary: everyone rushes to his assistance. The doormen hold the door open for him, the receptionists gush and grin fatuously, and the bellhops just about fall over one another in their efforts to locate his nonexistent baggage.

At one point a glimpse can also be caught, in this chaotic picture, of the maître d'hôtel saluting politely and the chef promising something or other now lost to posterity. Perhaps even the manager is there at one point, as if just to let Carl Laurids know that nobody here bears a grudge, and that even if no great amount of water has flowed under the bridge since he last tried to rob the hotel, rest assured, he can feel welcome here.

Through this tableau strides Carl Laurids, and in a way this scene can be regarded as symbolic of his progress through life during these years. The stage set—this hotel, the d'Angleterre—tries to convey an impression of deep-rooted nobility, while in fact it is nothing but a series of façades recently thrown together by Meldahl, that son of the proletariat. The idea was to create an environment in which Copenhagen's *nouveaux riches* could rub shoulders with its old shabby-genteel bourgeoisie and its bankrupted aristocracy, thus finding just a little of that security they all seek, the security Carl Laurids provides. This must be why he is admitted to this stage set that night; this must be why the waiter and the maître d'hôtel and the hotel manager and the receptionists bow before this man who does not even have any baggage. It is a dream of self-assurance, the early-twentieth-century dream of being allowed to bow down to a personality, if only it is strong enough.

And even to us, today, there is something alluring about this scene. There is something both modern and romantic about Carl Laurids's entrance. Imagine: he gains admittance to and residence in the most expensive hotel in Copenhagen, late one night, after a trip in a balloon; arriving with nothing except his beloved and, of course, his famous boyish charm—though probably without any prospect of being able to pay the bill! But once we have said this, if the picture is to be complete, then it is necessary to say something else: to add that there is also something comical about the whole situation; about Amalie, opening her eyes now and then, only to languorously close them again after having reassured herself that she is still in paradise; and above all about Carl Laurids, this gallant in his leather helmet and flying goggles. In his manic euphoria, he winks at the receptionist, blows a kiss to his old hotel bill, waves to the manager—not saying a word, but making it quite clear that he has come back here, of all places, because he has a mind to put his own immortality to the test. That, and because he doubts whether the little shrinking violet he has brought here has ever seen the like of this jerry-built whorehouse, and because it is going to be such a pleasure—heh, heh—to screw her in that bridal suite, where he has had so many other sweet young things before her. And the funniest thing of all is that by this time Carl Laurids is in fact floundering in the net; these fine airs of his are, in truth, convulsive twitches; as soon as Amalie looked at him for the first time—back there in the balloon, just before she turned her head away—something happened to him. That is what he is trying to cover up in the early hours of that morning, as the spring sun is rising over the Citadel and over the Royal Theater (another of those pies in which Meldahl had a finger); as he calls for a doctor, a specialist, a professor, to fatten up Amalie—someone who can turn this little cigar into a match for Daddy. And, of course, Carl Laurids gets his doctor and his nurse and a chaperone and even a cook, whose sole task will be to prepare dishes for Amalie from the diet prescribed by the doctor. Carl Laurids himself visits her once a day, then twice, then three times, then four, then five, and then as often as he can, not because this little escapade means anything special to him—far from it—but because the idea of this little Pygmalion story excites his curiosity; because just three-five-seven-ten-fifteen times a day he needs to see how she is getting on, his little chick, his spur-of-the-moment sweetheart. And the feelings he cherishes for her are really no more than ripples on the surface of that ocean of will and ambition harbored in the depths of his soul.

And it is precisely because she means nothing more to him than a little bit of fun to brighten his arduous existence that he can set the stage for her seduction as though it were a gala performance. He has the bridal suite lit by two hundred candles, and two silver ice buckets containing Dom Pérignon set next to the bed, along with platters of oysters—which he himself has never much cared for, but which fill the bedroom with an interesting aroma just right for what is about to happen: he, Carl Laurids Mahogany, is going to harvest this little pearl and then he is going to drop her, because, to him, the world is full of pearls and there's nothing in the least bit special about this one.

Rosy-cheeked and moist-eyed, Amalie smiles at him from the bed; she has put on weight, grown plump; he has had her dressed in a yellow basque made fashionable by the great diva Dagmar

Andersen, and in this she looks quite enchanting. She looks like, and is, a fruit ripe for the plucking—by Carl Laurids, in his studiedly nonchalant lounge suit. Beneath his casual veneer lurk the most painstaking of preparations. He has bathed and dabbed his underarms with eau de cologne and scrubbed his teeth with tooth powder and had his nails manicured and his beard shaved—though the sparse growth of this last presents a sad reminder that he is still not quite out of the throes of puberty. All in all, he has prepared for this coupling as a surgeon prepares for a tricky operation; without for one moment realizing that all these preparations represent one massive attempt to distance himself from the girl smiling up at him from the bed.

The date is June 15, the day on which, approximately seven hundred years earlier, the Danish colors fell from the skies—so nothing should go wrong. Nevertheless, as he crosses to the bed, Carl Laurids is aware that his interest in this girl remains fixed at eye level, that it will not spread to the rest of his body, and that for the first time in his life he is completely and utterly impotent.

What Carl Laurids had been hit by on that spring night, amid the two hundred candles and the champagne on ice and the scent of oysters and all the other symbols of irresistible masculine potency, was love. It had happened just as he lifted Amalie into the gondola, laid her on the chaise longue, and leaned over her. She had opened her eyes and recognized him as one of the young men who had been calling to her from her inner paradise her whole life long. Then she had turned her head away in dismissal and closed her eyes. And the thought that crossed her mind just before she lost consciousness, in the second immediately succeeding her first rush of happiness, was something along the lines of, So, he's here at last, is he, well, he certainly took his time about it and I really don't know whether I feel like talking to him, can't it wait till another day—and then she fainted. But Carl Laurids had taken it all in: both the admiration, which he was used to, and the flirtatiousness, with which he had never previously been faced and which shocked him that much more, coming as it did, from someone at death's door. And while he was trying to bring her back to life with a few more drops of cognac, while the balloon rose and rose, climbing toward the sunset, Carl Laurids tumbled into the abyss that yawned between Amalie Teander's adoration and her rejection.

During that fleeting moment when Amalie first opened her eyes and recognized the man in her life, then retreated into her own swoon—as if to say, I really don't have time for this, not right now—Carl Laurids encountered resistance on the part of a woman for the first time in his life. At Mørkhøj and, later on, in Copenhagen, he had learned that, like other people, women could be manipulated like tools. Being governed by values that were worthless, they were on the lookout for someone to whom nothing was sacred; and he had always been that someone—until he saw Amalie turn her head away dismissively. Or there may be another explanation for his falling in love: that for the first time, in Amalie, he found someone as ruthlessly egoistic as himself. A third explanation would be that from the first time their eyes met she had shown him a love that also embodied rage. And there is a fourth, and a fifth, and a sixth explanation—but none of them is as enlightening as the actual sequence of events. What happened was that Carl Laurids visited the bridal suite and Amalie, whose health was steadily improving, every day. He no longer ordered the candles to be lit, and after a while he also stopped the champagne, once he realized that alcohol had no effect whatsoever on his potency. He would chat condescendingly with Amalie, teasing her about her past; but he never listened to her answers, because his attention was turned inward, upon himself. All the while, as he was sending the nurse and the chaperone out of the room, and throwing his yellow gloves and his cane onto the furniture, and watching Amalie's lips move, he was like a tiger: lying in wait for his lust, which absolutely refused to manifest itself. Each day he left the hotel frustrated and forcing a smile. He swung his cane and tried to enjoy the summer weather; tried greeting passersby of his acquaintance, whistling a vaudeville tune, and thinking about his business—anything at all, so long as it stopped him from doing what he always did: getting drawn into endless monologues addressed to Amalie Teander. His fantasies always followed a particular pattern. He imagined sending her away, telling her, Your time's up, young lady, Daddy's paid for everything, and now you have ten minutes, I repeat, ten minutes, to get out of here. And as for me, I'm off, I'm a busy man, the world's waiting, I have to move on, I don't have time to waste on a little nun like you who's never even tickled my fancy; as far as I'm concerned, the world's full of women. Carl Laurids then pictured himself striding briskly away without a backward glance. But this monologue was always supplanted by another in which he added, Now, if you're ever short of cash, sweetheart, if you need your streetcar fare or fancy a piece of gateau at La Glâce, just you pop up to Daddy's office. Because if there's one thing we've no shortage of it's money. You just come to me. And Carl Laurids pictured himself helping her and her family, and the two of them walking side by side in a forest. Suddenly they come to a halt and she looks up at him with tears in her eyes . . . and here the fantasy always came to an end, just at this point, because he could not imagine what it would be like to kiss her. And always he would discover that he had been wandering aimlessly; that he was now halfway to Amager, or walking along Langelinie, or standing in the middle of Frederiksberg—far away from his office in Rosengården, where he was expected—up to his neck in confused and wildly romantic reveries which were intoxicating while they lasted but which left him with a dreadful hangover of self-loathing.

One morning Amalie received Carl Laurids fully dressed. She had dismissed the cook and the professor and the chaperone and the nurse, and she told Carl Laurids, with the air of a queen, that it had been interesting to make his acquaintance but now she had to leave; then went on to remark, coolly, that, as a real lady, she was not sure whether she should allow herself to remain alone with him in a strange hotel room. Carl Laurids looked over her shoulder, out of the window. The curtains were pulled back and a white-hot sun shone through the french windows, filling the room with suffocating heat and the illusory feel of a Sunday morning. From the street rose the distant clatter of horses' hooves and metal-rimmed wheels on cobblestones, and of a car being started with a crank handle. In sudden, wild delight at the distance she had put between them he took his first step toward her. They met halfway. With his first move, Carl Laurids managed to rip off her coat. With the second he tore off her dress, petticoat, and bodice. There then followed an involuntary and comical hiatus. She might not have been wearing a corset, but the basque which he himself had bought for her in Magasin du Nord—and which had cost a small fortune—was made of a silky stuff which, though cobweb-fine to the touch, resisted all his attempts to rip it apart. His eyes met Amalie's. Her dark curls shone in the sunshine, and from under her half-closed eyelids came a look of such scorn that fear of interruption sent a red streak of

madness flashing across his brain and he ripped the basque from
top to bottom. She bit his shoulder, hard, to keep him from going
berserk; then they dragged each other down onto the hotel bed,
whispering little curses while she teased him and urged him on by
saying no and yes at the right moments.

It took the sound of someone crying to bring them back to reality
and the realization that it was they who were still whimpering. Carl
Laurids lay still for no more than a moment. Then he shook himself
free of his vacant stupor. Filled with quiet triumph, he rose, dressed,
tied his bow tie, combed his hair, picked up his hat and gloves, and
walked out of the room without once looking at Amalie. He paid
the bill at reception—where the cash for that came from is something
to which we will return—and stepped out into the street. Whistling
in the dusty summer heat, he left the hotel behind while rational-
izing, explaining away, the upheaval into which his life had been
thrown over the past few weeks. The result of some minor biological
disorder, that's what it had been—brought about by certain chemical
changes—the consequence, he told himself straight, of pent-up lust.
So obsessed had he been with this odd Cinderella, this strange little
hunk of flesh, that he had neglected his love life. That was why he
had been so restless, why his keen powers of perception had been
blurred; sexual humors had built up in his blood—here he vaguely
recalled an article he had read on the subject—and this had over-
ridden his thought processes. Now, however, he had expended the
malignant juices; he was his old self again, fancy-free, unattached,
virile. The past was behind him, the future spread before him, he
had left that little canary for the last time, without saying goodbye,
without so much as a kiss. She'd got her comeuppance, got what
she needed of a four-letter word beginning with D. The score between them had been settled, and now he had to move on. Carl
Laurids flashed a roguish, carefree smile at a couple of passing
housemaids. Of course, she could always come to him if she needed
money, he told himself, no problem there. She could always be sure
of a bit of pin money if she called at his office looking suitably
humble. He wasn't the type to let an old flame down, dammit—
why, he'd subsidize her *and* her family. When she stood before him,
her dark eyes brimming with tears, he'd spread his palms benevolently. "Here you are, pet," said Carl Laurids. And only as he flung
his arms wide did he notice that he was making his way along

Vesterbro Street, and that people were standing in huddles watching him because he had been talking out loud and waving his arms about, and that he had gone astray, and that he had no idea where he was going, and that his mind was filled with pictures of Amalie, and that his longing for her was almost suffocating him. He tried to pull himself together, he really tried; all the way into town he tried to convince himself that he would turn off toward Rosengården; that in no circumstances would he continue on toward the King's New Square—all the time knowing that he could not trust himself. During this stroll, which must have taken about three-quarters of an hour, Carl Laurids learned that the essence of love has as much to do with the loved one's absence as with her presence. His vain attempts to bring himself under control felt like a physical pain, bringing tears to his eyes and making him wonder whether he had in fact gone mad.

For the last bit of the way, he had murder in mind. Walking down Strøget—bareheaded because he had unwittingly lost his hat—he pictured how he would place his hands around Amalie's throat and squeeze the life out of her, thus setting his mind at rest. But this fantasy was ousted immediately thereafter by another in which he avowed his love for her; and this was replaced by a third in which he was reading aloud to her from a French novel—though this last scene grew dim as he tried to remember what it had been like to make love to her. And as he was running up the stairs of the d'Angleterre he realized he could not remember what she looked like naked.

Having pictured every conceivable scenario for their reunion, he was at first unable to take in that the room was empty. Innumerable, made-up conversations, long since carried to their conclusion in his imagination, still rang in his ears, and it took a thorough search of every room and closet in the suite to convince him that she had gone. All she had left was a note; a stiff white card that she had tucked under the pillow. She had had the nerve to leave it there because she knew that he would not only come back but search high and low for any trace of her. The card's message was both naïve and haughty. Written with one of the hotel's rubber pens, it read: "I never want to see you again. Don't come looking for me, especially not at 17 Dannebrogs Street."

A week later they were married.

The wedding was arranged in typical Carl Laurids style. He had brought all of his supple efficiency to bear to ensure that even with so little time to prepare, the setting at least would leave nothing to be desired. And if the whole setup threatened to collapse at any minute, it was not because any of the practicalities had been left to chance. Carl Laurids had obtained all the appropriate documents, including—because Amalie was so young—written consent from Christoffer Ludwig. He had managed to send out invitations to all of the casual acquaintances from his balloon ascent and informed the newspapers, so that his wedding could also serve as an advertisement for his business activities. He had also booked the wedding ceremony; invited Christoffer Ludwig, Amalie's sisters, and Gumma (and arranged for a cab that could accommodate her tricycle); ordered the floral decorations for the church; and organized the wedding reception right down to the minutest detail. Why, then, did all these plans almost come to nothing? Why does it seem to me like a fluke that this wedding ever took place? Because on the morning of the wedding Amalie kept changing her mind, that's why, and was forever sending one of her sisters, who were helping her to dress, with notes to Carl Laurids in which she said, "I just *can't* go through with this, it's too big a decision for me to make in such a short time. And what are you really, Carl? No better than an animal, you and that past of yours, which you've told me nothing about, no, I just can't do it darling, we'll have to postpone it!"

Six times in the course of that morning, Carl Laurids drove back and forth between his room at the Hotel Royal—into which he had moved to escape the memories of his own weakness aroused by the d'Angleterre—and always got there to find her humming contentedly. No sooner had he returned to his hotel, however, than another note would arrive to send him racing back to Dannebrogs Street— where Amalie would say, "Of course there's nothing wrong, sweetheart, my little Laurids, Amalie's little honeybunch, you know I love you"—until Carl Laurids's hands were as shaky as they had been in the balloon just after love hit him like a heart attack.

In the church the bickering continued. At the altar, it was only with reluctance that Amalie said yes; and as they were walking down the aisle they were arguing so heatedly that the ceremony had to be interrupted for a moment while the newlyweds retired to a little room behind the vestry. Here, after Amalie said she had decided that she wanted a divorce, they had sex—brief and brutal—up against the whitewashed wall, before gliding down the aisle to a rather risqué bridal march, blushing and happy as kids.

The reception was held on Midsummer's Eve, amid the fake gilding and mirrored opulence of the Nimb Restaurant, overlooking the Tivoli Gardens. In its infinite vulgarity, this establishment conforms perfectly to 1920s *parvenu* dreams of putting on the ritz. Thus among the 160 guests were two professional teachers of upper-class etiquette, whom Carl Laurids had hired in one of a series of attempts to discover the code of conduct that would profit him best. Apart from these two ladies—who spent the entire evening observing the proprieties and ended up, therefore, speaking only to each other— it was a thoroughly indecorous affair. Entertainment was provided by three songstresses and a pianist from an establishment called Above the Stable in Charlottenlund. This quartet performed both before and after the meal, and their songs and dances filled the restaurant's private party rooms with just the right reek of the stables for most of the guests, who found self-conscious, cultivated conversation à la Debrett difficult, if not impossible. The twelve-course menu was devised by Carl Laurids's French chefs from the balloon and consisted of famous dishes from the previous century created at the same time as those unforgettable Parisian vaudeville shows that they so closely resembled, consisting as they did of a thin, appetizing layer masking lukewarm obscenity. The first course, Aphrodite Puree, was followed by Siren Shoulders and Casanova Kidneys, then a whole Saddle of Veal à la Eros and Skewered Hearts and Cul de Canard Reine de Saba, and various other dishes which I cannot quite recall, except for those last luscious titbits: Nipples of Venus à la Maxim. To wash it all down there was, as usual, champagne—champagne all the way; and afterward liberal amounts of a Sauternes so sweet that it climbed out of the glass all by itself.

Carl Laurids had put together this program of entertainment and food for his guests' sake. To him extravagance was but a tool; he was not an indecorous man. He never told rude jokes in company and never laughed when others did; sex to him was something private, something hush-hush; and if, as now, he exploited it socially, it was because he knew that in this way he could satisfy some need within his guests. One of the truths about Carl Laurids's character—even here, on his wedding day—is that he is a man

equipped with a kind of mental thermometer with which he is constantly and matter-of-factly taking the temperature of his surroundings. Besides which, almost all his attention was focused on the
invisible cord connecting him to Amalie. They may have looked relaxed—guests said later that they had been the perfect hosts: Amalie
vivacious and charming, Carl Laurids cutting such an imposing
and reassuring figure that everyone forgot he was only nineteen
years old—but beneath their easy equanimity they were watching
each other like two beasts of prey. Between them, binding them
together, ran a line taut as a piano wire. When Amalie laughed
her silvery, bell-like laugh and leaned over to place an arm on a
braided shoulder; and when Carl Laurids lit a cigarette fixed in the
end of a long, provocative cigarette holder, these actions were but vicious little tugs on the invisible steel wire linking them across the
room.

The party was a dazzling success. It escalated in much the same
way as the Midsummer's Eve bonfire on the Tivoli lawn, which the
wedding guests could look out onto. That is to say that it ignited
immediately, blazed fiercely, reached a ruddy culmination, and then
continued to flicker and glow until quenched by a shower of champagne. By then its content had complied both with what Carl Laurids
had desired, and to some extent planned for, and with the contemporary dream—which is also our dream—of affluence in the Copenhagen of the 1920s. The speechmaking had gone on and on,
continuing right through the night, even after everyone had stopped
listening and turned to dancing, or drinking hard, or screeching at
one another as they tried to make themselves heard above the jazz
band that had by this time taken over from the Stable entertainers.
That quartet had disbanded after the three songstresses disappeared
into the restaurant's intimate *chambres séparées* with three of the
male guests. These *chambres séparées*, too, had been hired by Carl
Laurids and were to come in very handy, very handy indeed. At one
point a young actress shed her corset and danced barefoot on a
table; still later, the two teachers of etiquette—and then Johannes
V. Jensen—departed in high dudgeon, refusing to be party to such
debauchery. By this the great writer, at any rate, meant something
he had accidentally overheard: the pianist from the Stable boasting
vociferously about his daily quota of arse—more than any toilet seat
in this restaurant on an average Saturday, he said, which remark

filled Jensen with such disgust that he had to leave—although not before venting his revulsion on the remnants of the festivities. But by then only Amalie and Carl Laurids were still sober enough to hear him, and they thought he was joking.

Neither Amalie nor Carl Laurids had drunk much at all, and even if they had, it is doubtful whether they would have become intoxicated. Enveloped in cigar smoke and music and the hubbub of conversation, they perceived everything with exceptional keenness and clarity. In Amalie's case, one of the reasons for this acute sensibility was that she still believed she was dead. Well, perhaps it is going too far to say she thought she was dead, but neither would it be correct to assert that she knew she was alive. Possibly I come closest to the truth in believing her to be convinced that those dreams she had been dreaming since her early childhood had now, at long last, taken the place of an inadequate reality. It was this conviction that inspired her nonchalance. She laughed insouciantly at the crude vulgarities of the male guests and sidestepped the women's curiosity and admiration and envy with a distracted gaiety derived from not really believing they existed. Instead, they seemed to her to materialize within her field of vision so fleetingly that she did not even manage to catch their names. Then they dissolved into a cloud of mist out of which Carl Laurids kept emerging as the only tangible feature; and even he, even Carl Laurids Mahogany, was ever so slightly unreal.

This gently distrait air about Amalie ruined Carl Laurids's appetite; it made his world contract until she was all he could see; and it filled him with a wild, childish, reckless desperation which at one point in the evening, when they came face-to-face in one of the deep-set bay windows, prompted him to lean toward her and bark, as though giving an order, "I love you." It was the first time in his life that Carl Laurids had ever uttered these words, and it goes without saying that even he—even such a cynic as Carl Laurids Mahogany—was hoping for an appropriate reply. But the momentous nature of the moment was lost on Amalie. With pouting, heavy-lidded indifference, she said, "Fetch me a glass of champagne, darling."

They left the restaurant just as dawn was breaking, by which time the party had burned itself out. They stopped for a moment in the doorway and scanned all the figures slumped in chairs, or lying across tables, or propped up against one another in corners. Carl Laurids noted, to his satisfaction, that no one was in a fit state to throw rice after their cab. Then he switched off the big chandeliers and they walked together down the stairs, past guests who were no longer capable of recognizing them, out to the waiting car—and away.

The house into which they moved had belonged to a bankrupt estate that Carl Laurids had taken over a year earlier. A large white villa with a black-glazed tile roof, it overlooked the fishing village of Skovshoved; lying about halfway between the large residence of Queen Louise, the Queen Mother, and coffee merchant P. Carl Petersen's mansion.

It was a big house. Even for the area around Skovshoved it was immense, with its balconies and sculleries, its garage and chauffeur's apartment and stylish, asymmetrical garden. And of course it had been designed by Meldahl—who else?

Carl Laurids had planned the decor. The large drawing room with the big bow windows overlooking the Sound was called the Hellas room. Here homage was paid to ancient Greece with two large pillars decorated with grapes and vine leaves—all in imitation marble—and an ornate stucco ceiling on which the flora of Greece bloomed in white plaster. The library evoked memories of far-off China, with its black bookshelves and blanc de chine paintwork and lacquered folding doors and fine porcelain—acquired, one way and another, through Carl Laurids's connections with H. N. Andersen and the Danish East Asia Company. The dining room, still on the ground floor, was decorated in the Moorish style with sweeping arches painted on the walls and a marble floor worked in the same pattern as the Court of Lions in the Alhambra. Then there was the billiard room with its wood paneling and hunting prints and, on the walls, rifles that had never fired a shot—supposedly reminiscent of an English country house; and the smoking room, which harked back to ancient Egypt. All these rooms were open to view, filled with guests, at the countless parties given by Carl Laurids and Amalie; and since they were also photographed, we can, today, reconstruct them right down to the position of every little knickknack. In addition, some of the second floor was on view to guests—but there the line was drawn; that was as much as anyone saw, so far and no farther.

The fact is that the house was sharply divided into the visible side, of which we have spoken, and the invisible—the toilets and bathrooms and kitchens and the tiny servants' rooms and the long corridors and empty nurseries and, most invisible of all, Carl Laurids's office, which lay on the third floor and which he cleaned himself because he would not even allow the chambermaids to enter it.

Carl Laurids designed his home in this fashion to suit the taste of the upper-class circles in which he moved. The people he met there had a need of such vast rooms; rooms designed for flaunting, in which they were surrounded by the treasures of good, solid civilizations—reminders that their lives really did have substance, and that history was on their side. They also had a need for someone—in this case, Carl Laurids—to keep the doors closed on everything to do with the preparation of food and excretion and hygiene and servants and cleaning. Everyone knew very well that these things were there—after all, their own homes were arranged in similar fashion—but no one ever mentioned them, since they had all entered into that unspoken European upper-class convention of living in a world divided into what they could see and what they pretended they did not see.

All of the many, many functions for which Amalie and Carl Laurids's house was to provide the setting had, like the house, their visible and their invisible sides. The visible proceedings were conducted in the dining room, drawing room, billiard room, and smoking room. And what did they involve? Has any reader wondered about that? What went on at these parties, with all these nobles and army officers and high-ranking civil servants and *parvenus* and famous artists? Well, they were not, as one might expect, discussing business. These people kept their work and their private lives strictly separate. As they said, we don't get together to talk shop but to enjoy ourselves. And that is precisely what the visible side of Carl Laurids's gatherings was about: it was about enjoying oneself; about getting the *feel* of one other. Across the green baize of the card tables and over cognac and liqueurs and across the big Steinway, these men and women *feel* their way toward one another. They reenact the convoluted rituals of middle-class culture, designed to foster that heart-

felt, tingling sense of belonging; combined with the realization—
and the impression—that at least we here on the inside, we who
have come in from the cold, stand united. There, outside, glint the
lights of Copenhagen, and this year alone the longshoremen have
been out on strike, and the bricklayers, and the federation of un-
skilled workers, and the deckhands—and that is just between Carl
Laurids and Amalie's getting married in June and their throwing
their first party here at the end of July. And in the northeast, beyond
Sweden—which they can, of course, see from here—the Bolsheviks
are committing their atrocities; and then there's the war they have
just come through, and the political situation on the domestic front,
with the Social Democrats now forming the second largest party.
All of which is just awful. Ah yes, but it is out there.

Over and above this, there was an invisible side to the party, carried
on at the invisible side of the house. Although perhaps "invisible"
is not the right word, since everyone sees what was going on; everyone sees it anyway: gentlemen and ladies throwing up in the toilets
after eating and drinking like pigs; men in evening dress chasing
housemaids along the corridors; married couples swapping partners
and withdrawing into the empty nurseries—while out by the summer
house in the grounds someone is crying as though her heart will
break. But this is all par for the course in Copenhagen. Carl Laurids
and Amalie's parties are not debauched, it is not as though they
have a bad reputation—quite the contrary. Just now there is an aura
of respectability around Carl Laurids—as there has been before and
will be again—and these parties simply typify the dreams harbored
by certain sections of the Danish upper class just after the First
World War. But if we are interested in finding out what made these
parties *special*, we will have to look elsewhere. If we want to know
what made them different from so many other parties held along
Strand Drive, then we will have to examine a number of details of
which very few people, if anyone, were aware at that time. Only
because we have so many descriptions of Amalie and Carl Laurids's
house have we been able to reconstruct them; and because I know
Carl Laurids so well that I know what to look for. Of course, once
again it comes down to cynicism, to the uncanny synthesis with
which Carl Laurids observes all the social norms and conventions,
abides by all the rules, even as he is looking straight through them;
as though he never does anything because he actually needs to do

it, but only because it might be worth his while. As, for instance, with a series of tiny, searing breaches of etiquette of which only he and we are aware, but which leave his guests with a vague niggling sensation at the back of their minds and help create a myth about Carl Laurids that will swell and swell, just like his balloon—until the day in 1929 when he suddenly disappears. These breaks with form are, in fact, very small; almost invisible. The house's mélange of cultural styles, for example, a mix that even by the standards of the day is possibly a mite overdone. It is as though Carl Laurids is saying, "You want culture? Well, that's what you'll damn well get. Here's Greece and the Etruscans and the Far East and Islam and ancient Egypt; that ought to make you feel really secure." And then there are the toilets, which are situated far too close to the living apartments. Thus, whenever anyone goes in or out, it is impossible not to see the toilet bowls—which Carl Laurids has had painted with rose petals and mounted on small platforms, all to satisfy some obscure wishes on Amalie's part. Carl Laurids never understands these wishes, but feeling the way he does about Amalie, he nevertheless complies with them. And then there is Amalie's bedroom, occupying what is really a *very* exposed position; with its double doors seldom closed, its Arabian Nights–style decor, and the erotic Indian miniatures on its walls clashing fiercely with the Raphael angels and Sistine Madonnas of the ground floor. And all of this the guests *see*. If it were not that they are but mere details within the greater whole, if Carl Laurids were not such a brilliant host and Amalie such a sparkling hostess, then their guests might have found it all pretty hard to swallow—both with what I have mentioned and a few other bits and pieces. But as things stand, no one apart from us is any the wiser. It never occurs to any of those invited to the house, not even regular visitors, that Carl Laurids occasionally seems like a very shrewd musician fiddling speculatively with the instrument of their souls.

Only in certain limited areas was Carl Laurids blinded by his love for Amalie. Where all—more or less all—practical considerations were concerned, his perception was crystal clear. Thus he knew right from the start that Amalie would never be capable of running a house. They had been there only a week when he appointed a housekeeper. He chose an African woman who went by the name of Gladys. Her skin was so smooth and shiny and she moved with such easy grace that it was left to her eyes to betray that she was probably more than half a century old. She came from Kenya and had been in service in Lord Delaware's house and, later, with Baroness Blixen; until, in 1915, she came to Denmark with this lady— later to become such a famous writer. And in Denmark she had remained (but don't ask me why; I have enough on my plate without trying to discover how Gladys ended up on Strand Drive), and here was Carl Laurids appointing her as his housekeeper. His gray eyes bored straight through the warnings given by his associates and all the talk of how much trouble one always had with servants and how Negroes were so unreliable and how there was no telling what might happen. He saw beyond the way Gladys mixed up Danish with English and her native tongue; homed in on her strength of will and her imperturbable air of authority. On her first day at work, he gathered all the staff—the three gardeners and the chauffeur and the housemaids and chambermaids and the two footmen and the cook and the kitchen maids—in the entrance hall, in front of the big fireplace. Carl Laurids's wealthy friends would have been surprised if they could have seen and heard him on this occasion. Gone was the affability, the charm, the confidence-inspiring manner; these Carl Laurids had quietly folded up and shelved. With the denizens of the house's invisible side he adopted another tone of voice, both paternal and threatening and much like the one he had once used with the staff at Mørkhøj. He said, "I have taken on Gladys here as housekeeper. You all know that you must honor me as you would Our Lord, and love my wife as you would Mary, Mother of God. And I tell you now that you must fear Gladys as you would a general. And if anyone here has any remark to make about her being a Negro, then you can go to your rooms now, this instant, and address your remarks to your trunk and then you can carry your trunk out to the driveway and I'll see to it that you're picked up by a cab and driven straight to hell—because you're fired, so get out!"

No one had any remarks to make, neither then nor later.

I should warn everyone against imagining that there was anything philanthropic about Carl Laurids's conduct on this occasion. There is nothing to suggest that he had any particular soft spot for foreigners, or took any special delight in the exotic, or had any desire to challenge the prevailing belief that the farther south from the Alps one traveled, the more inferior were the beings one was likely to meet. Carl Laurids acted in such an unprejudiced manner for one reason only: the usual one, that it was worth his while. With his unerring instinct for his fellowmen he had discerned in Gladys the gifts necessary for running a house such as his, on Strand Drive, firmly, efficiently, economically, and discreetly.

And so it was. In little or no time the house and its grounds seemed to be running themselves. Carl Laurids could be sure of seeing the staff only twice a month—because he insisted on paying them their wages personally. In fact, so effective was Gladys's understanding of how to respect and exploit the dividing line between the visible and invisible sides of the house that several days could elapse without even Amalie—who spent a fair bit of time at home—seeing any of the staff except her own maid, the chauffeur, and the footman who served her meals.

I would like to point out that Amalie is the first woman in the cast of characters to whom we have been introduced who does not need to lift a finger in her home; nor is there anything at all in her life that she *has* to do. It is tempting to say that here, for the first time, we come across the term "free time." And yet it can be difficult to say whether Amalie's time really is free—although I can say what she did with it: the same as her friends from Ordrup and Charlottenlund. Like her, these ladies lived in houses that cleaned themselves and where meals materialized without their having to give them a thought. They attended art classes and music lessons and took courses in the most attractive way of sticking flowers in water. They went riding—in summer, at Mattson's stables in the Dyrehaven park; in winter, at the Christiansborg Palace riding school. And always in a body. On second thoughts, I do not think we can say that these women spent every minute of their days in leisurely pursuits. Of course, it is tempting to get all hot under the collar and say, what are they anyway but a bunch of upper-class hothouse flowers, all wrapped up in cotton at a time when, in Copenhagen, people are still dying of starvation in the streets and in the tenement where Anna and Adonis have been living for some years. But it would not be fair. There is no doubt that all the riding lessons and tea parties and flower arranging and trips to the races and to Fonnesbech's department store served several important ends, the most important of which was that these women had a particular task in life: to show the world, and themselves, the true meaning of "femininity." In those salons and parlors and drawing rooms that others kept clean; in a world where the image of femininity changed from day to day—virtually from one day to the next—it was the heroic duty of these middle-class ladies to take, as it were, lifelong lessons in how to be real women. By frequenting the same riding schools and the same shops as former generations of the well-to-do and by making up bouquets like those created by Hans Christian Andersen they did their best to exorcise newspaper items on the increasingly outrageous bathing-suit fashions and the fact that more and more women were smoking cigarettes.

Amalie seems to have slipped pliantly into this circle of women friends; she seems to have assumed this lifestyle as though it had always been hers. The only thing that set her apart was the easygoing manner in which she accepted everything. Amalie's friends were ambitious. Their fathers' and their husbands' fortunes might have raised them beyond every form of normal, everyday life, and above every kind of financial consideration, but there was scarcely one of them who did not drag around some sort of invisible trunk stuffed with grinding, all-consuming ambition. Raised as they were in the belief that it was unfeminine to work for money, all these ladies from big white houses were passionately absorbed in developing their personalities; in *making* something of themselves; in making their own and their family's mark on the world. Most of us recognize this dream from our own experience—at least, I do—but for these women in and around Strand Drive in the Copenhagen of the 1920s it takes on a tragic dimension. Not infrequently it pushed them beyond the limits of normal behavior and regard for their own safety, sending them chasing off to Africa to run already insolvent coffee plantations, or spurring them to join the Sudan Mission, or to leave husband and children and travel to Paris to become writers or sculptors—all without ever being able to satisfy the demands they made on themselves.

But not Amalie. At which one might wonder, just a little—at least, I do—because if anyone is predisposed to such ambition it is Amalie, who suffered throughout her adolescence in order to demonstrate her own exceptional worth. But for some reason or other during these years she was very, very content. Whatever she undertook was done with grace, courtesy, and a smile and yet at the same time with the gentle air of distraction that had hung around her since her wedding and that left her only in certain specific situations—to which we shall return. In photographs from those years she bears a quite striking resemblance to the paintings on the walls in her own home. With her loose-fitting dresses and flowing tresses she is like a Raphael angel. Her hands seem flaccid and rather dejected and not at all capable of taking a firm grip on anything, let alone anything as starkly substantial as Carl Laurids must have been. The photographs have almost all been taken in profile, as though she did not want to meet other people face on. She is always gazing upon something or other, dreamy-eyed, in the manner of those contemporary Danish paintings of anemic women in churchyards in southern Europe; always painted against a backdrop of pine trees and gravestones, well into the afternoon at a point when even the light seems filled with a longing for something unattainable.

During these years Amalie's head was often in the clouds; the photographs do not lie, and this dreamy abstractedness was part of her makeup. On the long afternoons when the house seemed deserted, she could sit for hours in the garden. On such days, pictures of her childhood in Rudkøbing would appear to her and she would see them blend with her present surroundings into a quivering confirmation of the fact that she had always been one of the chosen ones and that, at long last, she had been proved right.

When Carl Laurids came home from work, Amalie was usually there. But he never came upon her right away. He had to pass from room to room searching, in the white light which, owing to the large windows and diaphanous curtains and the proximity of the sea, always pervaded these rooms, regardless of the season. Usually he was so desperate to see her that he simply slipped off his overcoat, dropped his cane, and, still in his hat and boots, began his search. He called her, he shouted, "Daddy's sweetheart," and "Where's my little wife?" and "Yoo-hoo," in a voice not merely hoarse with impatience but also breathless, because every single day, when he left the office in Rosengården, he started to fear that she would have left him. And this fear drove him to push the limousine to the limit along Strand Drive, to race up the stairs of the house—and not until he was inside did he force himself to slow down.

He always found her where least expected, on a landing, or in an alcove, or in a room that had been closed up, or on a bench in a far corner of the garden. She always looked at him in faint surprise, as

if to say, "Is that really you, Carl Laurids? How funny." This reception never failed to have its effect. Even though it was a ritual
which, in this aspect of their marriage, was as recurrent a feature
as the white light and mealtimes, Amalie never once failed to pro-
voke Carl Laurids with her apparent indifference. Disappointment
having taken the wind out of his sails, he would stand there, unable
so much as to kiss her forehead; and by the time he had regained
his composure she was already moving away from him, whispering,
almost to herself, "Actually I'm quite tired; it's been a terribly long
day." Carl Laurids would follow her, although he dared not run,
perhaps because she said, "I really do have a beastly headache, but
tell me about your day anyway." He cannot answer her, his mouth
is dry from the emotions that assail him, and so instead, slowly, he
follows Amalie, who has suddenly vanished, only to appear behind
a pillar or a dumbwaiter or calling to him from the floor above—
but always keeping a wall or a flower arrangement or a balustrade
between herself and him. On these afternoons they are like actors
privately rehearsing an assignation scene, and this image is perhaps
one part of the truth. As this cruel game of peekaboo progresses,
Amalie is possessed by an almost panther-like presence, and Carl
Laurids by increasing desperation—until, somewhere, he catches
up with her. As a rule, a struggle now ensues, in the course of which
Carl Laurids is always taken aback by the discovery that his wife's
delicate constitution and all her gaucherie are merely affectations
disguising a strength as great as his own. For what seems to Carl
Laurids an interminable length of time they reel around the vast
rooms, with the mirrors multiplying their clinches, transporting
them to other rooms, other floors, in a series of reflected pictures
that seem to embrace the entire house. And it is clear from these
pictures that if Carl Laurids finally manages to rip the black silk
underwear to shreds, it is only because, suddenly, at this stage,
Amalie is on his side and herself strips off the fabric. Then she digs
her teeth into him, and they sink to the floor and roll out of range
of the mirrors.

The relief afforded to Carl Laurids by their lovemaking was very,
very short-lived. By the time he came to, Amalie had risen, adjusted
her clothes, and already taken herself off, so that he had to go looking
for her. And by the time he found her, her face had already clammed
up again, grown distant and brittle. This filled him with rage—

white-hot but impotent. Meekly he had to make a tour of the rose beds with her, or drink tea with her while a voice within him screamed that only a moment ago they had been rolling around on the floor, dammit; a moment ago she had lost all self-control and clawed him to her. And now . . . what the devil had become of it all, what had become of her voracity . . . here, in the conservatory, where once again she resembled a nun, a schoolgirl? Once again she had abandoned him to memories he found himself struggling to credit, memories that compelled him, the next day and the next again, to reenact dreamlike chase scenes from which he woke alone, sprawled on the parquet floor with his trousers around his ankles, robbed of that sense of being in control which he had managed to sustain from first thing in the morning until this agonizing moment.

Amalie did not help him. For a while, in the early days, he had tried to make her acknowledge her desires, to no avail. Without ever losing her temper, she would skirt the subject, avoid answering, feel unwell, and say, "Carl, I honestly don't think this is something we can discuss; please don't refer to it again." Only once did he succeed in eliciting some sort of response. It happened one afternoon after they had made love on the big landing between the ground and second floors, when Carl woke up feeling more alone than ever before. He had come across Amalie sitting on a sofa, petting Dodo, her fawn-colored greyhound, with a tenderness that made him see red with jealousy. Unable to control himself, he kicked the dog away, hauled Amalie off the sofa, and yelled at her, "Do you realize you grunt like a pig when we do it!" Without a moment's hesitation, Amalie dealt him a blow that burst his left eardrum and sent him flying into the grand piano. Then she left the room, leaving Carl Laurids smiling sheepishly, because this very haze of pain in which he found himself simply confirmed that he was right.

But his triumph was short-lived, since Amalie never again lost her temper. From then on, she was prepared, both for his direct demands and for the veiled and unexpected effronteries by which he tried to get her to talk about sex.

For the first time, in his marriage to Amalie, Carl Laurids was forced to bide his time. Before this, he had found that he could always have his way, and that he could have it here and now, without delay. That the world was too slow and fuddled and full of woolly-headed objections made it possible for a young person such as himself to cut right through to the heart of the matter and get exactly what he was after; and the realization of this fact had turned into a rash and dangerous impatience. If, as often happened, he felt hungry between the meals served so punctually by Gladys, then he expected to be fed, on the double; he should just have to snap his fingers for someone to appear, to whom Carl Laurids would say, "I'd like lobster in mayonnaise, or asparagus with creamed butter, or strawberries and cream, or that porridge with cracklings that I used to have as a boy. Get it for me and make sure that it tastes just the way it did when my mother made it." Or he would suddenly take a notion to go riding and demand that his horse be saddled and outside the door in five minutes—"Five minutes!" he would yell— even though the horses were stabled over at Mattson's and it would take at least two hours to fetch them. Or else he insisted on going sailing—"Have the boat taken out of the boathouse and rigged up, I'll be down in fifteen minutes," he would say, even though he knew that it would take much longer, and twenty minutes later he had changed his mind and forgotten all about it. If, that is, he did not stride down to the little jetty he had had built out from the house's private beach and bawl, "What the hell are you doing, holding some sort of Bolshevik meeting, what the devil do you think I pay you for?" He was incapable of waiting; the one big discovery he had made at Mørkhøj had been precisely this: that there was absolutely no reason why one should not reach out and grab whatever one wanted, then and there. Now, however, Amalie was forcing him to forgo.

There were days when she would not see him at all; when she took to her bed and kept the door of her bedroom locked, and would not even come down to meals but left him to sit alone, first seething with rage, then alternately concerned for her health and speechless with mortification, until wolf-like restlessness drove him from the house. She usually put in an appearance eventually—although, often as not, in the guise of a convalescent, complete with ice packs, a feeble voice, and a deathly pallor that Carl Laurids suspected of being the work of a powder puff. During such spells he did not dare to lay a finger on her. While terrified that she would die in his arms of a frailty he did not actually believe in, he was also terrified of the strength he always sensed in her, even when she brought him close to tears by describing her ailments and insisting that she was dying.

218 [*The History of Danish Dreams*

Toward the end of such spells of sexual starvation it seemed to Carl Laurids that wherever he turned, he saw nothing but pictures of Madonnas and religion and chamber music and Dodo the sexless greyhound and Amalie's pale face and unwelcoming body under the orthopedic corset she never wore except at these times. And then he felt as though the world were an insipid stage set closing in around him.

At such moments he occasionally wished that he could have visited a brothel, or found solace in alcohol, or turned to one of the women from his former life. But it was impossible; that way was now closed to Carl Laurids. Ever since the moment in the balloon when Amalie turned her face away from him he had had no peace, not even in his dreams: Amalie's image was immediately superimposed upon every erotic fantasy, even more so during those periods when she held him at bay.

At such times he was visited by a jealousy which, in brief, hideous glimpses, showed him, as it shows us, that there were still some factors in his life and in his own character that had not been brought under control. At such moments he feared she kept him at arm's length because she had taken a lover; so he had her followed for weeks by four discreet, smartly dressed gentlemen usually employed by him to take care of difficult debt-collection cases. Their reports revealed nothing except that there were no men in Amalie's life besides Carl Laurids—and that, in a sense, was the worst thing they could have disclosed, since now there was no lover for him to kill. Then he turned his morbid suspicions upon Amalie's mental activities. She dreams of someone else, he thought; she's living in a fantasy world of unspeakable excesses—and he had peepholes bored in the walls of her bedroom so that he could spy on her features while she slept and, if possible, intercept snatches of whatever she might say in her sleep. He saw nothing except her sleep-smoothed, Madonna face and heard nothing except her slow, regular breathing, which made him grind his teeth in fury and desire, remembering as he did how rapid and urgent her breathing could become when they were together.

Having drilled a hole through to her bathroom that allowed him to spy on her nakedness, he came as close as he ever would to going mad. The general view held by the upper-class circles of his day was that women had no sex drive to speak of—this he knew. And until now he had filed away this scientific truth as just another illustration of the dunghill of misapprehension and humbug upon which society reposed and which made it so easy for him to forge ahead. With his eye to the peephole, he now reconsidered this assertion. Eyes pinned on Amalie as she passed a large sponge over her naked limbs, he began to doubt his own past. In desperation, he attempted to reassess his sexual experiences, from the forbidden couplings with Miss Clarizza on the white grand piano to his lonely awakening on the parquet floor. Maybe those women never really felt like it, he thought, maybe they only did it for my sake, and didn't get nearly so much pleasure from it as I did, and now she's washing between her legs. And it all became too much for him and he had to turn away.

When Amalie came back to him, it was always without warning, like some sudden, passionate explosion that could carry them anywhere; it could make Carl Laurids forgive her and forget everything, and fill him with a fierce happiness that was, more often than not, replaced by a certain arrogance, a sense of once again being independent, of having the upper hand. In this state he sometimes fantasized, as in the days before the wedding, of leaving her, and such fantasies could last for several days, until she rejected him again, and again sent him crashing down into his own abysmal dependence upon her.

It is important that we present a picture of Carl Laurids not only as a private individual but also as a businessman—and that is not easy because, throughout his life, he was very, very reticent when the talk turned to business matters. Anything he eventually did say has, of course, been remembered as a stroke of wit, a *bon mot*, which has then been passed on. But to me these utterances seem as obscure as the replies of any oracle. Take, for example, the time when Madsen-Mygdahl, then Minister of Agriculture, and the writer Johannes V. Jensen—both regular visitors to Carl Laurids's home —were extolling, as so often before, the virtues of free enterprise and the Good Old Days; assuring one another that the reason Danish agriculture is doing so well is that it has never had any help from the state and has had to learn to fight, and lash out to right and left, and stand on its own two feet; feet solidly planted in the Good Old Days that are now all but gone. There then followed a short break in the conversation while the two men's glasses were topped up with champagne, and during this break Carl Laurids places his hands on their shoulders and says, "Gentlemen, you need have no fears for the Good Old Days; we'll start turning them out again just as soon as demand is great enough." This sentence, like so many of Carl Laurids's other remarks, was committed to memory and was to crop up several times in Johannes V. Jensen's works, along with other pearls of wisdom regarding science and finance. But it is not clear, and this I feel I have to point out; it offers no clue to Carl Laurids's thoughts on business.

The doors of his offices in Rosengården, where he started his first company, were fitted with opaque glass. These panes blurred all contours and made it impossible for anyone outside to see what was going on—just as they block our view. Nevertheless, I am able to lift the veil and allow some details to filter out, to shine through— thanks, no doubt, to my persistence; although I should not perhaps mention that here, since it has nothing to do with this account, except inasmuch as I could not have written what follows if I had not felt that these smoke screens must not be allowed to stifle my urge to get at the truth. Carl Laurids is not going to get away with remaining an enigma. Since history shows that we are all only human—at any rate, the majority of us—I have not contented myself with anecdotes from his private life but have also picked up the tracks, all but erased, and thoroughly covered, of Carl Laurids Mahogany's business ventures.

As far as I can see, none of these enterprises are in any way connected. Carl Laurids would appear to have operated within one field for a certain length of time, after which he would leave it, completely and utterly, leaving no trace—only to pop up, a while later, in some new area. I cannot be absolutely certain, but I believe that Carl Laurids's first firm was some sort of consultancy business. As with so much else in his life, it has no antecedents. Unannounced, and without any visible preamble, he opened his premises in Rosengården. The sign on the opaque glass plate read: CARL LAURIDS MAHOGANY. IMPORT—EXPORT. In the front office sat a secretary; in the next, Adolf Hanemand, a Danish lawyer—that is to say, he held no law degree but had merely completed a short course of study culminating in an examination. Hanemand's presence was yet another instance of Carl Laurids never attaching much importance to the formalities. He had seen at once that Hanemand was full of legal guile and unhampered by all the usual concepts of right and wrong. Everything I know about what happened during the first years in the Rosengården offices was learned from Hanemand; and his willingness to talk can be attributed to the way it all ended.

One morning—after two years, and without any prior notification—Hanemand arrived at the office to find it closed. Since Carl Laurids objected to being contacted at his house, Hanemand went home. The next morning he was again confronted by locked doors. So he sent Carl Laurids a letter in which he demanded the salary owed to him plus compensation. Receiving no response, he sent another letter. To this he received a curt reply. On the reverse of one of his calling cards, Carl Laurids had written: "I regard all contact between us to be at an end." Hanemand then paid Carl Laurids a visit. He took the streetcar out to Charlottenlund, walked up to the house, and rang the bell. Carl Laurids himself opened the door, and, standing on the marble steps, Hanemand came straight to the point. While smiling pleasantly at Carl Laurids, he told him he had various documents tucked away that would have to be termed damning; what he, as a lawyer, would call extremely damning. And the only thing that would stop him from handing them over to the police was an explanation from Carl Laurids, along with his outstanding salary and some compensation to boot—and it had better be right now, this instant. Carl Laurids stood there with his hands behind his back, rocking back and forth on the balls of his feet and absently watching the goldfish in the pond. Then he said, "Are you threatening me?" and as Hanemand started to reply, Carl Laurids hammered a large set of brass knuckles into his open mouth. The blow sent Hanemand flying down the steps and into a lifelong dread of Carl Laurids. This dread prevented him from going to the police, and when I was interviewing him—when he was sitting opposite me, telling me about Carl Laurids—it seemed in no way diminished by the fifty years that had elapsed since that afternoon on Strand Drive when he saw his employer for the last time. But, as with so many others who have known Carl Laurids, the Danish lawyer's dread was mingled with admiration; his voice held what was almost a note of awe as he told me how Carl Laurids looked his clients *in the eye*: these clients were inventors; in fact, it would appear that Carl Laurids's company had acted as a link between inventors and investors. In those days, according to Hanemand, Copenhagen was home to many an ardent soul obsessed with the idea of technological progress. Carl Laurids put these people in touch with well-to-do civil servants and merchants keen to invest in the future, and the appropriate contracts for these alliances were drawn up at the offices in Rosengården. During these years, Carl Laurids's offices provided a gathering point for the most extravagant dreams of the future, and one could be forgiven for thinking that this is the very crux of his business; it is hard not to think that he must have derived a certain satisfaction from being confronted on a daily basis with people such as these, who took as gospel that what is to come is better, much better, and at any rate more profitable, than what has gone before.

But if that is how Carl Laurids felt, then he has kept it well hidden, since Hanemand certainly cannot recall Carl Laurids ever making any comment about his work. According to Hanemand, his employer never exhibited anything other than remarkably dispassionate powers of concentration; and what he remembers best of all is that Carl Laurids always looked his clients in the eye. "Damned if he ever looked at the *article*," said Hanemand to me; "he never looked at the *inventions*."

There is reason for believing that Carl Laurids possessed not so much as an iota of the technical knowledge one would assume to be an essential requirement in running a business such as his. On innumerable occasions he has sat opposite proud and nervous eccentrics while they demonstrated their lives' work to him; and only very occasionally, in the course of the conversation, has he lowered his gaze to the jumbled mass of springs and ball bearings and steel and ebonite and wood and spools and wires deposited on the newspapers spread across his desk. Instead he has used the time to study the individual before him. And so these interviews never lasted long, since a few minutes was all Carl Laurids needed in which to learn enough either to send this inventor away or to ally him to one of the growing number of investors who contacted him with increasing regularity. After that he would draw up one of the contracts on which, during those years, his income must have depended.

During those years, a fair number of the early twentieth century's dreams of technological omnipotence passed through Carl Laurids's offices. Harebrained idealists presented their plans for floating cities, and bombs that could avail themselves of the need of every atom to free itself of the past, and a printing machine so sensitive that it could print the Lord's Prayer on the yolk of a fried egg. These ideas Carl Laurids rejected: not necessarily because they had no future but because he felt this future lay too far off. Instead, with his sure sense for what the present day and the immediate future could handle, he backed projects from inventors in whom he detected the right blend of madness and realism; hence, in Rosengården, a great many contracts were drawn up for projects involving the improvement and production of rapid-fire machine guns and coal-fired refrigerators and artificial fertilizer and internal-combustion engines and more machine guns and phonographs and bicycles and pressure cookers and cosmetics and more machine guns—in fact, arms production appeared to be turning into quite an industry for Carl Laurids, until the day Hanemand found the office door closed.

In the ensuing years, Carl Laurids became a factory owner and company director. We know that he bought up, on the cheap, a plot of land on Christianshavn, right opposite the tenement where Anna and Adonis Jensen lived. And we know that on this plot of land he erected factories for the production of ersatz substances. Somehow or other he had managed to acquire formulas and inventions and rights to the manufacture of chemicals for—in the first instance— substitutes for tobacco and phonograph needles; although we know this only because all of it came out during the investigations into the collapse of the Copenhagen Merchant Bank in what was—in all senses—the chilly month of January 1922. No charges were brought against Carl Laurids; naturally, nothing could be proved, and by then he had disposed of the factories and his hands were clean. Thereafter, he had embarked upon the ambitious project of producing ersatz coffee from shredded peat—which I have only been able to unearth because it was disclosed when the Farmers' Bank crashed and Carl Laurids was mentioned as being a personal friend of the bank's president, the financial wizard Emil Glückstadt. Very soon thereafter Carl Laurids was only a former friend of the bank president, when the latter was arrested and accused Carl Laurids of being party to a number of fraudulent activities. It turned out, however, that Carl Laurids had already quit the ersatz-coffee business and, furthermore, that nothing could be proved. And it is the same story in the following years, with the failure of a number of financial institutions revealing that Carl Laurids has been producing synthetic bicycle oil and aromatic substances, and running a nationwide marriage bureau, while at all times inhabiting a gray area between the dubious and the downright illegal. Until, finally, a sentence is passed on him: a mild sentence, a judgment so tentative that it might almost be termed a friendly warning. It is passed on him because in his old building in Christianshavn—which he has reacquired—he has manufactured a large consignment of shampoo from a caustic soda base. This he has then sold cheaply and, in the opinion of the court, in good faith—such good faith that he escaped with a modest fine. And this although there were people walking around Copenhagen, and especially its poorer districts, wearing hats and woollen caps in an effort to hide the fact that they were, thanks to Carl Laurids's shampoo, Complete Hair Formula, bald, totally bald.

After this conviction, he left the manufacturing industry and entered the entertainment business. A week after sentence was passed on him, he sent a letter to the Dyrehavsbakken Stallholders' Association, suggesting that he be permitted to set up an establishment for the staging of an exhibit of dwarfs. He must have been working on the idea for some time, since the letter was accompanied by detailed sketches of the two-story wooden building intended to house this unique attraction. The ground floor of this building was to contain a stage on which the dwarfs would dance and sing, while on the second floor there would be smaller rooms fitted out with scaled-down furniture. A miniature boxing ring was also to be constructed. It is not known where Carl Laurids had come by this idea, but he had timed it to perfection. While it was creating a stir and being mentioned in the newspapers and brought to the attention of the authorities and becoming a matter of public debate, he signed contracts with forty dwarfs. He traveled a great deal during these months, locating dwarfs in Denmark and northern Germany— whence he conveyed them to Strand Drive in one of the big limousines and installed them in empty rooms in the gardeners' and chauffeur's quarters and in the pavilions on the grounds. There, every day, Amalie could see them strolling across the smooth lawns.

Carl Laurids had selected his employees with care. Some of the dwarfs were freaks of nature, with tiny bodies, short legs, and great, balloon-like heads; others were, in every respect, well proportioned, but only three feet tall; and still others looked like insane scientific experiments. But they were all gifted and exquisitely polite people who spent their days paying impeccably correct calls on one another, or in reading Euclid's *Elements* or teaching themselves to dance or to play chamber music on the diminutive instruments Carl Laurids had purchased for them, to help them prepare for their show business debut.

All the indications are that this debut was a success. By the time the Danish authorities and the stallholders' association and the newspapers and the rest of the Danish public turned on Carl Laurids's project, it had attracted attention worldwide, and pictures of the dwarfs with the chivalrous manners had circulated in the international press. Shortly after the Copenhagen city fathers definitively rejected the proposal, Carl Laurids was visited by two men representing a major film company. They came from Hollywood and gave the lie to every one of the widespread 1920s preconceptions of America's barbarous Western ways. Even in the summer heat they were smartly dressed in jackets and waistcoats, and they spoke in quiet, cultured voices. They spent a whole day in the conservatory, watching the dwarfs through binoculars, and then they left. They must, beyond a shadow of a doubt, have made a deal with Carl Laurids, because, only a week later, he shipped the dwarfs off on the liner *Frederik den Ottende*, bound for America. Carl Laurids himself accompanied his cargo to the boat—with the black limousine and the dwarfs attracting a fair amount of attention on the wharf; and there were many who cast curious glances after the tall figure in the dark coat who stood alone gazing after the ship. This figure is Carl Laurids, and he is standing on the very spot where Anna and Adonis once stood, dreaming their way to foreign lands. But whether Carl Laurids dreamed there is no way of telling. It may be that he came to the quayside only to make sure that this shipment went without a hitch, and even then he must have been hatching plans for the next consignment.

This took place two months later and consisted not just of dwarfs but of all manner of freaks. Carl Laurids may have come to a prior arrangement with the two representatives of American culture. Or he may have been acting altogether on his own initiative, trusting solely to his sure instinct for the future—which, this time around, enabled him to anticipate Hollywood's demand for monsters for the wave of gothic horror movies that was beginning just as Carl Laurids dispatched his third and fourth loads to the Promised Land. These individuals—some of whom would, a few months later, be staring down at Danish audiences from the silver screen, in the guise of reptiles or lepers or test-tube monstrosities or the Hunchback of Notre Dame—had presumably been found by Carl Laurids in the rural areas; in German—and in some cases Danish—hospitals; and in the lunatic asylums of Jutland and the islands. And he must have been extremely quick and extremely discreet, because he left virtually no trail. A handful of institution superintendents recalled him as being a warmhearted humanitarian desirous of adopting some poor handicapped person; still others took him to be some relative appearing out of the blue; but nowhere did anyone quite catch his name. And so no connection was ever actually made between those few complaints and inquiries which, when they did eventually surface, seemed to be scattered, indiscriminate outbursts. Only to us do they form a pattern.

At a fair guess, Carl Laurids signed up around two hundred individuals, dwarfs included. In putting together his second and third batches of these bizarre actors he had, however, to abandon any thought of intelligence and nice manners. True, in an attempt to increase their value, he did arrange to have his discoveries instructed in the skills most necessary for their future careers: speaking English and eating with a knife and fork; but he soon gave up every effort in that direction. He lodged them in four large army tents he had had erected outside the villa, and employed a team of hefty male nurses to keep them in order.

Even Amalie found it hard, during this period, to remain lost in her usual carefree reverie. These people whom Carl Laurids had unearthed were not your average cripples—these were people suffering from water on the brain or rare, incurable growth-retarding illnesses or mad, capricious fits. During the day they wandered around the garden and at night they invaded Amalie's dreams, until she dispensed with her usual reserve and slept with Carl Laurids, to draw from his presence the strength to convince herself that these wretched creatures were a hallucination. She soon had to stop holding her tea parties in the rooms facing onto the garden; then had to abandon them altogether because, despite their limitations, these cripples could get around with such amazing agility on blocks and crutches and rollers and the stumps of their arms and legs that they could easily give their nurses the slip, and hence could appear at any minute, outside any window and even inside the house—where the reaction they elicited from the assembled ladies was one of both repulsion and irresistible attraction. At one point, Amalie complained to Carl Laurids, and, after looking at her for a moment, he replied, "That's why I'm going to put them in films, darling; audiences will want to see them again and again, just to make sure that they need never see them anymore."

The fact that he actually took Amalie's question seriously enough to give her an answer—even if it was just this vague remark—is thanks to the transformation that had taken place in their relationship since Carsten's birth. He was born in May, after a winter in which several of the big financial houses with which Carl Laurids had links had gone into liquidation. With all the feverish rescue operations of the winter months, Amalie's condition had not registered with Carl Laurids, apart from his noting that she kept him at an even greater distance than usual. And it may be that he did not want to see anything else. To coin a phrase he himself often repeated: people see only what they want to see; and perhaps he had some intuition of what was to come.

And what was to come came in May, with Carsten's birth, and tossed Carl Laurids into such hellish agonies of jealousy that here, again, we have confirmed for us the observation that in love—and hence, here, with Amalie—everyone, even Carl Laurids, is only human. The first thing he noticed about his son was the spastic ugliness common to all newborn babies, and this left him cold. But the next thing he noticed about the little boy was the infant's ruthless craving for its mother; and in this craving, Carl Laurids recognized himself. Despite its being unheard of, despite all warnings from her women friends, and with complete disregard for Carl Laurids's attempts to forbid it, Amalie insisted on breast-feeding the baby. Deaf to the doctors' admonitions that it would ruin her figure, she gave free rein to that staggering strength of will previously shown only to her family and Carl Laurids, and put the baby to the breast whenever and wherever necessary. The first time Carl Laurids witnessed this, it made him sick with distaste. In the way his son clutched at Amalie's swollen breast he saw his own helpless dependence, and when Amalie drew the child to her he saw the unconditional tenderness he had never received in anything but meager doses. At that moment he wanted to leave Amalie, but at the same time he was more powerfully attracted to her than ever before. Meekly he complied with her wish that they should all three sit together in the garden and be quiet; "Be quiet, Carl," she said if he tried to talk his way out of his misery. Likewise, he had to join them on their long walks along the promenade or through the center of Copenhagen, when Amalie would not let the nanny come but insisted on pushing the baby carriage herself. On these walks where, from a distance, they resembled our common dream of a happy and well-to-do husband and wife, Carl Laurids made one of his life's most unpleasant discoveries. With his usual keen perception he saw through the contemporary illusion of the baby's innocence, pene-trating to the truth, which was that—from its carriage, or wherever else it might happen to be—this little creature, his son, who still looked to him like an earthworm or a hairless insect, exercised a calculated dominance over Amalie. Helplessly Carl Laurids realized that the child's gurgling and inarticulate wails, and its hunger, and its bowel movements were all part of a campaign by which it seized power over his wife and shut him out. On these days with Carsten and Amalie when, the spring sunshine notwithstanding, Carl Lau-rids shivered in his own isolation, he saw how the child was steering Amalie back toward reality, something only he had ever been able to do. In the face of everything and everyone, apart from Carl Lau-rids, Amalie had preserved the dreamy air of distraction which had surrounded her since the balloon ascent and which often made the invisible servants, and even her guests and her women friends, won-der whether she really was aware of their presence. Carl Laurids now realized that when she was with the child she radiated an awareness of which he himself had only ever caught glimpses. When she was tending the child, and changing it, and washing it—again regardless of the nanny whom Carl Laurids had employed, who was all but superfluous—she displayed a puzzling and terrifying effi-ciency; it made him feel as though she were a chasm into which he had never peered.

It was then that Carl Laurids started to tell Amalie about his life. During that spring and summer a breach appeared in his character, and through this crack flowed confessions that would previously have been unthinkable. It might be going too far to say that he talked in order to unburden himself. It is probably closer to the truth

to believe that Carl Laurids—discreet, ever-secretive Carl Laurids
—was now trying to do what so many other reticent men, both of
his own day and later, have tried to do, which is to reach the woman
he loved by means of a new, hitherto unseen candor.

This candor had no effect on Amalie. Why she held Carl Laurids
at bay will always remain something of a mystery, but she did not
return his confidence. Perhaps she was never aware of it; perhaps
she knew that Carl Laurids's love burned because of and not despite
the gulf between them; perhaps a bit of both. Be that as it may, she
kept him firmly on the fringes of her relationship with Carsten;
which is why, later, she was able to recollect only snippets of what
he had said and so was unable, later, to repeat very much of it. Even
so, these half-remembered or three-quarters-remembered confessions—which have then been passed on to me at third or sometimes fourth hand—represent vital source material for my account
of Carl Laurids's boyhood at Mørkhøj and for his business activities during the period following the fourth shipment of cripples,
that being absolutely his last contribution to the entertainment
business.

That same summer he opened a couple of art galleries in the
center of Copenhagen, and because he was so frank with Amalie,
we also know how he came by his paintings. To some extent, during
these years, Carl Laurids was again running a factory. He had the
big garage fitted out as a studio in which, day in, day out, six painters
were hard at work. No one knows where these men came from or
who they were. The signatures on their pictures were pseudonyms,
and I have been unable to discover any evidence of Carl Laurids's
having met them prior to this summer, but by now this missing
chapter is not to be wondered at. It is Carl Laurids' trademark; it
is what we keep running up against—just like the high level of
expertise we encounter here, in these six men, as we do in all of
Carl Laurids's employees. In no time and doubtless without giving
it a second thought, he had snapped up six men—six specialists—
who just happened to be stuck in an era to which they did not belong.
Every one of these painters possessed an incurable and hopeless
love of the nineteenth century. When Carl Laurids took them on,
they were pale and undernourished young men in threadbare coats,
who thought and painted and starved in the manner of the Golden
Age Romantics. Carl Laurids licked them into shape. He provided

them with paints and canvases and three square meals a day and a regular wage. In return—in the big garage, which still smelled of lubricating oil and leather upholstery—he set them to painting nude models. During these years an uninterrupted stream of well-built young men and women passed through Carl Laurids's garage, there to be committed to large-scale canvases. During these same years these paintings were to fulfill the artistic needs of a new moneyed class, whose knowledge of pictures was restricted to childhood memories of cheap religious prints stuck inside the lids of their parents' dower chests. These members of the *nouveaux riches* harbored an irrational fear of the wide expanses of bare wall in their big flats on Søtorvet, or their villas in Charlottenlund, but Carl Laurids knew what these people wanted. "They want the usual things," he said to Amalie, "above all, security and the assurance that there is something—come to that, anything—that will last forever. And that," he explained, "is what these paintings can give them. Just so long as they aren't modern and aren't meant to represent pulverized brains or a world that's falling apart." At his behest, his artists painted a warm, rounded reality composed of well-known motifs: women in a state of undress, in their boudoirs or in Turkish baths or by little lakes or in mythological settings. And the only thing that set these pictures apart from those of the previous century was that the painting of physical features—the hair between the legs, for instance—was scrupulously lifelike: not least because Carl Laurids had insisted on precisely this detail. It was he, too, who engaged the nude models and with his own hand composed the traditional-style still lifes that were so popular, arranging freshly shot pheasants and dead-eyed hares on tables alongside expensive porcelain and the latest Mauser rifles—ever so casually disposed. In these arrangements, the timeless country-house atmosphere with which Carl Laurids had grown up was brilliantly combined with the most modern technology.

Of course, there is no way of knowing how many pictures Carl Laurids sold, but it was a lot—lots and lots—that much, at least, Amalie remembered his saying; so there is little reason to doubt that once again he has struck gold, just as he had done on every other occasions. Nevertheless, one day it was all over. One day Amalie looked out of the window to see that the garage doors were standing open and that the big studio, which had for years been full of canvases, was now completely empty. I doubt whether Amalie has thought much about this. From where she stood, right in the thick of things, I dare say the situation did look just as she described it when replying to inquiries from her women friends: "Carl's full of ideas; he's always coming up with something new; I wouldn't give it a thought; Carl's work is so boring; the best way to get to know Carl is socially, preferably over a good dinner," she said. But to the rest of us, standing back from it all, it is quite another story; and I, who am obliged to tell the truth, must now point out that it is very difficult to discover why Carl Laurids acts as he does. Up to this point one could get away with thinking that he is driven by the same motive by which everyone around him thinks they are driven: the wish to accumulate sufficient wealth and build up a business so sound that they can face the future with confidence. But it becomes difficult to maintain this point of view; there are grounds for suspecting that, once again, far too little of the truth is being disclosed. Well, why else would Carl Laurids keep moving on? It is pretty much a foregone conclusion that he could have earned a decent living and supported both his home and his marriage in any one of the areas that he sped through; he would have become a millionaire wherever he was, and for most of the time he probably *was* a millionaire—if we disregard his financially obscure beginnings around the time of the balloon ascent. And yet he stays only so long in any one place before wiping the slate clean and moving on to something else, and from that to the next thing, and then on to the next—until all the signs are that he is searching for something in particular; that what he wants out of life is something other than money, something else, something that as yet remains a mystery.

It was at this point that he sold his cars, keeping just one, a limousine convertible, with a cream-colored hood and a capacious trunk; an odd move, and one that coincided with his giving up the offices on Ny Øster Street from which he had been operating ever since the Rosengården days. He had retained one of the painters, a taciturn little man with a profound grasp of graphic techniques. With this man as his sole employee, Carl Laurids now ran a business about which we know very little, and upon which I do not wish to comment, apart from citing one of Amalie's recollections. She seems to remember Carl Laurids once telling her—while half-asleep— that he was printing banknotes. She remembers how she—also half-asleep—had felt so happy because she thought he must have been taken on by the National Bank. There is, however, nothing to suggest that this was the case—far from it. It seems certain that Carl Laurids was still his own boss, but apart from that we know nothing, not even where the business was based.

There are a good number of photographs of Carl Laurids from those days, and even a painting executed by one of his painters; similarly, people who met him during this period remember him clearly to this day. He was tall and slim and broad-shouldered; he had a smooth, fresh complexion; and the gaze he directed at the camera lens was very, very penetrating. People who had known him since he first appeared on the scene have said that the years had not touched him; that when they looked at Carl Laurids they still saw the youth in the white tails and flying helmet, giving an unforgettable speech from a pile of champagne cases. To me, sitting here with the photographs, it does not look quite like that. To me it is obvious, very obvious, that the intervening years can be discerned in Carl Laurids's face. It is as though that ruthless self-assurance has grown even greater and, with this, the face has grown calmer. But at the same time that little facial tic has spread and can no longer be hidden by his mustache. This tic, which stems from his time at Mørkhøj, has gradually become more marked and has, by this time, started sending sudden quivering spasms across the lower part of his face. But, this apart, I think it is true to say that Carl Laurids's features do seem remarkably youthful—or perhaps time-less would be closer to the mark. He seems to stand outside, or to one side of, the processes which age his contemporaries and which, for want of a better term, we call the passage of time. Where, during these years, Carl Laurids's peers seem to be consolidating, he seems to be branching out. While those businessmen who are, in a way, his colleagues—or at any rate his guests and neighbors and admirers—are accumulating most of what life has to offer—or at any rate, cars and paintings and houses and titles and directorships and mistresses and vintage wine, as well as less tangible things such as security and peace of mind and, of course, capital, above all, capital—these are the very things which, during these years, Carl Laurids either cuts himself off from or does not seem to worry about. Thus the only point at which, from a historical point of view, we can pin him down to a normal pattern of behavior is in his relationship with Amalie; and even this point is no longer as constant as it once was, because in the years after Carsten's birth Carl Laurids is away from home more and more often and for longer and longer periods.

In reality, Carsten's childhood ought to have been different. If this family had not been as it was, then his childhood ought to have been like that of other children on Strand Drive or on Bred Street or on Søtorvet—in other words, permeated by all the secrets which people kept from one another, and most particularly from the children. This reticence was designed to protect that sensitivity and innocence which would, some years later, lead the Children's Panel and, hence, Carl Laurids and Amalie's neighbor the merchant P. Carl Petersen to so thoroughly misjudge young Maria. Carsten's situation was, however, somewhat different. As a consequence of Carl Laurids's absences, and his indifference, and as a consequence of Amalie's fierce love for her child, and her dreamy, untroubled view of the world, during these years, nothing—or almost nothing —was hidden from little Carsten. Amalie utterly ignored the opinion of her friends and the psychiatrists and the general public that the best thing for children is to be kept out of sight, kept out of the way, kept down—apart, of course, from those occasions when they are trotted out in their role as the most important thing in the world, the coming generation. She took Carsten everywhere with her, and since she categorically refused to hand him over to nannies, Carsten saw everything: he saw her friends; sat in on drawing and flower-arranging classes; accompanied her to Fonnesbech's department store and to the racecourse and to Amalie's riding lessons at Mattson's—where Gladys sat with him in her arms so that Amalie need never lose sight of him. During these years, the entertaining at the house on Strand Drive reached new heights. There was a frantic air to these years, as if (and here we are talking with the benefit of hindsight) Carl Laurids, and perhaps also his guests, sensed that while he may be the one who brings them together, whom they lean upon and whom, at this time, they are even trying to have nominated for Parliament, he is also about to leave them. These parties constitute some of Carsten's earliest memories. He recalled the food and the monocled men and the old women smelling of camphor and cloves and the young matrons—radiant blossoms with women's faces—and the officers in uniform, complete with saber; no party was complete without a saber. He also sees the servants, the secret matrimonial confrontations in the invisible corridors, the frenzied couplings on the smooth lawns, and the dreadful drunkenness; and that he saw and remembered these things is yet another indication of a fact we have stumbled upon so often before in this context: that children take in a great deal more than we give them credit for. Obviously, all the women kissed the little boy in his lace-collared sailor suit and linen cap, and the men shook his hand; but since he was a child no one really paid any attention to him, and those who did remember anything about him remembered a pale-faced boy with large, pensive eyes. And that is as much as we can possibly discover about these years of Carsten's life: that he is pale and has large, pensive eyes; and that he never leaves Amalie's side; and that he sees everything—pretty much everything—apart from his father, Carl Laurids, who is barely glimpsed, because he is so busy; and if he is around, then he is either leaving the house or coming in, or crossing to the grand piano with a glass of champagne for some diva who has just finished singing. Or else it is afternoon and he is kicking Dodo the greyhound out of the way, to get to Amalie that much quicker. But he never notices Carsten. Nor does he notice those big, inquisitive eyes with which, a moment later, Carsten sees his parents' ever-present, permanently pulsating passion ignite and explode, right there at his feet—on the floor—in broad daylight—in that huge house; which is deserted except for the invisible servants and, of course, himself. And it is now, right now, that Carl Laurids starts to fade away.

It is now that he stops paying the rent on premises that lay we know not where, and in which he must have wound up his last company—which dealt with we know not what, apart from that sleepy hint that it might have been in the banknote-printing line. Soon Carl Laurids will be gone, never to return; soon I will be left even more alone than before; and even though all that has been taken from me are the partially erased tracks of a long-dead historical character, still I can already feel the loneliness that comes from my never having understood Carl Laurids and from my inability to let go of what I have not understood. All I can do, to catch a last glimpse of him, is open my eyes wide and try to peer into the dwindling light, though it reveals nothing other than those inscrutable photographs of him and the knowledge that, toward the end, the Copenhagen chief of police was a regular visitor to Carl Laurids's home; and not only the chief of police but also certain foreign gentlemen with whom he conversed in English and German.

There are many indications that during this period his business dealings hinged upon his many and most diverse contacts rather than on merchandise—apart, that is, from the sporadic deliveries to the villa of certain boxes containing weapons. It was from these boxes, the day before he disappeared, that he took the parts for the machine gun that Carsten helped him to assemble. It seems likely that he was at this time acting as some kind of consultant, promoting the sale of armaments from Scandinavia to certain European powers that were then planning an armed solution to the problem posed by the future. He may also have been acting as a vital link between Danish and European police forces and intelligence services. And at this point it is tempting to say, aha, so that's what Carl Laurids was up to, that's what he was aiming at; so he did believe in his own speeches, after all, and now he is going to wind up feeding the flames of the fire from whose ashes the new Europe will rise. But this would be a mistake, because there is nothing to indicate that Carl Laurids was politically active. As far back as Mørkhøj, he had realized that every phoenix rises only to be, a moment later, charred to a crisp—and once reduced to ashes, one species of bird is as good as the next. He would never dream of committing himself. Confronted by the chief of police and the foreigners with the smoldering eyes and voices thick with hopes of the future, he was, as always, courteous, laconic, and totally dispassionate.

On the evening prior to his disappearance—after he and Carsten had assembled the big machine gun—Carl Laurids went for a walk. This was no farewell stroll but a walk he was in the habit of making. Everyone else—including me, I think—would have headed into the countryside, through the budding beech woods, but Carl Laurids walked down to the cold and leaden Sound. He stepped out briskly, past the private beaches and the white bathing tents and stone breakwaters. His movements are loose and easy, and it is evident that this moment of leavetaking—during which most people try to put off what is to come, if only ever so slightly—did not present a problem to Carl Laurids. On his return to the villa he hung up his cane and his straw hat in the vestibule as he always did and went into the drawing room to say good night to Amalie; the only inconsistency here was that he did not stay for a minute, sitting on the chaise longue or standing in the doorway in his usual wearisome but obligatory attempt to gain permission to follow her up to bed. He simply said good night, then turned on his heel and walked down the corridor and out of this story.

Amalie was only fleetingly surprised by his curtness, and not even later—when she was desperately going over the events of the last few days in her head, trying to come up with some motive for his disappearance—not even then did she understand that this last gesture on his part was, in all probability, a sign that he had succeeded in his greatest and most significant undertaking: to make himself absolutely free of her, the only person he had ever loved.

Then Carl Laurids is gone. Of course, it took time to ascertain that he had mortgaged the house to the hilt, sold all the stocks and shares, emptied all the bank accounts, and taken the car, although all of this was merely a formal confirmation of what the whole world knew by the very next evening. The rumor spread along invisible channels, leaving behind it a dull paralysis that would take many years to turn, very slowly, into pain and loss and wonder and triumph among all those to whom Carl Laurids had been important.

Amalie had known since early that afternoon. She had been in Copenhagen with Carsten to collect a prince's outfit which she had forced Carl Laurids into having made up because she had fallen into the habit of calling her son "my little prince." In the shop, while Carsten was trying on the outfit, Amalie saw the warm spring sunshine change color and grow white and cold. Seized by a sudden feeling of unease, she left immediately, with Carsten in tow. They found the villa empty, and Amalie sat down to wait. After an hour, they heard the outer door. Then she looked at Carsten, sitting opposite her on a large sofa, all forlorn, in white velvet trousers, white velvet jacket, blue cape, white cotton stockings, patent shoes with big buckles, a little sword, and a tin crown on his head.

"If he doesn't come now, he's never coming," she said.

They sat perfectly still for a few minutes, until there could be no doubt that it was the wind that had slammed the door.

Then Amalie said, "He's left me."

The shadows in the grounds lengthened; the rumor of Carl Laurids's disappearance spread in Copenhagen; Carsten got up and walked softly around the empty rooms with his sleeves dangling over his hands because the tailor had not had the time he needed—and Amalie sat on in the big armchair, staring into space. She sat on as the sun set, sat on right through the night, and while she was sitting there the house held its breath, the invisible servants held their breath, the world held its breath, and we hold ours—because it is so obvious how little Carl Laurids has left her. He has run off with much more than the limousine and the bank accounts and her respectable standing as a married woman and a mother. He has taken her romantic bliss. For when Amalie treated Carl Laurids with distracted disdain, when she played with him and kept him at arm's length and kept his desire simmering, painful and uncontrollable, it was only because she was sure that she and he were floating in a bubble in eternal space. She had been so sure that there would never, ever, come a moment such as this one, when everything around her seemed to be melting away, even the house. Already, that night—with telepathic clarity—she sensed her husband's final, heartless mortgaging.

That night, there are very few of those who know Amalie, and knew Carl Laurids, who have any doubts about how things will turn out. In their opinion, Amalie is, of course, finished; it is not just that she is a woman on her own with a child and the shame and poverty; no, what is worst of all is that she has been abandoned by Carl Laurids Mahogany. That is the most awful thing. Carl Laurids always knew how to get out in time, and who has ever dared to pick up the pieces after him? And so, around Strand Drive and in Gentofte and on Bred Street no one gives much for Amalie's chances; despite the fact that these people love to gamble, not one bet is taken on whether she will make it or not, because, obviously, she is finished; all that is left for her is a heroic suicide, or a rapid descent into social obscurity. Then they lay their heads on their pillows and switch off their bedside lights.

Nevertheless, they all dreamed of Amalie—inconsistent, confusing dreams, only a few of which have been preserved for posterity, and which I will not waste time on here, especially since we have the eyewitness reports of the invisible servants, who put off leaving the house, and Carsten, who spent the whole night sitting on the sofa opposite his mother. Amalie said not one word in the course of that night, and during those first hours—as the sun went down and it grew dark, as she relived her crazy love for Carl Laurids and her longing for him—she resembled everyone else's picture of her: a frail young woman who calls to mind the dewy Madonnas from the paintings on their walls, and who might at any minute fall apart and dissolve into a pool of tears. Then she would admit to herself that a woman in Denmark in the 1920s is nothing without her man—especially not a fey dreamer like Amalie, whose father has squandered everything, virtually everything, so that she does not even have a fortune to compensate her for the fact that she has been dishonored.

Then one of the expensive, mortgaged clocks struck midnight, and the first despairing Danish dream of the abandoned wife was supplanted by a new dream, with Amalie's face turning into a white mask of bitterness as she saw her life as being wasted, her youth misspent, her marriage futile, and Carl Laurids a fiend. In this state she could, right there and then, have killed, and if she had become fixed in this wrath her life could have become the tale of the avenging wife and mother—which might also have been interesting, but that is not what happened; we must stick to the truth. Which is that as the night progressed, Amalie's face grew increasingly calm and increasingly determined. With the first faint light of dawn she caught sight of Carsten, who had fallen asleep on the sofa across from her; then she drew her legs up underneath her and a strange light came into her eyes. As the first rays of sunshine struck the tops of the trees in the grounds, Dodo the greyhound began to growl menacingly. It had been sleeping on the rug in front of the fireplace and now, having been woken by the sun, it lifted its head and saw Amalie. She was still sitting in the armchair with her legs folded beneath her, looking both alert and relaxed as she stared straight ahead, without blinking. At that moment she looked so much like a big cat that the greyhound did not recognize her, and when she shifted one paw lazily, the dog slunk out of the room. Then Amalie got to her feet, lifted Carsten, and carried him up to his room. As she covered him with the quilt she said, matter-of-factly, "What I am about to do I do for you."

That same afternoon she rang the stockbroker at his office and asked him to call on her that evening. She knew he would come, and for the last half hour before the appointed time she watched from the windows of Carl Laurids's deserted office on the third floor as he paced back and forth, a little way down Strand Drive, referring at brief intervals to his watch, so that he could knock on her door with a punctuality of the kind which her grandmother in Rudkøbing had taught herself and tried to teach her children, but which was, for this man and his family, a two-hundred-year-old matter of course.

He was a member of a Jewish family that had resided in Copenhagen for several hundred years and that had built up in that city a banking and stockbroking business with the most spotless reputation. Once, shortly after he arrived in Copenhagen, Carl Laurids had visited the tall, narrow building on Gammel Strand to suggest, with his patent assurance, a collaboration. He had been turned down flat by the very man who was now waiting outside his house on Strand Drive, the man who had at that time just assumed leadership of the stockbroking company after twenty years with the Ministry of Finance. At the ministry he had developed an allergy, a dry cough, that would start up whenever he found himself in the same room as an unsound business. Just at the sight of Carl Laurids's hat coming over the Marble Bridge he started gasping for breath; and when Carl Laurids was standing in his private office his whole body broke out in an itch so unpleasant that—once Carl Laurids had left—he had to loosen all his clothes in order to scratch, an unheard-of act for such a tightly buttoned-up lawyer. Not being one to give up hope, Carl Laurids had invited the stockbroker to his balloon ascent. He had come, quite without knowing why he did so, and it was there that he first laid eyes on Amalie. After that, Carl Laurids kept on issuing invitations to him, presumably to borrow a little luster from his respectability, and the stockbroker had kept on attending the parties on Strand Drive—still without knowing why. He always turned up somberly attired, never danced, drank nothing, ate modestly, and spent the evening sidling from room to room along the walls without any hope of meeting anyone he knew, and making no human contact other than a casual handshake from Carl Laurids.

What none of the guests knew, and what the stockbroker himself did not realize—what, in all probability, Carl Laurids did not even grasp—Amalie recognized immediately. With his stiff collars and his stiff gaze and his stiff movements, this powerful, prosperous citizen and civil servant was trying to keep at least some sort of grip on himself, to stop himself from breaking down into his basic components—these involving, first and foremost, a powerful craving for Amalie. She knew that this craving was the sole reason for his turning up, year after year, at the hedonistic parties on Strand Drive and, once there, enduring the loneliness and the dreadful itching and the coughing fits that assailed him when confronted with so many unsavory businesses assembled in one spot. And when he sidled from room to room with his back to the dance floor it was, Amalie knew, solely in order to follow her every move in the wall mirrors. Up till then she had never paid him any attention. She had noted him and added him to her mental list of admirers, but he and she moved in different worlds. Now she raised him up into her reality.

She let him in and showed him around the villa, chatting to him all the while about religious matters: opening maneuvers which, however, lasted only for as long as Amalie deemed necessary. In the bedroom, she disrobed him so gently that his garments seemed, to him, to fall off unaided. With the unfastening of the last buttons he fell apart, and Amalie picked him up and took him in her arms. He cried inconsolably while they made love and continued to cry like a child throughout the night. When morning came, he sat in Amalie's lap in knee-length silk underpants, sucking on a white cloth while she gently rocked him. At that point she could have asked for anything whatsoever; he would have given her everything, but the only thing she asked of him was to be her confidant and financial adviser during these difficult times. Thereafter, she helped him to dress and knew, when he left, that he would always come back.

Without a moment's hesitation she then picked up the telephone and told the professor to come. The professor belonged to a noble family whose members had been generals and admirals since the time of Christian IV—and still were. He himself had been a colonel in the Army before opting for a professorship in architecture, and he girded himself with learning and medals and a hoarse bark and boasts about his family's wealth, along with various other signs of unassailable virility—all of which Amalie had seen right through, despite having met him on only a handful of occasions, at parties given by Carl Laurids to which he lured this coxcomb, this Knight-of-the-Dannebrog-at-such-an-early-age, by pandering to his vanity—by no means a difficult undertaking. On these occasions

Amalie had seen past his decorations to the mistreated and hard-pressed mongrel hiding behind the stiff fabric of his uniform and the gold braid. She knew he had noticed her, and she knew that he would come because he remembered her and because, when she spoke to him on the telephone, she had not invited him but given him an order. He arrived as punctually as the stockbroker had done the day before, in full court dress. Without wasting any time on the formalities, Amalie led him to the bedroom, ordered him to take off his uniform, and when he hesitated, slapped his face, hard, several times. At this he broke down; then she made him pull down his trousers and she spanked him. He cried when, after a little while of this, she stopped—"But that's all you're getting," she said, "a few small slaps on that white army bottom," and then he had to button up. In the drawing room she allowed him to drink half a cup of tea, to help him pull himself together, while she sat opposite him, her face hard and inscrutable. Then she ordered him to leave. She did not get up to show him out, but as he was leaving she told him coldly that his only chance of being allowed to come again lay in taking care of certain urgent expenses for her. From the hallway, through the closed drawing room door, he begged her to let him write her a check, and once he had done so she had the footmen throw him out.

On the next evening she was visited by an influential government minister and on the next by H. N. Andersen; and since these two men are well-known figures whose memories are protected I will refrain from mentioning here a lot of things that could be divulged, or what Amalie demanded of them. All I will say is that her demands were modest. And so it continued: she made demands, but they were never high.

On the fifth day—which was the last, this time around—she received the Copenhagen inspector of schools, and from him exacted the promise that when the time came—in other words, in over ten years' time—he would procure a scholarship for Carsten to one of the most prestigious prep schools in the country.

Then she went to bed and slept for the first time in five days.

The simplest thing now would be to say that evidently Amalie must have decided to become a prostitute; naturally, that would be simplest, since we all believe we know what that word entails. But

in her case this would not be correct; it would be a gross simplifi-
cation of Amalie's activities in the years ahead. Beginning with the
stockbroker and the professor-colonel, these amounted to a series
of moves—let us say business transactions, or let us say amorous
transactions—that were a great deal more subtle and complex and
difficult to comprehend than ordinary prostitution. Amalie *understood* her customers, that much can be said here and now; she
understood that the stockbroker had to be handled like a frightened
child and that the professor had to be denied precisely what he
thought he had come for and that the government minister should
be allowed to talk, just talk, and that H. N. Andersen wanted her
to recount for him fictitious incidents from his youth among the
brothels of the East Indies—incidents he could now relive only in
this way, with a strange woman and the sough of the Sound in the
background. And she gave these men exactly what they needed,
without losing one vestige of her own dignity.

In the course of that one night on which she had said farewell to
Carl Laurids, she lost any resemblance to the Madonnas on the
walls and slipped away from our dream—and the dream of her own
day and age—of a delicate, symbolic woman. In a sense, she continued to look as she had always done; she corresponds in every
respect to the ideal of her day, her customers' ideal and ours, of a
beautiful woman: an ideal that calls for shapely hands, soft lips, and
regular, delicate features, and so on and so forth. But there is no
longer anything the least bit delicate about this woman as a whole,
and we must differentiate between Amalie before and Amalie after
Carl Laurids's disappearance. Previously, in her dress, she had followed the daring fashions of the day; she had mastered the art of
being both distant and absolutely up to the minute with her bobbed
hair, loose-fitting, low-waisted dresses, and boyishly flat chest. But
from the night on which Carl Laurids disappeared she altered her
appearance. She tied a turban around her hair until it grew long
enough to be piled up in elaborate coils; and from then on, she wore
only black dresses—not to show that she was in mourning, not to
look like a widow, but because black represents solidity and, during
these years, it was solidity for which Amalie was reaching out. Her
dresses were tight-fitting, clearly delineating her figure and emphasizing to anyone and everyone—including us, whose knowledge
of her appearance is gleaned mainly from photographs—that she

grew to look more and more like a big, beautiful cat. That was how she received her first customers and, later, the long ranks of those who succeeded them.

It was to be the case with all of Amalie's business relationships that her demands were moderate. With most of her clients, she could have asked for anything at all, but did not. She now practiced in her business affairs the same restraint that had become an ideal for her since she decided, after Carl Laurids's disappearance, to bid farewell to her extravagant ways. Do not expect me to explain this. I am only reporting the truth—even if, as here, it does consist of riddles: riddles such as how Amalie managed to take these steps into reality and, in just five days, ensure that she and her child could stay on Strand Drive and in stylish society, and in comfortable circumstances, when everyone, even I, would have expected her to drop out of the villa and into some humble public office and into another district and out of this tale.

On the seventh day after Carl Laurids's disappearance the workmen arrived, and for the week during which they were at work Amalie received no one, absolutely no one. During that period she left her five first clients—who had safeguarded her future—to yearn for her; left her and Carl Laurids's acquaintances to speculate over just when she would be forced to move out. These workmen were the same foreigners who had, at the beginning of the century, installed her grandmother's water closet. They were much older now, and spoke with less and less exuberance, but they worked with the same impressive dexterity. It has not been possible to discover where they came from or how Amalie found them; when they were finished she paid them in cash—with H. N. Andersen's money—and then they vanished.

Anyone less strong than Amalie would undoubtedly have been tempted to have all traces of Carl Laurids removed. There were other women—who do not come into this story, but whom I mention here because they, like Amalie, felt that they had been abandoned by Carl Laurids—who continued to wallow in the despair out of which Amalie pulled herself. They burned every picture of Carl Laurids and every present he had given them; they even burned their sheets and made all sorts of excuses to their husbands for cleaning their homes from top to bottom. They did not, however, succeed in cleaning the vanished cynic's ghostly charm from their hearts, and in the end they went as far as to burn the rugs and the drapes and had the furniture re-covered, to get at least a bit of peace. Amalie did not need to do any of this. She put all the photographs of him in a drawer, gave away most of the things he had left behind in his wardrobe to the Salvation Army, and locked up his office, which still held traces of his burning of the last of his papers. Then she set the workmen to work on the task for which she had really engaged them: to make the house into a barred incubator for Carsten.

Before this, Amalie had never worried about Carsten, regarding him, as she did, as a child of the gods. In her world—which I have never understood and which she does not appear to have had a clear grasp of, either—Carsten was a kind of small Achilles. So convinced was she that he was not of this world, that he was on a plane above it, that she let him do whatever he liked; let him fall and burn himself and bump himself and cut himself; and laughed at his tears and kissed his scratches, saying, "There, now, Mama's kiss will make you all better, my lamb," and was sure that it really would. But from one day to the next, after Carl Laurids disappeared, she grew afraid that something might happen to Carsten; and this would prove to be a lifelong fear. When she rang the stockbroker, and thereby stepped into reality herself, she got it into her head that she must have pulled Carsten down to earth with her and that he was no longer invulnerable. That, at any rate, is part of the explanation for her seeming, all at once, to see the white villa as a landscape fraught with deathtraps for a sensitive child such as Carsten. It seemed to her, now, that the windows yawned vacantly onto an abyss into which Carsten might plummet at any minute, so she had the workmen put up grilles; first on the second-floor windows; then on the ground-floor windows, because she thought they were also too high; and then on the basement windows, to protect him against kidnappers. She started to heed the doctors' warnings against too much sunlight and had heavy drapes hung over the barred windows; then she had the sharpest and most dangerous-looking dragons' heads cut off the furniture and the doors to the back stairs locked so that he would not tumble down them. With all this done, there came a day when she thought she heard the cutlery rattling aggressively in its drawers—so she had all of the knives replaced by a special type with rounded tips and then had all of the drawers and cupboards con-

CARL LAURIDS AND AMALIE] *245*

taining the kitchen utensils fitted with padlocks. By the time the
workmen were finished, the house had been altered beyond recognition. For years, after they had left it, only very few changes were
made; so we know, from the eyewitness accounts and from the
photographs, just how it looked. In these photographs the rooms are
unrecognizable—these cannot be the suites that Carl Laurids had
decorated so provocatively and with such aplomb, we tell ourselves.
But they are, and if you look very closely you will be able to recognize
one piece of furniture after another, until it dawns on everyone—
just as it dawned on me—that the change has been wrought by the
new gloom behind the heavy drapes and by certain details that
Amalie herself arranged with a sure touch. The only thing she asked
the workmen to do—other than the grilles on the windows—was to
paint over the Dionysian excesses on the walls of the garden pavilions. Everything else she attended to herself; which meant that she
first of all removed the Indian miniatures from her own bedroom,
partly because she did not want to scare her clients and partly because they reminded her of what she had had with Carl Laurids,
which she knew would never come again. Then she moved certain
of the most naked modern paintings out of the drawing room into
less-frequented rooms; hoisted a large, crude chandelier made out
of old bayonets farther up, and shifted some of the improper lifesize
bronze figures into the corners of the rooms, out of view. The weird
modern chrome and ebonite lamps in organic shapes that Carl Laurids had brought back from his trips abroad, or received as gifts from
his American contacts, she shoved to the back of the shelves—and
with these and some other minor alterations she changed the house
completely. Just two months later, she gave her first dinner party.
If I were to describe the entertaining done during Carl Laurids's
time in one word, then the word that comes to mind is "loose."
Everything about Carl Laurids's parties was loose: the number of
invited guests was loosely estimated; their titles were loose, and their
fortunes and their conversations and their connections and rules for
how one ought, in general, to behave; so that the party was like a
large, brightly colored, unpredictable creature that pulsated: now
screeching and ferocious, now muttering and cautious.

Amalie's first parties, and all those that came after them, were
very different. On the first occasion, she invited twelve people—six
married couples; on subsequent occasions she again invited twelve,

or sometimes eight, and on rare occasions twenty-four people. The guests were, that first time and thereafter, officers in the Army and heads of government departments and commodores and judges and professors and company directors and undersecretaries, with now and again a politician, and now and again a writer—almost all of whom had wives who could sew and cook and run a household with a firm hand. These people regarded themselves as the very flower of Danish Officialdom and pillars of the Danish State System. They arrived on time, somberly dressed; they ate sparingly, drank little or nothing at all, and conversed quietly on the chances of avoiding pneumonia by sprinkling powdered sulfur in one's socks in the morning, and on the lovely plaster casts of Greek antiquities in the National Art Museum. After dinner, the men sat together in one group and the women in another; there was never any dancing at these parties, and at eleven o'clock everyone left—everyone, without exception.

One might wonder at Amalie's giving these dinner parties. At the time of the first she had—at least to the best of my knowledge— between ten and fifteen regular clients whom she herself referred to as Friends of the Family and whom she allowed to visit her once or, at the most, twice a month. And the amazing thing is that it is these very men and their wives who constitute the core of the social circle that she builds up over these years. Why, I have asked myself, was it necessary for Amalie, who was otherwise so discreet, to run such a risk as this must have involved: taking on the role of hostess, thereby bringing herself into the public eye, and then, as if that were not enough, putting her clients around the same table, along with their wives? The answer has to be that she herself wished to be a part of this company. She had been let down twice in her life, first by her father—who had lost everything thanks to his need to rebel—and then by Carl Laurids, with his lack of respect for anything whatsoever; both of whom were men who had challenged some of the fundamental values in life. Now Amalie turned to face these values and their servants, these buttoned-up men and quiet women—but she was not content merely to meet them in her bedroom. Her wish, for her son and for herself, was that he and she should also be respectable and share in the traditions of these people. And at first glance this wish seems incredible; how can Amalie be both courtesan and healing spirit for these men—drying their tears and giving them satisfaction or spanking them or bathing them or talking harshly to them—and then sitting with them, shortly afterward, around the dinner table, amid all that polite conversation and good taste? How can she? Because both she and her guests are schooled, primed, utterly perfect, flawless exponents of a particular type of behavior: one that forms an important part of the Story of Danish Dreams; one that is usually called the art of reticence. Carsten notices it for the first time at Amalie's first dinner party. He also sits down to this dinner, to this one and all the others—Amalie insisted upon it, even though she knew it was a breach of a protocol that was, in all other respects, followed to the letter. That she would not yield on this point is, of course, because these dinner parties are held for his sake, since she means him to draw nourishment from the presence of these people, and learn from them, and perhaps become, first of all, like them and, later, even better—preferably even better. Amalie's ambitions are at this point extremely far-reaching, and that is why Carsten attends these dinners. He is only five years old, but nevertheless, like many children, he is extremely sentient. Though unable to put what he experiences into words, he has immediately perceived that this party is not like the ones he is used to; he notes the composure and the dark colors and observes (to his disappointment) that the women are fully clothed, and that there is no music. Later he also notices something else. At some point during the dinner, when he has long since given up trying to follow the conversation, he senses a tension, senses that the very furniture, in this room and the others, is trying to stay absolutely still: the grand piano does not resound to the conversation as it usually does and only a very few sounds penetrate from outside—and all because these people, none of whom he knows, are surrounded by a force field of suppressed energy. Vibrating beneath the dark surface and their table manners and the disciplined gestures there is a tremendous pent-up power, which forms an intrinsic part of these people and of the truth about Danish Officialdom, and which disguises itself with dark clothing, restraint, and well-considered remarks. Only on the thin outer crust of Amalie's parties is there anything banal. Beneath this crust power surges. While her guests discuss the excellent warming qualities of angora and the merits of sulfur powder and how the Copenhagen museums have so many lovely plaster figures, what they are in actuality discussing is the big questions in life: love and money and religion and life and death—only it is hard to catch this because they speak so softly. While keeping within the bounds of Society and making sure that no one could hold them responsible for anything whatsoever, because they have spoken so obtusely and with such tremendous discretion, they carry on conversations in which dramas no less intense than those of Carl Laurids are played out. And this Carsten understands. Not on that first occasion, I grant you—at that point he is still too small and merely senses the tension in the room. But as time goes on, within a few years, he is old enough to grasp what is actually being said, and to recover from his first feelings of confusion, which stem from, among other things, the command over time possessed by these people. Their ancestors once served in the bureaucracy of the absolute monarchy, and, what with family tradition and their own endeavors, they have become so proficient in subjecting themselves to King and Country and Duty and God and Morality that they can speak of seventeenth-century imbroglios as though they themselves had been responsible for their outcome, and of events far into the future—such as their own retirement or their children's retirement—as if they were just around the corner. This is also why the men are now able to forget where they actually are: in a house decorated with a wild extravagance that is toned down only perfunctorily by the drapes; a house in which, at other times, they were received in very different ways, before being led to the bedroom, where their tears or wails or cries of joy or grunts reveal something about the price of forgoing the unpredictable, personal side of life in favor of Duty.

These parties worked because, of course, Amalie was the perfect hostess. These days she was never distant, as she had been in Carl Laurids's day. On the contrary, she exerted such a presence in the room that every single guest felt that he or she had been particularly favored. Not one of the men suspected for a moment that he was not the only man in Amalie's life. Such was the treatment Amalie accorded her clients—so individual and so sincere—that not one of them ever realized how, no matter what else went into their relationship with her, it all came down to business; it was a matter of survival. Moreover, whether there is anyone else in Amalie's life, and why she does what she does, are questions to which they give little if any thought during these dinner parties. This is owing to the extent of what we agreed, a little earlier, to call reticence. So all-embracing is this reticence that, on these occasions, the other truth about Amalie—the truth about the bedroom and the professor with his trousers around his ankles, and the stockbroker crying like a baby, and H. N. Andersen's brothel stories—does not exist; it is in no way whatsoever the truth. As far as the wives are concerned, the manner in which Amalie conducts herself and the good food and the carefully observed protocol make every one of them feel as though she were Amalie's bosom friend. It never occurs to them that, in any number of ways, Amalie knows more about their marriages than they do themselves. Indeed, on these evenings, it never occurs to Amalie either; she even deceives herself; even to her, on these evenings, her guests are just very good friends.

I would like to suggest a single word to epitomize Amalie's dinner parties. I know how dangerous such a word can be, that it is an oversimplification; but I have noticed that it is my way of remembering. It is a word that can be used as a sort of heading, a pointer to a more precise explanation. The word I would like to suggest is "consistent." The way in which her guests and she herself are polite, in which they observe all the many rules of social intercourse, and in which they avoid striking any note other than the right one is just that: *consistent*. I would like to add that this is a social convention, a way of life, that requires a great deal of energy, since one is constantly having to combat any tendency toward inconsistency—and life is full of such tendencies, even in those days.

So in a certain sense, Amalie is a consistent person. With her uncompromising discretion and her will to get on in the world, she is very, very persistent. But it now appears that she did have certain soft spots, a few weaknesses, and it is precisely these that make her story so interesting. If, all along, she had been as strong and intransigent as the people she wants to imitate, then she might have left fewer traces of herself, or at least different traces. But she found it hard to maintain absolute reticence. Somewhere within herself she must have been shaken by the deceit and the struggle to act as if everything were idyllic. And so, now and again, she confided in Carsten.

She did not tell him the truth, or at least not the truth as I see it; she did not present her situation in quite the way that I have done, that is, by admitting that she was a kind of high priestess tending a ritualized hypocrisy that was not actually hypocritical. Instead, she tells Carsten about her lovers as though there were only one. This must have been because she was ashamed; on those quiet evenings with her son the proprieties were there in the bed beside her. She —who bound her clients to her with an invisible rubber band that would, sooner or later, bring them catapulting back to her precisely because she would do anything whatsoever and never feel shame —felt ashamed when faced with her son. When she was confronted by him, her strength deserted her and she told him, not the truth, but her dream of the truth, which was that there was only one man and that he was not her client but her lover.

She undressed herself and Carsten almost completely, and lit candles; then they snuggled together in the big bed and she lowered her voice and told him about a man so generous and cultivated, the handsomest man in town, who had a most particular smell about him, a smell of Russian leather, which she tried to describe to Carsten. And every detail she had gleaned from her host of clients. Because she took such pleasure in her own dream, and because it was important to her that Carsten believed her, she embellished her portrait with insignificant minutiae until it seemed frightfully improbable, even to Carsten. Of course he knew she was lying; he is an astute boy and, in any case, he has seen everything—right from her meeting with her first customer, the stockbroker. He had witnessed his sobbing through one of the peepholes in the bedroom wall which Carl Laurids bored, once upon a time, and which Carsten had even seen his father using. That he had never forgotten. So although he listens entranced, he does know the truth, perhaps even better than Amalie herself, as she talks herself into her own hopes and invents a lover with none of her clients' neuroses, a lover who is terribly reminiscent of Carl Laurids.

Again I have this urge to shout at Amalie, across the expanse of history, "What the hell do you mean by treating a little boy like that, making him your confidant, using him the way your customers use you—like someone you can pound away at and exact relief from? After all, he's only a small boy who, while all this is going on, has only one thought in mind: how to earn his mother's love and take his place at her side, replacing the real Friends of the Family and her make-believe lover!" But I restrain myself. It is too late anyway; there is nothing to do but shut up, clench one's teeth, and stick to the facts, which are that sometimes, while Amalie was describing her ideal husband, she would burst into tears and pull Carsten even closer to her and say, "You are the only man in my life, you are all I have, all my hopes are pinned on you, and one day you are going to make a new life for yourself and for me and boo-hoo-hoo"—she would bathe him in a flood of tears while he lies there, at the age of six or seven or eight or nine years old, wondering how on earth he is going to manage to carry the whole world on his shoulders.

During these years, the contradictions amid which he grows up are typical of the Danish upper class. His life is conducted in a dark tunnel with a white dot of light both ahead of him and behind. The light behind him is the days before Carl Laurids disappeared, and the light ahead is the future that Amalie sketches for him on an almost daily basis in the big bed, once her client has been dismissed and she has brought Carsten in beside her. In her vision of the future he will become a great lawyer and earn a fortune, and will, in some unspecified way, raise her above her present circumstances. The picture of Carsten's becoming a lawyer is very clear to her, so clear that often, in Carsten's presence, she will practice saying to her mirror, "My son is a lawyer," or, "My son is a trial lawyer, or a judge, or Chief Justice of the Supreme Court." This has its effect on Carsten. Before his sixth birthday he knows what he is going to be, and this knowledge forms that patch of light ahead of him in the tunnel. The tunnel itself is this house in which he has grown up, supposedly a good home and a sheltered nest for a child. That is how Amalie refers to it—"our cozy nest," she says of this monstrosity which, during these years, gives the impression of being deserted, having been built for a large family and lots of servants and a vast household; not for one son with a mother who has kept on only Gladys and a kitchen maid and a part-time gardener, and to whose dinner parties only six married couples are ever consistently invited.

The house is a monument to a particular picture of child rearing which is very widespread in Denmark at this time and in earlier days and which is based on the concept that it is possible to protect a child totally during its sensitive formative years; to keep it untouched by any and all influences while at the same time rearing it to face the big, bad world and all its temptations. It is to protect Carsten that Amalie has had the windows barred and the drapes hung; and even when either she or Gladys takes him out for a walk—since she believes fresh air is important—she insists that he carry a parasol to protect him from the sun. And, still for his own good, they keep him inside, or at least inside the grounds, and stop him from playing with the other children, who are, of course, the same upper-class children in lace collars, Little Lord Fauntleroy outfits, and sailor suits whom Carsten had always played with before. Now, however, Amalie imagines that they might harm him or somehow lead him astray or have a bad influence on him. So Carsten grows up in the dim rooms of the cozy nest, and during these years he becomes remarkably good at playing on his own, or with his nice, safe wooden blocks and his blunted tin soldiers and scissors with rounded tips, because he has no choice. He has no one else to play with because, since Carl Laurids's disappearance, the world, according to Amalie, is full of bad people and evil characters. And that is why Carsten can now only wave through the balcony grilles to his former playmates—P. Carl Petersen's masseuse's daughter and the little princesses who swim outside the Queen Mother's house and whose nakedness under their floppy bathing costumes he now has to content himself with imagining. Or, rather, he *almost* only waves from the balcony, because it so happens that now and again he manages to slip out. Now and again he is let out—always by Gladys or the gardener or the kitchen maid, because they had always done this sort of thing before, and because Carsten was on such close terms with the invisible inhabitants of the house, and, of course, because they loved him. So now and again they let him out into the grounds or into a neighboring garden or onto the street, but only ever when Amalie is not at home. It cannot have happened all that often; Carsten himself denied it later, and the only reason that I know anything at all about this is that the servants remember it.

Here it might be enlightening to point out that it is just around this same time that Maria, in Christianshavn, is defying her mother's ban against playing in the courtyard. It is interesting that the desire to protect children from other children exists both in Charlottenlund and in the tenements of Christianshavn. But one must beware of confusing the reactions of the two children. Maria's is a true rebellion, she does what she likes; by this time she has all but stopped depending on her parents. But Carsten's situation is somewhat different. At this point the most important person in his life, bar none, is his mother, against whom he would never dream of rebelling; he merely emits a few little cheeps and tugs ever so slightly at his leash.

The way Amalie sees it, all of the hazards in Carsten's life are outside: the sunshine, the other children, ditches just lying in wait, and the rolling countryside. Inside, it is safe. And so Carsten's childhood becomes a wide plain of endless afternoons on which he knew that one of the Friends of the Family was paying Amalie a visit. During these afternoons he would wander restlessly around the house beneath the bristling bayonet chandelier and etchings of bloody hunting motifs and toys—with the vast rooms shrouded in silence, apart from the distant sounds from Amalie's bedroom and the echo of that menacing reticence.

Amalie really struggled to raise Carsten in line with these secrets, which are an integral part of the bourgeois soul and which at this point, in the early 1930s, crop up in all walks of life—with a particularly refined variety flourishing in the families of civil servants. Now, of course these secrets had their purpose, though what this purpose might be, it was up to the children of the day to try to guess. The children have to feel their way to table manners, and where one may play and where one may not play and, most especially, what games one may not play; then they have to sense why the servants and the corridors and the toilets and the bathrooms are invisible and why naked walls are a threat; and why one never talks about money and never swears. Thus—by leaving the children to guess, instead of just telling them, straight out—one creates a tension and ensures that one's children will grow up imbued with a vibrant vigilance. This schooling in vigilance should guarantee that the young people may well relax, but never to the extent that they become lax and forget themselves and grow inconsistent. Part of the truth behind this reticence is that it creates an abiding state of tension. I find it hard to come up with any better explanation than this, nor do I think anyone should expect me to; who am I to explain this phenomenon that extends far beyond the Story of Danish Dreams and into the entire structure of Western culture? What I can do here is to say that Amalie was only partially successful in rearing Carsten in this fashion because she is not strict enough, not consistent enough; although she does try, something inside her always yields; there is something *porous* about the whole of this life that she has constructed for herself and Carsten. She tells him much more than she ought to, because she cannot bite her tongue; and since she cannot control her temper, she rants and raves at him, and throws china at him, instead of freezing him out, giving him the cold shoulder. She tells him about her fantasy lover, including physical details which he should not know the first thing about at this point, but which he is supposed to learn through guesswork several years from now. Even those things of which, once he had learned to walk, he ought not to have had the faintest inkling—her nakedness, and her body, vivacious in bed—even those she could not keep to herself.

To a certain extent, she keeps him cooped up, and he actually does have to spend the major part of his childhood in these dim rooms. When he reaches school age, she hires private tutors for him, so that she need not release him; she takes the first crystal set he builds away from him, to prevent him from hearing the shocking news reports, and she sends him to bed when her guests start talking about the world at large. Yet she cannot keep her own interest in politics hidden from him, and in sudden attacks of eager weakness she confides to him that the Dane Svend Olsen, whom she once met at a party, and who told her he loved her, had taken second place in weightlifting at the Olympic Games, and that a Social Democrat government minister, a Friend of the Family, has made a splendid impression at a meeting in South Jutland, and that she has recognized Carl Laurids in a photograph of influential Nazis grouped around Hitler. She lets him see the photograph, and he can sense that even while she thinks Carl Laurids's new status and elevated rank among these braggarts is all wrong and quite scandalous, still she finds it quite, quite fascinating.

So Carsten has a very mixed upbringing. In a way, the big villa is a kind of dank, moldy cellar that never sees the light of day, and there is something rather deformed about Carsten—slightly reminiscent, in his paleness, of a sucker shoot, he has the same look of well-bred distinction as a stalk of asparagus. But at the same time he has, of course, swallowed some good mouthfuls of fresh air, especially as a small child. He has felt his way through the world in a different way from that of his upper-class contemporaries, and hence there is a sureness to his movements that only the child who has been able to explore without constantly being stopped can acquire. All things considered, we should all be grateful that this is not a novel, since Carsten is far too complex a character to figure in a novel. It is a hard enough job portraying him as a historical character. He is a quiet boy; everyone who has met him says so, even Amalie. Carsten is a nice, polite boy, they say—by which they mean that one hardly ever notices him, and if one does, whatever one sees is just as it should be. But he is also someone who absorbs things; there is something absorbent about him as a person, and particularly about the large, dark eyes. He ingests every piece of information: the expensive lessons from private tutors, the dinner party conversations, and what, in bed, Amalie tells him he is going to achieve—with an urge to devour knowledge that must have something to do with his having grown up among adults. Although I cannot know for sure, I would imagine that growing children have need of other children; but around Carsten, the void created by interminable afternoons in that big house was only ever broken by adults. When he is very young he plays with building blocks, then with tin soldiers—and then he starts to read. It so happens that the big house contains quite a number of books. In all probability, Carl Laurids bought them to go with the furniture, and these books provide Carsten with yet another huge straw to dip into the adult world. What he reads, in fact, is gilt-edged Danish literature, in which grownup men describe the same loneliness as that which surrounds him. In a vague way, he recognizes his own situation in these books, although he never succeeds in doing what writers from the Golden Age onward have recommended: taking a masochistic pleasure in this loneliness. Throughout his childhood Carsten missed having playmates, and neither Amalie nor the books nor the visitors to the house were able to convince him positively that the outside world is something to be avoided, or at least approached with caution, and in any case to be guarded against.

If it is correct that the middle-class breeding and decent upbringing and good manners that Amalie abides by during these years is a strain, then perhaps I can describe what happens next as a sudden lapse. One evening, just after sending a guest home, Amalie went down to fetch Carsten. There is nothing at all unusual in this; she usually comes to fetch him around this time and normally finds him hunched over a book, or sitting, staring decorously into space, in some corner, with his white face a pale, gleaming patch in the darkness. But not this day; this day she finds him naked, having taken his clothes off and wrapped his body—which is slender and white with a greenish cast, through lack of sunshine—in black velvet. He has taken the velvet fabric from one of the long and ingeniously draped curtains that had, just a moment before, been covering the windows: pulled it down and cut it with the harmless scissors. To Amalie's thunderstruck face he says simply, "Darling Mother, I wanted so much to be just a *little bit* naughty," and thus avoids getting into trouble; thus he charms his mother and makes her forgive him on the spot. And one thing leads to another. Amalie wraps a bit of the sheared velvet around her head like a turban; later she loosens her dress; later still she calls for Gladys and gets her to help her undo the corset she has started wearing because she has put on weight and because her clients feel more comfortable in the company of corseted women. At this point she and Carsten dress up Gladys in some of the black velvet, and when there is not enough, the other curtain is cut down, allowing the waning evening sunlight to fill the room with a reddish, wistful light that reveals its Moorish wall decorations and patterned floor *à la* Alhambra. And perhaps that is why the game these three people are playing turns into a harem scene, with Carsten ordering the two women about and displaying an imperiousness that makes me think this middle-class propriety is full of surprises. Their game ends with Carsten laying his head in Amalie's lap while Gladys sings one of her tribe's wailing, feet-pounding songs. Obviously, all of this takes place indoors, and what makes this scene so astonishing is that it is precisely the kind of thing that Amalie is usually at such great pains to prevent. Picture, if you will, the sight of Amalie, the great—at this point almost naked—whore, and Carsten, the pale, dictatorial little boy, and Gladys, the sturdy African with the dreamy eyes and rhythmic movements, dancing and singing in the rays of the setting sun in these outlandish surroundings.

The next day everything is of course forgotten and has never happened and presents no problem; but from then on, Amalie and Carsten play abandoned games of this nature with increasing regularity. Often they play them in the bedroom, where Amalie gets Carsten to pretend to be a lawyer presenting cases in imaginary courtrooms against fictitious opponents who have insulted her sacred honor. Or she gets him to sing, or to dance childish little minuets that he has learned during some of the endless one-to-one classes with his private tutors. As time goes on, the character of these games alters. Sometimes they act out abduction scenes in which he kidnaps her and they ride on the tasseled bolsters across Amalie's bed, which is as vast as a desert. Or she tells him about the life he and she will share once he has distinguished himself and completed his education and been appointed to a permanent post. It is during this period that she persuades him to take her photograph with a camera she has been given by one of her clients, and more and more often she tells him, "There have been three men in my life: my father, Carl Laurids, and you; but the other two let me down." After a while she seems to forget both Christoffer Ludwig and Carl Laurids, and it is then that she switches to saying, "There has only ever been one man in my life, and that is you."

They start to go on outings. A Friend of the Family has loaned Amalie a chauffeur-driven car, and in this she and Carsten take drives through the woods of North Zealand, sitting in the backseat sniggering like children, unaware that they are heading into the land of lost souls that lies just beyond the bounds of good breeding and reticence.

It was on one of these outings that they paid a visit to Christoffer Ludwig. It was spring, and the cool air and the sunlight and Amalie's feelings for Carsten, which by this time had long since eliminated her good judgment, filled her, one Saturday morning, with a sentimental urge to see her father—and Carsten assented. Amalie had begun to ask his advice, and that morning, when she asked him if he would like to visit her father, she added flirtatiously, "I'm asking you because you are the man of the house."

Visiting Christoffer Ludwig was like stepping into another age. Dannebrogs Street languished, as always, in the same indeterminate light, and Amalie had the feeling even while still outside the house that she ought to have stayed away. The door of the apartment was not locked, but the foyer was almost completely blocked by books. There were books everywhere in the apartment, thousands of volumes stacked from floor to ceiling, and the reams and reams of paper had drained the air of moisture, leaving a crackling dryness that seared the throat. Carsten and Amalie could see, as they passed from room to room along the passages between the books, that the apartment looked as though it had always been deserted. Finally

Amalie took a deep breath and led Carsten past the teetering piles and into what had at one time been her father's study. Christoffer Ludwig was still sitting at the round table, at the same spot and in the same position as when Amalie had sought him out so many years before, to tell him she had seen her great-grandfather's ghost. He was very old and his eyes glistened with senility. He was barely capable of grasping that there were living creatures in the room. It was evident that he had been forsaken, surrounded by books which said that love is eternal, and by crumbling bits and pieces from his life, such as the yellowing cut-out paper creatures and half-printed forms and little toys. A great hush hung over the room, and in this hush Amalie compared her own picture of old age with the truth about her father. Like most other Danes, then and now, she had her own favorite fantasy about growing old. In this she pictured a silvery-gray, cultured couple—husband and wife—surrounded by timeless green plants, and rooms filled with forgiveness, and children and grandchildren—a dream that was, of course, a lie. She had been able to make-believe that Christoffer Ludwig was living in a state of well-deserved dignity, but only because she had not seen him for ten years. Now she saw that the little porcelain-headed dolls and rocking horses around him were toys that had belonged to her and her sisters. Then she dispensed with reality. With an invisible gesture she wiped her mental blackboard clean of everything to do with Christoffer Ludwig and the loneliness of that apartment and the thought that a fully accomplished life can end like this; then she turned on her heel and left. Carsten stayed where he was for a moment longer, taking a good look at the books and the old man and the feeble hands fumbling with the bits and pieces lying on the table in front of him. Then he turned and walked away; walked out, and into disaster.

It struck on a Sunday, in the afternoon and in the most straight-forward and imperceptible fashion. Behind them Carsten and Amalie have all the inventive ploys of the weekend, with dressing-up games and hours spent in the big bed; and the games they are playing now, on a Sunday afternoon in Charlottenlund, are no dif-ferent from those they have played so often before. Amalie is wearing a black health corset, and at one point Carsten takes this corset off. She resists—of course she resists—but it is just for show, and then Carsten flexes his muscles. It is as though he is stronger than he has ever been and Amalie has to struggle to prevent him having his way. Now they are standing swaying together on the floor, and to us this wrestling match is reminiscent of the erotic clash between Amalie and Carl Laurids. Then suddenly Carsten has the upper hand. He has clearly become stronger, much stronger, and now he pulls the corset off Amalie—and pulling a corset off a woman, even when she is merely making a show of resistance, takes almost all a grown man's strength, at least as far as I have been able to ascertain. Amalie is now naked; in a flash, Carsten, too, is naked and they are swept away by forces greater than themselves. No bells start to peal, no warning lights flash, because they have been through all this before; for years and years they have been exploring the boundaries of the mother-son relationship and have become so familiar with them that no brakes are applied now, as they overstep them.

They wake up side by side, both of them feeling clearheaded and exhilarated. While still in bed, Amalie suggests that they should go away together this very day. Initially this suggestion seems relaxed and natural; it seems as though Amalie had been given this idea by nothing other than the birdsong and the fine weather. But deeper down it has a nasty ring of desperation about it—to me, at any rate. Amalie and Carsten are standing with one foot in reality and the other in an intimacy between mother and son of a sort which is out of the question but which, nevertheless, they now attempt to hold on to—as Amalie cancels her appointments for the week and Carsten calls to order a car without a chauffeur, because he wants to drive himself. Then Amalie packs. When Gladys tries to stop them, they pay her no heed; then they carry their cases out to the car. Everything is now ready for what they have both almost certainly thought of as a honeymoon, although they did not say this to each other. They force Gladys to take a photograph of them standing in front of the car, a two-seater Daimler convertible. The photograph shows just how bad things were: Carsten is dressed in clothes that are much too big and a bit old-fashioned—obviously taken from Carl Laurids's wardrobe. They are both smiling, giddy with happiness. In Carsten's smile it is possible to discern a hint of triumph—at his new conquest and at being out in the sunshine after a boyhood spent indoors. Amalie is obviously proud and happy; I do not know why, but I am afraid that she is smiling with satisfaction at once more finding herself in a respectable relationship with a man. Then they get into the car. Carsten sits on four cushions, so that he can see out of the windscreen. He cannot reach the pedals, but Amalie works them; she has taken her shoes off and is trying to remember how it looked when Carl Laurids drove. They drive down the graveled driveway, past the dilapidated pavilions in which Carl Laurids's dwarfs once lived, and through the overgrown grounds—the little boy and the beautiful woman, Carsten and Amalie, that is, looking as though they are en route, with style and dignity, from one success to the next. Just as they reach the gateway, Carsten looks back and waves triumphantly with his straw hat— which has, as it happens, belonged to Carl Laurids—and drives head on into the right-hand gatepost, one of the two substantial pillars that flank the driveway. This does not budge an inch and in fact turns out to be even more solid than all the other pillars in this house. The car concertinas. Both Amalie and Carsten are hurled forward and bang their heads off the windscreen. When Amalie comes to, a moment later, she checks to make sure that they are not badly hurt. She takes Carsten in her arms; his eyes are closed and blood is trickling in a fine, sinuous thread down his face, which is pale and very young. And this is precisely the point when Amalie sees him as being very young. Here, in this crumpled car, she re- discovers the outlook on life held by her acquaintances; like a tidal wave, her common sense, her good judgment, and her strength return to her and for a moment she sways unsteadily on the seat. Then she straightens up and draws Carsten to her. He is still un- conscious and oblivious to everything, but Amalie has once more transformed him into a child. At that moment Gladys reaches the car and helps mother and son out.

Part Three

MARIA AND CARSTEN
AND THEIR CHILDREN

The house by the Lakes
(and other matters)
A longing for order
1939–1989

ON AUGUST 10, 1939, Amalie said goodbye to Carsten and sent him off to Sorø. In parting, she shook his hand—shook his hand, no more than that, not so much as a kiss on the cheek. Since their car accident in the grounds, shaking his hand was as far as Amalie could go, although to Carsten she explained this away by saying, "It isn't quite proper for me to kiss you now that you're all grown up."

Carsten was dressed in the white summer uniform of Sorø Academy: white trousers with no pockets, dark blue jacket and vest, white shirt, and white-crowned cap with gleaming peak and shiny leather strap; and from a distance he looked like a naval officer. Several of their neighbors from the adjoining villas witnessed their leavetaking, having grown accustomed that summer to keeping a sharp eye on the goings-on in the white villa. Now they were trying to guess whether this smartly turned-out naval officer, this lieutenant or captain, was Amalie's lover or just a friend. It never occurred to any of them that this was Amalie's son, that this was just Carsten—the boy who had, not so long ago, been playing with their own children— standing here in front of the big six-cylinder Hudson that Amalie had borrowed for the occasion, looking handsome and broad-shouldered, with one forelock fluttering free of his cap.

At this moment of parting, Carsten has the look of a young man leaving his mother and father to start a life of his own and that was how Amalie wanted to see him, even while life without him was out of the question. Which was why she had done everything she could to prepare for his departure, to assure him and herself that even though she stayed behind, still, in a way, she would be with him. Some weeks earlier she had gone, by herself, to Sorø—well, of course she had gone down there, driving off in the same showy car that Carsten would ride in, which she had borrowed from a client, without having the faintest idea of where Sorø lay. At school she had been too faint with hunger to pay attention during geography lessons, and in later years Carl Laurids and her son had been her only clear focal points; she really had had more to worry about than where Sorø lay. Nor, strictly speaking, had she any idea what kind of place the academy was; the director of education's descriptions had gone over her head, and the only thing she was sure of was that it was very, very respectable.

She had been happy with what she saw. Driving up the avenue, she noted how, with its park and library and church and main academy building and headmaster's residence and pavilions, the huge school looked like a cross between a university, a country house, and a reform school. But the external structure was not her main concern. Her childhood in Rudkøbing and her marriage to Carl Laurids had taught her to be somewhat skeptical of buildings and interiors and had shown her how much more power she had over people than over their surroundings. Which is why she paid the headmaster of the academy a visit.

She found him in his office. He was a scholar, a strict Latinist who had assumed the academy's classical tradition, shouldered responsibility for the future of young people, and taken up all the challenges of his day. These burdens had bowed his shoulders and endowed him with the characteristic gait that had, among the students, earned him the nickname of the "Shuffler," and as soon as Amalie saw him she knew she had won before she had even started. He began by assuring her that he was her humble servant and that, yes, he had received the letter from the director of schools in Copenhagen, whom he knew very well and for whom he had great respect; he then went on to express his regret that every place at the school was filled; furthermore, the academy entrance examination —which was compulsory—had long since been held; finally he said quite bluntly that there could be no thought of accepting her son at the academy. And not for one second during this long-winded, Germanically convoluted speech did he raise the visor of academic arrogance that covered his face—a mask that reminds me that Sorø Academy has, at different times, been both a monastery and a lunatic asylum. As he was winding up his speech, Amalie was drawing closer and closer to his desk, wanting to get around all these objections, to get so close to him that his nearsighted eyes would, for the first time, be able to see her, and to envelop him in the thick folds of her radiance.

"Headmaster," she said, "I've been so much looking forward to meeting you."

By the time she left the school, everything was, of course, in order. The great philologist accompanied her all the way to her car, his gait grown youthful and spry. As Amalie drew her fur-trimmed driving cape around her shoulders, he spread his arms and said, "Madam, *'mea virtute me involvo'*—you wrap youself in your virtue." "You're so sweet, Raaschou," said Amalie and blew him a kiss. Then she drove down to Sorø town, to see Curre the watchmaker, whom the headmaster had recommended as having an excellent family with whom she need have no worries about lodging Carsten.

She spent an hour at the watchmaker's house, making an indelible impression. She introduced herself and presented the letter of recommendation the headmaster had given her; then she described how sensitive Carsten was and how his stomach tolerated only the best-quality produce and his skin only the cleanest of sheets and his lungs only the freshest of air and his good looks only whole nights of unbroken sleep and his health only the finest treatment imaginable—until she had given the watchmaker's family the impression that this prospective lodger was some superior being who might at any moment die on their hands. While Amalie was speaking, her eyes were scanning the house, noting the neatness of it, with the pictures of the King and the Crown Prince on the wall; noting the provincial seemliness that she knew from Rudkøbing, and the humility with which the watchmaker and his wife showed that they would consider it an honor to have a student of Sorø Academy in their home. Later, in Copenhagen, Amalie explained to her women friends and to the Friends of the Family that it was this air of scrubbed subservience that had made her decide in favor of the Curre family, but in actuality other factors had been at work here. What she had ascertained, during that hour in which she had spoken nonstop, was, first and foremost, that the family's only daughter was just seven years old and that Mrs. Curre was a workhorse—small and thin, with large red hands and all the steadiness of the works in her husband's clocks, but totally lacking in that feminine menace from which Amalie would do anything to protect Carsten. Because there were to be no women in his life except her—at any rate, not right now; at any rate, not for the next three or four or five or six or seven years; there's time enough for that sort of thing, she thought. Then suddenly, after having seen every inch of the house and every member of the family and talking nonstop and terrifying everyone, she softened. With a startling change of mood, she turned the brilliance of her smile—which was by this time becoming famous in certain circles in Copenhagen—on the watchmaker's family, whom she had just flattened completely. Then she raised Carsten's rent from 75 kroner to 150 kroner per month —of the stockbroker's money—and shamelessly complimented the watchmaker on his wit, the watchmaker's wife on her charm, and their daughter (who had not uttered a single word) on her intelligence. Thereafter she slapped the watchmaker on the back and said, "Damn, I'm glad the little darling's going to be living with you," before sweeping out of the door and into the car. The Hudson roared to life, and she drove off, back to Copenhagen. So lost was she in her own thoughts on this journey that she arrived home still none the wiser as to where in the world Sorø might be. All she knew was that the place was in order—in every respect in order.

And now she is saying farewell to Carsten. She had picked up his uniform herself, the day before, from the tailor recommended by the headmaster. In his suitcase he also has a winter uniform, again with pocket-less trousers—a style that by this time is already outdated, even at Sorø. Nonetheless, Amalie has opted for these, having been told by the headmaster, "Here we teach young people to get to grips with things; here we teach them that one cannot walk through life with one's hands in one's pockets."

At the last moment Amalie decides that Gladys shall accompany Carsten. "Gladys is coming with you," she says, "and that's all there is to it. She'll drive down with you now and come back with the car in the evening"—the reason for this being that she can then make Carsten's new bed just the way he likes it, and unpack his suitcase and put his clothes away in his closet and hang up his shirts. The main reason, however, is that Amalie wants, somehow, to prolong this parting and give her boy some substitute for the embrace she can no longer give him, afraid, as she is, of losing all her self-control.

And so Carsten drives out into the world, and, seen from our point of view, it is both too early and too late.

At one point, as they were driving along Roskilde Road, they overtook a green Buick, one of the Copenhagen Police Department's paddy wagons. Just as the two vehicles drew level, a pale face could be seen behind the bars of one of the tiny windows. It was the face of a girl, at one and the same time calm and wary, and for a few seconds she and Carsten gazed into each other's eyes. Then the big Hudson had left the police van far behind, and the girl was gone.

It was Maria Jensen. At that point, sitting in the paddy wagon, heading along Roskilde Road, she was fifteen years old, and two years had elapsed since her mother disappeared and the tenement in Christianshavn sank into the ground.

Often, in my conversations with Maria, I have returned to the question of what her life was like during these two years, but she has never been able to give me a coherent answer. Nonetheless I have been able to figure out that after she turned her back on the vanished tenement, and on her father, and walked into the Copenhagen autumn, her life took roughly the following form: to begin with, she slept in railroad cars and in parks and on stairways, while winter was setting in. She was very close to perishing when she met Sofie, a girl of her own age, who looked like a sylph or a fairy-tale princess until she opened her mouth and gave vent to a voice as raucous as the sound of trains being switched. She introduced Maria into a club life which, until then, Maria had only ever viewed from the outside, while holding her father's hand. The club meetings at which the two girls stepped out were held in Vesterbro. Cloaked in the anonymity of the legislation governing private clubs and tax dodges, these men-only societies met in some of the scores of cow barns still standing in this part of town. For these meetings, the cows were shooed into adjoining premises or into the barnyard, so that the empty stalls could be pressed into service as the wings for shows performed by young girls—girls like Maria and Sofie, who danced and sang, without a stitch on, to the music of a concertina played by the society chairman, a young man who smelled of Esprit de Valdemar and who, in the intermissions, was wont to fiddle absentmindedly with a blackjack. After the show, a dance was held in a closed-off coach house. The chairman played and the young girl performers accepted invitations to dance until daybreak, or until the police arrived, or until they had found a gentleman who would see them home. Maria and Sofie performed a song that Maria had learned from the whores in Christianshavn as a little girl. It went like this: "Tahiti is paradise on earth, hm hm," and the girls made the "hm hm" sound by blowing through their noses in imitation of Polynesian wind instruments. They performed in grass skirts and nothing but grass skirts, looking so innocent that even the society members—who had come only because their lust was so hopelessly bound up with a taste for young meat—had tears in their eyes and felt contrite and thought: These two sweet little girls shouldn't be here, they should be at home with their mother.

After the show they both danced with great and genuine joy, before allowing some gentleman—who had to be both elderly and well off—to escort them home. They had rented a room together on the outskirts of Vesterbro—lying at the very heart of a series of increasingly murky courtyards, at the end of a black passage—and it was to this that they led their prince for the night. Usually the victim did not notice where they were going because he was so busy ogling the two little girls, whose innocence seemed to him to shine in the darkness, and trying to figure out whether they realized what all this was about and where it was leading. "How does a sweet little girl like you come to have such a rough voice?" he would ask Sofie as they were leading him through the last of the courtyards. "All the better to tell you how pleased I am that you walked us home," Sofie would reply as they walked up the stairs. "How does a little flower like you come to have such a firm grip?" he would ask Maria as they were walking along the passage. "All the b-b-better to hold y-y-your hand," Maria would reply. Then she would close the door behind them, take her police helmet from the chair where it lay, and put it on. Usually it was at this point that she let go of the man's hand and butted him in the face with the police helmet, snuffing him out like a candle in a draft. But sometimes Sofie would hold her back, because she had become what is termed, in the police reports, physically aroused. In that case, she would let the gentleman undress her, after which she would undress him and take advantage of him while Maria sat silently in the dark, playing with the wallet she had fished from his clothes, waiting for the sign from Sofie to tell her that she could now bend over the stripped man, feel around in the dark for his head, and bash him in the face. Then they would pull off his underclothes, roll him down the stairs, pile him onto a handcart, wheel him out, and dump him in the nearest ditch.

They stopped going to the private-club dances when they realized that they could pick up better-off victims in the city dance halls. So they started to frequent Figaro's and the Marble Café in Store Kongens Street; started to wear high heels and evening dresses and makeup and learned to steer clear of overzealous officers from the vice squad. Other than that, the drill remained the same: they would lure some elderly gentleman into seeing them back to their room —where they went on living, even though it was like a black hole in the darkness. Once there, they usually knocked him out without any further ado, and took his wallet. In the summer they would also take his clothes and his shoes, then wheel him off on the handcart and throw him into a ditch on the outskirts of town. Only rarely did a victim ever recognize them later, and if such a situation did arise, they could soon shut him up, with Sofie saying, in her gravelly voice, "You do know we're under age, don't you?" and Maria stammering softly, "Y-you know what they do with old pigs like you who pester little girls, don't you? They c-chop it off, so you'd better piss off."

During these years they see so much of society's underside that they begin to doubt whether it has a topside. Thanks to their cunning and hardihood, they succeed in evading the police and the vengeance of their victims and pimps and other prostitutes and the owners of the establishments where they picked up their customers, while still retaining a sort of innocence. When they are alone, or with children of their own age, they behave as what they in fact are: two little girls who would much rather jump rope or play hopscotch or take the streetcar out to Charlottenlund or the train to Hornbæk, to watch the well-to-do and dream about what it must be like to toss a ball about with the rich children in their gardens, or play with them on the beach. And no matter how strange it may seem, Maria remains sexually innocent. Even though she witnesses everything, or almost everything, that Copenhagen has to offer in the way of fornication, still she remains every bit as untouched and virginal as the day she was born, and this she achieves, quite simply, by keeping her distance. When Sofie yields to temptation and makes love with a victim on the bed in which, every night, the girls sleep arm in arm, curled up like puppies, Maria sits on the floor staring vacantly into the darkness, the sounds of copulation arousing no feelings whatsoever in her. And it is the same story if Sofie brings home one of her beaux—an errand boy or a wrestler or a baker or a schoolboy; Maria vacates the bed and goes down to the courtyard to play hide-and-seek with the other children. She does not appear to have been shocked, not even when Sofie takes her with her to the rooms above the circus building and has intercourse, or something that passes for it, with all twenty-three stableboys one after the other. And while all this is going on, Maria sits in a corner playing with a little puppy, letting it pee on her police helmet while she babbles baby talk to it.

Eventually they also stop going to dance halls. There came a day when they were seen home by a man of property—what the French would call a *rentier*—who, having seen through their baby talk to precisely what they were, offered to let them live in his apartment, "with room and board and an allowance in return for your sleeping with me," he told Sofie, "but we'll have it put in writing—everything has to be in order." The girls spent four months in this apartment, which was as big as a barn and dirty as a pigsty, and at the end of that time Sofie was so overwrought that a breakdown looked likely at any minute. It happened in the kitchen where, after having subjected her to certain particularly degrading variations on intercourse, their landlord had demanded that she eat with him. Now he is insisting that she sit before him, naked, while he eats, fully clothed. He is eating white bread; first he spreads it with a thick layer of butter, then he licks the knife; next he spreads it with liver pâté and licks the knife, then he adds a layer of vegetable salad and licks the knife—and then Sofie lunges at him. In the same moment, he has in his hand a little pistol, one he always carries because he has never trusted the girls for a second—or anyone else for that matter. Sofie opens her mouth and screams and, terror-stricken, he shoots her in the throat. Then he just stands there, not moving a muscle, as though he is working something out. He does not try to defend himself when Maria grabs hold of his collar and beats his head against the yellow kitchen tiles: once, and his nose breaks; twice, and his lip splits and several teeth shatter; three times, and his jaw cracks; and four times, and a good many more. Then Maria stammers something at Sofie and takes her in her arms and realizes that she is dead, that yet another person is gone from her, in a life that seems to her to consist of a long line of losses, one after another. Then she empties the cigar box in which the *rentier* keeps his money and clears out.

The police found her at the Marble Café, where she had been sitting for three days in a row, from morning till night, waiting for them to show up. Those three days had seen a change in her. Her stammer had become so bad that it was almost impossible for them to question her. They took her to the police station and sent for a policewoman. She had a long talk with Maria, after which she said that the girl seemed normal enough, but such a little slip of a thing that she could not possibly be fifteen, as she claimed. Once Maria had stammered out her name, they had unearthed all the vague reports in their files in which the Stutterer was mentioned, but the policewoman—who was regarded as an expert on children, and especially girls—rejected this material with a wave of her hand, saying, "There's no way this puny girl could be that notorious gang leader—look at her, she couldn't fight her way out of a paper bag." And so it was concluded that she could not have beaten up the *rentier*, who had brought the charges that led to her arrest.

After keeping Maria at the police station for the two days it took before the search for Adonis Jensen was called off, they drove her to Annebjerg reform school in Odsherred, with the policewoman as escort. It was during this journey, through the barred window of the van, that she saw a big white car overtake them, and, for an instant, looked a handsome boy in uniform in the eye—though neither she nor he could have known that they were meant for each other. And by the word "meant" I mean nothing other than that the future will shape itself in such a way that they will, in many ways, turn out to be each other's destiny.

For the first time, during this drive, Maria realized that she was actually on her way to a home for girls. She had thought, just as I did, that it was bound to be a reformatory and a prison and a sort

of school, where brute force and ill-treatment and inhumane practices were the order of the day; where it would be discovered that
she had never learned to read and write, and she would be punished;
where she would plunge into a coal cellar of misery—and *that* she
could not bear because since Sofie's death she had grown soft and
incoherent.

Her fears were borne out by the manner in which she was received.
This home for girls faced onto Nykøbing Fjord, whose waters were
black, windswept, and lit by a moon that seemed to Maria to be
weeping, all alone in the heavens—and that such a sentimental
thought should occur to her says something about how close she
had come to the end of her tether. Silhouetted against the night
sky, the actual building looked like a vampire's castle, and Maria
was left to wait, alone, in a cold, dark hallway, under a large painting
so darkened by age that all that could be discerned of its subjects
—men, all of them looking like demonic buccaneers—was the
bloodshot eyes gleaming down upon her. After a while Miss
Smeck—one of the home's two headmistresses—appeared. In the
dark she seemed tall and pale as a statue. She had been a missionary
in China, and she treated Maria to a brief speech in which she
described the time she sailed up the Yangtze River alone on a mission
for the Society for the Eradication of the Rituals of Primitive Peoples;
and how she had met the other headmistress, Miss Ströhm, who
had taught her that in our lives, as in our dreams, we are totally
and utterly alone. Thereafter she locked Maria—who had not understood one word of her speech—into a solitary-confinement cell in
the attic; and there, beside herself with fear, Maria fell asleep.

In fact, this reception had been a trick, a ploy, from beginning to
end. The home took thirty girls at a time, most of whom arrived
foaming at the mouth like lions and fell into the same class as poor
dead Sofie—believing that they had seen everything there was to
see in this life and harboring no hopes. The two headmistresses
thought it expedient to give these girls a shock before leaving them
to wake up as Maria did the next day—to a morning as beautiful
as Creation.

When she opened her eyes, the sun was shining in through the
attic window, the birds were singing, and the distant sky was blue.
She got out of bed to find that her door was no longer locked, and
when she stepped into the corridor she was handed her uniform.

She slipped, first, into this and then into her first day at the home, which was to be more or less like all the others, consisting as it did of ample meals and flag-raising and working in the orchard and the kitchen garden and the rose beds and games on the lawn and community singing and Miss Smeck's accounts of her years in China.

From her very first day, time lost all meaning for Maria. She forgot how long she had been at the home; she barely remembered which day of the week it was; the future did not exist. Time counted only in terms of the number of days left until she had turned up first for flag-raising and for morning assembly so often that she would be presented with a silver "King's mark" badge, a defiant symbol of Danish patriotism bearing the monogram of King Christian X. She spent three years at Annebjerg, and for nearly all that time she believed she would stay there forever. To her the home was a paradise over which the two headmistresses kept watch with an authority and love that have something to do with this being 1939 and not forty years earlier—the time from which all the ubiquitous rumors of reformatory callousness stem.

In many ways Annebjerg corresponds to that period's dream—which is also our dream—of how to treat young girls who have wandered off the straight and narrow; who have sunk into the morass of the city and have neither father nor mother, but who have now been moved to the countryside and given blue blazers and white skirts and raspberries and cream under the acacia tree in the garden. These girls were taken for saltwater dips in the fjord; they weeded the rose beds and fed the twittering birds and inhaled the scent of wheat and, in some way, rediscovered both their fathers and their mothers in the two headmistresses, thus being allowed to be just what most of them were: little girls.

There were only two things the two headmistresses dreaded. One was the outside world, which for them began where Annebjerg ended—down by the wicked highway, which only the two oldest and most trusted girls were allowed to go anywhere near, and then only if they had to weed or water the outlying rose beds. In these the two spinster ladies had ordered the planting of roses of the large pale-yellow variety, to make visitors aware that Annebjerg was a house of innocence. Ordinarily, these visitors amounted only to errand "boys" delivering milk and groceries to the home, and *they* were of the same age as the ladies—over fifty, that is. This was tied up with the other thing the two ladies dreaded: the other thing, the only other thing, of which they were afraid was the young girls' sensuality, which they regarded as an illness on a par with tuberculosis. Not least among all the many functions they believed the house ought to fulfill was that of being a sort of sanatorium, where their little girls could recover from their attacks of sensuality. And to prevent any relapses, two different devices were employed. One was Miss Smeck's missionary voice, the one in which she had kept time for the rowers going up the Yangtze; the one she now used to say to two girls who were sitting too close together, "What are you two doing, sitting rubbing up against each other like that?" This was a very effective device, if we then add that the two headmistresses were also present in the bathroom every morning, when the big girls washed the little ones; and that they made frequent, unheralded inspections of the dormitories. The other device was a strict curfew—the outside world was absolutely out of bounds. Very few of the girls had any home to go to, but even those who had were rarely given permission to leave Annebjerg. Trips beyond the grounds of the home were few and far between and usually took them to the beach or nearby spots of historical significance, which should, preferably, be deserted, with no other human beings in sight: ruined castles, for instance, or rune stones or ancient burial mounds, which Miss Smeck would use as a springboard for accounts of her time in the tropics, while Miss Ströhm, not unlike a nervous gundog, flitted back and forth along the fringes of their bevy of girls, keeping a sharp eye on the surrounding world, to ensure that it would not show its worst side by sending their way what they dreaded most of all: a man.

The majority of the girls preferred this kind of life; it would be inappropriate and wrong to feel outraged and think: Those poor girls, what a pity there weren't any boys. The belief that keeping the two sexes apart can do great and irreparable damage belongs to a later date; it was not generally accepted in 1939, and certainly not among the girls at Annebjerg, whose experiences with men had been so unpleasant that they much preferred to be protected.

For Maria Jensen, life during these years could not have been better. She became the headmistresses' favorite and was in every respect a model pupil. On her very first morning she had handed over her police helmet. She had still had been carrying it when she arrived at Annebjerg because, with the Copenhagen Police Department having long since gone over to new uniforms, Maria's helmet was regarded as an antique; and since it never occurred to anyone that this fragile, weeping girl-child had once bashed in a colleague's face in order to get said helmet, she was allowed to keep it. At Annebjerg she gave it to Miss Ströhm, who hung it on a hook in her office, and there it remained, because Maria forgot all about it and never thought of asking for it back. Instead she let her fair hair grow and acquired rosy cheeks and suntanned feet and dazzlingly blue eyes; in every way resembling the headmistresses' dream—and ours—of a little girl who has been lost and has now been saved. Her voice, when she said grace and morning and evening prayers, was full of conviction—as it was when, at the headmistresses' request, she led the community singing. After a few days at Annebjerg she had begun to prattle like a preschool child, and now and again she would coyly pretend that she could not speak properly. All in all, it seemed that at Annebjerg—which contained almost everything the tenement in Christianshavn had lacked—Maria relived the childhood she had never had, because Anna had been searching for her childhood instead of looking after her daughter.

Twice a month, the girls entertained one another. These entertainments were held by candlelight, after they had had tea and cake and sung, accompanied by Miss Smeck on the guitar. They danced cotillions, and the minuet from the play *Elverhøj*, and Maria sang "Tahiti is paradise on earth, hm hm"—a song that went down just as well with her fully dressed in the large drawing room at Annebjerg as it had done with her naked in the cow barns of Vesterbro. Strangely enough, Adonis Jensen was often onstage—far from Annebjerg—on these selfsame evenings; and as the applause swelled around Maria, she was infected by the same stage fever that Adonis was experiencing at that very moment. At such times she felt she was in some way linked to her father. These evenings were the only times she ever thought of her family—or rather, of Adonis—but then she felt so close to him that she could have spoken to him, if she had wanted to.

These evenings were also the only times at Annebjerg that it was considered acceptable and quite in order for the girls to touch one another, that they were actually encouraged to do so—when it came to ballroom dancing. Maria normally took the man's part, and it was on these evenings that she received her first premonition that things could go wrong.

When I talked to Maria about her time at Annebjerg, she did not speak about premonitions; she stressed what a happy time it had been and how kind everyone had been to each other, and only after a while, once she was well into her story, did she suddenly mention these disturbing details—as, for instance, with those evenings when she sang and danced the man's part and thought about her father, and when the notion struck her that she was missing something. These feelings of want were few and far between, and when, presently, I mention them in context, it must be remembered that they cropped up as tiny incidents in the happy flow of Maria's time at Annebjerg: of winter in the warmth of the tiled stoves with spice cakes and snowball fights, of spring and summer rich in roses and sea bathing, and a golden, wistful autumn that tasted of apples. During this time Maria reaches the age of sixteen, then seventeen, then eighteen, and even though she has, in due course, been given a room of her own and three silver badges; even though she is now entrusted with pruning the yellow roses near the road and still prattles like a toddler and now knows Miss Smeck's anecdotes by heart and would thus seem to have become a part of Annebjerg, still, when all's said and done, she really is a big girl now.

And then the electrician appears on the scene. He turns up on a day in March—a bitterly cold day but a spring day nonetheless. He is a young man, and young men are not in the habit of visiting Annebjerg—even the police officers and child welfare officers who bring the girls are elderly men, because that is what the headmistresses have stipulated. Nevertheless, this electrician is young, because Annebjerg has not had electricity for very long and the headmistresses have therefore not been able to come to their usual arrangement with his company. In other words, Miss Smeck has not been able to call it, as she usually does, and say, "We would prefer you to send a woman, but if you send a man, then he must be a family man and over fifty years old, otherwise we cannot do business. Now I'll leave you to think about that. Thank you and goodbye." Then she would hang up knowing full well that she would get her way.

But the electrical wiring is new, its failure comes as a surprise, and it is the slightly less consistent Miss Ströhm who makes the call; which is why, now, a young man in blue coveralls cycles up to the home. He does not report to anyone, he does not make for the office to check on anything—if he had done, he could have been stopped. Instead he parks his bike, takes his toolbox, and goes straight down to the basement to change the blown fuse—that being all that is wrong. He lights the little paraffin lamp he has brought and sits down in front of the main switch—and then he notices the girls.

They are all around him in the darkness, and they do not make a sound. That is what is wrong; that is what makes this moment magical and terrifying for the young man. He knows girls who giggle and girls who shout and girls who turn away in disdain, but never before has he come across girls such as these, who stare without blinking. The girls, too, find the situation surprising; if they hadn't, they would have acted in a more normal fashion—by running away, or passing some sly remark or looking at the ground—but they have followed him down into the basement and suddenly they are very close to him, closer to a man than they have been in a long time.

I do not know how long this moment lasted. Maria is at the very front, closest to him, and to her it seems like a long time—but not nearly so long as it does to the electrician. All at once he has the impression that these eyes are staring at him in a very *hungry* way, and suddenly, up from the depths of his consciousness, wells the nightmare of his sex: of Valkyries and Amazons and shield-maidens and women who have been without men for a long while and so must, he thinks, be wild with hunger for my body. Then he feels the cold sweat of fear beading under his blue coveralls and, with a gesture taken from another dream—the Westerns at the movie theater in Nykøbing (double bill, Saturday afternoons)—he drops his tools, blows out the paraffin lamp, fights his way through the darkness, stumbles out to his bicycle, and weaves off down the driveway, pursued by the imagined howling of wolves.

Back in the darkness, the girls sit on, unable to make head or tail of this. For a moment there is silence, and then they start to giggle—all except Maria. She is still thinking about the electrician.

Then comes the soldier.

It is a day in May, one in a never-ending string of bright, humming, warm spring days at Annebjerg, and Maria is watering the roses next to the highway. She has been entrusted with this job because the headmistresses now have complete confidence in her and because she has been at Annebjerg so long that she should be armed against exactly what happens next, which is that a soldier comes walking down the road. His gait is unsteady because he is just about dislocating his neck in his efforts to drink in Maria's suntanned legs and sun-bleached hair and capable hands and roguish blue eyes, and so on and so forth. For his part, he is fair-haired and blue-eyed and broad-shouldered, dressed in tight white trousers and blue regimental shirt. He is a Marine, looks as though he can hold his own, and in every way resembles the Danish dream of the charming soldier.

But he is German. That may make no difference to Maria—later on, she barely remembered it—but it registered with me: this soldier is German, and it is the first indication Maria receives that, at this point, Denmark has been occupied by Germany for more than a year.

In this instance there is no time to think, no gazing at each other wondering this, that, or the other. What happens is that Maria leaves the watering can where it is and falls into step behind the soldier; then, once they have been walking like this for a while, smiling at nothing in particular, she moves up alongside him. But by then Annebjerg is out of sight; by then they have walked right through Nykøbing and out the other side.

While they are disappearing down the road, without Maria's ever once turning around, I find myself wondering why she did it; why did she run away, instead of staying at Annebjerg, where she was happy? I mean: both then and later it is obvious that Maria's dreams of happiness all deal with a life like the one she led at Annebjerg; with a regular sense of security and regular meals and singing and dancing twice a month. So what is it that makes her follow the soldier, in spite of all that?

It would be simple if the answer really were a longing for love. But that answer is too simple; besides which, it does not fit with the actual events. Shortly after her running away—later that same day—Maria and the soldier are sitting on the back of a flatbed truck; he tries to hold her hand but she pulls it away; he tries to kiss her and she turns her ripe red lips away; and then he thinks, this little buttercup, this *Snuggiputzilein*, is obviously asking for the direct approach. So he tries to unbutton her uniform blouse, and before he knows it, he is sprawling in the roadway; before he knows it, he has been ditched, he has gone overboard, and sees the truck disappearing into the distance. So if it was love that Maria was after, then it was certainly not love at any price.

Left alone on the back of the truck, she started to regret the unaccountable impulse that had prompted her to follow the soldier, and that very afternoon she did try to get back to Annebjerg. By this time she had had three years of feeling like a little girl; that is how she looked and how she behaved; no one would have taken Maria Jensen for anything but that. And it was this girlishness that was to lure two lusty farmhands into making a big mistake. They were sitting on a load of hay, alongside Maria, and this load of hay was being drawn by that rarity: a tractor heading in the right direction, away from the setting sun and home to Annebjerg. The two hands had tacitly and cheerfully conspired to rape Maria, all for her bonny blue eyes, and when one of them grabbed hold of her arm and pulled off her skirt, it was the first time in a very, very long while that Maria had been subjected to violence. She reacted instinctively by relaxing and letting things drift, but at the same time her innards contracted into a knot and, for the first time in a very long while, her eyes took on a glazed expression that would have served as a warning to children and adults in Christianshavn. And with that she drifted away from the security of Annebjerg and into the dream of a girl who can take care of herself. As the man forced one of his legs between hers she drove one knee into his crotch, then she put her thumbs to his eyes—which were wide open with astonishment —and pressed. He rolled off her without a sound. She stood up and stepped into the center of the swaying load of hay, and there she took on the other man, who had brown-stained plug-tobacco teeth and a wicked-looking hard-on jutting out of his open fly. A pitchfork had been stuck in the hay and this Maria hauled out. The man circled warily around her. It had dawned on him that he was up against an unusual opponent, but he did not know how unusual and so he miscalculated. Maria feinted a lunge and he was knocked off balance, giving Maria the chance to bend down, pull his trousers down around his ankles, and jump clear before his long, flailing arms could get to her. Now his movements were restricted. The next time Maria feigned an assault he lost his balance altogether, and when, at that same moment, Maria took a menacing step toward

him, he toppled backwards and sailed out into space. Aware that
the first man had staggered back onto his feet, Maria then pirouetted
around and hammered the pitchfork against his chest. The blow
sent him flying off the cart. Later, she thanked the friendly tractor
driver for the lift and told him that the two hands had jumped off
back down the road. The man noticed that her voice seemed to have
deepened and that a faraway look had come into her eyes. Maria
simply thought that there was no reason to go back to the home,
and that she felt like having a look around among all these country
bumpkins and that there was nothing, absolutely nothing, to be
afraid of. Then she starts walking along the highway, toward the
sunset and Sorø.

By this time, Carsten has been at Sorø Academy for two years,
and even though it is tempting to get straight to the crux of the
matter and describe his first meeting with Maria, that is not how
history is written; that would mean succumbing to the temptation
to which love will always give rise—and I will not have that laid at
my door. So we will have to start with Carsten's reception at Sorø,
two years earlier, on August 15, 1939. On that day, he lined up with
all the other academy pupils—in class order, under the supervision
of an inspector—before being allowed into the assembly hall. There
he stands, along with the other new pupils, shaking in his shoes
with apprehension, beneath a coffered ceiling painted with distant
stars and with the portraits of former headmasters gazing austerely
down upon them from the walls. Here, the headmaster delivers a
speech from a raised lectern. This speech is obviously aimed at the
new boys, the new little counts and sons of diplomats and customs
inspectors and pastors and company directors and sawmill owners
and office managers, and in some cases—Carsten's, for example—
of widows. He speaks to the sons of all these people, who do not
know one another but who have this in common: that they are
bursting with ambition on their children's behalf, and so have had
the choice of sending them to Herlufsholm or the Metropolitan
School or Sankt Jørgen's Gymnasium or Sorø Academy—and have
chosen the academy because this place is shrouded in the spirit of
history.

And it is this very spirit that the headmaster now touches upon
in his speech, which he embarks upon after the singing (accom-

panied by the music teacher on the piano) of one of Ingemann's
lovely hymns, set to music by the composer Heise, who was once a
music teacher at the academy; and after the headmaster has—
among the mass of crew-cut heads and boyish faces that he does
not normally see very clearly—located Carsten's. He recognizes him
almost immediately, because Carsten has his mother's eyes, and
those eyes are still glowing in the old Latinist's soul. He flings out
a hand in one of those gestures that derive from his being a kind
of a god, and from the fact that he is backed up by a cultural tradition
that he and the rest of the teaching staff do not believe has altered
in three hundred years; one that will, in all probability, last forever—with a few small changes along the way perhaps, but in effect
forever. Then he says to the crowd of sixteen- and seventeen-year-
old boys, "Gentlemen, I would like to welcome you to this school.
I say 'Gentlemen' because, as members of this academy, you are
expected to act like gentlemen. You will soon fit in here, if you
are at all suited to boarding-school life, and the first thing you will
learn is that from now on, no one is going to hold your hand, you
will have to fend for yourselves, pull yourselves up by your own
bootstraps; if anyone gives you advice you must accept it as a gift,
deserving of gratitude." His eye falls on Carsten, and for a moment
he is silent, thinking of Amalie; then he continues: "You can win
respect through personal proficiency in the classroom and on the
playing field, but, gentlemen, should it be noted that you are flaunting this proficiency, you will discover it will do you no good. Critical
as your schoolfellows are, any humbug will soon be exposed, and
everyone will come to occupy the position determined by his personal
worth; you will grow to love this place, this playground of your
boyhood and youth; you will grow to love having such a picturesque
setting for your daily routine: this historic site, with Bishop Absalon's
church and its graves; these fine examples of Danish architecture,
dating back to the first half of the nineteenth century; these venerable
old trees whose age, in the childish imagination, becomes much
greater than it actually is." And here the headmaster again falls
silent, overwhelmed by memories of his own youth at the school, a
time he always recalls with particular vividness at just such moments
as this, when he is welcoming a new intake of students. Finally he
continues: "There is boarding-school life itself, cradled on its fundamental affinity with this, the academy—an affinity made all the

stronger by the fact that your lives here will be so different, and not without a certain harshness, in the face of which it is so easy to seek comfort and balance in the countryside spread at your feet, a countryside so gentle, so charming, that it seems made to be loved. But what makes this academy quite special, what makes it so utterly splendid and unique and unparalleled in Denmark, is its inner life; it is the spiritual continuity, an uninterrupted line stretching from Bishop Absalon, via Christian IV and Frederik III and Holberg and Heise and Hauch and Ørsted and Ingemann, right up to the present"—and here the headmaster waves an arm in the direction of the teaching staff.

There are a good many teachers, and at first glance, standing there along the end wall of the hall, they look like a collection of powerful eccentrics. Despite the summer heat, they wear threadbare alpaca coats, or jackets and waistcoats, or stiff collars and lorgnettes and pince-nez or lightly tinted spectacles; some are wearing white coats, to demonstrate their connection with the sciences, and some sport bushy beards and sideburns grown in emulation of dead scientific heroes—but all of them stare straight ahead, looking very, very serious. The seriousness of their gaze fills the new students with respect, and that is the intention. If, however, one looks more carefully (as do some of the older boys) something else becomes apparent, something more; then other truths emerge from behind these formidable façades and one realizes that there is something rather worn and shabby about these men and that their eyes, which look neither to right nor to left, harbor no small measure of madness. And all of this betrays the fact that these custodians of the Spirit of the People are also something other, something more, than awe-inspiring sages; that they are, in fact, poorly paid clerks in the dream factory that is Sorø Academy. The dreams manufactured here are those the headmaster has given such an excellent account of in his speech: the ideal of spartan boarding-school hardiness and the ideal of brilliant Athenian-style scholarship and the ideal of an ardent, tremulously fragile love of Nature. And a good, hard look will reveal that the teachers' lineup in the hall underlines this line of thought: closest to the headmaster we have Cultivation and Tradition and the National Spirit—in other words, the famous Plato scholar whom the students call "Meph" (short for Mephistopheles), who likes little boys and who, on a daily basis, boxes a good number—actually, a very large number—of ears, this being the only physical contact permitted at the academy between teachers and pupils. Then we have the French teacher "Don" (short for Don Juan, because of his foppishness and his great interest in little girls), then come all the other philologists and scientists, several of whom have written text-books or distinguished themselves in the field of research. Now they are distinguishing themselves in human terms by their jumble of neurotic idiosyncrasies, epitomized by the students in such short and significantly compact nicknames as "Gnasher" and "Doggo" and "Slobby": names with which Carsten and the other new pupils are not as yet familiar but which they will get to know. Around this group of men, whom the headmaster has just described as having a direct link with Bishop Absalon's day, a space has been left, a bare stretch of floorboard, unoccupied because this bare section is meant to mark the gap and the drop in prestige that brings us to those stocky, barrel-chested men standing with their arms folded; men called Møller and Thomsen and Sprakkesen. These men are the PE and woodwork teachers and they have no nicknames, perhaps because their madness is so obvious that there is no need to draw attention to it. These are the school Spartans, men full of enthusiasm for the physical culture of the ancient world and for the English public-school spirit. It is they who, with unflagging energy, will take the lead in the cricket matches and gymnastics sessions; and in the year-round dips in Sorø Lake, which will inflict unaccountable and agonizing rheumatic twinges upon many of the young people gathered in the assembly hall, before they have even graduated. These men despise the rest of the academy teaching staff, considering them to be weaklings; and so the naked floorboards that separate the two groups of teachers also manifest the school's picture of the division between body and soul.

In one corner stands the grand piano and at the keys sits the music teacher. He and his piano, complete with the Danish songbook—which contains a number of songs written by or set to music by former academy students—symbolize the third dream mentioned by the headmaster in his speech, which is fostered here: the dream of the lovely and beloved Danish countryside.

Most of the things I have mentioned here are my own observations, not Carsten's. I am basing them on my conversations with former pupils and, indeed, with Carsten, but the pictures of how everything fits together are my own. Of course Carsten saw how the teachers were lined up, he saw their vacant stares and all their tics and twitches and trembling hands and their odd habit of muttering to themselves and moving their lips during the singing, to hide their fear of uttering a sound anywhere but from their own, elevated lecterns—of course he saw all of this. But it did not arouse any particular feeling in him; nor did he hear a single word of the headmaster's speech, and afterward he was unable to recall which songs he had sung, because he had been so busy bringing all his well-meaning energy to bear on one single thing: trying to do more or less what he had been doing for as long as he could remember —his duty. He focused all his concentration on looking as though he were listening attentively, and on not looking conspicuous or forward, and on glowing with expectation at the thought that for three years, here, at the best of all possible schools, he would be given the chance to do exactly what the headmaster and the teachers and the students and—first and foremost, behind them—his mother expected of him. So immersed was he in these efforts that he received no clear impression of anything until, suddenly, a wiry little boy from a class senior to his hissed something under his breath. Shocked by this show of disrespect, Carsten turned to look at the boy. He is met by a pair of dark eyes, and then the boy says, coolly and without noticeably lowering his voice—while nodding his head in the direction of the headmaster, Mr. Raaschou-Nielsen, the Shuffler, on his raised lectern, "Can't you just hear the spiritual snot clogging his mustache?"

This seemingly meaningless, throwaway, chance remark sticks in Carsten's mind like a burr. And it embodies a fourth dream from Sorø Academy: the dream of rebellion.

It might be supposed that it is the students who dream of revolting, that they are the source of rebellion, but that is not the case—or at least it is not that simple. On the whole, the students are of the same mind as the teachers. Despite the spiteful nicknames, despite the secret, forbidden rituals, and despite that unseverable bond between academy boys, past and present, to which the headmaster is at this very moment referring—still, the teachers and the students form a united front. In actuality, the solidarity of the boys and their traditions and rituals are an expression of their delight at being chosen, of being among the best in the country, *primi inter pares*, thanks to their attendance at this delightful school set amid countryside which, it is quite true to say, they will grow to love with an ardor that will, in forty years' time, readily bring tears to the eyes; this school, whose teachers they do, at heart, respect, because, at heart, they believe them to be ministering to values at which one might well poke good-humored fun but which are, in reality, sacrosanct. And that the pupils hold such a view has something to do with Sorø Academy's still being at this time—despite all the rhetoric that a man's a man for a' that, blah, blah, blah—a school for the upper and upper-middle classes. So the rebellion stems, not from the general run of pupils, but from certain boys, such as the boy standing behind Carsten in the assembly hall.

Boys such as these are described, in the parlance of their day, as black sheep, rotten apples, and bad characters, and I can see that they do exert a powerful fascination. I would like to be able to say that Carsten became such a rebel, and that this transformation began on that very first day in the assembly hall and went on and on. But it would be a lie; the dream of the insubordinate student belongs to a later day and age; almost twenty years will have to elapse before Danish writers begin, smugly, to depict themselves as long-legged delinquents who can rock back and forth on the balls of their feet and have the last laugh and run rings around the teachers. In 1939, at Sorø Academy, such boys were regarded as undesirable elements, a blight on youth and on the academy's hearty, scoutmaster ethic.

Carsten is the very opposite. He is obedient and conscientious, and even on that very first day in the assembly hall he turns away from the boy behind him in vexation, and tries to forget him.

And so he enters academia. Two years go by, and during these two years Carsten is awarded two prizes for diligence and two prizes for proficiency, and he becomes something of a legend at the school. This is not to say that he was *talked* about; a great deal more *talking* was done about the boy who was standing behind him in the assembly hall. During these two years, he has arranged for as many minor scandals as there are weeks in the year and more large ones than Carsten has had prizes, until finally his parents are asked to remove him from the school—which is a nice way of saying that he was kicked out. He, too, became something of a legend and *he* was talked about, but Carsten's fame was of a different sort. It stemmed from his doing his duty to an absolutely unheard-of degree, from his fulfilling his obligations to such an extent that he realized Sorø Academy's false pictures of diligence and studiousness in the previous century. In the course of these first two years at the school, Carsten turned up on time every single day, and not only on time but *early*, not to prepare his work—that he had, naturally, done the day before, or even before that, during the free-study periods—but to have that day's lesson absolutely fresh in his mind and to be able to come out with his answers smartly and without hesitation. He chose to read the classics, since, despite the academy's democratic spirit and its respect for the sciences and the useful modern languages, Latin and Greek were nevertheless still, somehow, better. But it was not only in the classical languages that he excelled; he was also brilliant when it came to other subjects and to PE classes—when he took his winter dips without flinching and pulled his white shirt straight over his wet body without drying it first, because Møller, the PE teacher, considered using a towel unmanly and sissified. And then there were the Sundays in the watchmaker's house, when he ate a roast and dessert with the watchmaker and his family in the front room (from which the echo of Amalie's visit had never truly faded), politely recounting what he had learned at the academy. All in all, wherever he may be, he is a model pupil, his behavior immaculate. There is nothing one can point a finger at, not even in his free time, when of course he is an active member of the academy's voluntary study groups. These concern themselves with the strength of Denmark's claim to South Jutland, and with readings from that essential work *Study of Denmark's Southern Boundaries*, which traces the root of South Jutland's severance from the mother country to Knud Lavard, around 1129. Carsten attends these study group meetings as well prepared as for the obligatory classes.

His behavior was exceptionally well suited to the academy's teaching style, which was based on learning incontrovertible truths by heart; a system modeled on the conjugation of the Latin verbs—which, thank heaven, are incapable of change, that language having died out long ago. Attempts were made to apply this model to all aspects of school life, not least to Danish lessons, where it was held to be an incontrovertible truth that no literature of any merit had been written in the Danish language since the year 1900—and certainly nothing worth studying in senior secondary. Here lessons involved getting pupils to memorize the brilliant social history notes of the eminent literary scholar and former member of the academy Vilhelm Andersen, in such a way that they could (as Carsten did at his final exam) be tested on one of Grundtvig's poems and would, like Vilhelm Andersen, be able to say of the passage "And with wealth we can say it is progress indeed, when few have too much and still fewer are in need" that *here*, precisely *here*, Grundtvig is presenting an economic program with far-reaching consequences.

Obviously another kind of reality existed beyond the walls of Sorø Academy, but this was of no great interest to the academy boys or the teachers or the headmaster. Naturally, they knew of its existence, and naturally, the school subscribed to certain newspapers—which, now and again, someone might read—but there was something unreal about the outside world; it was as though the news reports from outside were just vague, fanciful rumors. Carsten had been at the school for a year when the Germans occupied Denmark, and if one asks, as I have done, what effect this had on the day-to-day routine of the school, the answer is: Virtually none. On April 10 a detachment of German soldiers set up machine guns in Sorø town square and a German military band played, and the boy who had been behind Carsten in the assembly hall went over and spoke to the German soldiers. A few days later, at morning prayers, Carsten was presented with a prize for diligence, and the headmaster said, "You have applied yourself in a manner the like of which has not been seen in this century, and I predict that when you fly out into life you will perform great and wonderful deeds in Denmark's name, gladdening your mother's heart"—here the headmaster paused briefly—"and bringing honor to the school. And now I would like to ask all of you"—here the headmaster reluctantly looked up from Carsten's brown eyes—"as far as is possible to save on toilet paper, which has, because of the current situation, been rationed."

The "current situation" was the term used at the academy when referring to the German occupation, about which very few knew what to think until the Boy from the Assembly Hall wrote in the school magazine that this occupation was an insult to democracy, thus prompting the headmaster to confiscate every single copy, thereby making it clear to those who did not know what to think that it was best not to think anything at all. This moved the boy to retaliate in a little leaflet that he produced and duplicated himself, using a typewriter, one finger, and carbon paper. In this he wrote that it came as no surprise to him that the school did not call attention openly to the criminally violent nature of this Fascist occupation of Denmark, since he for one had always been very well aware that the academy's blithering brand of nationalism had no time for modern history but would rather dwell dolefully on the Spirit of 1848 and the Defeat of 1864 and the Reunion of 1920. Furthermore, he would like his fellow members of the academy and schoolmates to know how rife was sympathy among the school's teachers for Aryan notions that the ancient peoples actually stemmed from Nordic tribes who had migrated south—the very notion put forward by that trashy novelist Johannes V. Jensen. In his opinion, wrote the Boy from the Assembly Hall, this notion was stupid, unsubstantiated, and arrogant. Naturally, this leaflet, too, was confiscated, to be used, not long afterward, as an argument for asking its author's parents to remove him from the school. It is mentioned here because it made a deep impression on Carsten, so deep that when I spoke to him, almost fifty years after reading it, he still knew its contents by heart.

It is tempting to ask whether Carsten and his schoolmates were happy at the academy, and it is a question I have in fact put on several occasions to former students who attended the school at the same time as Carsten. Most of them have answered, "Those certainly were grand days," or, "We were treated in a civilized fashion, treated like adults"—and clichés such as these caution me against addressing the past with a concept of happiness from our own day and age. So I will let that question pass and try instead to give an objective account of what life at this time was like for Carsten. For Carsten, life at the academy came as a natural continuation of his life with Amalie after Carl Laurids's disappearance. Here, too, there were adults who expected—and rewarded—a particular mode of behavior, adults who paid homage to the same ideals as Amalie, namely, Cultivation and Good Taste and Order and Diligence. Because the academy was closed off, set apart—constituting a kind of cultural and historical island—it was possible to preserve the notion that even if life does go on outside the walls, everything that really matters is going on here, on the inside; and what goes on is pretty much the same as what was going on in the previous century. Carsten had grown up amid human relationships as unpredictable as the weather: with Amalie's capricious temperament continually sweeping through the house like a sort of indoor thunderstorm bringing sunshine in its wake; and with the love affair between her and Carl Laurids having its own unreliable meteorology. As far as he was concerned, it was, in many ways, deeply satisfying to come to Sorø, where the time was spent teaching students about those things which are completely and utterly stable and immutable. The idea of the Spirit of the People was immensely appealing to him: the idea of a kind of lineage, a thread running from the men of the runes and Absalon right up to the present day, a tangible thread that glowed on those two occasions every year when the great Vilhelm Andersen gave a lecture at the school. He always began—amid breathless silence—by placing his silver-topped cane on the lectern as though it were some great treasure, some significant archaeological find. Then he would hold the entire student body spellbound, listening for two hours, while he revealed that the world was not, as they thought, incalculable and unreasonable and awkward and difficult, but, on the contrary, clear-cut and coherent and sound as the Spirit of the People itself—especially if one belonged to the Flower of Danish Youth. This idea of belonging to the Danish elite appealed to Carsten. Despite his modesty, despite there being, for most of the time, something self-effacing about him, something that appealed both to his schoolmates and to the teachers—for modesty was one of most prized virtues at Sorø—despite this, he feels his heart beat fast at the thought of belonging to the flower of something, even a phenomenon as hazy as Danish Youth.

And really, such a sense of pride is not surprising; in fact, in a way, it came as an enormous relief, because he felt he was on his way. And what did he think he was on the way to? Well, naturally, he was on his way to becoming what he and most of the other boys at the academy dreamed of becoming, what they had promised themselves and their mothers they would become: a great man. Every time Carsten heard the headmaster or Meph or Gnasher or Vilhelm Andersen say, "You are the standard-bearers of Democracy and Danish Culture and the Spirit of the People," he felt he had taken yet another step in the right direction, and it was because he wanted to hear these words as often as possible that he had become a model of diligence and anonymity.

In spite of everything, however, something of the outside world did infiltrate Carsten's life during these years. For instance, concerts

were held at the school, usually chamber music evenings at which
the headmaster invariably welcomed guests by saying that Our
School is an island in the sea of time, and on this occasion the winds
have blown our way Mr. Opera Singer this or Mrs. Pianist that, and
our very own music master will wield the violin bow. On the subject
of these evenings, the Boy from the Assembly Hall wrote in the
school magazine that what the seas of time washed up onto the
academy's shore consisted mainly of wreckage from the foundering
of bourgeois culture, and he recommended an alternative to all his
readers: the movie house in Sorø, where three or four films could
be seen on any one weekend. After giving it a try, Carsten kept going
back to it, as did many of his schoolmates. And what they found in
Sorø's movie house was love.

The word that covers Carsten's attitude—and that of his
contemporaries—to love is "chaste." All the talk of boarding-school
years being the jolly days of French postcards and wild school dances
and booze and condoms and eighteen flushed-faced boys whacking
one another off in a twelve-foot-square bathroom is, in all probability, a myth—at any rate, it was not true of Sorø. No one here
spoke of love. Or, rather, of course they spoke of love—the entire
bourgeois culture is, in some sense, one long, mumbled discourse
on love—but they spoke of it in terms of Ingemann's poems and
love of one's country and the countryside around Sorø, which
seemed made to be loved. But the love that is filtered through Ingemann and one's country and the Sorø countryside is watered down
a little, so if we ask what the boys *really* knew about love, the answer
has to be: Very, very little. Now, of course one does not need to
know anything about love; personally I am inclined to believe that
intuition will take you a long way—if, that is, you have permission.
But that—having permission—is exactly what it boils down to, because at Sorø permission was never really given. This was obviously
partly because of certain prohibitions and regulations stating that
girls were not accepted into the school; and that those dances to
which girls from the town were invited had to finish at a decent
hour; and that the drinking of alcohol was not allowed; and that
study periods had to be observed; and so on and so forth, but all of
this falls short. The most important rules were unwritten and unspoken and perhaps quite simply unperceived, and these rules were
implemented by the boys themselves and had to do with not referring

to love other than through jokes that left behind more confusion than clarity, and bearing love's burden with a smile, or at any rate not letting it show.

Carsten always went alone to the movie house, as did his schoolmates; and even if, now and again, he walked down there with someone, he always left by himself—to be alone with the storm of emotion, both splendid and embarrassing, that he was convinced was unique to him. It was the same emotion he experienced when he read, again preferably in absolute privacy, those contemporary authors whose works were not studied at the school—apart, that is, from Jakob Paludan's novel *Jørgen Stein*, a veritable textbook on sexual and social impotence that both teachers and students regarded as presenting an exceptionally accurate picture of adolescence. Carsten knew that other literature on the subject also existed. Several times in Copenhagen he had seen the magazine *Sex and Society* at the newsstands. However, Amalie's guests and most other people described this magazine as pornographic trash, so he had never read it. And in any case, it would probably not have said a great deal to him. Carsten and his contemporaries read what they read and felt what they felt, not because there were no other books or feelings, but because what affected them most deeply was H. C. Branner and films based on Kipling's stories and Karen Blixen's tales and Cooper's Leatherstocking Tales, all of which pointed the way back toward the chivalrous romance of earlier times.

Now, this romanticism was widespread throughout Denmark, so do not make the mistake of imagining that it was a dream that Carsten dreamed in such an out-of-the-way place as Sorø. I have mentioned it precisely because it corresponds to the yearning felt by so many Danes this spring, when the academy decides to hold a Midsummer celebration, just like the Midsummer celebrations of Ingemann's day; the spring when one of Amalie's friends, the Copenhagen chief of police, and the Danish police and Parliament and the Supreme Court all conspire to turn a blind eye and thumb their nose at the Constitution and arrest Danish Communists and Communist members of Parliament. I do not mention this last event here because Carsten would consider it important—not right away. In fact, he is not even aware that it has taken place, but later— later—it will be of some relevance to him, which is why it is included here.

There are many reasons why the academy—that is to say, the headmaster—made the decision to hold a celebration. One reason was the occupation. The Midsummer festival would provide an opportunity to celebrate being Danish, by coming together, standing shoulder to shoulder, singing Danish songs, and feeling the Spirit of the People. Another reason may possibly have been that, with this celebration, an attempt would be made to revive an ancient tradition. During these years a passion for tradition prevailed among both students and teachers—a grand desire to go back in time, far back, to the days when uniforms did not have pockets and everyone could still feel the Spirit of 1848, and values were clear and distinct and not, as now, increasingly blurred.

And this, too, the headmaster mentions in his speech. He speaks to the entire academy, which has assembled on the banks of Sorø Lake, just before the boat trip that is to be the high point of the evening. And he says, "This evening, Ingemann's spirit hovers over these waters. This evening we are reaching back to the classical peaks of Danish Culture." Then all the rowboats push off. They are decorated with greenery and flowers and colored lanterns, and their crews have brought along guitars and lutes and books of Latin and Danish songs and a passionate longing to commit suicide or to die like Shelley in the waves of the Ligurian Sea. The moon rises over the shining lake and out on the water; the boys sing college songs from the last century in which they assure themselves that the future is theirs, and praise Woman and Wine—which, in the main, they know of only from hearsay.

Before the headmaster's speech and the boat trip there has been a *smørrebrød* supper and—possibly because nostalgia has run away with him—the headmaster has ordered the serving of a punch made from fruit wine. Carsten has drunk some of this wine, and even though the punch is weak, even though it is what Ingemann would probably have called children's punch and left untouched, still it has its effect on Carsten. This effect is such that, having drunk his first and then his second glass, he, who is not given much to speaking, feels called upon to propose a toast to er . . . to er . . . to the Ladies, and everyone heartily salutes the handful of schoolmasters' wives and the six day girls, who cannot join the boat trip because Father wouldn't like it, but must be back home in an hour's time. Drunk with joy because his toast has gone down well, Carsten drinks four more glasses in rapid succession, and by the last glass it seems to him that someone has lifted off the detachable top of his skull and that a cross between a firework and a plume of feathers is now sprouting out of his glowing head. It is in order to savor this headgear in peace that—after the headmaster's speech—he gets into a boat, pushes off from the shore, and glides out onto the lake alone. But this gesture also has something to do with his and his schoolmates' need to experience any kind of emotional moment in solitude, and as Carsten glides out onto the lake under the moon there is an air of great and impossible loneliness about him.

Across the lake comes the sound of voices singing in harmony and of soulful solos accompanied by a lute, and of faint shouts along the shores of the lake, where bonfires are now being lit. Then Carsten sails past a reedy islet. On the islet sits a young girl with fair hair and eyes that even in the moonlight are an undeniable, striking blue. Because Carsten is so close to her before he so much as notices her, he does not have time to react in any of the predictable ways. He does not have time to be shy or rush off or say good evening or act as if he has not seen her or sink into the ground or jump into the water. Instead he falls straight into a sort of coma of benumbed ecstasy, in which state he first of all rows slowly around the islet once and then again, while gazing intently upon the girl in total silence.

Of course the girl is Maria Jensen, and between her and Carsten at this moment there lies both a few feet of dark water and an abyss. This abyss is created by his coming from a rich family while she comes from a poor family, and from his having learned to beware of girls like her and from her having learned to beware of men in general. It also comes from his having gone to school for so many years more than she, and from the distance between Christianshavn and Strand Drive, and from his having learned—not least at the academy—to despise anyone of his own age who is not cultivated, and from her having learned—to be on the safe side—to hit first and talk later. And so many other things have gone into its making that there ought to be absolutely no chance of its being bridged— but then, as he is starting to row around the islet for the third time, Maria says, "Hey, chum, got any room for a girl to stretch her Marlene Dietrichs?"

Then Carsten surfaces with a plop and pulls up alongside the reeds, and Maria climbs aboard in a skirt that is still sopping wet because she has waded out to the islet, and with cheeks that are hollow with hunger because she has not eaten in a long time. Then they head out into the lake.

A lot of bonfires are now blazing along the lakeshore; wistful chords reach their ears from the other boats, and then Carsten gets to his feet in the boat and sings. He has his work cut out keeping his balance, and in normal circumstances he would never have had the courage to sing on his own—and in no circumstances, no circumstances whatsoever, in front of a girl. But he is still in a sort of trance, and he has been drinking punch, and he has been picked for the school choir—which has made two tours of South Jutland —and so now he sings that lovely verse of Ingemann's:

> *"In the depths of the soul a sea does lurk*
> *Frozen hard by the world's chill squalls"*

and the distant lute takes up his key and accompanies him as he continues with:

> *"And hidden in tomblike silence and murk*
> *That which no earthly sun can recall"*

and now the crews of the other boats have also fallen silent to listen.

Then Maria's big moment has come and, sitting in the stern, she lifts up her celebrated soprano and sings that ditty so well known in Christianshavn and Vesterbro and Annebjerg:

> *"Tahiti is paradise on earth, hm hm,*
> *Thither my thoughts often go . . ."*

And the listeners on the banks say not a word. Once more Maria is onstage—like her father, Adonis—and with her face turned to the big spotlight, the moon, she sings:

> *"Where birds of paradise build their nests*
> *And love's magic blossoms grow"*

and then they have floated past all the other boats and are heading for the center of the lake.

And floating there—to those watchers on the lakeside who may see them—they are just a boy and a girl in a rowboat on Sorø Lake. But to us they are much more, to us they are, first of all, two different collections of wishes and hopes from two different classes, and it is thanks to these hopes that they now find themselves in the same boat, and that Denmark is as it is. What I believe is that a whole series of factors have made it possible, now, for them to vanish from view together—including that none of the teachers has called them back, even though they have seen them; and that Carsten has been drinking punch and has not been stopped from going out in a boat on his own; and that Maria has had the necessary, boyish daring to wade out to the reedy islet and to talk to a boy in a boat; and that she has run away from Annebjerg because, in her mind, she cannot reconcile her wish to be a little girl with her knowledge that the only way of surviving in this world is to be as tough as a boy; and that she has been able to stay away and at large for more than a month by stealing, as her forefathers did; and that Carsten believes emotions have to be experienced in solitude; and that he, together with the rest of the school, wants to revive Ingemann. And that all of this should be reason enough for the Rich Boy and the Poor Girl, Carsten and Maria, that is, to meet here has something to do with the point in time—that is to say, the spring of 1941.

Carsten rows for a bit, then he lets the boat drift, then rows a bit more, and they talk off and on, then lapse into silence, then exchange a word or two more. While they are gliding along, and the banks are growing distant, although they are still sitting where they have been sitting all the time, they are drawing closer to each other. Carsten tunes in to what lies beyond the girl's rough manners and her directness and the fact that she blows her snot straight into the water; and she sees past his side part and exaggerated politeness; and with every sweep of the oars both of them are moving further to the other side of their own prejudices—until, finally, they are very, very close to each other.

At no time do they touch, and in the end they have also stopped talking. When Carsten rows the boat in to the bank the faintest hint of dawn can be seen in the east.

Neither of them has anything remotely resembling an appreciation of their situation—and so they do nothing to ensure that they will meet again. They part without knowing each other's first names.

A year later, Carsten graduated from the academy, and being thus finished with Sorø he should have left for home. That was what

everyone else did, and hence, only a few days after commencement
with all its speeches and prizes for diligence and songs, the academy
was empty of pupils. But Carsten stayed behind. He said nothing
to the watchmaker's family, even though they were obviously expecting him to leave any day now. He stayed on for a week, strolling
every day around Sorø—and the academy in particular—with
clouded eyes. He wore the suit that he, like everyone else, had had
made for commencement, but only because he was no longer entitled to wear the school uniform. Because naturally he would have
preferred his uniform. Carsten was a creature of habit, he thought
of himself as a *member of the academy*; it was impossible for him
to picture himself naked, or in a dinner jacket, or in anything other
than the shirt and waistcoat and jacket bearing the academy's Phoenix buttons.

He stayed on at Sorø in an effort to combat the process of dissolution. He stayed on because he hated—more, feared—the
thought of things falling apart and proving to be incoherent. He
stayed on because he could not absorb the fact that he no longer
belonged here—at the school and in its grounds and in the assembly
hall and in the big, sunken bath where, once a week, there had been
compulsory communal bathing. If there had been anyone in whom
he could have confided, he would have said that at Sorø he had
learned about Eternal Values and the Significance of the Individual
and Human Fellowship—and here he was, discovering that even
the fellowship of the academy could be dissolved, from one day to
the next, and all the familiar faces fade from view. Next year it
would start all over again, with the message being imparted to new
faces, and he, Carsten, would be forgotten, even though he had
received an A-plus in every subject and the collected works of Vol-
taire as a prize for diligence. But he did not feel as though there
was anyone to whom he could talk; despite being surrounded by
crowds of people he felt totally alone. So instead he had to talk to
himself, muttering his muddled thoughts under his breath as he
strode around, imagining that he had, as a listener, a girl with fair
hair and blue eyes who was far, far out of reach.

He gave no thought to the future, he just could not believe that
his Schooldays were over—and his Youth—and that, somewhere,
Life and Responsibility were lying, slavering, in wait for him; he
knew that he wanted to stay here, in these secure surroundings

where he was familiar with the faces and the truths, and where he was close to the Spirit of the People and Culture and that reedy islet on Sorø Lake. When, after five days, the big car that had, in a distant past, driven him to the school arrived, he hid in the academy grounds and watched from a distance as Gladys hunted for him. He heard her call, like an echo from his childhood, but kept well out of the way until she drove off late that night.

The next day, the Girl from Sorø Lake made him leave for Copenhagen. Not that she spoke to him; nor could it be said that she appeared to him—it was more as though she were some sort of siren in reverse and that the memory of her told him that if he wanted to see her again, he would have to make a move, get away from this place, and, in the first instance, go home.

Carsten took the train to Copenhagen, then crossed the city by streetcar. He noted with dismay and absentminded wonder that the streets were swarming with German soldiers and that several city monuments had been walled in to protect them from explosions. Amalie met him in the grounds of the villa, where she had said goodbye to him, and shook his hand as she had done then. And with this handshake she was trying to say, "I know what we two share, my pet. The years have passed and you have grown tall and broad-shouldered, and you wear a suit now, but everything is the same as it has always been, and that is how it will stay." Then she left him to his own devices. Not because she had nothing more to say—quite the contrary: more than anything she would have liked to lead him straight to her bedroom, lay him down on the bed, draw him to her, and pull him across the years and the events that lay between them at this very moment. But she controlled herself, she refrained, because her maternal instinct and foresight told her that by leaving him alone now she would stand a better chance, later, of getting through to him and of attaining that goal around which everything had always revolved: their shared dream of the future.

During the following days it was brought home to Carsten that he had grown older. On lingering exploratory tours of his childhood home—where everything was coated with a thick but transparent layer of memories—he discovered that it looked just as it had always done, and yet it had changed irrevocably. The villa was still large —it was huge—but still it was much smaller than he remembered;

it was still pervaded by the scent of strange flowers, but that scent was no longer the same, because now it reminded him of wood shavings and coal-tar soap in the academy's frothy communal bath.

What Carsten became aware of during these days was that phenomenon he had already sensed at Sorø, the same phenomenon that had kept him there for an extra week: the relentlessness of time. Anyone else might have seen the white villa in a different light, but Carsten was as he was, and what now confronted him—sighing and wailing, and yet silent and uneasy—was the traces of a bygone time and the pain of knowing that it will never come again, that it had gone, taking with it his childhood. And then and there he began to picture this childhood as a gentle, undulating boat ride across a sea of unconcern. This longing for an imaginary past was to remain with Carsten all his days, transforming, as time went on, into a pale, faint melancholy. The actual, searing pain lasted only for those first few days after his return from Sorø. Thereafter it was replaced by something else: by an odd sense of weightlessness. Although he did not know it, this sense was something Carsten shared with his classmates and with thousands of graduates throughout Denmark. During these very days they were making the discovery that they weighed nothing. They woke up on the morning after their commencement parties convinced that they were dying. They had tombstone hangovers and felt embalmed for eternity by alcohol, and yet they got out of bed, stood upright, their feet planted on the floor, and then it happened: they discovered that they were spry and nimble, not merely in good shape for mummies but alive and kicking and sort of—how shall I put it—free? It was as though there were no responsibilities and no one above them and nothing they had to do; it was as though, all of a sudden, they had grown up, just as one dreams of growing up—reaching out beyond all boundaries, out to freedom—and they were seized by a sense of freedom that pulled upward, in the opposite direction from gravity and parents.

And I am tempted to say that it also pulled in the opposite direction from reality, because this sense of freedom was, of course, nothing but a vacuum—a void, an air pocket, giving a short-lived illusion of floating. For Carsten this illusion was even shorter-lived—shorter than for most of his contemporaries. He seemed almost to be jumping on the spot, straight into the air—taking off, rising, hanging there for a moment, with elevation, and then falling. With so many different forces at work in Denmark in the 1940s, it would be absurd to refer to freedom as anything other than a tiny jump.

He landed in the conservatory, which had been built onto the villa during his absence, and as he entered this glass-walled room filled with flowers, the thought struck him that his mother had had to abase herself and submit to a fate worse than death for this room, and, just in the nick of time, he managed to fend off this thought before reliving, in his mind's eye, the scenes he had witnessed as a child by peeping into Amalie's bedroom through Carl Laurids's spyholes.

Now, it may be that this was precisely why Amalie had arranged to meet him here—to call forth these memories; it may be that she wanted to get him into the right mood by reminding him of the past, since what she wanted to speak to him about was, of course, the future. This set in like some law of gravity that has, just for a moment, been suspended, because that is what Carsten's future was like, like a law of nature, with room for the odd, minor deviation, but not for anything that could really alter its course. To be sure, it was presented as a choice. Amalie said, "I'm so happy to have my big boy home, it hasn't been easy, being a woman on her own in the big city"—and here she gestured vaguely in the direction of the conservatory and Carsten's images of what a woman alone in Copenhagen, Amalie, that is, must have to put up with. "But now it will be easier, just knowing you're here, just being able to see you every day"—and here she stole a glance at him to see whether he had been entertaining any dreadful ideas of leaving home—"I feel so much easier, just knowing that there will be someone here—Mother's own boy—to look after me if I should fall ill *again*," she says. Carsten remains silent, acquiescent—and then it comes, what all of this has really been leading up to, when Amalie says, "Now, my dear, of course you know that, for centuries, there have always been three choices open to a boy from a good family wanting to make his way in the world: the Army, the Church, and the Civil Service." Then she looks questioningly at Carsten, but there is no question, he *has* landed, he has come back down to earth.

He is going to study law, well, of course he is going to study law—and he *will* start, in a moment, but first there is just one other thing: even now, in July, now he has just left school, one thought has begun to gnaw at him—that he might risk wasting time.

There is something strange and disturbing about this idea of time being as tangible as the real coffee that Carsten could drink, the occupation notwithstanding, because Amalie numbered among her acquaintances a man who had access to everything. But not even that coffee could be wasted—no spills on the white embroidered tablecloth, thank you—but that is hardly as strange as the idea that time should not be wasted. It startles me, this idea—partly because, well, time isn't a concrete entity, is it?—but mostly because this passionate interest in Carsten's future does not really appear to be necessary. It does not seem possible to pinpoint any *compelling* reason for Amalie pushing Carsten and Carsten pushing himself—to study, and complete his studies, and become a great lawyer. It seems to me that Amalie had long since proved she could take care of herself. The villa had a new conservatory, and there were sacks of coffee in the attic, and smoked hams and racks of wine in the cellar, and no sign that she was likely to run short. Nor was there any *ethical* reason for Carsten to run like a horse at the racetrack. Without anyone but herself being aware of it, Amalie's status has in fact been altered. She had maintained her coterie of Friends of the Family and had even expanded it. But she never went to bed with her clients now, or at least almost never. Slowly and imperceptibly she had used her power over men to make the path to her bedroom less and less accessible to them, until finally she closed it off altogether. But she had retained her influence; she had become a wise counselor and interlocutor and healing spirit and friend and philosopher—everything except what she had originally been, a shrewd whore.

She had kept up with her old friends—she still saw the stockbroker and the professor—and she had widened her circle by the addition of such celebrities as that controversial and thus risky acquaintance, the architect and journalist Poul Henningsen. And up until his death in 1942, Prime Minister Stauning would visit Amalie Mahogany to have a rest and to beg for one thing and another, and she denied him nothing apart from the one thing that she never, or almost never, gave to anyone at all now.

But all of this she kept from Carsten. She quite simply did not tell him. Instead she depicted her life as a journey through a vale of tears, and that is what is so strange. Because she is not the only one; at this point in time, Denmark is full of petits bourgeois brandishing whips and frantically chasing their children into the future so that they can have an education and *amount to* something, to something more than their parents.

Now, don't get me wrong, I can understand some people having this dream and I think it makes good sense, where the parents are janitors or shoemakers or shipyard workers and can remember hunger and the thirties and the Old Days and stories of the cholera epidemics of the last century, and hence fear the coming of a new Depression; fear that the country and they themselves and their children will sink down into the kind of poverty that Adonis and Anna once knew in Christianshavn. But not everyone, not even the majority, are in that position; most of those who are wielding the whips are people who, in a sense, are comfortably off and have no trouble making ends meet, people whose minds ought to be so pleasantly free from worries about where the next meal is coming from that there should be room to think beyond a career in the Army or the Church or the Civil Service. But no—they do what Amalie does, more or less what Amalie does, and this I cannot quite understand.

Amalie knew, as only a mother can, how to appeal to Carsten, and this she did by speaking to his guilty conscience and his love for her and his fear of wasting time—and he was all ears. He applied for a student job with the Department of Statistics and was given it on the spot because, statistically, and in every other way, his marks in his final examination had been so exceptionally high, and because he made the sort of confidence-inspiring, orthodox, and at the same time personal impression that can be made only by someone who has from a very early age inhaled the Culture of the Danish Civil Servant.

He had to start work at 7:30 a.m. and finished at 4:00 p.m.— which meant that he could squeeze in yet another job, the day was not yet over, there was still time to roll up his sleeves and do a good job of work before attending night school classes at six o'clock in the city center. And here Carsten did something he knew he would never be able to tell his mother about: he took a job as a messenger. Now, *that* Amalie could never have lived with. She told Carsten what she had once told Carl Laurids, "It is not called *going to work*, we do not know what *work* is, it is called *going to the office*."

And this is where his law studies start.

They began with the *Filosofikum*—the preliminary examination in basic philosophy that everyone wishing to study at Copenhagen University had to pass. The idea was that this course should provide an insight into the foundations of learning and the Eternal Truths upon which the teaching at Sorø Academy had also been based; and this insight was conveyed to the students—Carsten and a great many of his contemporaries, that is—through the study of formal logic and psychology and, first and foremost, Professor Dr. Harald Høffding's splendid book *History of Modern Philosophy*. The most recent entries in this book dated from the previous century, thereby emphasizing the view that Carsten had brought with him from Sorø: that the past, and not least the nineteenth century, is better, significantly better, than the present. At the examination, questions were put to him by a professor who persisted in squashing imaginary moths on the desktop throughout, and he was given a question on "The Subconscious," to which he gave the answer expected of him—neither more nor less than that the Subconscious is like an iceberg with a small section sticking up above the sea and the rest underneath. The professor then nodded benevolently and said, "Thank you, you can go, and be so kind as to close the door behind you, as quickly as you can, to prevent any more of these irritating insects getting in."

As I said earlier, after commencement students were expected to be capable of discerning the foundations of learning—possibly only far off on the horizon, but intimated nevertheless—and this was also to hold true for Carsten. He thought he could see the law, albeit pretty far off, but looking like the Copenhagen Law Courts: solid, with touches of ancient Greece and Rome about it—and of something else, something that was both terrifying and indestructible—and all based on the eighteenth-century philosopher Montesquieu's theory that the state is composed of the legislative, the executive, and the judicial bodies—this last, in Denmark, being the law courts, which are one hundred percent autonomous. Carsten considered this autonomy to be a most important concept. Of course, he knew very well that the judicial system was bound up with society, but at the same time he had the distinct feeling that it was above it. And even higher up, he felt, was *jurisprudence*, which bore some resemblance to mathematics and to Latin grammar and classical antiquity, inasmuch as it dealt with eternal truths; he felt, here at the beginning

of his academic studies and later on, too, that lawyers, like mathematicians and philosophers, were—let's not beat about the bush
—higher beings, inhabiting a rarefied air in which one became
exceptionally clear-sighted and farsighted.

The course of study was designed in such a way as to support this
view. It was run by professors who were never seen. Some of the
older students said they had once heard from still-older students
that they had heard from even older students that once upon a time,
in a far distant past, these professors had given lectures in almost
empty auditoriums, working their way through dense jungles of legal
detail only to discover eventually that there was no chance of ever
getting through the syllabus, and that they had, several months back,
lost the last of their audience. After that they had withdrawn from
reality, away from tiresome, compulsory lecturing and into what
Carsten imagined must be an elevated, academic silence, which they
only broke in order to do what—guess, no, wrong, not to publish
the results of their research: no interesting papers on Danish jurisprudence had been published since the previous century—but to
publish bulky, expensive compulsory textbooks in which they conducted blood feuds against one another and by which they secured
themselves a large and steady extra income.

And so a void had been created in the law faculty between the
students—standing, or perhaps, rather, crawling, on terra firma—
and the faculty professors who set the exams and determined the
framework of a jurisprudence which Carsten envisaged as an aerial
version of the city courthouse, but which, as far as I can see, was
more like a sort of bubble that had cut itself adrift from society in
the previous century or perhaps even back in the Middle Ages.
Obviously, this void had to be filled, and the individuals who had
taken on the task of building a stairway to the temple of justice were
the *private tutors*. Even in those days, it was whispered of these
individuals (who have long since become creatures of legend) that
they were strange shoots on the law's beautiful tree and to that I
would have to say, you're damned right they were. They were eternal
students or former students or lawyers with ailing practices and
shady pasts. They were all, each in his own way, a bit peculiar,
reminding even the inordinately polite Carsten of exhibits at the
Zoological Museum—in the vicinity of which, in the city center,
around Store Kannike Lane, their classes were held. But they did

have certain things in common, qualities which were not to be mocked and which would have looked good anywhere, even hung on a wall or preserved in alcohol: their incredible memories and their flair and their keenness to earn money. They knew the textbooks backwards, they could talk and talk and rattle off notes at a cracking pace, occasionally saying, "Turn the page," because they knew that they had moved on to a new page in the textbook. Or they might ask a question along the lines of, "Where do the shutters go up in Civil Law?" and then go on to quote every instance in the thousands of clauses where shutters are put up. But it was not just that they had good memories; they also knew how to run a business, they were traders and hucksters who had rented space in cheap, privately owned premises, expected payment a month in advance, and neglected—with a judicial appreciation of income tax technicalities—to issue receipts. The fierce rivalry that existed among them had elbowed the most inept out into the gloom of the occupation, and those who were left were odd but talented teachers who always sent observers to exams and had a good feel for what would be handed down from on high and thus an almost prophetic talent for predicting exam questions.

One of these tutors—Tyge Lubanskij, who taught civil law—was to become a significant character in Carsten's life. I do not think the relationship between these two men could be called a friendship; all of Carsten's relationships with other people were marked by an innate distance and politeness, so it would be more correct to say that he and Lubanskij were acquaintances. This acquaintanceship —which also involved a third party—was struck up early on, during one of the first tutorials on the YWCA premises in Store Kannike Lane, amid the sunshine and sweltering heat of late summer. Seated right in front of Carsten is one of the few female law students, a girl whose hair is parted into two heavy, fair plaits, thus revealing the back of her neck, which is somewhat concave and very distracting. It reminds Carsten of something and diverts his attention from the open book in front of him, in which he has had a bookbinder insert hundreds of blank pages now awaiting notes that are unforthcoming because he has noticed that the girl, although she cannot be said to turn around, occasionally sends him what at this time was known as a "sunbeam glance." It is at this point, however, that Carsten actually *hears* Lubanskij's voice for the first time. Now, there is no saying why this should happen right now, but it does, and the girl is forgotten as Carsten becomes captivated by the tutor's penetrating voice and his brilliant command of the law and the flicker of madness with which, again and again during this lecture, Lubanskij ventured to the limits of legal thought. For the first time ever it occurred to Carsten that even the cleverest of men might not hold the answers to everything, and when the class was over he remained in his seat staring at the blackboard, which the tutor was wiping clean. Then he realized that his neighbor had also kept his seat and, turning, he recognized his former schoolmate the Boy from the Assembly Hall. Carsten stares long and hard at him, wanting to make sure that it really is he and looking for any marks of the awful venereal disease that rumor had once bestowed upon him. But the Boy seems to be healthy, in fine fettle, radiating an air of concentrated zeal, and Carsten feels an odd flutter of pleasure at being so close to this energetic little body and these provocative opinions with which he is as yet unfamiliar but of which he already has some inkling. Shortly after this, Lubanskij sits down beside the two boys and starts to tell them his anecdotes and stories from Copenhagen nightlife and of his contempt for the legal institutions, and somehow or other ersatz coffee and pastries appear (probably paid for by Carsten), and they talk on and on as the summer draws to a close and turns to autumn, then winter, then spring again. Later on, Carsten is to recall these conversations as one long, intoxicating stream of words.

The Boy turns out to be a Communist—well, of course he is a Communist—Carsten realizes, to his delight, that the Boy will always push as far out as it is possible to go. But that is not the whole story, that is only the beginning, and in no time he has also told them that he is a freedom fighter and a member of the resistance. With childlike eagerness he shows Carsten and Lubanskij his false identity cards and illegal newssheets and his stolen German Parabellum, so heavy that he has to use both hands to raise it and so big that it looks as though he has a nasty growth under his Icelandic sweater. And of course Lubanskij is not to be outdone; he, too, explores the limits and tells them, contemptuously, about the absent law professors and the legal collaborators and of life as a lawyer— which may be tough and dirty, he says, but it's realistic. At some point he also tells them how, in '41 and '43, the Minister of Justice,

Thune Jacobsen, and the head of the Supreme Court, Troels G. Jørgensen, helped the Germans with the unconstitutional arrest of three to four hundred Communists, thus demonstrating that insignificant as the Danish police force might be, it can still carry out a piece of high-quality European workmanship, and Lubanskij says this with a sarcastic little smile, implying that of course this is unspeakably sordid, but that's life.

Carsten never forgot this story; through everything else that was said, through Lubanskij's cheery cynicism, this event sticks in his mind. One of the reasons for this may perhaps be that Lubanskij mentions Louis von Kohl, whom Carsten remembers as one of the men who visited Carl Laurids before he disappeared. At any rate, this story sows the first seeds of doubt in Carsten's mind concerning eternal justice and the Supreme Court and middle-class values; in some way this tale links up with his lonely days at Sorø Academy after commencement and gives rise to a vague, inexplicable feeling of disappointment.

During these evening and nocturnal discussions—after the tutorials, in the blacked-out city center—Carsten always sits between the other two. On one side of him is the Boy, all fired up with enthusiasm for Stalin and the millennium and world Communism and Russia's battle with the Nazis, as he condemns the policy of collaboration and the King and the collaborators. And on the other side of the table Lubanskij is agreeing with him, it's immoral, damned if it isn't, but it's also a realistic picture of life, and what do you say to some coffee and pastries? Carsten never *says* anything at these meetings, he listens and listens but makes no direct contribution to the conversation—because he has nothing to say. The real world referred to by the Boy and Lubanskij is one he knows of from these meetings and these meetings only. The rest of his life is taken up by work at the Department of Statistics and his messenger job and civil law and meals with Mother and the deep sleep of oblivion. Nor does he feel any need to say anything; he is bewitched by these two impressive individuals, their knowledge, their points of view, their ardor and idealism and cynicism, and at the same time he is overwhelmed by a sense of how little he himself does and is and knows. He feels like some kind of insect, sitting out there in the darkness, seeing the light of the other two burning brightly but without the strength even to flutter anywhere near the lamp. During this time, which seems so short but which must have lasted for a couple of years, Lubanskij and the Boy were his ideals, just as his father and mother and Mr. Raaschou-Nielsen had been; the only difference being that these two lads in the YWCA rooms are tempters of a sort, whose stories and viewpoints seem to call to him and lead him close to limits he would rather not reach.

During these years, Carsten's relationships with other people are relationships with role models, since that is how he has been raised. He has been taught to take his cue from ideals. If Amalie had had her way, Carsten's world would now consist of that handful of people one looks up to—the geniuses—and the many who are to be despised and feared—laborers or tobacconists or those who do nothing at all. But Carsten's world is not quite so simple. Amalie has not had her way in all things and he cherishes some dreams of tenderness for which she would not have cared—one of which concerns the girl on Sorø Lake, who is neither an ideal nor someone to despise but something else again, something indefinable that is now drawing closer.

One day the Boy did not turn up for a tutorial. He had never been absent before. He did not come the next day either, or the next again, so a search was conducted and a number of telephone calls made; then his parents turned up at a tutorial, red-eyed from weeping, to ask if anyone knew anything—but he was nowhere to be found, until Carsten happened to remember the name on one of his false identity cards. And then they found him, or, rather, the girl with the plaits found him. She went from hospital to hospital, repeating the name Carsten remembered, until she came to the Nyelands Street first-aid station, where she was told that the boy had been buried the day before. Thereafter she walked back into town in a kind of trance, walked up to the classroom, and interrupted the lesson to tell them that the Boy was dead.

It had happened during a liquidation attempt on an informer. The plan had been for the Boy to ring the doorbell and then blast the informer when he opened the door. That would have been the standard method, the sure method, but of course the Boy did not take the direct route; instead he had to make a quick detour around the edge of the abyss, walking up and down outside the informer's apartment, parading his audacity and his semiautomatic the size of a pumpkin and his belief in world Communism—until the informer opened his window, took leisurely aim, and shot him stone cold dead. The girl's lips, telling all this, were framed by a set white face that revealed how even she, who had never exchanged one word with the Boy but had for two years kept her back to him, was deeply affected by the influence exerted by people who truly believe in something, who burn for a cause—for their own sakes and for ours. Having unburdened herself by speaking to these people, to whom she had never spoken before but whose hearts she felt must also have been touched by the Boy, she broke down, and then the class broke up. Lubanskij fought his way through the confusion and the sudden sense of fellowship to Carsten's desk and began to speak, softly and feverishly, about living and dying and religion and this life—which was hard but just; and even though Carsten felt dizzy, as if from loss of blood, still, at some point, Lubanskij's voice got through to him as it had done so many times before, and it dawned on him that the man before him, this brilliant teacher and tutor and expert on civil law, was in the throes of some kind of breakdown. Sitting there, blubbering, he described, in a manner that was both penitent and gloating, how he had misused his clients' funds, and why shouldn't I, he said, I mean it's all there in the bankbooks, after all, and of course it's not right, but that's the way of the world.

At this point Carsten had to leave. He walked down Store Kannike Lane and through the city center and past the brick shells protecting the monuments, and out and in among bicycles and producer-gas cars and sudden shouts and scattered bursts of firing while his brain whirled like a centrifuge, trying to absorb the fact of the Boy's death and Lubanskij's confessions. It is late June 1944, the sun is shining, people around Carsten snarl like animals, the big general strike is just in the offing—but Carsten notices none of this because he has retreated into himself, managing both to be lost in thought and to keep on walking with no idea of where he is going. It would be wrong to say that he is thinking; I would say, rather, that he is looking for something—and I suppose that what he is looking for would best be described as a higher order. To Carsten the Boy's death, Lubanskij's confessions, their afternoon discussions, those last days at Sorø, and—even further back—Carl Laurids's disappearance are all pointing in the same direction: toward a dreadful suspicion that law and order are no longer to be relied upon. Carsten is not looking for religion, or for King and Country—this is 1944, after all—no, he is looking for something else, for Good Middle-Class Common Sense, for the deeply rooted Danish faith that all—or almost all—men want the same things: law and order and a steady job and respect for the Spirit of the People and the Eternal Truths. Carsten does not picture anyone's having to initiate these values; it is rather as though he imagines them manifesting spontaneously, as though they ought to *crystallize* when enlightened people are gathered together—enlightened people like Lubanskij and the Boy, who have let him down this very day by dying a meaningless death and by making meaningless confessions. The thought reduces Carsten to tears, and as he walks, weeping in the June sunshine, across the Town Hall Square—which looks like a bomb crater, because it has been dug up for the building of new air-raid shelters—he becomes, for me, a symbol of how difficult it is to be a good little citizen in Copenhagen in the middle of the twentieth century.

Not until he had actually entered Tivoli did it dawn on him where he was—but his presence there was no accident, and he, too, was aware of that. There was something about the Old Garden's neatness and its lovely buildings and the lake and Lumbye's music that reminded him of his home and of Sorø Academy and of the order he sought. As he walked along the gravel paths and evening fell, he let his loneliness wash over him. He passed the glass hall where young people—clearly not weighed down, as he was, by *Weltschmerz*—were dancing the jitterbug, and then he gave vent to his tears and to that well-known, that Danish, that standard why-does-nobody-like-me feeling. When my soul is so beautiful, embracing an ocean, he said to himself, and—speaking of oceans—he found himself down by the lake, thus calling attention, all unwittingly, to the strange fact that so many significant events in his life are played out near water. Because as he walks past the tearoom, with its terrace jutting out into the lake like a little peninsula, there she is.

She was far away, surrounded by mist and protected by a bodyguard of men in blue coveralls, open-necked shirts, rolled-up sleeves, and tattooed forearms, and, to begin with, Carsten just stood there, stock-still. It was the girl from Sorø Lake, she was a long way off, and this time he had no boat and he was sober and unhappy and the men around her are starting to take notice of him, and they are workers, they are obviously workers, he should just keep walking, nobody likes him anyway, the chances he has never had have long been wasted, he might as well slop off with his inner sea. And having thought it through this far, he sets off toward her. He bumps into lampposts designed by Amalie's friend Poul Henningsen, stumbles down the marble steps, gets in the way of waiters who spill ersatz gateau and glasses of wartime fruit wine over him, steps on a hundred outstretched, ladylike insteps, and totters through a biblical hail of curses. All in all, he goes through hell and high water before he finds himself standing in front of those Dietrich legs. Behind him, the restaurant is in an uproar; disaster approaches, yelling fit to burst; a storm is brewing—but he does not budge, because he knows that he has a grip on something, and that if order and rationality are anywhere to be found in this life, then they have something to do with this girl. So he salutes the tattooed gallants and the waiters and the screaming ladies with a courtesy and firmness completely lacking in condescension or fear or anything at all except a tremendous determination to make a date with this girl. And this he does. "Tomorrow, about the same time, same place, pal," says the girl. Then the waiters are on him and Carsten is sent flying through the doors to float homeward through *la bella notte*, drunk with happiness.

And it is this happiness that brings me to mention this episode here, since there were few truly happy nights in Carsten's life during these years—and so it ought to be mentioned. But even though Carsten thought, that night, that he had reached the end of the rainbow, it turned out to be nothing but a cobweb of hopes and dreams; and these were blown away the next morning when a series of bombs exploded in Tivoli, flattening the glass hall and the roller coaster and the concert hall—complete with several of Lumbye's original scores—and catapulting a blazing grand piano across the lake and down into the tearoom, sending it up in flames along with Carsten's hopes. From the windows of the Department of Statistics he saw the smoke and heard the explosions and gave up any idea of going down there, since obviously you cannot meet a girl in a cordoned-off ruin. Besides which he did not dare, and besides which she'll never turn up, he thought, but there he was wrong. Maria would meet anyone, anywhere, if it suited her, and she wanted to meet the handsome boy with the center part and the desperate eyes; so she jumped over the barriers and waited in vain for Carsten in the still-smoldering burned-out shell of the tearoom. It was midnight before she gave up and vanished into the dark city.

Not counting that time when the two cars drew level on Roskilde Road, Carsten and Maria have now met twice, and there will of course be a third meeting, something which they themselves never wondered at but which does surprise me. After all, who would believe that this historic romance could resemble all those folktale romances in which everything comes in threes. And who would believe that the opportunity for this third meeting would present itself, when such a meeting must, at any rate from a statistical point of view, have seemed unlikely, now that Carsten—who no longer had the Boy or the Girl from Sorø Lake to call to him from way out there, where reality begins—had stuck his head in the sand, buried himself in his books, and worked his way to safety through his studies and on Strand Drive and at the Department of Statistics. He no longer raised his head when Lubanskij paraded his wry wit just for him, having woken up to the fact that the tutor was a mermaid whose song, now woeful, now triumphant, lured one into whirlpools and unlawfulness and death and mutilation and love wasted and the smoke from the blaze fed by Lumbye's scores. The only memory Carsten retained of the last year of occupation was of the clause-infested terrain of his studies. He spent his days in a kind of invisible tunnel which he carried with him wherever he went and which he could, at any time, draw his head into. He rose in the mornings and went to work at the Department of Statistics; blind to everything, he rode his messenger bike past bonfires in Isted Street, through battles between agitators and the private security guards and past the news of the invasion; then he went to tutorials and covered his blank inserted pages with meticulous notes; and after that he went home to bed, with nothing to show for the day but a small bouquet of legal curiosities.

I started out with the notion that the occupation must have been a significant time both for Carsten and for Danish Dreams; and again and again in my conversations with Carsten I have tried to find out what he remembered, until, eventually, I have had to accept, resign myself to, and admit that, for Carsten, the occupation was no more or less than a few scattered observations that left no lasting impression—not even of the Liberation, of Friday, May 4, when he had a tutorial in the late afternoon as usual. When the newscaster on the radio announced that Germany had capitulated, Lubanskij was expounding a particularly tortuous legal case involving a man who let his dog out by lowering it to the street from the fifth floor in a basket. While the noise outside swelled and the streets filled with people, Lubanskij explained that if this man were to do the same thing with his neighbor's dog and if that dog were then to jump out at the third floor and be mashed to a pulp, then this man would be held responsible. Shots were fired into the air outside and most of the students had left the room, but the tutor talked on, even when only Carsten was left. At one point, outside, a streetcar went past the windows: a streetcar that the crowd had derailed and was now pulling along Store Kannike Lane—but these two, Lubanskij and Carsten, could not see the streetcar for fragmentary points of Roman law, even though Maria was sitting on its roof. She saw Carsten, but Carsten did not see her, and the next instant she had been pulled on down the street and Carsten understood perfectly what *diligentiam quam in suis rebus* meant but had no idea that Denmark was free, or at least to some extent free; nor that the love of his life had ridden past outside the window on the roof of a streetcar.

In June, Carsten graduated as a bachelor of law—magna cum laude, a dream of a degree, awarded on only a very few occasions this century: before Carsten, to a couple of walking legal encyclopedias—now professors—and, some years after Carsten, to a jovial if rather reserved boy by the name of Mogens Glistrup.

Amalie was not on hand to congratulate her son. Paralyzed with fright at the thought that he might be awarded anything less than the very best degree, she had, for the first time in her life, got drunk on a full bottle of sweet Madeira from the century before, and had then locked herself away in her bedroom, where she had drawn the drapes, climbed into bed fully clothed, and pulled the quilt over her head. But still she could not rest—not even in the darkness and her sticky, cloying drunken stupor—when ahead of her all she could see was the disgrace and the humiliation if her little pet should let her down by only getting a first-class degree.

But of course Carsten did not let her down. Quietly, and without any exultation, his upbringing and his years at the academy and his university studies and his mother's hopes for him reached their culmination on the actual day of his final examination, when it was proved that he knew his four thousand closely written inserted pages of notes absolutely by heart and, furthermore, that he was possessed of a rare breadth of legal vision *and* that all these demonstrations of diligence and innate brilliance went hand in hand with a most proper respect for and academic humility toward his professors. At critical moments, when these soap-bubble balloon captains—who had descended from their remote medieval heights to set exams based on textbooks they themselves had written—began to feel that the toothy smile of the boy facing them was just a little too wide and that his view of the subject matter was just a little too lighthearted, then, just like that, Carsten could capitulate, bow his head, draw in his horns, and the appropriate beads of anxious sweat would break out on the bridge of his nose, convincing the two professors that the voice they heard—his, Carsten's—came to them from the dust and the depths of humility and altogether from far, far, far beneath them—and so, naturally, he graduated magna cum laude.

He did not go straight home after the exam. He felt like a bottle that had been uncorked and is now bubbling over. Now, it might be considered only natural for Carsten to savor this champagne feeling in the company of his friends or at any rate with other newly fledged graduates, but that was not Carsten's way. Just as in the days after his commencement, this free, floating sensation was something private that he wished to experience alone—filling him, as it did, with inner turmoil. And so, on this his big day, he wended his way through Copenhagen, growing more and more confused, thanks to the sort of postwar anarchy that reigned in the city—with an Englishwomen's drum corps marching through the streets and a hundred thousand workers demonstrating outside the Parliament buildings at Christiansborg Palace for a forty-hour workweek —forty hours, thought Carsten, hurrying away, forty hours!—when he has been working seventy, no, more like eighty or ninety hours a week. Not that it makes him mad, he simply does not understand it; just as he cannot comprehend the rioting, or the dancing in the Town Hall Square, which he passes a little later—dancing that has lasted from the Liberation until now with no interruptions other than those arising from the occasional police baton charge, one of which happened to occur just as Carsten was passing, forcing him to sidestep the fleeing crowds and all the police officers, our very own boys in blue, who had been away, interned in German concentration camps, and thus in the good books for a year or two, but who were now back, with their shiny buttons and the batons that Carsten just managed to avoid by making for Frederiksberg.

It was evening, almost night, when he arrived at Lorry, that celebrated restaurant complete with private party rooms—and there he ran into a party which was being held by his fellow students and to which he had been invited. He had declined this invitation, fearing that it would be just exactly the kind of party it turned out to be—with a jazz band and hordes of people shouting at the tops of their voices and silent couples collapsing onto tables and chairs and benches and hedges, reminding him that he was all, all alone.

Of course, this was a party for well-bred children from top-drawer families, with (to begin with) drinking in moderation and nice young men in light-colored sweaters and sports jackets who said, "May I kiss you?" and who still, even after five or seven years at the university, had difficulty with brassiere fastenings. But for some reason, the gathering also included another sort of element. No doubt this had something to do with the Liberation and this spring's short-lived sense of love for our fellowmen, because the party also included workers in oversized suits and factory girls with beads in their hair. And at one point one of these girls stepped up onto the stage and sang a song about far-off Polynesia. It was Maria Jensen.

Later on, she and Carsten danced together. It was the first time in his life that he had ever danced; at school dances he had always managed to glue himself to the wall and stick there, even though there had always been girls tugging in the opposite direction. Now, however, he did not care; now he let go and yielded to Maria, who led him onto the dance floor, and there he discovered that there was no problem, that his body seemed moved by one long, effortless memory of always having danced. Then they clambered over the fence into Frederiksberg Gardens. Behind them the sounds of the party grew muffled and the distant racket of the police assaults on the dancing in the square faded away and the city lights grew more faint. They walked along the gravel paths, past the whispering trees and the filmy patches that Carsten recognized as the ghosts of Danish writers who had wept, in Frederiksberg Gardens, the Danish writers' lament that says, "Why can't I have more mistresses? Why can't I have more money?" But on this night even the ghosts were silent, perhaps on account of Maria's straightforward way of un-hitching the moorings of a little boat and pushing off, so that she and Carsten glided out onto the glittering water. They did not do anything, they merely sat gazing into each other's eyes until Maria knelt down in the boat, removed his jacket, and pulled down his suspenders. When she unbuttoned his fly Carsten said, "I would like to point out that I am, if I may say so, a classic sexual neurotic."

He delivered this monstrous remark not without a certain pride, but Maria ignored him and placed her hands on his penis. She eyed it carefully, as though its rigid whiteness afforded her some glimpse of the future, and then she took it in her mouth.

Maria had arrived in Copenhagen the previous winter, and she had arrived on skis. Until then she had been at Annebjerg. After her meeting with Carsten on Sorø Lake she had made her way back to the home, meek as a lamb. She had been hugged and forgiven; her fair hair had been brushed and her blue eyes had wept, and in an attempt to explain her inexplicable disappearance the two head-mistresses had decided that there must be something wrong with her metabolism. So they fattened her up on stout and double cream and then had her operated on for Graves' disease at Nykøbing County Hospital. After that everyone calmed down; after that the dust settled; and the couple of months when Maria had been away could be referred to as that time when you were ill and had to have an operation. Then all sense of time took off and floated away be-neath white fluffy clouds and across yellow wheat fields and roses in the sunshine, and life in the country, where, the occupation not-withstanding, there was butter and cream aplenty. And there Maria looked after the little ones and sang and danced the man's part in the minuet from *Elverhøj* and resumed her place as the meek and mild little Danish girl, a happy girl, a proper little gem, and the apple of the headmistresses' eyes, for a period which must have lasted about four years and which came to an end one Christmas Eve.

It was a Christmas Eve with glazed turkey, golden-brown candied potatoes, a Christmas tree as big as a house, and Miss Smeck's legendary tales of a Chinese Christmas in a heat that beggared belief; there were little presents for all the girls and later there was candy. Then Maria was taken aside and handed a long, cylindrical paper parcel, and in the parcel was a pair of skis. This is a classic scene: the poor little orphan girl being given a pair of skis by the two good headmistresses; it is moving—even I find it moving. And it might be hard to understand, nowadays—when Christmas is all about spending money we do not have on things we do not need to impress people we do not like—but it was different in those days, at any rate at Annebjerg, where Maria is now crying fit to burst and the headmistresses are also reduced to tears. They were grand skis, made of ash, and they and the headmistresses seemed to be saying to Maria, "You will stay here at Annebjerg forever, you have a mission, you have survived life in the outside world and the viral attacks of sensuality, and now you must stay here and help the weak." Not that this was said in so many words, but it seemed somehow to hang in the air as Maria donned her outdoor things, because she could not wait to try out her skis. On her way out, almost as an afterthought, she lifted her police helmet—everyone had forgotten whose it was—from the hook on the back of the headmistresses' office door and put it on, just to keep her head warm.

Outside, it is cold and silent and white with snow—a star-bright, moonlit night. Maria steps out into the snow and she has never skied before, so Christ knows it's anything but elegant, but she makes headway, she heads away, and soon Annebjerg is nothing but a distant point on the horizon—snow-white even though it is the middle of the night. Maria does not turn around, and she never returns.

She skied all the way to Copenhagen, but don't ask me how she managed it or why she ran away. All I can say is that there are these two sides to Maria's character. She is capable of playing the Little Match Girl and her mother's dream of the perfect daughter for years, but now and again something goes wrong and then the other side appears, her eyes take on a glassy look, she dons her police helmet, lashes out like a prizefighter, and is capable of leaving all she has in this life to shuffle on skis from Nykøbing, Sjælland, to Copenhagen one hallowed Christmas Eve.

In Copenhagen she became a factory girl. She stayed with friends around and about in the city and in boardinghouses and in single-room occupancies—though she never spent more than a few weeks in any one place—and she worked in the Danish Cotton Mills and

at Boel and Rasmussen's chemicals plant and Dumex Pharma-
ceuticals and in various chocolate factories and at Latichinsky and
Son's soap works, and at an unaccountably large number of other
places. The story of the Danish factory girl in the 1940s has not yet
been written, and it would be going too far to tell it here, but Maria's
experiences were anything but trivial. She spent these years in a
sandstorm of asbestos and in vaporous clouds of grinding oil and
alongside conveyor belts where pregnant women struggled to stretch
beyond their eight-months-gone stomachs to pack ersatz coffee, or
where young girls painting phosphorescent radium fluid onto watch
hands kept licking their brushes to keep a point on them, and were
eaten up by stomach cancer before they could become engaged—
if, that is, they had not been fired for refusing to stick their backsides
out far enough for a pinch when the president inspected his troops.

But no one messed with Maria. During these years she switched
jobs every bit as often as she switched her lodgings; whenever she
thought a place was starting to smell ugly or the work was too
exhausting or too boring or too sordid, she rapped her bosses over
the knuckles, demanded her wages, grabbed her coat, and left. And
the next day she would start all over again somewhere else. Or she
might take a break, during which she would live on next to nothing.
She was by no means a *dedicated* factory girl. Being dedicated and
class-conscious and a member of a trade union requires a certain
peace of mind, it requires one to stay in one place and get a grip
and hang on and believe that this will be worthwhile—but that was
not Maria's way. For us, looking back on it, identifying the labor
movement and its history is easy enough, but as far as Maria was
concerned there were only good or bad girlfriends, honest men or
rogues, an endless succession of workplaces, and the tough, illusion-
free egoism that enclosed her like a shell until she met Carsten.

It was not long before this that she had her first affair—with a
Russian who had been liberated from a German concentration camp
and whom she met at a performance of Russian music and dance
in the Copenhagen Sports Club hall. She had gone along because
she found the emaciated foreigners attractive and because they ex-
cited her curiosity—and perhaps also because they aroused her sympathy. At this show she met a disabled Asian who danced on the
stumps of his shot-off legs. He was also missing an arm, and for the
few weeks that he spent in Copenhagen he was her lover. Then he

and the other refugees disappeared, leaving a chink in her armor and a wild song, heavy with homesickness, in an incomprehensible language.

And then she met Carsten.

On the day after their boat trip in Frederiksberg Gardens he had to report to the draft board, and there he was assigned to the Supply Corps. At first it looked as though his military service might present a problem for him and Maria, but as it turned out, it did not. Because naturally Carsten was first in his class at drill school, which meant that he could choose where he would be stationed, and he chose Copenhagen's own old Citadel so that he could come home every evening. Nor did he have any problem with his bracing stint of basic training at Høvelte Barracks, because he came home on weekends and because he had not knuckled under as he had feared he might. On the contrary, like more or less all the other conscripts, he found himself enjoying the exercise and the hearty outdoor life and the shared hate of the NCOs and the bluff camaraderie that constitutes the most common of all Danish army buddy dreams: the dream of our common obligation to do our bit for that needless, that stupid, that in all respects absurd military service, which I personally have cheated my way out of by feigning an injured knee but which in Carsten and Maria's case in fact presented no problem.

Their problem was Amalie Mahogany, Carsten's mother.

Initially, Carsten did not tell his mother about Maria, and that, I suppose, was quite natural, since he was not sure that the affair would last. But even when it did prove to stand the test of time, he did not say anything, let's just wait a week or two, or a month or two, he thought, let me just finish my military service—and this he did, but still he said nothing. Obviously, he underwent certain minor changes, but she'll never notice, he thought, it can be put down to army life and having a law degree; but as time went on, he began to suffer. He grew thinner and paler, dark circles appeared under his eyes, he slept badly, and, worst of all, he caught himself answering back to his mother and at times all but breaking out of his polished decorum to snap at everyone around him, in a fever of exasperation brought on because he and Maria had not as yet spent a whole night together. He had returned home from their first lovers' tryst in Frederiksberg Gardens before dawn, knowing, as he did, that Amalie would be lying wide awake under the quilts waiting for him and for his examination result, and thereafter he had continued to go home each night, preferably not later than midnight, because Amalie would be lying awake and he was all she had.

Of course, love will always find a way and a time, being not solely a nocturnal pursuit, so—in keeping with Maria's nomadic existence—the two young people learned a great deal about venetian blinds and keyholes and which sofas creaked and which did not, but it was not the same as being able to stay together all night long. In time, the sleeplessness and the strain began to tell, and then Carsten told his mother.

By then his affair with Maria had been going on for some years and Amalie had known about it all along—of course she had known about it, but she was waging a war she believed she could win by dint of exceedingly long-term planning, and hence she had waited patiently for this moment. She listened to Carsten's rambling hints and then she said, in a voice that laid a sugar coating over prussic acid and icy polar winds, "But we must invite her to dinner—oh, do let's invite her to dinner."

Now, it might be thought that Amalie would have chosen to meet Maria alone—it would surely have been only natural to keep it to just the three of them, she and Carsten and Maria—but no, instead she chose to call upon a phalanx of intellects; she wheeled out the heavy artillery.

This dinner had been planned for two years: seating plan, menu, choice of wine, everything. She said nothing to Carsten, simply telling him to say to Maria that it would be an informal little get-together, and so Maria turned up, in all good faith, with neatly brushed hair, a freshly ironed summer dress, and a little posy of flowers, for what turned out to be Amalie Mahogany's grandest parade to date. There were flambeaux lining the driveway and gleaming cars and twenty-four guests, including the winner of the Nobel Prize in Literature Johannes V. Jensen (and his wife); that great authoress Baroness Blixen (unaccompanied); Prime Minister Hedtoft, the man who had—reluctantly, but with a little smile—maneuvered Denmark into NATO; Professor Rubow, a professor of literature and one of Amalie's Friends of the Family; and Professor Niels Bohr, who had been awarded the Nobel Peace Prize—no, I beg your pardon: the Nobel Prize in Physics—and nigh on a score of other guests with this in common: that each of them, just like the

Baroness and Jensen, considered that *he* or *she* was the only truly intelligent person at this party—which every one of them was convinced was being held just for his or her benefit. This evening, however, they are actually all puppets in a masque directed by Amalie, a drama that is one of the most regularly staged productions in Danish history, entitled *The Mother-in-Law's Pulverization of the Undesirable Daughter-in-Law.*

Dinner was served in the new conservatory extension, which boasted sixteen green marble pillars and doors of Brazilian rosewood with ivory door handles—all purchased with the money Carsten had earned during his university years in the belief that, by so doing, he was saving his mother from a life of prostitution. Amalie had given Maria Professor Rubow as her dinner partner, and the great scholar talked and talked, leaving Maria, who knew no one except Carsten, isolated amid a sea of French quotations and blasé witticisms, until Amalie presented her. With a wave of her hand she reduced everyone to silence, even the Baroness, and in this charged hush she introduced Maria and forced her to address this gathering of *beaux esprits*, thus revealing that she spoke the language of the Christianshavn tenements mixed with a bit of Zealand dialect from Annebjerg and that she was, in fact, a little rambling rose, a lily from the gutter. She was then permitted to sit, until Amalie asked for her comments on the food—how was the *saumon*, would you care for some more saddle of veal, what do you think of this Sauternes?—until Maria's stammer became so pronounced that she could not get a reply out.

Carsten held his tongue throughout the meal. Naturally, he wished he could have done something, he wished he could have risen to his feet and pounded on the table, but it was this very table—with its Royal Copenhagen Flora Danica service and crystal glasses and the invisible barbed-wire fences erected by table manners and an age-old dread—that kept him firmly in his seat, while the Baroness told him of a story she was working on, about a dinner that raised its guests up into a new sphere of freedom.

Over coffee and brandy, Amalie stood up and said to Maria, "I understand from my son that you sing, so I have persuaded my friend, the great writer Jacob Paludan, who is a connoisseur and lover of music, to accompany you." And it seemed now as though Amalie had indeed crushed Maria, because she stood up and walked stiff-legged past the guests and over to the grand piano, to Paludan and the prospect of the vast room. Maria had turned up at this party as a young girl, a nice little shrinking violet, prepared to make a good impression, but now something happened to her; it was as though her eyes swam out of focus, and then she stared in Amalie's direction and said, hoarsely, but with her stammer more or less under control, "I've heard about y-y-you, Amalie, they t-t-talk about y-y-you at Latichinsky and Son's when they're wrapping the perfumed soaps, and they say you're the biggest whore in C-C-Copenhagen." And with this, Maria stalked out of the room, although she did turn back just for a moment, in the doorway, to meet Carsten's gaze. He had risen half out of his chair and for a moment he stayed suspended in midair, in a sort of no-man's-land, or as though he were a piece of scrap iron caught between two magnets. But then, with a jerk, he is on his feet, strides over to Maria, and fulfills all our expectations of how, if things are to turn out as they should, sooner or later a boy has to leave his father and mother and follow his love.

Where did the two young people go after they left Amalie's? They went to an apartment on the fourth floor of a villa by the Lakes in Copenhagen. It has never been easy finding an apartment in Copenhagen, nor was it any easier in those days. Then, as now, you had to have contacts, and the lease on this apartment was also in the nature of a bribe from one of the numerous law firms who were at this time angling for Carsten. The building was big, grand, and ramshackle and will turn out to be a fateful spot in Maria and Carsten's life. It was not situated in poverty-stricken Nørrebro, nor yet in the elegant confines of Frederiksberg, but somewhere between the two, and it had not been built in the last century, nor yet in this one, but somewhere at the turn, by a family that was neither aristocratic nor common, well-to-do without being really wealthy. It had been built on a piece of ground with an uncertain future, and it was still standing there, surrounded by tall linden trees and dog shit and a faded three-quarters grandeur. It had a large, neglected garden, thickets of plaster on the ceilings, rot-riddled floors that sagged like hammocks, water pipes that emitted a ghostly hiss, interconnecting rooms, and tall windows—and in the light that pours through these sit Carsten and Maria. The apartment is empty of furniture; they sit in an echo of emptiness and nebulous hopes—well, what happens next? Sunlight streams through the window and for a moment the universe is put on hold: they have not actually moved in yet. They have slept together; they have known each other for several years and they really ought to have been married by now, but they have just not got around to that yet. Carsten has completed his studies and really ought to have found a job, but as yet he has not done so. Maria can clean and cook and generally keep house, even such a bogus spook-ridden box of tricks as this, but she has not made a proper start yet. With respect to this situation, I would choose to say that Carsten and Maria are waiting. They are not waiting for any-thing in particular—neither for life nor for the future nor for each other—they simply seem to have suspended all progression mo-mentarily; and this waiting time, brief as it may be, is characteristic of this place and this time, in the late 1940s in Copenhagen. Both Carsten and Maria have been aware of this feeling before, but it has never been as strong as now, and this has to do with the fact that something is afoot and that something is, of course, the Welfare State and a freedom that is, at any rate to some degree, greater than ever before in the history of the world. And then there is something else that is hard to explain. Of course Carsten and Maria will marry and have children and work and assume their place on the beaten path—it is still a natural law of sorts—but it is as though, before all this gets under way, they are struck by a certain hesitance. And in the sunlight in the house by the Lakes the reluctant air of these days induces the giddy sensation of falling in love and a faint, far-away, tentative realization that all the old values are disintegrating.

The next instant this feeling has gone and they have moved in and bought furniture and Carsten has found a job.

Once Carsten graduated, everyone was after him. Of course, they had heard of him long before this, even the professors of law had heard of him, and now everyone wanted to employ him. The Min-istry of Justice wanted to employ him, the Foreign Ministry wanted to employ him, as well as all the big law firms, and at the Citadel he met the head of Army Intelligence, that deep-frozen Cold War warrior and later colonel, Lunding—and he, too, wanted to employ him. All of them were, of course, attracted by his astronomically high marks and his incredible diligence and his winning nature—all the *promise* of a meteoric career that hung around Carsten like a radiant aura. But there was something else, too, something they could never quite put their fingers on—not even wily old Lunding —and that was Carsten's innocence. There was not one of these individuals or bodies who did not, deep down, feel the earth giving way beneath his feet or sense that a new age was dawning—even for the Danish state system, which had otherwise managed to maintain its dignity and remain well preserved since the days of the absolute monarchy. And so they all dreamed—at night, at any rate, and on the sly—of a phenomenon such as Carsten; of a new generation of civil servants whose belief in the middle-class worldview remained intact.

Carsten turned down all of them. He shook his head and said no, thank you, and politely shook the outstretched hands before immediately releasing them again; he enjoyed his popularity and the strange waiting period, and then he made his move and accepted a position with Big Fitz.

There are several conceivable reasons for Carsten's choosing this particular law firm, one of them being that Fitz was one of Amalie's friends from the time she was beginning to refer to as the Good Old Days. But the most important reason lies, I believe, elsewhere: in the fact that Fitz's chambers were like a lighthouse, a bastion, in the current of time. These chambers were situated in a mansion on Sankt Annæ Square, close to the Amalienborg Palace and the royal family, and indeed Fitz was lawyer to the royal family. He was a very old man, the sixth-generation senior partner of a firm weighed down and glossy with distinction and solid tradition. The firm acted as State Counsel, Fitz and his colleagues being the government's legal advisers and, in their opinion, having conducted every big case of any significance during this century and the end of the previous one. They had administered Lady Danner's estate and had been instrumental in winning that glorious case, *The State* vs. *Herman Bang*, that writer from the gutter—and homosexual to boot—who had on that occasion been convicted of pornography for his novel *Generations without Hope*. They had conducted the Count at Mørk- høj's probate case and the celebrated case in which the Burmeister & Wain shipyard tried to get out of paying the engineer who had improved and installed the diesel engine in the world's first diesel-powered ship, the *Selandia*. They had seen to the small print in the sale of the Danish West Indies colonies to the United States, and

Fitz had personally addressed the court in the open-and-shut case against Norway concerning Denmark's rights to Greenland, in which it was eventually established at the international level that of course Denmark owns Greenland. The firm took care of legal matters not only for the royal family but also for the proud old Danish aristocracy, added to which Fitz himself sat on the board of Burmeister & Wain, Otto Mønsted Margarine, the Margarine Company, Hirschsprung and Sons Tobacco Company, the Private Insurance Association, and the Trifolium Dairies; and, for his day and age and for Carsten, he represented a happy blend of the best of the old traditions with modern-day big business. The existence of Fitz and his firm, its customers' titles, its marble mansion and polished brass nameplate, all amounted to one huge affirmation that everything was perfectly in order.

So Carsten started work at Fitz's chambers, and at just around the same time the new decade—the fifties, that is—also started. Of this time Carsten and Maria have both said, independently, that it seemed to consist of nothing but Sundays. Now, obviously that cannot be true, but it says something about how this period was peaceful in a way even I can sense, and it makes me think that if I had been living then, I could have said: Come, dear reader, take my hand and let me lead you along the lakes and in through the riotously overgrown, romantic garden and into the grand entranceway with its ground-glass panes etched with elaborate floral designs, and up to the second floor to a Sunday afternoon idyll. The apartment has been beautifully done up because Fitz knows the president of Lysberg, Hansen and Terp. It has been painted, at Carsten's request, in the same pastel green and terracotta as old Pompeii, with white woodwork, veneered rosewood furniture, pictures on the walls, and books on the shelves—an apartment that breathes like some great beast. Slowly and comfortably it fills its lungs, expanding and contracting and expanding around Carsten where he sits working, enveloped in a cloud of smoke and the delicate aroma of latakia tobacco; and around Maria, who is sitting embroidering—yes, just so: she is sitting embroidering, since that is what she does with her time during these years, when she is not keeping house and cooking and, in every conceivable way, *being* there for Carsten. She embroiders and he works and only rarely do they look up, they are concentrating deeply, but they each *know* that the other is there.

On some of these Sundays they take the streetcar or the train out to see Amalie, who seems to have forgiven everything and who, during these years, is growing to look more and more like a big black panther—although, despite dyeing her hair and despite the expertly applied makeup she now has something rather moth-eaten about her. This only serves to reassure Maria, who now feels more relaxed in her mother-in-law's home than ever before and can sink back into the sofa and enjoy the little chocolate "Sarah Bernhardts" from Rubow's patisserie. The next day Carsten has to go to work, and when he comes home his dinner is waiting for him, good Danish dishes which, despite whatever else may come along, he still prefers; dishes such as meat balls and pork sausages and chitterlings as only Maria can make them, with just the right little touch of wine vinegar. Afterward they drink coffee and listen to the radio and Carsten has a bit of work to do and, outside, it is summer or winter or something in between but always, in some way, pleasant weather; and, to me, these two young people—who love each other and who have just recently been married at the registry office in Copenhagen Town Hall—seem to combine with their comfortably breathing surroundings to create a unified whole that is apparently very, very harmonious.

Although one could perhaps have looked at it in a different light. We could perhaps have latched on to certain details that shatter the idyll. As, for instance, the fact that, in the entranceway, on the way up the stairs, we pass the door of the ground-floor apartment, which bears a sign that says: THE DANISH STANDARDIZATION BOARD SUB-COMMITTEE FOR THE STANDARDIZATION OF WINDOW ENVELOPES AND PRINTED FORMS—which is in fact a cover for one of Colonel Lunding and Army Intelligence's electronic surveillance stations. Or we could, in Carsten and Maria's apartment, have latched on to the disquieting hiss in the water pipes and the muffled sound of distant telex machines and the rotten floorboards that have been known to give way and crash down into the apartment below, thus affording Carsten and Maria baffling glimpses of electronic consoles bristling with large lightbulbs and radio valves, until the army workmen patched up the hole—sealing it off until the building gave way in some fresh spot. One could also point to Carsten and Maria's wall, on which hung a very large reproduction of Picasso's *Guernica*. Not that it is any business of ours what people hang on their walls, and it may be that the young couple have been given this picture as a wedding present and feel that it is interesting and modern, but when all's said and done, it *is* a picture of war—with severed limbs and bombs and dead horses and suffering. And that it should be hanging here, in the living room, indicates an odd kind of disregard. But then again, this may be no more than a stray thought, which I cannot back up; and life in the early fifties, here by the Lakes in Copenhagen, was no doubt above all idyllic. And it flows out into a bicycle trip.

One summer they decided, on the spur of the moment, to load up their two bikes and take off into the countryside and sleep in a tent—although they could just as easily have stayed at a hotel. They started out by riding south. The larks were singing and they rode for a whole day alongside the crumbling ruins of a wall, which happened to be the wall around Mørkhøj; they reached Southern Fyn and, at one point, ate their lunch beside the statue of the great physicist H. C. Ørsted, in the square in Rudkøbing; later they came to the fishing village of Lavnæs, to which a paved road now ran; and they passed through the town with the inn where a vengeful Ramses—Maria's paternal grandfather, that is—found his father. And from all of these marketplaces and walls and squares and houses the past came rushing out and shouted after them, but it always arrived too late, to find that they had just disappeared around the corner and the past had missed its bus. They did not even notice the spots where old WANTED posters had defied the Danish climate—among the world's worst—to tell Maria that the hunt had been on all over northern Europe during the previous century for her paternal grandfather or grandmother or great-grandfather. Carsten and Maria did not pull up at one single place to be reminded of the past, because they had no knowledge of it. They had only the vaguest ideas—or none at all—of where their ancestors hailed from, and why, and no town or place-name or buildings or posters could jog their memories. At one point they passed through Sorø, which, as far as I can see, ought to have been vibrant with sweet memories, but all that happened was that Carsten pointed toward the academy entrance and said, "I used to go to school there," and then they looked into each other's eyes and laughed lovingly and then they kissed, *mmm-wuh!* Then off they rode, leaving behind them the

town and the academy and the lake and the unanswered question
of why it did not even occur to them that this was where they met.

Riding there, side by side along the country lanes, under the sun
and the sky and the larks, and eating liver pâté with cucumber on
country bread in the fresh air, they resemble the fifties dream, our
dream, of young love; and the only thing that might seem surprising
is that their past did not really exist; that they rode through Denmark
without any sign of recognition and without visiting one single person and without really *seeing* anything at all except each other's eyes
and each other's sun-kissed freckles. And perhaps this says something about the price of that impending freedom which was already
making its presence felt; it says something about the fact that the
country which this double infatuation cycled through was already a
strangely anonymous Denmark. And a moment later their infatuation was no longer doubled but trebled when, on the top of that hill
called Himmelbjerget, Mountain to the Heavens, Maria suddenly
found herself with something in her hand, something light-
colored—her diaphragm—and she drew her hand back and sent
the soft rubber disk spinning far off into space. And because, that
summer, everything fell into place with such perfect and intimate
timing, she became pregnant that very evening.

Her pregnancy lasted for six years—yes, you heard right, six
years—and when I have said to Maria and Carsten, "That can't be
right, it's impossible, a pregnancy lasts for nine months," they have
said, "Well, have you ever been pregnant?" And although that is
no kind of an answer, still it reminds me that what we are talking
about here is how they *experienced* the pregnancy, and by their
reckoning it lasted six years—six years that saw the advent of the
Affluent Society. There came a day—although it may in fact have
been several days—when Fitz called Carsten into his office and said,
"I would like to warn you about something, I would like to warn
you about James Joyce's novel *Ulysses*. It is one long, scandalous
piece of verbal diarrhea—which is why I myself have never read
it—and if you, Mr. Mahogany, steer clear of everything in any way
associated with this obscene pamphlet, then I predict a golden future
for you." Then he congratulated Carsten on the completion of his
three-year apprenticeship, and on being, now, a qualified lawyer;
he gave him a raise in salary and invited him to take a seat on the

first of a number of boards that would, during these years, bid him welcome; and then he asked him to take over some of the day-to-day running of the firm.

It was just at this time that Maria started working. It is hard to say what made her start, but to begin with, it looked good, resembling as it did the fifties picture of an independent woman who wants equal pay and wears the pants—as Maria did, pants that were let out at the waist to accommodate her stomach. There are various factors to do with her work that can be wondered at: in six years she was taken on at 170 different workplaces and worked nowhere for longer than three weeks. It is almost certain that she worked a few stints as a construction worker, making herself out to be a man and passing the swell of her three-year pregnancy off as a beer belly; and for some weeks she also worked as an attendant in another of those places where the history of Denmark was being written: the public toilets in the Town Hall Square. All of this points out that the story of Maria's working career is not just that of an energetic young housewife, and that something, somewhere, was not quite right. But getting to the root of what was wrong would be far too laborious a task, and from another and simpler point of view, everything was in order—and it is this point of view I now opt for: Through the fifties the little home by the Lakes continued to sail through an uninterrupted succession of Sundays, during which, somewhere along the way, they buy their first car—a Volkswagen Beetle—and their first vacation home.

They may not have seen much of each other during these years, nor much of that side of life which lay beyond the everyday routine. When they were together in the evenings it was all they could do to stay upright long enough to eat before falling into a deathlike sleep in the big double bed—in which, through all these years, Maria had to lie on her side in a kidney-shaped arrangement of hard pillows that took the weight off her stomach. During this period they also saw less of Amalie, and the only regular contact they had with other people came through Colonel Lunding, who would come up to visit them on the dark winter evenings—red-eyed and pale from lack of sleep—for a glass of milk and a cup of coffee and a good cry. The burly soldier always started off by telling one of his hunting stories, and then he would switch to bemoaning these changed days, and then he would start to cry, and Maria had to draw his grizzled head across her stomach to her breast and dry his tears and wipe his nose, while he wept and said, "Now the Reds are slinging mud at that righteous war in Korea, and those swine have altered the Constitution so that a woman—boo, hoo, hoo—can succeed to the throne, and these days you can't even damn well arrest people because of their political convictions, how the hell do they expect a man to do his job, and every hour more and more Ivans are pouring over the border, damned if we won't all end up being infected, I'll probably end up in the booth voting Communist myself one of these days." But in Maria's arms he calmed down, and in the presence of Carsten's well-dressed amiability and the smell of success and the old days he pulled himself together, brightened up, and managed to gloat over the rebellion in East Germany and say, "Still, it's an exciting time, what with the crisis in Poland and all, and could I have another glass of milk and I'd better be getting back, duty calls, you have to keep up the morale if you're going to act immorally."

Maria and Carsten never really understood what he was talking about. To them events on the international political scene were nothing more than a faint hum from the electronic equipment in the apartment below, and as far as they were concerned, the future of Denmark was safe in the hands of such a sensitive man as Colonel Lunding. Then Maria gave birth.

She gives birth in an expensive private maternity home, and because it happens to be New Year's Eve, only she and the midwife and a nurse are present. "I'm afraid both the consultant and the doctor on duty have been called out to an emergency," the nurse apologizes—this emergency being, of course, that they are dead drunk, and not only that, but dead drunk at the home of Amalie Mahogany, who is holding a big New Year's party. "But don't you worry, madame," says the midwife, "we have all the most up-to-date equipment on hand"—as Maria can see for herself, from where she lies in state surrounded by gleaming tiles and glaring spotlights and glittering steel and buzzing autoclaves. As further reassurance, they also have access to countless X rays, since, with Maria's stomach being so inordinately huge and her pregnancy having lasted for six years, the consultant has taken somewhere between fifteen and twenty good X rays of the fetus, just to be on the safe side, and because he regards the fears held by certain of his colleagues regarding radiation as unscientific old wives' tales.

And so the midwife knows in advance what is about to happen, which is that Maria gives birth to twins, a dark girl and a fair boy, and—bearing in mind the bombardment of X rays to which the babies have been subjected and also how long she has been pregnant—it is not without some relief that I can report that both babies have the right number of fingers and toes and appear to be healthy and normal.

Maria refuses to be anesthetized; even when she is cut and stitched, the only sound that escapes her is a faint moan, and when the nurse moves in with the mask Maria wags a menacing finger at her and hisses, "Beat it and take that thing with you!" And so all is quiet in the maternity home; the only sounds are Maria's moans and the faint hum of the apparatus and the gentle rustle of the midwife's starched gown and, at one point, the wails of the two babies, which subside when they are laid to the breast and a bright-eyed, triumphant Maria gazes into space and thinks: I've done it, I've given birth.

Then another sound starts to swell, faint but nevertheless quite distinct, the soundproofed door notwithstanding. It sounds like an animal screaming, but it is, in fact, Amalie Mahogany. She has abandoned her guests, having all at once been struck by the feeling that her grandchildren were being born at that very moment. She has not even taken the time to kick the consultant into life, she has simply taken a taxi, and now she is standing outside, and wanting in.

But she does not get in. Maria has said, "I want to be alone, absolutely alone, my husband has to see the babies before anybody else," saying this in the same voice with which she had waved the ether mask away—a voice that will not take no for an answer. Nevertheless the nurse tells her, "Those noises you can hear, madame, it's your mother-in-law, she's very upset, should we let her in?" But Maria shakes her head and hisses, "There must be some mistake, my mother-in-law is not even in Copenhagen, not even in this country, she's stationed on Greenland, she's far away, and she would never carry on like that. That woman out there is someone who sometimes shouts at me in the street. Will you please have her removed."

So Amalie is taken away by the police. After all, this is a private maternity home and they are paying through the nose for Maria's confinement; besides which, Amalie definitely does not seem normal, and so—regardless of her evening dress and her pearl-embroidered shawl and her furs and her hat and her jewelry—three porters and two police officers shepherd her out onto the street, where she screeches, "Those are my son's children in there, they're my grandchildren." Then, when one of the officers grabs hold of her arm to lead her away, she takes a swipe at him, yelling, "Let go of me, boy, piss off and polish your cuff links before you lay a finger on a real lady!"; after which she is handcuffed and taken to Store Kongens Street police station to spend a wrathful New Year's Eve in custody.

While all this is going on, Carsten is at work. At this point, holidays no longer exist for him, and today he is working particularly hard, to avoid the thought of blood and slime and pain and all the mystery of womanhood. But he arrives later, some time after midnight, when the birth is over and the twins have been washed and fed and Amalie put behind bars and Maria wheeled away from the abattoir-like delivery room and into a lovely private room. Then they put a call through to him and he turns up, utterly confused, wearing a green loden coat and carrying flowers. He kisses the children and he kisses the children's mother—his wife, that is—and then he starts to cry, and at that moment the little family has no problems.

But I have. For while the Mahogany family is stronger and more collected than ever before, its history is more confused than ever. Hitherto I have endeavored to make my account exhaustive and keep it simple, and although it has never been easy, it is now more difficult than ever because, at this moment, in and around this maternity home, an overwhelming, bewildering number of pictures of these newborn infants now present themselves.

To all appearances, Carsten and Maria are alone with their children; to all appearances, there is no one else in the world but them, but that in itself is complicated enough. Because, without realizing it, they both have their own ideas about the children. They may, at this moment, be smiling at each other and hugging each other, but

Maria feels that, strictly speaking and deep down and at heart, they are her children—wasn't she the one who threw away her diaphragm that day and hasn't she carried this sweet burden for six years? Not that Carsten would disagree with her on that point: in a certain, physical sense they *are* her children; as far as everything to do with the metabolism and the nurturing and the screaming is concerned, they are Maria's, their mother's; but in another, deeper sense he feels that they are his children—isn't it primarily he who has to put clothes on their backs and Maria's, and food in their mouths, and isn't he the husband? And, he thinks, in a wider, legal sense these two creatures are citizens, responsible adults of the future, and thus, to some extent, they belong to society.

These, therefore, are the divergent dreams of two parents, and if that had been all there was to it, then it would not have been so bad. But in the room next door the midwife is talking to the consultant, who has now put in an appearance; and even though his surroundings still look rather greenish and curved to him, as if viewed through an empty champagne bottle, yet he is in no doubt the twins were born amid examination tables and gas cylinders and respirators and autoclaves and disinfectants; thanks to the X rays and his (and the midwife's) training; in the secure, white-tile surroundings of the maternity home—and so, naturally, modern medicine can lay claim to their future. And somewhere in Store Kongens Street, the previous generation—Amalie that is—is banging on her cell bars, yelling, "They're my son's children and mine, and if you knew what I've suffered and sacrificed for that boy, and every one of you will be fired tomorrow, I'm a good friend of the chief of police, you know!"

And that's no lie. Back at Amalie's house on Strand Drive at that very moment, the chief of police is singing a song with a *"Parlez-vous"* refrain and toasting the newborn children whom his hostess has taken herself off to visit. He, too, has his ideas about the children's future, as do the other guests; and as does Colonel Lunding, who calls the next day with a bunch of flowers and a card inscribed "To two little soldiers from Uncle Lunne"; and Ramses and the Princess and Adonis—wherever they may be—would have had their own hopes; and Carl Laurids perhaps could not have cared less; and Fitz, counsel to the Supreme Court, will be happy just so long as no one ever reads modern literature aloud to them; and Progress and the Welfare State and the 1960s—which are just in the offing —provide no solution; they do not point toward anything other than freedom of choice.

Thus, gathered around the twins' cribs, we find all the hopes of the poor and the rich and the middle class and those on the neth- ermost rung. There are hopes pointing backward and hopes pointing forward, all mixed up into such a clamorous chorus of contradictory expectations that I hardly have a moment's peace in which to say that, at this point in time, in Denmark, so many dreams are making themselves heard that it may no longer be possible to present them through the two-dimensional medium of paper; and that is my problem.

Nevertheless, I will carry on, I will turn a deaf ear to my doubts —well, what else would you have me do? Instead, let me tell you about the success of Carsten's career, which took off in earnest just before the twins were born, when Fitz called him into his office. The old lawyer's face gleamed, weary and opalescent, among the brown paneling and brown leather furniture and brown wash draw- ings, as he announced to Carsten that he was going to retire and that he felt certain that Carsten was now capable of assuming his burden when he relinquished it. Carsten had no idea that Fitz had any sort of life outside of his chambers and the law courts, and so he did not understand what he would retire to, but he did not ask, just as he had no comment to make on being ordered to take over the firm; he simply nodded and obeyed as he had obeyed Carl Laurids and his mother and Raaschou-Nielsen and the professors of law and the army officers.

He was on his way out, and had opened the innermost of the office's double doors, when Fitz called to him. This time the old man gave his successor a somewhat speculative look before saying, "Carsten, I would like to bequeath my spiritual legacy to you," and Carsten felt himself start because, for the first time ever, Fitz had used his first name.

The old lawyer held a long and well-considered pause and then he said, "I have summed up my experience of life, and what it amounts to is a dreadful truth, known only to very few, that being that our legal system is the Monte Carlo of justice!"

Carsten stared at him dumbly; then he gave a little bow and left the office. He had not understood his employer's cryptic farewell remark but had not had the necessary courage to ask him to elaborate upon it. Several times, during the period that followed, he almost brought himself to ask, but still did not dare to; and then, one day, Fitz died in his office, sitting in his office chair, and suddenly it was too late.

That same year Carsten was made a counsel to the Supreme Court, the last occasion on which this ostentatious title was conferred. Carsten had applied for this only because he knew it was what Fitz had wanted; for his own part he was not greatly interested in this or in any other title, and if you were to ask me, "So what was he interested in, then?" the only answer I can safely give is "Work."

He was the perfect counsel—well, of course he was perfect, since the courtroom proceedings, then as now, constituted a dance; a strict and unvarying sequence of steps that his whole life had been geared toward learning. He was the consummate trial lawyer. With manic and unfailing energy he could prepare his prosecutions and defenses in minutest detail and then wait, with infinite patience, for his turn to come. When it did, he would stand up and start to speak in beautiful, faultless Danish while pacing back and forth across the floor, knowing that he was following this theater's predetermined plot and making use of whatever modest room for improvisation it afforded—to which end he employed his good looks and his charm and his courtesy and the weight of that civilization which he felt backed him up and gave him cause to hold his head high.

Right from the start he acted for the big companies. It was he who won Faxe Limestone Quarries' creditable case against the state, and the big trademark suits brought by the American Coca-Cola Company, prior to and during its infiltration of the Danish market. He was also lawyer to the Wealthy—with his schooled discretion and politeness and personal modesty he was better qualified than anyone else to take care of the Really Rich Danes who, their enormous fortunes notwithstanding, were the most delicate of plants where money was concerned, willingly pursuing a lawsuit for years to force some little retailer to take back a pair of shoes and then, after losing their case, needing a diplomat as charming as Carsten to dissolve the glue that kept their small change stuck to the linings of their pockets.

Like Fitz, Carsten was family lawyer to the old aristocracy. For the money and—more often—for the prestige and, not infrequently, out of sympathy, he administered the dwindling revenues derived from exploitation in a distant past for old people who had been born and brought up like the Count's children at Mørkhøj and hence had never learned to look after themselves. Now they sat in empty, debt-ridden, unheated manor houses the length and breadth of Denmark, staring at telephones that they could not figure out how to use because the operators had been replaced by automatic switchboards and the thought of dialing six numbers left them baffled.

The world showered honors on Carsten. He was given the most prestigious cases, was elected to the last of those boards to which he did not already belong, and was mentioned in the press. He was still only in his thirties, and seemed to harbor no doubts, and there was something totally *natural* about his social acceleration. He was well dressed without having to work at it, athletic without training, suntanned without ever seeing the light of day, relaxed although he never took a vacation now, and always, always in command of the situation.

And of course, once again, he became a symbol. His manner was proof that old-fashioned integrity and industry and rectitude could be combined with modern business techniques and modern-day society. In the courtroom the judges were hard put to it to conceal their emotions, and at board meetings hardened company directors and business executives and *éminences grises* and Scrooges regarded him with brimming eyes, and now and again a tear was shed. When Carsten really went to town, when he actually stood up and unfurled his eloquence like a garland and started pacing back and forth across the floor, the old money men would suddenly feel their crusts starting to crack, as the young lawyer unraveled the most complex situation for them, or devised a plan of action that would give one of the labor unions a bloody nose. Then, all at once, they would feel their emotions running away with them, because, they thought, this kid's a golden boy, he's a boy wonder, just the kind of young lion that is needed; he's the guiding star, our insurance policy, he's the plug in the hole, they thought and blew their emotions into their handkerchiefs. Then Carsten sat down and the meeting could continue in all serenity, now that all doubt had been erased. When the twins were a couple of years old he bought the piece of ground next to Amalie's villa on Strand Drive and had a big house built of yellow brick. And, with this, the road to the future should have been clear.

Maria falls into line with these developments quite admirably. She has to stop working because she refuses to let anyone else look after the twins; obviously, they could have had four or five nannies looking after them, or been placed in a luxury-level nursery school, but that is quite out of the question. Maria wants to keep the children with her at all times, and since no employer is going to accept that, she has to give up working and stay at home. Although the fact that she never really comes to look upon Strand Drive as "home" proves to be one of the family's little problems, and she refuses to acquire a driver's license for the little Mercedes two-seater that Carsten has bought for her, and she will not have servants, she intends to look after this house—which she does not particularly like—herself. Carsten tries to convince her, to no avail—and this obviously has something to do with Maria's upbringing; she is very, very reluctant to take orders; somewhere in the house, on the back of a door, her police helmet still hangs, and even though Maria never puts it on now, it still acts as a reminder of something.

Nor does anyone ever succeed in making her truly *socially acceptable*. Amalie did try, but after her first attempt, many years before, she had resigned herself to an I'm-lying-in-wait-armed-to-the-teeth attitude toward her daughter-in-law, an attitude that caved in on only a handful of occasions—as, for example, with the birth of the twins. But other people also try to turn Maria into Mrs. Mahogany, wife of the counsel to the Supreme Court, Carsten among them—or at least he makes a few feeble attempts, and on one single, solitary occasion he does manage to coax her into attending a society function, for the first and last time. It is a dinner with roast pheasant and gateau from La Glâce and everyone talking about this wonderful game of golf until Maria, clutching at a fragile straw, leans toward her dinner partner and asks, with a glint in her eye, "And do you play golf, too?" Unfortunately, the man seated next to her is Kristian Mogensen, later to become such a celebrated lawyer. At this point he is young and up-and-coming and he says, "No, my dear lady, not yet." And so Maria stands up, with a twin on each arm, and then she starts to cry and screams across the table at Carsten, "Why the hell did I have to come here and who are all these boneheads, they talk just like machines, well, we're off, the twins and I are leaving, and you can stay here and enjoy yourself with your floozies and your gateau and on the way home I'm gonna tramp right across that bloody golf course, so there!" And Maria makes her exit.

Carsten never again tries to take her into society, and the episode is soon forgotten because things are happening fast for the family during these years; this unfortunate little incident is put behind them just like Maria's upbringing and the war and Carsten's periodic bouts of forgetfulness and Amalie's anxiety and the seedier parts of Copenhagen, and Colonel Lunding—and now the road ahead does seem to be clear.

One January day Carsten received a visit. It was a Sunday and he was alone in his chambers on Sankt Annæ Square. He was sitting writing, and around him everything was very still—well, of course, everyone else took Sundays off, but Carsten was covering sheet after sheet of yellow legal paper with his individual, speedy, legible, and somehow attractive and arresting hand. He had had a very busy week, with court sittings and negotiations every day; and the settling, at long last, of the estate of the big ersatz-coffee merchant who had, at one time, taken over Carl Laurids's factories; and the winding up of some big property deals in which Burmeister & Wain and the state and the Danish Sugar Refineries had swapped around the ownership of half of Christianshavn at their discretion and under Carsten's guidance. Throughout this week he had managed to grab no more than a few hours' sleep, and those he had taken while waiting to be called, having long since learned how to sleep standing up with his eyes open and an attentive expression on his face and having also learned to awake from this uncanny sleep—of which only he was aware—totally alert. During this week, when night and day had run together into one, he had seen his wife and children only once, and that had been in court, during the processing of one of those small cases that went hand in hand with the big ones—a damages suit involving a job applicant who had, during an interview for a job, insulted the president of the company and then knocked him down. In a way, such a case was beneath Carsten's dignity, but he considered it an honor to conduct it and to win it, since, when we protect one company's or one individual's legal interests, he said, we are protecting all of them, and we pursue it to the hilt. By this time he had been working nonstop for five days in a row, and still he was smooth-shaven and neatly pressed and in top form. Not until just before the pronouncing of sentence, when the case was as good as closed, did it become obvious that he had been living on nothing but black coffee and willpower. Only then, when the defendant leaned forward and said, "Damn! You look awful, sweetheart," did he realize that it was Maria and the twins who were sitting there, because once again Maria had gone looking for work with a child on each arm, and had, once again, been rejected.

Such an experience would have moved most other people to wonder whether a prolonged coffee-only diet provides the right kind of sustenance, and whether once a week in the courtroom is the right time and the right way to see one's family, but not Carsten. Sitting there on that Sunday, in the empty building, planning for the coming week, which would be even more full and ambitious than the previous one, he felt well content with what he had achieved. You have done your duty, and more, he said to himself, not without a certain satisfaction.

He had reached the point where going into his own private little dressing room, taking a shower, and putting on a clean shirt and a fresh silk tie did not help him, because he still felt so dirty; and even though he had shaved very thoroughly, the stubble still showed blackly through the transparent skin of his face, and he thought: I'd better go home now.

It was then that he received his visit. Not from any person, but from his own store of memories, which came pouring in through the double doors to show that they, like Carsten, knew nothing of days off. First to appear was this little episode: there had been a minor case in the court, a trivial matter, a case conducted for the ersatz-coffee manufacturer's daughter, one of Denmark's richest women, who owned half of Town Hall Square. The other party was a nanny. The case boiled down to a matter of a few hundred kroner and, said the ersatz-coffee manufacturer's daughter, *the principle of the thing.* "I *won't* pay," she had said to Carsten when he tried to dissuade her, it being clear that this paltry amount was the nanny's obvious due. "We are pursuing this suit on grounds of principle," she had insisted, and Carsten had pursued it; and even though he pursued it in bottom gear, knowing that they ought to lose the case, he won it anyway.

Now it came back to visit him. It had been a trifle, and it ought to have been gone and forgotten, it really had no business here in Sankt Annæ Square, but it slunk in anyway, manifesting itself as a scent. Carsten sniffed at the closed doors and windows and caught the scent of ersatz coffee, which does not smell too good at the best of times—but on this Sunday it smelled particularly bad. Carsten opened a window overlooking the statue of Christian X, but the smell just became worse and he began to feel unwell. It occurred to him that he never should have conducted that case, nor, possibly, the case against his own wife. It might even be that cases of this kind ought not to be conducted at all: they marred the picture as a whole, sowed doubt about the justice of the legal system, and nurtured the Monte Carlo idea of Fitz's bitter legacy, which now, all at once, Carsten thought he understood. Then, just next to him, he heard someone speak, and there was his former friend and intellectual mentor Tyge Lubanskij, tutor and lawyer, and beside him, the Boy with his uncompromising opinions; over by the filing cabinet waited the lonely days at Sorø after the academy closed down; and there was Colonel Lunding, weeping in the kitchen by the Lakes; and the stockbroker, seen through the peepholes in the wall of his mother's bedroom—until Carsten's office was full. "I hope there is room for all of you, and you are most welcome, just as long as there is a chair left for me," he said to the visions and sat down.

He sat on, without moving a muscle, until the cleaners arrived the next morning, and even then he did not move; they had to clean around him. He was still sitting there when the secretaries and the messengers arrived, and then the chief clerks and the other lawyers, and he remained sitting there all day, because no one really dared speak to him.

In the evening, Maria came to fetch him and take him home. By then his hair was graying and naturally he was unshaven. They had him admitted to Montebello Sanatorium in North Zealand, where he remained for six months.

While Carsten was away, Maria discovered that she and the children were, to all intents and purposes, alone in the world, and this she discovered after she had spent two days sitting gazing out of the window in hopes of a visit from someone, only to find that no one came. The telephone rang once. It was Amalie, and the brief, inane conversation with her mother-in-law left Maria feeling more alone than before. She began to think things over, and it dawned on her that she had no friends—a revelation that is, in a sense, banal, because of course she has no friends; her childhood home has been swallowed up by the earth, and her mother and father have disappeared, and she has grown up in a home for girls and on the street and has had somewhere in the region of 250 different places of employment, and she is married to a man, Carsten, who moves in circles as remote from her as another planet, so there is nothing to wonder at: of course she is alone. And yet, at the same time, it does seem odd, since she has moved around so much and met so many people and most of the time she is forthright and gregarious and sincere, and so still it surprises me that she has not formed just some kind of attachment that might have lasted until this moment when her husband had been admitted to a sanatorium and she was left alone with two children. I believe that this is a significant feature of Denmark and the sixties, this quite natural anonymity which, having paralyzed Maria, now pins her to the sofa. It says something about Denmark and about progress. Without claiming to be able to explain it, still I am inclined to think that it is important, since it is the first time in this account that I have come across someone in want of company—not any company in particular but just any old company.

If Maria had told someone of her plight—Carsten, for instance (who was in the sanatorium), or Fitz (who was dead) or Amalie (who was not even an option)—no doubt they would have said, as Miss Smeck had once done, that at heart we are all alone. That, however, is no real comfort but more of a middle-class attempt to lessen the pain of being anonymous. Maria chose to solve her problem in a very different, and radical, fashion. She left home with the twins, who could now walk—at least for short stretches; she took a taxi to Christianshavn and wandered around her old childhood haunts, which had been razed to the ground and built up again using matchbox buildings that looked like monuments raised in honor of the right angle and the idiotic contribution architects have made to the loneliness of the big cities. She kept walking until, in the mouth of a basement entry, she recognized the face of eccentric old Miss Poulsen, who had been living on the street throughout Maria's childhood—and, in fact, since the turn of the century—and had dedicated her life to feeding the city's cats. Maria dragged her along with her across the square, where she recognized one of those park-bench tipplers who have been working since the First World War to accustom their bodies to the denaturants in alcohol, and, armed with these two finds, Maria climbed into a taxi and drove back to the villa, where she installed them. The next day she went back to Christianshavn again and came upon two of the sailors she had known as a girl. Then, on the way home, she passed by Central Station, where she picked up an organ-grinder and his wife, and in the days that followed, with a child on each arm, she called on Kofoed's School for Indigents and the Heaven Express Hostel for Men and the Copenhagen Refuge for Men and the Salvation Army Hostel and invited the homeless back to Charlottenlund.

They brought fresh color to her cheeks, those days, and she felt fit and well and happy, not least on those long evenings in the big drawing room in front of the blazing fire, when all of her guests gathered for the dinner she had prepared and then made themselves comfortable in Danish designer Hans Wegner's beautiful chairs and smoked and drank and stared vacantly at the domestic coziness and the paintings and the leather-and-steel grand piano designed by Amalie's old friend the architect Poul Henningsen.

If there is anything touching about this scene, it is unintentional—and my depiction of it is less than accurate, since Maria did not act out of charity but simply because she lacked company. She entertained no deeper feelings for her guests, and when they vanished from her life, they vanished without trace. She was having one of her glassy-eyed periods; life seemed to her to be trouble-free. Of course these people must come home with me and taste the fine brandy and the cigars, she thought, but at the same time she was distant and restless and the real reason for her bringing these people to Strand Drive was that at this time she was obsessed by the notion of refurnishing her life that had been coming over her in spells ever since she was a little girl—a notion that masked a deep sense of dread.

Over the six months of Carsten's absence, at least fifty people stayed at the villa. One day, Maria came by the house by the Lakes and invited Colonel Lunding's successor to come over and put the villa's second floor to whatever use he saw fit, and since Maria was a well-known figure in army circles, her offer was accepted and a couple of new electronic data processors and a sensitive piece of monitoring equipment were installed on the spacious second floor, thus adding an extra, military element to the comings and goings on Strand Drive.

Only once did Amalie try to stop her daughter-in-law. She pulled a blanket around her shoulders, walked through the little gate in the hedge, strode across the lawn—past the wheelbarrows full of junk and the barrel organ and the Jeeps and the unmarked cars— walked in without knocking and set about speaking her mind. Then she found Miss Poulsen at her side, putting an arm around her shoulders and saying, "You know, the other day I had the runs something awful, I was feeding the cats down by the road and it just started to come. It fair *squirted* out, I can tell you"—and Amalie had to turn and go home.

Two weeks before Carsten came home—in connection with the surveying of the house for the foreclosing—the police put Maria's guests out of the ground floor and the Army Intelligence officers on the second floor moved their equipment back to the Lakes.

And Carsten and Maria moved back with them.

They only intended to stay there temporarily, and in a way that is how it was. When Carsten returned to his family he was also able to settle back into his office chair—the one in which Fitz had died —and he resumed his post as counsel to the Supreme Court and the resolving of delicate matters for the royal family and the Margarine Company and the Danish East Asia Company. He seemed to be his old self again: serene, attentive, and ambitious; and before too long he bought a lovely little mansion in Gentofte and he and Maria and the children moved in. Up there they could enjoy the breeze off the Sound and Maria did not have far to go to get to the job that she had, with her unstinting tenacity, found for herself with Nordic Insulin. And here they stayed until again, one Sunday night, Carsten did not come home and was found by the cleaners on Monday morning sitting in his chair with a face as gray as plaster, grown stiff and motionless as the statue of Holger the Dane awaiting his country's call in the bowels of Elsinore Castle; petrified by good intentions and overwork and the dawning awareness of how hard it is to carve a career out of the difference between right and wrong and still remain as pure as the driven snow.

He was taken to Montebello, and the sight of the yellow-painted hospital set in its leafy grounds made him feel as though he were coming home.

This time the mansion was not sold, even though he was away for the best part of a year; this time the company paid for the house and for the servants who had become necessary shortly after Carsten's second admission to the sanatorium.

Up until that point, Maria had always had the strength to reject the idea of help in the house, but one day she began to cry. Without a word to anyone she sat herself down and quietly fell apart at the seams, and out poured a relentless flood of tears that would not be stanched. After three days she was driven to the nursing home where she had once given birth. Here she was met by Amalie's old friend the radiation specialist, who had, at the time of the twins' birth, been a gynecologist and obstetrician but had since, because of personal experience and current trends, become more and more involved in psychiatric work. So he had given up his professorship and his consultancy and converted his maternity home into a little private psychiatric hospital. And here he kept Maria for three days, helping her out of her grief and back to a slightly shaken reality with the aid of electric shock treatment—which he regarded as a kind of psychiatric pat on the back—and the help of modern psychiatric drugs, with their mysterious names and surprising and inexplicable side effects.

By the time she came home from the nursing home a team of servants had moved in and she did not have the strength to throw them out, so they were still there when Carsten came home.

On his return he and Maria and the twins moved back, for a time, to the house by the Lakes, not because it was strictly necessary but because, for some unaccountable reason, they felt at ease in those uneasy surroundings, resonant as they were with the hum of the city and the deep vibration from the diabolical electronic equipment on the ground floor. Later on, of course, they moved back to Gentofte and the mansion and the servants and the law chambers and the new job that Maria had found, and, of course, they believed that this time it was for good; now they could take it easy—but of course they could not, and although they did not know it, the house by the Lakes was already calling to them again, as Montebello was calling and the radiation voltmeters and straitjackets were calling and the bankruptcy auctions were calling—all because this husband and wife, Carsten and Maria, carry the weight of so many dreams that refuse to amalgamate, and so they are doomed to spend the greater part of their lives swinging between affluence and poverty, stability and disintegration, Gentofte and the house by the Lakes, an average existence and the nursing homes—and it is these swings of the pendulum that form a framework around the twins as they grow.

The twins had not been baptized—Maria had been dead against it—but they had been named Madelene and Mads. Amalie, who had suggested Madelene, wanted to call the boy Max or Frederik or Ferdinand, but Maria had bared her fangs and said, "Nothing doing, one weird name is enough. He'll have a good Danish name—Mads"; and thus a compromise was struck that tallied with the children's looks, which were a kind of genetic compromise, with Mads being fair and Madelene not dark but black and, Maria could tell, the spitting image of the Princess.

I do not know exactly when they started school—as I have said, now that I'm getting close to my own time, the story is trying to wriggle out of my grasp—but it must have been sometime during the first half of the sixties, and it came at a time when the family was once again living by the Lakes, so the children were enrolled in a nearby school, by the name of Bording's School, which is still there, towering over the houses around it and casting a shadow far across the lives of present and former pupils.

Bording's was a "free school," which meant that its teachers were freed of the trammels that would, in the ordinary state schools, have restricted their right to whack little children on the head; and so the twins—who had, prior to this, never been struck—found themselves growing up amid liberally administered smacks and modern Danish Grundtvigianism. This meant that the pupils were given no books, thus allowing the teachers to be all the freer in their own, very personal, interpretations of the History of the World and the Creation and Biology and the Norse Myths—which were presented as a justification of the school's own particular brand of discipline, which dated from Grundtvig's own day.

Despite this strictness and the teachers' delight in the odd little slap, school for Mads was, on the whole, reprisal-free, inasmuch as he proved to be a bit of a tightrope walker, able to balance on the very narrow path between what was forbidden on the one hand and what was also forbidden on the other hand; and this balancing act of his is reminiscent of his father's. He was blessed with Carsten's good manners and intelligence and diligence, and although it cannot be said, as it was of his father, that he was never late for school, I can at least vouch for the fact that he was almost never late; in all of his nine years at the school, with almost no exceptions, he was always on time for morning assembly, at which he sang loud and true in his clear child's voice, gazed intently upon the great Free School man, educator, and headmaster Frede Bording with large, lustrous eyes, which had nothing to fear because Mads always did as he was told and what was expected of him. He soon learned to read and would read aloud in the sweetest of voices; he had delightful penmanship and a sweet temper; played with the other children without allowing himself to be lured into fights and without crossing the line drawn in red across the playground close to the gate; a line that said: This far and no farther. He was singled out for special mention at parents' meetings, and twice—in the middle of a school year—he was moved up into a higher class that could do greater justice to his swift powers of comprehension and mature temperament. He was rewarded with little bags of fruit for his nice drawings, and pats on the back of his crew-cut head for his nice singing—and only the fact that he is fair-haired rather than dark and that there is nothing timid about him prevents him from being an exact replica of his father.

Madelene, on the other hand, turned up for her first day at school armed with a kind of contrariness that the teachers misunderstood and interpreted as lack of intelligence; and when they moved Mads up a grade, they moved Madelene down. From the very start, and for all of her time at the school, they viewed her defiance as one long incitement to push her under and to try to prevent her snorkel from breaking the surface. She learned to read and write, but only with reluctance and at a snail's pace, and when the bell rang she had to be chased out into the playground against her will—only, then, to start a fight or lock herself into the toilets with four other girls or leave the school grounds, even though this was forbidden. All in all, during these years, Madelene seems possessed of a mulish hostility toward authority. Nevertheless, for the first few years, even the most slaphappy teachers, even the headmaster, Mr. Bording himself, hesitated to punish her, because she was a girl and Mads's sister, and because her father was an influential and well-known man. But she was afforded this protection only until the day when, on one of her rambling expeditions in search of rules to break, she found her way down into the engineering access tunnels running far beneath the school and, once there, lit a fire, partly to disperse the darkness and partly because children and other underdogs have always dreamed of stealing fire from the gods. This then ignited the lagging around the water pipes. Madelene had to cut and run, to escape the poisonous fumes, and on ascending to ground level she was met by the fire department, the headmaster, and the heavy open-handed blows which, to the end of his days, he maintained had done no one any harm.

Thereafter the charmed circle around Madelene was broken. The teachers were convinced that she must be an exception to the golden Danish rule that all little girls of good family with long, curly hair are well behaved—so they let rip and swiped at Madelene whenever they had the chance, they dragged her up to the blackboard and through humiliating inquisitions for which they knew she was not prepared, and then slapped her in the side of her head and sent her back to her desk only to call her back for another couple of swipes—after all, isn't prevention better than cure?

On winter mornings, Mr. Bording waited in the playground for latecomers, and there he and Madelene encountered each other time after time in the glare of the floodlight that played across the blue-white snow, as she came trotting up, having lost one mitten and left her bag on the bus—fifteen minutes late and still unmoved by the situation, unmoved by the headmaster and the Checkpoint Charlie atmosphere of the deserted playground; and looking just what she was, an underage Gypsy in the snow, taking beatings and detention and reprimands without displaying remorse or anger or anything at all except an air of let's-just-get-this-over-with.

One could perhaps ask what it meant to this brother and sister to be treated so differently and to find themselves drifting apart, but I do not have the answer to that question. It does not seemed to have mattered greatly to them. During all of this and through everything that follows, they seem to have remained good friends—that is as close as I can come to it, and it may be that that is just what they were, good friends. There was never any suggestion of a particularly deep love between them; they never did realize the sixties dream of love between brothers and sisters, and one of the reasons for this was that from very early on, quickly and in different directions, they both ventured out into unruliness.

For the twins, the school was one of the last places where life was still ordered and predictable. At the school it went without saying that the things in life that really mattered were Christianity and the Danish Song Treasury—sparkling and gleaming in the pages of the *Folk High School Songbook*—and a culture redolent of the last century. And of course the children had to learn to sit still on their asses for nine years running at school, followed preferably by three years at senior secondary or preferably even longer; of course they had to be rendered knowledgeable and intelligent, and learn to sing on key and fill in the background in their drawings in art lessons; and if, like Madelene, they were disobedient, they should be given a whack in the head, after which they ought to be contrite and set to with renewed diligence and joy—for hadn't Grundtvig said that the man has never lived who has not had something drummed into his big thick skull that he had no liking for to begin with, so you'd better like this, they told Madelene, because if you don't we have ways of whetting your appetite.

Only very slowly did it dawn on the school and its teachers and their pupils that this attitude was gradually becoming somewhat antiquated, but there came a time when they began, albeit unwillingly, to see the light; there came a time when the real world began to seep in—because, when all is said and done, this red stone building by the Lakes was not Sorø Academy and this was not the forties but the sixties. And Mads's answer to this dawning realization that the school was not the world, and that disorder awaited him on the outside, was to push himself to the limit.

He turned to sports, attacking them with manic intensity. First he took up handball and soccer, in both of which his game rapidly improved; but then, once he began to feel that the ball was like a piece of modeling clay that he could pull any which way and send spinning into the goal from the most ridiculous angles, he gave up these games and turned to fencing—because there one is alone and masked, facing one's opponent who is also alone and masked, and by this time he was beginning to think that the problems life throws our way have to be solved alone. He became a brilliant foilsman, capable, though he was just a child, of presenting a threat to the adults in their own tournaments, with them thinking that they had this overconfident little boy in retreat, until suddenly there would be a parry and a riposte and *smack*, the light went on, it was touché to Mads, and they had lost to this babe in arms who was now, no doubt, going to get a big hug from Daddy and Mommy, who, they thought, must have come to hold his hand. But there they were wrong; Mads came alone, since at that point both of his parents were in the hospital and his home temporarily dissolved. The only constants in his life were the school and this sport, which he now gave up in order to concentrate on track and field, which he gave up to become a competitive gymnast, until he was lured away by mountaineering and skiing and wound up spending the holidays of his adolescence in places where the Alps take on the look of a gaping maw crammed with teeth—until, one morning on the North Face of the Eiger, he found that he was tired of the wind and the altitude. So he came back home to find some new and incalculable project that would provide him with the illusion that if only he persevered in trying to solve this mystery, then he would, eventually, find the peace for which he was searching.

All of this was of course possible only because Carsten and Maria paid the bills. Beneath all the years of the twins' unsettled childhood there hung a safety net, which sagged now and again when Carsten was admitted to the sanatorium and the house in the northern suburbs had to be sold off, but if one cannot pay cash one can always borrow, and so in fact there was always money, even for the craziest caprice. And so there was no great problem, either, when Madelene was kicked out of school.

This came about on the day that she hit back; when the school called the police, and she hit the policemen, too—hit them with a brick. Thereafter a meeting was called of the teachers' council and the parents' association, where all were reminded of how Madelene had almost burned down the school; and of the summer when, before anyone else, she had gone barefoot at school; and how she had eaten copper sulfate to learn something about chemistry and be registered as sick; and had come to school gaudily dressed and got drunk during school hours and smoked narcotic substances in the toilets and started coming and going as she pleased and unsettled her school-mates by being photographed naked for an obscene weekly magazine, although she was only thirteen and thus needed her parents' permission—which she had been given. "And that does not do the school any good either," said the chairman of the teachers' council, and went on to add, "We have hesitated to expel her before now, only because we trusted her parents and her brother, but now we have reached the end of our tether." The next day he told Madelene, "Now you can pick up your bag and go around to all the teachers and thank them for the time you have spent here." Madelene stared sullenly at him, left the school, and entered the first in a long string of private schools in and around Copenhagen which, over the next few years, she was accepted into and kicked out of, until Carsten and Maria gave up and tried boarding school instead. But the boarding schools could not cope either with her lack of respect for regulations of any kind whatsoever, and they had to ask her to leave, to be on the next train out of there and never show her face again. Finally even the educational authorities shrugged their shoulders and left her to go her own way, in a world where, for the first time in this account—and perhaps the first time in history—the future was not all mapped out and where there was no knowing what the next moment might bring.

The family provided the twins with their only gathering point. It was hard to say in advance where they would gather, since sometimes it was in the affluent surroundings of a villa in Ordrup or Klampenborg or Gentofte and sometimes in the house by the Lakes, and once, when they were all at a low ebb, it was in the fearful cold of a shack on the edge of Amager Common. A full complement was rare, since often Carsten would be missing, or Maria, or both of them—if Madelene was not wallowing around in some distant mire and if Carsten had not gone too far afield on some headstrong hobbyhorse. And sometimes there was more than a full complement because Maria, in an attack of compassion, had invited a dozen poor wretches home with her. But sometimes they were themselves again; sometimes the family really did gather together in a drawing room lit by oil lamps and candles, with Hans Wegner's chairs and sofas designed by Børge Mogensen and a Golden Age painting that immersed the wall in a deep, sentimental landscape that cannot be dismissed as a romantic lie, any more than this family idyll can be dismissed. There actually were moments when they really did experience *Hygge*, that particular Danish blend of warmth and coziness and pleasurable feeling, moments when it became a reality. The twins' lives and those of Carsten and Maria would be incomprehensible and improbable if we did not accept the existence of these evenings, where they are all in the one room with someone reading aloud and someone knitting and with some music from the record player that might be Mahler; or where they just sit looking at one another and the story ceases to rattle on and the room is pervaded by something I am not ashamed to identify as happiness. They truly are happy, and the peace and contentment of these moments fiercely contradicts the persistent rumors that this family had lost all meaning and that it was heading toward its own disintegration.

Sometimes, on such evenings, Amalie is also present, and it says something about the harmony of the moment that this old panther can warm herself alongside the little lambs, Maria and the twins. And Adonis and Ramses and the Princess also put in a brief appearance. Maria herself has found them; for some years they have been living like itinerant prophets, doing the rounds of the provincial fairs to proclaim the blessings of modern electronic technology, presenting slide shows and 16 mm films which avow that in America, only a few years from now, it will be possible to transport everything, almost everything, by television cables. Operating the equipment is Ramses, now an extremely old man, while Adonis performs wistful songs that say, who knows, perhaps we are all electronic signals in a beeping machine controlled by some inscrutable being, and our love no more than an electric whisper in an integrated circuit. And while he is singing and the slides keep changing, the Princess stares fixedly at some point beyond the heads of the spectators, who no longer know that she was once a circus princess and the most notorious female criminal of her day, or that she must by now be more than one hundred and fifty years old.

Maria also makes an attempt to find Christoffer Ludwig, Carsten's grandfather, whom she has never met, and she actually does track down the apartment on Dannebrogs Street, and the door is open, but she is stopped by the books. By now these form a wall that has closed off the narrow corridors along which Amalie and Carsten found their way, many years before, to Christoffer, and no one is ever quite clear about what became of him and of Gumma and Amalie's two sisters.

Of course, this peaceful family life was short-lived; before too long the picture would dissolve as Carsten got to his feet because he had some work to prepare and a moment later he could be heard pacing back and forth across the floor above as he presented his plea in a forthcoming case to the walls, saying, for how much longer is the Ministry of Agriculture going to abuse our patience; and Maria had an appointment with her psychiatrist; and Mads had to get up to do 150 push-ups and then retire to prepare himself mentally for the morrow's 400-meter final; and Madelene had already left. Everyone had left—except Amalie, who sat on alone, deep in thought, because she had happened to pick up a newspaper only to have her eye caught by a picture, a fuzzy portrait of a South American dictatorship assembled around its President. Standing slightly in the background was a man she recognized, even though he was black-haired and sported a gaucho mustache and the features were obliterated by the coarse grain of the picture. There was no doubt, it was Carl Laurids, his eyes boring, with unremitting watchfulness, through the graininess and the filters and the differences of time and place and through Amalie's pounding heart and out into the future.

At that moment Ramses and the Princess stepped back out into the hullabaloo of the world, back to extolling the virtues of technology and modern times. It was just a short step, because they walked out onto a highway and were run over by a truck, and as they were picking themselves up they were run over again by another truck; once more they tried to get to their feet and this time were run over by a vehicle that might have been a combine harvester, or one of the Army's armored personnel carriers. And after standing quietly by the side of the road for a moment, Adonis turned and disappeared, because he had always found it hard to face up to the trials and tribulations of life.

Madelene, too, disappeared, at least for a while—for the time it took to have a hand in breaking into a pharmacy and then experimenting with the spoils and plunging into a chemical high from which she emerged much later with a charred taste in her mouth. This she tried to get rid of by allowing herself to be admitted to the hospital, until she grew tired of the mirrors in the locked ward— burnished steel plates with a filmy surface in which she could not see her face—and discharged herself. Then she sank from view for a while, leaving no trace until she popped up as the representative of a political party which, like so many others, believed that the Welfare State was an evil conspiracy that had to be done away with; and to be better prepared for assisting in this execution she took off to a training camp in Lebanon, from which she returned with freckles and a sunburned nose and ten kilos of plastic explosive that could have wiped out anything and everything, but did not—because now she discovered her most abiding passion, instant gratification. Instant gratification, she told Mads and her parents, instant gratification is the sole enduring principle, she said, and though it sounded vague, it camouflaged an attempt to test the limits of love. These proved to extend a good long way: to men and then women and then children and finally a calf, a beautiful, newborn, dewy-eyed black-and-white calf that shit enormous cow pats all over the fifth-floor apartment in which it lived with Madelene, alongside the loose connections and the forgotten lump of explosive that lay sweating in the sun on the windowsill.

This apartment could be seen from the house by the Lakes, and from there Mads could glance across at it when he was visiting his parents—when they were not in the hospital or at work or living somewhere else or unavailable for some other reason. And he was to glance in the direction of Madelene's apartment particularly often during the spell when he set himself up as his parents' servant, wanting to heap coals of fire on his own head and to breathe some meaning into life. He looked after the house by the Lakes, dressed in striped livery and with a napkin over his arm, but this whim did not last long because, at the time that this one overtook him, Mads's whims were following hard on one another's heels. After leaving school he had entered the university, only to leave not long afterward because chess was taking up all his time, until that was supplanted by another course of study, and then a third—this last being succeeded by Mads's apprenticing himself to a joiner. This he gave up in order to study philosophy, and that, in turn, he gave up to write a mathematical thesis, and that, too, he gave up to move back in with his parents in the house by the Lakes, and be, for a little while, a pale and worn-out butler who really only relaxed when all the family was gathered together—and even then only for short spells because it dispersed so quickly.

The last time—or no, I had better stick to what I know for sure and say, the last time to date—when they were all gathered together was at the launching organized by Maria and Carsten. In saying that Carsten and Maria organized it I am already going too far, since, in actual fact, there is no proof that they were the moving forces behind this event, but at any rate there was a boat, that much is sure, and a ceremony was held, and an event that was televised and reported in all the newspapers; and the press gave the impression that all credit was due to Maria and Carsten. This event bore all the characteristics of a truly solemn occasion; in other words, besides the boat that was to be launched down a long ramp, it was graced by the presence of the mayor of Copenhagen and the Prime Minister and a number of famous actors and writers; also present were Carsten and Maria and Madelene and Amalie and Mads, and, indeed, so many people were present that one might even say the Nation itself was in attendance.

If we are to go by the newspaper and television reports, this boat was a gift from Maria and more especially from Carsten, who wished, in this generous fashion, to mark his retirement from a long and strenuous working life during which he had earned a fortune; a fortune in which he now wanted the city of his birth, Copenhagen, and the land of his birth, Denmark, to have some share. And that was just what the mayor said: "May I, on behalf of all the people of Copenhagen and of Denmark, thank you for this glorious gift, this historic Danish ship," he said. And even at this point something was obviously not quite right, since this ship was not historic—a fact easily verified simply by taking a closer look, although it would seem that Mads was the only one to do so. And what he saw was that this proud ship was a big, flat-bottomed boat; that, if anything, it was some kind of barge, and one which might have sailed the rivers of France or Holland's canals but which had, most definitely, never been Danish. But now it had been given a slapdash touch-up with a coating of tar that only just concealed the dry rot and blue rot and shipworm holes. Then, when the Prime Minister spoke, the feeling that something was far wrong grew even stronger—at least for Mads—because the minister regarded this ship and its launching as a great cultural event and political manifestation, a salute, in fact, to Denmark's voyage into the new millennium. And even though we have our problems, the minister said, we have reason to feel satisfied, since things are moving, more or less, in the right direction—with the odd detour here and there, of course—but we are pretty much on track. Then it was Carsten's turn to speak, and his speech made it clear to Mads that the boat was neither a gift nor a cultural event nor a salute to anything at all, but that it was being launched because Carsten and Maria had decided to leave Denmark, and that they had decided to sail away because, as Carsten said, we met on a boat.

Then Maria smashed a bottle of champagne against the hull of the boat and named it the *Spindrift Dolphin*, and that flat-bottomed bumboat slid down the ramp to float on the choppy little waves so typical of Sortedam Lake in Østerbro—for it was into the old city moat, that pathetic pond, with its lazy wading birds and unhealthy carp, that the boat was launched. And now Mads elbowed his way through the crowd of well-wishers, making for his mother because he had given up on his father. Having reached her, he tried to stop her by saying, "What kind of a ridiculous, inane affair is this anyway, and why has everyone in your family always had to draw so much attention to themselves, and what makes you think that you can get away from Denmark, from yourselves, and start a new life just by sailing out onto Sortedam Lake in a floating bathtub?" But Maria waved him off. "Beat it!" she said, to her own son, and even he had to get out of the way.

And now Maria and Carsten stepped on board, together with the mayor and the Prime Minister and Amalie and Madelene and a good number of other people; an orchestra played and, as though to order, the moon rose up into the sunset sky. And, in honor of the occasion, an amusing film was projected onto the big, flat cloud that hangs permanently over Copenhagen. Then Mads turned and left as so many children before him have done—although, of course, he is not a child any longer. He walks back to the deserted house by the Lakes and up to his room, and sits down by the window. He can still hear the music and, far off in the distance, his family are sailing in the moonlight and even though they have put to sea on Sortedam Lake he does not feel sure that they are coming back. When he closes his eyes he can see them quite clearly; he notes how Carsten sniffs at what he takes to be a trade wind and how Maria is singing a song about Tahiti for the Prime Minister, and how

Madelene lays a hand on the mayor's thigh—since love will even stretch that far. Somewhere close at hand a calf lows forlornly; and in Charlottenlund on Strand Drive, Dodo the hairless greyhound is howling; and at Bispebjerg crematorium, in a white-hot blaze, Ramses and the Princess are transformed into an anonymous heap of ashes that will end up in a common grave because no one has been able to identify them; and somewhere on some highway Adonis is walking away, not wanting to be a bother to anyone. All of this Mads senses, at this moment, with the kind of clarity that follows a bad hangover or a long illness—not because he is clairvoyant but because he was born to the sensitivity and confusion of this century. And I know what I am talking about, because I am he—from now on, you can call me Mads. And if I persist in writing the history of my family, then it is out of necessity. Those laws and regulations and systems and patterns that my family and every other family in Denmark has violated and conformed to and nudged and writhed under for two hundred years are now in fact in a state of foaming dissolution. That is why my father and my mother and my sister and my grandmother and various friends and acquaintances and several primarily accountable personages can, at such an inane ceremony, launch their longings onto a waterhole in the heart of the city. Ahead lies the future, which I refuse to view as Carl Laurids did: down a gun barrel; or as Anna did: through a magnifying glass. I want to meet it face-to-face, and yet I am certain that if nothing is done, then there will be no future to face up to, since although most things in life are uncertain, the impending disaster and decline look like a safe bet. Which is why I feel like calling for help—don't we all have a need to call out to something?—and so I have called out to the past.

It marches by me like some sort of procession. Through this room pass Anna's longing to be a child and Adonis's impotent charm and Christoffer's paper creatures and Amalie's femininity and appalling ambition and Thorvald Bak's misplaced love and the Count's fear of time passing and the Old Lady's fear that it might stand still and the Princess's motherliness and Maria's tears and police helmet and Carsten's willingness to do his duty and Madelene's lawlessness and Carl Laurids's cynicism—and naturally I am afraid because sometimes, as they are gliding past me, I get the feeling that these people and their imagery are very like me; now and again the thought strikes me that perhaps I have never really *seen* other people's expectations, that I have only ever seen my own, and the loneliest thought in the world is the thought that what we have glimpsed is nothing other than ourselves. But now it is too late to think like that and something must be done, and before we can do anything we will have to form a picture of the twentieth century.